The Honorables

HONOR AMONG
Thieves

Elizabeth Boyce

Bestselling author of *Once a Duchess*

Crimson Romance

New York   London   Toronto   Sydney   New Delhi

CRIMSON

Crimson Romance
An Imprint of Simon & Schuster, Inc.
1230 Avenue of the Americas
New York, NY 10020

ISBN 978-1-4405-8497-8
ISBN 978-1-4405-8496-1(ebook)

To Michelle, for the friendship and laughter—but mostly for the greatest pun that's ever been punned.

Acknowledgments

My eternal gratitude to Sarah and Jesse Zuba, whose generous hospitality breathed new life into this project. Without their support, this novel would still be languishing on my hard drive.

Thanks to Synithia Williams, who listened to me ramble the whole way to Atlanta, and said a romance novel about corpse theft sounded like a great idea.

I sing hymns of praise and thanksgiving to Tara Gelsomino. Thank you for your enthusiastic support of this novel and of The Honorables. Every author should be lucky enough to have an editor like you in her corner. Thanks, too, to Annie Cosby, and the rest of the team at Crimson Romance, who always go above and beyond on my books.

Many thanks to my parents, my husband, and my children. Thank you for loving me, even when I'm on deadline. I couldn't do this without you all.

Finally, my heartfelt thanks to my readers. Your kind notes, comments, and questions mean so much.

Chapter One

1816, Middlesex

The grandfather clock in the corner thunked a steady rhythm, and Lorna sipped her tea. Around her, the parlor's shabby sofa and chairs stood empty, waiting for callers who wouldn't arrive. No one mourned the passing of a madman.

A series of hollow gongs announced ten o'clock. At the cemetery, the vicar soon would pray over Thomas, with only poor little Daniel and a manservant in attendance.

The droning chimes faded. Silence filled Lorna's ears, a soothing balm to her frayed nerves. Her brother's screams and curses had filled the house for months before the end came. Belligerent and wheedling and sinister by turns, the incessant noise had threatened to pull the whole house into insanity with him. Even when he no longer opened his lids because light hurt his eyes, his lips moved, spewing blasphemies and mad rants or begging for something—the services of a prostitute his most frequent request.

On one of these occasions, her resolve to ignore his revolting words had failed her. "Hasn't your whoring done enough?" she'd snapped. "There will be no more of that for you, brother."

Thomas growled in protest and squirmed against the lengths of linen bound to his ankles and wrists. One eye cracked open, rolling in the socket until it settled on Lorna. It looked like a watery poached egg floating in a ring of crusty lashes. Gaunt, stubbled cheeks pulled back to reveal slimy teeth. "Then give me *your* mouth." The thin, soiled nightshirt wadded around his thighs outlined a jutting erection.

Lorna's cheeks still burned in shame to recall her brother's suggestion. He'd laughed at her shocked indignation, all the while lewdly grinding his hips in circles. "You're too scrawny to fuck, and your cunt's dusty like a harp in the corner, waiting for someone to play it. But your lips are pink and ready." She'd never heard two of those words before, but it took her only a second to interpret them.

Lorna took a cake from the table of refreshments meant for sympathetic neighbors. Cook insisted on providing the late Baron Chorley a respectable funeral, despite the disgrace he had heaped upon the family while he lived. Lorna nibbled slowly, relishing the sweetness against her tongue.

Of late, her meals had been gulped down without tasting the food. Almost every waking moment had been spent at Thomas's bedside, watching the restraints. Twice he'd escaped. The first time, he kicked through a window, shredded his leg, and nearly bled to death before they wrestled him back into bed. The second time…Lorna winced at the memory of the maid's ruined face.

After that, Thomas was kept under constant supervision. Lorna hadn't thought it fair to leave the last remaining footman, Oscar, and the old butler, Humphrey, entirely in charge of tending him— especially since the servants worked out of loyalty now, rather than for a decent wage.

Lorna swept a few crumbs from the skirt of her black dress. The garment began its life a pale rose, but the necessity for mourning weeds had seen it dunked into a stinking vat of vinegar and dye just yesterday. Mrs. Lynch, the housekeeper, had smoothed an old sheet over Lorna's chair before she sat, lest dye bleed onto the faded upholstery.

A knock sounded at the front door. Lorna set down her teacup and folded her hands in her lap a few seconds before Humphrey's stooped form appeared in the parlor door. "A Mr. Wiggins is here, Miss Robbins," he said, presenting the caller's card.

"Show him in," she said.

The name sparked no recognition, but Lorna did not know most of Thomas's acquaintance. Fifteen years her senior, her half-brother had been mostly absent from Lorna's life. She'd made rare, brief visits to London, and he came home with even less frequency, despite the family seat being only a handful of miles outside of Town. They'd spent no length of time together until six months ago, when one of his London companions unceremoniously dumped him, soaking wet and raving, on the portico. From what Lorna had been able to piece together, Thomas had no friends, only people to whom he was indebted. If this Mr. Wiggins had come from Town to pay his respects, though, perhaps he'd been a true friend to her brother.

Humphrey returned with her guest. The man was not much taller than she, several inches over five feet. Stringy gray hair inadequately covered a balding pate, and the man's middle paunch had a sadly deflated quality to it, like an empty wineskin. His apparel looked fine at a distance, but when he took her hand in greeting, Lorna noted frayed cuffs and thin places at the seams. *Not that I've room to judge,* she thought, glancing at her own tatty furnishings.

"Miss Robbins," he said, "please accept my condolences for your loss." His accent carried the remnants of a working class upbringing.

"Thank you, Mr. Wiggins." Lorna took her seat and gestured him to a chair. "May I offer you some tea?"

"With my gratitude." As Lorna handed him a cup, he said, "I was hoping I might see Lord Chorley."

"Oh." Lorna faltered, grasping for delicate words. "I'm afraid that won't be possible. The viewing has ended. My brother has been moved to the church for burial. Unless…" She twisted her fingers together, uncertain about the protocol of graveside services. "If you hurry to the churchyard, you might be able to see him before…But I really don't know."

Wiggins gulped his beverage and smacked his lips. "I'll wait," he announced. "I've got no pressing engagements."

Lorna frowned. "I'm sorry, sir. Do you mean you wish to see the new Lord Chorley, not the deceased?"

"Just so," Wiggins replied. "I've no wish to peep at a soul case." His eyes narrowed on Lorna in suspicion. "Unless this is another ruse to get out of paying his notes. Has he skipped to Calais?"

Lorna suppressed a groan. So Mr. Wiggins wasn't a friend, after all. "If it's money you're after, sir, I'm afraid I cannot help you."

The man nodded. "Then we're all right, miss. I wouldn't dream of treating with a lady, so if you don't mind passing me one of those cakes, I'll just await his lordship's return."

One of her cakes, indeed. Lorna raised her chin a notch. "You mistake me, Mr. Wiggins. I run this household, not his lordship. Any understanding between you and my late brother is none of my affair, and I refuse to be drawn into his financial mishaps." She stood, calling upon every ounce of her girlhood comportment training to maintain a polite tone. "I do thank you for your condolences, Mr. Wiggins, but I'm afraid I must bid you a good day."

Wiggins wagged a knobby finger. "Now, now, missy, that dodge will never hold up in a court of law." From a pocket he produced a stack of notes, which he handed to Lorna.

A cursory examination showed amounts to make her stomach clench. A hundred pounds. Fifty. Five hundred twenty. All carried her worthless brother's signature, all dated within the last eighteen months. "Thomas was…sick," she said, her throat catching around the allusion to his insanity, "when he borrowed from you."

Wiggins sneered, all pretense of politeness dropped. "He's not the first taken by the French disease, and he won't be the last, but I'm out the coin anyway. My business is with Chorley. If the baron I knew has escaped to hell, then I'll speak to the new man in charge. He'll make good on these notes, all right, or I'll have the law on him."

The threat against Daniel turned Lorna's despair to rage in an instant. "*The new man in charge,*" she said, venom dripping from her words, "is a boy of seven. You cannot hold him responsible for another's debts." She threw the stack of notes right back in Wiggins's face, where they exploded like confetti.

A shadow darkened the moneylender's features an instant before he chuckled. He reclined in the chair, more at his ease than when she'd offered him tea and pleasantries. "Oh, but I can. Lord Chorley is responsible, and it doesn't matter a whit to me if he's a babe in arms. I'll bring suit against the estate. It'll cost you dear to have a barrister speak for you, and you'll still have to pay up in the end."

She closed her eyes and scratched at her head with both hands, an anxious habit she'd abandoned years ago—until Thomas came home. Now thin weals crisscrossed her scalp. She winced as her nails dragged across them; the pain brought clarity. Lorna rounded on him. A faint smell of vinegar wafted from her skirts as they swished around her legs. "All right, Wiggins, look." If he could drop the social façade, so could she. "I have perhaps twenty pounds to my name. Take it or leave it." She looked down her nose, raising a brow in challenge.

He guffawed.

"Twenty pounds, the chit says!" He wheezed through a laugh, his face going puce with the force of his amusement. "If that's not the best demmed jape I've heard this age and more." He wiped tears from his cheeks with the ratty cuff of his coat. Then he gathered up the promissory notes and tucked them into his pocket. "I'll leave your twenty and take the fifteen hun'ret I'm owed, miss."

He smiled as he rose to his feet, but the malice gleaming in his eyes sent ice to Lorna's toes. Wiggins stepped toward her. Lorna instinctively retreated. "I will have my due. Need be, I'll take this house and everything in it; I happen to know it ain't entailed. Better for you to sell on your terms, than give it to me on mine. You have two months, then it's pay up or else."

Sell Elmwood? Everything inside of Lorna rebelled at the notion. For years, she had worked to keep the estate's ledgers balanced. She had scrimped and cut back and done without, all to provide Daniel a safe, happy home. Thomas never did anything for his half-siblings. He couldn't be bothered to visit the small property more than once every few years. No, it had been Lorna's duty to keep everything running. And now Thomas was threatening to ruin her carefully ordered world from beyond the grave. She wouldn't allow it.

"Absolutely not," she declared. "I won't give up my home."

"Then you'll have to cough up the blunt some other way." Wiggins gave her an appraising look. "Might be you've something else to sell."

Lorna took leave to doubt that.

In response to her dubious expression, Wiggins turned cajoling. "You *could* use some meat on those bones, but there's some as like the skinny ones. Not to mention being the first to breach the walls, as it were, commands a higher rate—"

She shoved him, hard, toward the door. He stumbled and cracked his shin against a side table. The impact drew a hiss of pain from Wiggins.

"Get out," Lorna said in a low voice. "Take your notes and your filthy mouth, and get out of my house."

Wiggins rubbed his injury through his pant leg. "You're gonna wish you hadn't done that. I'll be back. Fifteen hundred. Cough it up, or I'll choke it from you." The moneylender limped from the room.

An hour later, Daniel found her. His dark eyes were wide and solemn in his slender face. Oscar the footman patted the new baron on the shoulder before leaving him in Lorna's care. When they were alone, Daniel curled up beside her, heedless of his formal black suit. Her arms twined around her young half-brother, pulling him into her lap, where he nestled against her. He was getting too big to fit comfortably, but neither of them was ready to give up the familiar closeness.

While Lorna had a few scant memories of her own mother, Daniel had none of his. His mother, their father's third wife, had died only hours after his birth. Following her burial, their father took a drunken ride. Never much of a horseman in the best of times, he was thrown from the saddle and broke his neck. At the age of fourteen, Lorna became the only parent Daniel had ever known.

She pressed her hands to the boy's face. "Your cheeks are cold, darling," Lorna murmured, lightly rubbing the pink skin to warm him.

"Yours are wet, Sissy." Daniel's chilled fingers smeared a tear toward her ear. His pale features pinched together. "Are you crying because you miss Brother?"

Lorna gave a watery laugh. As if she could miss the wastrel who had only brought them ruin. "No, sweetling, I'm crying because I missed *you*."

His slim arms circled her neck. "It's a silly rule, that ladies can't go to a burial. Now that I'm baron, I'm going to change it. You should be able to do anything you please."

She nuzzled the top of his head. His hair, honey-tinged brown, smelled of wind and dry leaves. "My own little knight in egalitarian armor." Fierce love thundered through her body. She would protect Daniel from Mr. Wiggins and anyone else who threatened her family. No matter what, she would keep Daniel safe and give him a home.

Even if she had to sell herself, body and soul, to do it.

• • •

After tucking Daniel into bed, Lorna swathed herself in Thomas's billowing black cloak and stepped outside. The early November evening carried a bite in the air, but she welcomed the brisk chill.

Her sturdy boots carried her across the lawn and down the familiar path through the small home wood to the lane heading into the village. The gathering dusk didn't signify. Her feet knew every root and stone along the way.

Since the funeral, Lorna had kept a semblance of calm about her for Daniel's sake. After the harrowing months they'd endured, the boy needed a return to the order of their life before Thomas's illness. All through the day, though, anger built inside her, until she felt her ribs would crack with it. The fire in her belly drove her onward.

Avoiding the village high street, Lorna slipped down the alley beside a tavern. Yellow light and sounds of male conversation seeped from chinks between the boards. She shrank from the light and noise, clinging to the shadows.

Two turnings brought her to the church, and a quick sprint across dead grass took her to her brother's grave. A little nosegay Lorna gave Daniel for the purpose lay atop the mound of earth. Thomas had a place in consecrated ground, blessed with the peace he'd ripped away from her.

Rage bubbled up from her gut, filling her throat and choking her. She wanted to scream at Thomas, to lash out at him for destroying the home she'd worked so hard to keep. How was she to find the money to pay the wretched Wiggins, except to sell her home or herself? A terrible choice. An impossible one. Marriage wasn't even a viable option. Lorna had no suitors. No man came sniffing after the homely daughter of a poor, country baron. Even if she started hunting a husband now, she would never marry in time to save Elmwood from Wiggins. No hero would swoop in to deliver them from ruin—it was up to Lorna to protect her family. She wished she knew the vile words Thomas knew. Nothing in her feeble lady's vocabulary was profane enough to express her outrage.

But she did know a couple, she recalled, compliments of her dear brother.

"Cunt." The word felt guttural, like a good, cleansing cough. "Fuck." Lorna didn't know how to use them in a sentence, but they were the worst words she'd ever heard. She hurled them at her dead sibling repeatedly, imbuing them with a healthy dose of hatred. When she'd had her fill of obscenities, she spat on his grave, in defiance of God's law and man's.

"How could you do this to us?" she demanded of her sibling. The anger that had sustained her all day turned to apprehension. "What shall I do?"

The more Lorna considered the hopelessness of her situation, the more she felt herself swamped by dread. Suddenly, her chest seized; her lungs refused to draw air. Fear clawed at her throat. *Have to get away.* Escape was the only thought left to her. If she stayed in this spot, she would surely die. Some distant part of her mind recognized no immediate threat, but the larger portion of Lorna's consciousness was overcome with the certainty of impending doom.

She whirled in a billow of black wool and launched herself into a dead run, her skin crackling as if from an imminent lightning strike. Lorna's feet only carried her a short distance from Thomas's resting place before she fell to her knees. Her vision narrowed and her ears rang, and then she knew no more.

Some time later, Lorna awakened to darkness. Her eyes felt gritty and her head ached, after-effects of the terrifying episode she'd suffered. She was in the cemetery, she recalled, curled inside Thomas's cloak. She pulled it from her face and choked back a yelp.

A huge hound loomed over her, slobber dangling in twin strands from loose jowls. It pressed a cold nose into her neck and snuffled. Lorna shoved at the beast's head. "Get off," she hissed. The dog licked her face.

"Hey, wassat?" The voice was nearby. "Coop," it called in a whisper. "Bluebell found somethin'."

"Body?" answered another voice—Coop, Lorna surmised. "S'not like the digger to leave one out. Might be one for the pauper pit. Pretty Lem, see what's what."

Lorna tried to back out from under the slavering Bluebell, but her hairy captor simply flopped down on her chest, pinning her. A few seconds later, a figure appeared with a shuttered lantern, illuminating the tan and black bloodhound. "Good girl, Blue. What you got? Is it—oh, shit!"

Lorna just made out the surprised face of a young man before he ran in the other direction. Bluebell heaved herself up and loped after Pretty Lem. "It's a lady, Coop! A live one! Pack it up, boys."

"Can't yet," said Coop. "Bob's in the ground."

Lorna scrambled behind a nearby gravestone. When no one immediately pounced on her, she peeked over the top. It was still night, dark except for the light of two lanterns illuminating a group of four men. They wore roughspun clothes, with scarves, gloves, and hats shielding them from the cold. Pretty Lem frantically gestured to where he'd found Lorna. One tall, lanky man propped himself against a shovel driven into the ground, as casual as you please. A third stood at the light's edge, minding a mule team hitched to a wagon. The fourth man, average in height and build, exuded an air of authority. He had to be Coop, the leader. That one listened to Pretty Lem and peered into the darkness. Lorna ducked behind the stone.

"Fartleberry, the second we've got the goods, start filling. Lem, you and me'll load." Coop issued orders with military efficiency. "Out o' the earth bath, Bob."

Bob's in the ground, he'd said a moment ago. The hair on her nape stood on end as she peered once more over the gravestone. An elongated, white shape emerged from the dank ground. In a sickening rush, Lorna realized they had opened her brother's grave.

Before she could consider the folly of it, she was pounding toward the gang. "Stop!" she cried. The too-large cloak tangled around her legs; she went sprawling, face first, into the loose soil that used to cover her brother.

The gangmen glanced her way, but continued their grisly work. Coop dragged Thomas's wrapped body away from the grave, while the thug he'd called Fartleberry gave a hand to a fifth man emerging from the ground.

Lorna sputtered dirt and swiped at her nose. She'd spat on Thomas's grave just hours before, and thought it the worst insult possible. Compared to this atrocity, it seemed a tender caress. "Put him back!" she demanded.

The hulking brute fresh from the ground leaped the open hole and grabbed Lorna around the middle. He hauled her away from the dirt, which Fartleberry began shoveling back into Thomas's empty grave.

"What'll we do wif her, Coop?" the big man's voice rumbled.

Fartleberry chucked dirt into the hole at an impressive rate. Lorna noted the shovel the man used had a wooden head, not iron. "We oughter do her and sell three, 'stead of two." His words were muffled by the scarf covering the bottom half of his face. The calm way he suggested Lorna's demise made her lightheaded.

"We're not doing nobody," Coop said.

He and Pretty Lem loaded Thomas into the back of the wagon, alongside another corpse. Bluebell propped her front feet on the wagon bed and sniffed the bodies, while Lem retrieved another shovel and joined his comrade in moving dirt.

"Ten quid ain't worth our necks." Coop wiped his hands on his baggy trousers, then swatted Fartleberry on the back of the head. "Use your breadbox 'fore you go spouting off, fool."

He sauntered toward Lorna with a lantern. She twisted in her big captor's hands. For her pains, Bob merely lifted her from the ground and held her more securely against his filthy coat. He smelled of death and worms. Her head swam.

Coop hoisted the lantern to her face. Lorna squinted at the light. "You picked the wrong night for a midnight stroll, girl."

As her eyes adjusted, Lorna took in details. Coop had a large nose, spiderwebbed with blood vessels. His ruddy cheeks were covered in gray stubble. Pale, suspicious eyes squinted at her.

"I wasn't strolling," Lorna informed him, "I was visiting my brother's grave." She kicked her boot heel into the big man's shin, earning an "Oi!" in return. "Tell your ruffian to let me go."

"Set 'er down, Bob, but keep a hand on 'er."

As soon as Lorna's feet touched the ground, she ducked out of Bob's grasp and darted to the wagon. She tugged at the dingy linen covering her brother. "Put him back! He isn't wearing any valuables, nothing worth stealing."

Bob reached her in a few quick strides and snatched her arms. Bluebell bayed and pranced around them in a circle, as if they were playing a game.

"Beggin' to differ, miss, but we got what we came for." Coop's nose dripped; he swiped it with the fringe of his scarf. "Daft Jemmy," he called to the mule handler, "get the team ready to go." To the men filling Thomas's grave, he said, "Double time, lads. We're gone in five. Harty Choke Boys won't be none pleased when they find we've picked their garden."

Fartleberry grunted in reply. He wielded his shovel like a fencing master with a foil, graceful and swift. The hole was nearly full again. Beside him, Pretty Lem methodically arranged the soil neatly at the edges so it resembled the undertaker's original work.

"What do you mean, you've got what you came for?" Lorna demanded. "Who's the other body? And why do you want them? Thomas wasn't important. He wasn't…"

She trailed off as Coop chuckled. Behind him, Pretty Lem gently replaced Daniel's nosegay atop of the grave. Once the gang cleared out, no one would ever know tonight's macabre crime had taken place. No one but Lorna.

From the wagon bed, Coop fetched a coil of rope. "Your Tommy might not've been worth anything to you," he said as he approached, "but he's worth ten quid to the anatomists. Maybe twelve, if we can offload 'im fresh."

The implication shocked Lorna to her core. She barely noticed as Bob spun her so Coop could tie her wrists. The hempen rope bit into her flesh, snapping her mind into focus. What the thief said horrified her. Appalled her.

Intrigued her.

"Wait just a minute!" Once more, she kicked large Bob's abused shin and wrestled around to face Coop, flinging her arms free of the rope. Annoyance pinched the boss's lips, but Lorna was riding high on the sudden deliverance laid before her. "Be perfectly clear, sir. You mean to sell my brother's body?"

"Yeah, that's right. Now turn around like a good ewe and let me tie you up. I wouldn't argue with a third quarron, so don't make me do somefin unfortunate, eh?"

The threat hadn't much weight behind it, but who knew what these miscreants were capable of? Lorna licked her lips, recognizing a moment of decision was upon her. This was a group of thieves, she told herself, not murderers. If Coop and his gang meant her violence, they'd have done it already—wouldn't they?

Squeezing her eyes shut, Lorna summoned the image of her little brother. Daniel relied upon her. She'd sworn to do whatever it took to provide for and protect him. And so she would. The decision made, a strange calm settled over her.

Pretty Lem hopped to the driver's seat and took the reins from Daft Jemmy. The remaining men and the dog clambered into the bed with their frightful cargo, leaving room on the front bench for Coop. And Lorna, if she got her way. "Bob, help me into the wagon, please," she instructed her burly captor. She strode the short distance to the wagon, leaving a protesting Coop to trail in her wake.

"What in the bleedin', blazin' hells is this? Bob, don't you lift a finger to help her."

Lorna turned on a heel and shot Coop a quelling look. "Thomas's body belongs to his family. If anyone is going to sell it, it will be me."

Chapter Two

London

Wiping his hands clean, Brandon Dewhurst bid his anatomy students a good day. As the young men filed out of the dissection theatre, he noted that several still looked a touch greenish from their first postmortem operation. One of the fellows who'd stayed behind to help clean up wasn't faring very well with his duties; he gagged while bundling up the body. Brandon had seen it over and over again in his several years of teaching: New students of surgery and anatomy steeled themselves to boldly handle viscera, only to be done in by the unexpected stench.

Death stank abominably, but this was nothing compared to the choking confines of the Army's surgery tents in Portugal, where Brandon had learned his trade. There, the pounding heat took the scent of hundreds of unwashed men and cooked them with the surgery's fetid air of sickness and rotting meat until the aroma was an entity of its own, a loathsome thing permeating the camp, filling his throat, and clinging to his hair and skin, no matter how he scrubbed after a day's labor. Having spent the five years of his service breathing those noxious fumes, the scent of a lone corpse barely registered in Brandon's nose.

His father, Viscount Marcel, had complained that he'd not purchased a commission for his youngest son to become a sawbones, but Brandon had preferred healing to killing other men in battle.

The last of the students gone, Brandon climbed a flight of stairs to the upper floor of McGully's Covent Garden School of Anatomical Studies. For the past three years, he'd worked under the Scottish surgeon-anatomist Douglas McGully. Brandon rapped on the door of his mentor's private dissection room.

"Come in, lad."

Warm sunshine bathed the chamber with twice as much light as the schoolroom, owing to the tall windows on three walls and skylights overhead. Brandon filled his lungs. The faint scent of polishing wax hung in the air, with the barest metallic whiff of blood. Only the freshest specimens graced Douglas McGully's table. His were far more expensive and difficult for Brandon to obtain than the corpses used by the students. Many were dead only hours before their mortal secrets were uncovered by the eminent surgeon.

In the center of the room, McGully worked at his table, peeling back the layers of a young woman's abdomen.

Beside Brandon's mentor, another gentleman perched on a stool with a sketch book in his lap and an array of his own tools—charcoal sticks, pencils, pens, and small bottles of ink—neatly lined in a wooden case on a smaller table. The artist, Mr. Culpepper, constantly glanced back and forth between his own work and McGully's. He had the long fingers and light touch of a surgeon, and would have made a fine one, had he not been of an artistic bent. Still, his collaborations with McGully were great contributions to the world. Together, the surgeon and artist had produced five volumes exploring various conditions or systems of the body. Each book was revered as anatomical gospel.

The old Scotsman folded the last layer of tissue covering the abdominal muscles, then stepped back while Culpepper finished his sketch. "Take a look," he said, wiping his hands on a towel. "Care to guess how far gone the lass is?"

Brandon's chest constricted at McGully's invitation. He confronted death day in and day out. He lived amongst the dead and fought to save the dying. He had seen men's intestines spill from their bellies and had sawed off limbs without flinching while his patients screamed. There was little left in the surgical world that bothered him, but the pregnant ones got him every time.

In the recesses of his mind, he saw another woman, writhing in the back of a cart. Long, black hair clung to her sweat-drenched face. Her mouth was locked in a rictus of pain, yet no sound escaped her lips. Dark eyes rolled until they settled on him, filled with silent pleading, as her life drained away between her legs. Around him, people shouted in Portuguese and English, arguing, demanding, begging. Their voices barely registered. There was only Brandon, the woman, and the child.

Brandon slammed a mental door on the memory, willing his mind into a place of cold reason. Gently, he laid his hands on the exposed muscle and closed his eyes. He pressed in and down, probing for the top of the womb. Just above the pelvic bone, a firm roundness pushed its way into the abdominal cavity. He drew a breath and opened his eyes. McGully peered at him with a steady gaze. "Not very long," Brandon said soberly. "Two and a half months, three at the latest."

"Tried to slip the babe." McGully sniffed, fished a handkerchief from his pocket, and honked into it. "Drank a hokum potion— brewed by some incompetent midwife, no doubt. I smelled it in her mouth." His voice, muffled by the cloth over his nose, communicated his derision of these inferior practitioners. McGully stuffed the handkerchief up his sleeve while he gazed at his specimen. "Poisoned to death before she bled, poor lamb." He patted the girl's hand as if to comfort her.

On the other side of the table, Culpepper sifted through his pen nibs, which clinked together with cheery, tinny sounds.

"I need more," McGully said. "And later. You've brought me four in the early stages, but I must have specimens farther gone. We need to examine the fully blossomed womb to track the process of fetal development." McGully's furry eyebrows drew together in a white caterpillar. "I say, Dewhurst, are you quite all right?"

Brandon nodded and wiped the sheen of moisture that had popped out on his brow as his employer spoke. Intellectually, he knew the work was necessary. Vital, even. Too many women perished during pregnancy and birth. The only way to combat these fatalities was with knowledge. But, God above, he hated seeing the pregnant ones.

"Yes, sir," he said. "My contacts are keeping their ears to the ground for the wom—" *Cold, distant,* he reminded himself. "For the specimens you require."

"Excellent. Thank you." McGully clapped Brandon on the shoulder. "I'm counting on you, lad."

Unbidden, the face of the dark-eyed woman flashed through his mind. *So was she.*

· · ·

Soft tapping at the alley door woke him at once. Brandon rarely slept more than a few hours at a stretch, and then never deeply. Within seconds, he was out of bed and wrapped in his great-coat. He stumbled from the basement room in which he resided, scooped up the lantern in the hallway, and wrenched open the door, letting in an icy gust of wind.

On the stoop stood the leader of the Artichoke Boys. He wore trousers ripped at the knees and a muddy coat. A muffler wrapped about his head framed his red, chapped face. "Evenin', sir." The man bobbed his head.

Brandon nodded in return. "Slee." He lifted the lantern and peered toward the mouth of the alley. He made out the shadowy figures of three other men pulling bodies from the back of their wagon. Brandon was part of a noble profession, but this aspect of his work, coldly dealing in stolen human bodies, sometimes made him sympathize with the penny dreadfuls' lurid depictions of surgeon-anatomists as ghoulish fiends. Of course, understanding public disdain didn't make it any easier to swallow. "I trust you got my message this evening, about a fishwife."

Slee chortled. "Indeed I did, sir. She weren't no one's wife. Not in the proper sense, aye? Sold more'n fishies, too, right?" He rocked back on his heels and grinned, displaying brown teeth and gaping holes.

Slee wasn't normally so jovial at three in the morning. His odd mood put Brandon on edge. "Did you bring her?"

"Weeeell, that's the question, though, isn't it?" Slee stepped back to let his men come forward with two wrapped bodies. "You wanna 'spect the goods?"

"Is one of them the woman I asked for, or not?" he demanded.

"Not as such." Slee wrung his hands in a manner Brandon supposed was meant to pass for ingratiating. "It seems one of our competitors—a professional rival, you might say—acquired the body before we were able to claim it."

"It was them Crib Cross Gang," announced one of Slee's brutes. He huffed a cloud into the cold air and rearranged the burden slumped over his shoulders. "They've cut us out lots, ever since that 'ristocrat." The brute's face crumpled in thought. "He was a baron or somefin, ain't that right, Slee? The one we didn't get for Mr. Dewhurst a week back? A baron?" Slee made a sharp gesture at his subordinate. "Well, it's true," the hireling muttered dolefully. "And 'snot jus' us. Crib Cross is running circles 'round all the gangs."

"How can this have happened?" Brandon demanded. "I heard of this woman barely an hour after she died, sent word straight to you, and another gang *beat you to the body?*"

"We went first thing tonight," Slee protested. "Earlier than we should've, even, but Crib Cross beat us by hours. Took the lady in broad daylight, we heard. God's own truth, I can't see how they pulled it off."

Brandon slammed the side of his fist against the door frame. At least McGully didn't know about the body. What would he say if he learned Brandon had let an eight-months-pregnant specimen slip through his fingers?

He waved the men carrying the bodies inside. When Slee tried to step in, Brandon blocked his way. "This cannot happen again," he warned. "When I tell you to get me a body, you get it right away. I don't care if you're in the middle of your own wedding, you get me the damned body."

Slee chuckled, but his laughter died on his lips when he met Brandon's furious gaze. He ducked his head. "Yes, sir," he said, abashed. "Won't happen again, sir."

After the Artichoke Boys left, Brandon took himself back to bed and groaned. He couldn't believe the bad luck. The resurrection gangs weren't the only ones with professional rivals. At this very moment, another anatomist had his hands on the corpse that should have been Brandon's.

How had the other gang done it? He tried to imagine a group of rough, dirty louts waltzing out with a fresh body in front of the deceased woman's neighbors, but couldn't conjure the picture. Body snatchers didn't operate like that. They kept to the dark and scattered like cockroaches at the first sign of trouble.

"The Crib Cross Gang," Brandon whispered into his dark room. This was not the first time the gang had thwarted him. He'd been disappointed to miss out on the baron's corpse. Aristocrats tended to be in overall good shape when they died, making them plum specimens. According to the Artichoke Boys, Crib Cross had been wildly successful of late. They were beating the other resurrectionists to the best bodies. How? Brandon couldn't let a bunch of ruffians stymie his or McGully's careers by cutting their access to corpses.

Brandon would have to get more directly involved. He didn't trust Slee and his lot to outwit their rivals. They had no reason to risk themselves on Brandon's behalf—unless they had proper incentive. It would take some doing, but with his usual cold, surgical precision, Brandon would uncover Crib Cross's secrets, and put a stop to them.

Chapter Three

At a dirty table in a dirty tavern, the Crib Cross Gang was in high spirits. Coop pressed a tankard into Lorna's hand. She had no desire for more ale, but the other men wanted to toast her. How many was this tonight? Three drinks? Four? Lorna had never had ale before falling in with the resurrectionists, but they quaffed the stuff like it was the only thing saving them from certain doom.

"I can't," she protested, sliding the mug back toward Coop. She felt uncomfortably full, though she'd had little food today.

"My treat," Coop insisted. Lorna had learned the gang leader's name was Nat Cooper, but he looked mortally offended the one time she called him Mr. Cooper. "Business has never been brighter, thanks to you." He winked and nudged the beer. "Least I can do is keep our Blackbird watered."

On one of her first nights with the gang, Daft Jemmy had commented that Lorna's skirts flapped like a blackbird's wings. The others quickly adopted the nickname, informing her that every resurrection man needed one.

"Aww, go on," cajoled Pretty Lem from across the table. He flashed her a dazzling smile and raised his drink in salute. "To my 'sister,' lads."

Lem really was as handsome as his moniker suggested, with mischievous, hazel eyes and golden curls. His ready smile showed a row of white teeth, their neatness interrupted by a chipped front tooth, which only made his dimpled grin more endearing. Tonight he looked especially fine, thanks to the thorough scrubbing Lorna had insisted he undertake before this afternoon's outing. Every barmaid in the establishment cast doe eyes at Lem, and he had no compunction in returning their appreciative regard.

"Stroke o' genius, it was," Coop said, "claiming to be sibs come to fetch your dear sister's mortal remains."

"Tears an' all!" Fartleberry grasped his hands together at his chest, blinked his eyes rapidly, and set his bottom lip to quivering. "'Oh, ma'am,'" he said in a falsetto, "'my dearest sister *must* have mentioned me an' our brother! We were *ever* so close as chil'ren.'" His imitation of Lorna's voice set the table to laughing. He trailed his fingertips down his cheeks to indicate tears. "'I can't believe this, both her an' the babe. Boo hoo!'" Fartleberry clapped his hands to the tabletop and laughed, face red and eyes streaming. "Goddamn!" He wiped his nose with his sleeve. "Ain't an actor on Drury could squeeze a tear better—God strike me blind if it ain't so."

Bob tossed a crust of bread at Fartleberry's head. "Naw, we need your eyes, but He can 'ave your nutmegs," he said, setting off another round of hilarity.

Lorna forced a laugh for the sake of her company. Meanwhile, her stomach churned with the cheap ale and the memory of another dead woman's bulging stomach. This was the second heavily pregnant woman this week.

To her right, Daft Jemmy turned wide, innocent eyes on her. She hated seeing him in his cups; it was like watching a child imbibe. But there was no stopping the gang from providing him drink. He leaned over, his full, soft lips almost touching her ear and whispered, "Still sad, sweet miss?"

A lump formed in her throat. Lorna nodded.

"I used to cry, too," Jemmy continued softly. Lorna strained to hear him over the raucous merriment in the public house. "But then Coop tol' me they're all jus' sleepin', an' sleep ain't nuffin' to cry over, 'less you're 'fraid of the dark." He nodded sagely and patted her hand.

Lorna's head and heart ached, and she feared she would toss her accounts if she lingered any longer. "I must go now," she announced. She thrust out her hand. "My share, if you please."

Coop chuckled while he dug in his pocket. "You caught on right quick, eh? Just as blunt about blunt as the rest of 'em. All right, then, le'see." He flipped through a stack of bank notes and peeled two off. "We got eighty for that one—best I ever done on a single stiff. Ten's your share." He added a coin to the paper bills. "An' a bonus for your fine performance."

Eleven pounds was barely a chink in what she owed Wiggins, but was by far the largest take she'd earned in a night. Altogether, she'd earned about fifty in a week. It felt like a fortune, but she hadn't yet earned even a tenth of her debt. She had to get more—lots more, and fast.

She shoved the money into the pocket of her cloak and bid the men good night. Her black mourning attire drew a few curious glances from the other patrons, but this was the kind of establishment in which people knew better than to nose into someone else's affairs, and eyes were quickly averted again.

A pool of light spilled from the door when she opened it, illuminating a man who had been reaching for the handle. He didn't belong here any more than she did—that much was evident by his straight, confident bearing. In a fleeting second, her mind sketched an impression: tall, but not odiously so; striking in appearance, but not particularly handsome.

Their eyes met. Somehow, he saw right through her. His gaze laid her bare. She felt as if an invisible fist drove the air from her lungs. Then she started to panic.

Lorna ducked her head and shouldered past the man. She stomped through an icy puddle, dragging the hem of her dress through filthy slush.

"Stop!" called the man in an authoritative tone. "Miss… ma'am, stop!"

Her mind screamed, *Runner*. Why else would a gentleman be here? If he was an investigator with Bow Street, if he had weaseled out the Crib Cross Gang…Never mind losing her home, what would become of her little brother if Lorna was arrested? Daniel would be left without a soul in the world.

Lorna's feet picked up speed. The warren-like East End was still unfamiliar territory, despite the nighttime excursions that had brought her here numerous times of late. Getting lost was preferable to getting caught, though, so she lifted her skirts and sprinted down one street, and then another. Heavy footsteps pounded behind her at first as the man called out again. Lorna turned another corner and ran faster, nimbly avoiding other pedestrians. Her black bonnet fell backward, catching itself by the bow around her neck. Hair tumbled from pins and whipped around her ears. Her heart slammed against her ribs, and her throat burned with the cold air heaving in and out.

Ramshackle tenements teetered over the narrow, muck-filled street. Fetid smells of emptied chamber pots and rotting refuse assaulted her. The sounds of a woman and man screaming at each other poured out of one window, while a child's wail fell from another. Lorna couldn't hear her pursuer any longer. Had she shaken him? Just to be safe, she took one last turn.

She raced forward, only to find the back of a building looming ahead, ending the alley. Lorna pivoted to retrace her steps. As she turned, her boot found some slick mire; her foot shot out and she fell sideways, landing on hip and elbow. A sharp hiss escaped between her teeth, but she didn't dare cry out. She scrabbled to regain her footing and lurched onward.

A man—*the* man—skidded to a halt at the mouth of the alley. "There you are!" He took several quick strides toward her.

Lorna backed away just as quickly. Her breath came in choking, rasping half-sobs. Lightheaded with fear, she searched frantically for some means of deliverance. In a rubbish heap mounded against the wall, a small shadow pounced.

She dove into the midden and grabbed the cat by the scruff of the neck. It yowled and spit, dropping a fresh-killed rat. Lorna snatched the rodent by the tail and flung it at the man; it bounced harmlessly off his thigh. The cat she grasped under its front legs, flailing claws aimed at her adversary.

"Back away!" Lorna shouted as she advanced, wielding her furry weapon with as much menace as she could muster.

"Did you just throw a *rat* at me?" The man sounded more perplexed than angry. He started forward again.

"Stay back!" By now she was only a few feet from the man. If she could throw him off balance, she might buy herself a precious few seconds to dash past him and out of the alley. She lunged, and the furious cat swiped at the man's face.

He dodged the claws. "Miss, please," he called over the feline clamor. "I mean you no harm. I only wanted to give you this." He extended a hand. "It fell from your pocket when you left the tavern."

Lorna glanced at the proffered hand. It contained a wad of bills, her night's pay. Her arms drooped as the manic fear slipped away. "Oh."

The cat twisted in her grasp and lashed out again, this time catching the man's fingers. He sucked a sharp breath and snatched his arm back. The money fell to the ground.

Startled, Lorna released the cat, which crouched and bared its fangs before it sprang back to the refuse pile. "I'm so sorry!" Without a thought, she grabbed the man's hand to assess the injury.

"It's nothing," he protested, breaking the contact.

"No, no, let me see," Lorna insisted.

She yanked off her dirty gloves and took his hand again. His warmth surprised her, and felt marvelous in her chilled palms. It was so dim in the alley, she couldn't see enough to be of any use, but she made a go of examining the cuts, anyway. She just barely detected the thin claw marks, which showed as dark lines against his skin.

She cradled his injured limb, palm up. It was a lovely hand, she thought, as she traced long, slender fingers. There was a rough spot on the pad of his index finger, a small callus, but none on any other. What caused this one thickening? A bead of blood spilled over his middle digit. Lorna patted it with her cloak. "I'm afraid I don't have a handkerchief," she said as she looked up. "Do you—"

Her words died in her throat when she saw his expression. Even in the near-darkness, she recognized his intensity. He held himself perfectly still; only his eyes moved, following her every gesture. Once more, she felt hunted.

His hand fell as she stepped back. She stooped to retrieve her money, this time stuffing the bills into her gloves as she donned them. All the while, he remained still, watching. "Thank you for your kindness, sir."

"Not at all, Miss…"

She shook her head. No names.

"May I escort you somewhere?" His voice was all politeness, seemingly unfazed by the mad chase she'd led him on through the seedy side of London.

"Thank you, no." Lorna stepped wide to move around him. Her head redoubled its pounding, and her stomach roiled queasily. "I must be going. Home. To my brother. I must…I must take care of my brother." She knew she was babbling, but couldn't seem to stop herself. What was it about this man? Perhaps he really was an inspector, or…Well, at the moment, she couldn't think of anything more terrifying than an agent of Bow Street.

Around her, the city crept back into her awareness. The fighting couple still yelled. A man's boisterous, drunken voice echoed nearby. A dog barked. The air stank. And it was cold, so cold. She shivered and wrapped herself tighter in her cloak. "Sorry about your hand," she said in a voice just over a whisper. The need for escape would not be contained another moment. "Good night."

The weight of his gaze bore down on her as she fled.

• • •

Brandon watched until she disappeared in the murk. "What the hell just happened?" he muttered.

His conscience nagged at him for allowing her to go off by herself. The East End was no place for a lone woman, especially at night. But she was so skittish, he feared he'd frighten her again if he insisted on accompanying her.

The scratch from that infernal cat stung. So much for the warm glow of performing a good deed. "If this festers," he said in the animal's direction, "I shall take great pleasure in hunting you down and skinning you alive. That's my cutting hand, you wretched beast."

As he worked his way back through the maze of alleys and streets, Brandon's mind lingered on the strange young woman. She seemed to be in mourning, swathed all in black as she was, so what on earth was she doing in a disreputable public house? He wondered, too, who it was she mourned. Had she lost a parent? She might even be widowed, he supposed.

Beyond her dress, he'd been able to make out little detail. She was so slender, at first he thought her no more than an adolescent. She ran like a sprightly youth, too. Brandon had been hard-pressed to keep up with her, and could not hope to match her agility in dodging obstacles. Only his longer stride allowed him to follow her.

Her hair, once loosed from the dowdy bonnet, revealed itself to be a mass of tight, shoulder-length curls that seemed to have a life of their own. She'd looked like Medusa in a fine pique as she threatened him with the cat. He couldn't determine the shade of her eyes, but they flashed clear and bright with the bits of light they caught. Slightly upturned nostrils flared indignantly when she warned him away. Altogether, she might be considered to possess only passing looks, but when she turned her face up from tending his hand and he got a close look at her mouth…Lord, those lips. Wide and lush with a gentle, elongated bow, rather than the pronounced pout popular with the fashionable set. That was when he determined she was no adolescent girl, but a grown woman. No child possessed such a mouth.

He hoped she made it home to her brother in one piece. It would be the worst pity imaginable for something unfortunate to befall the owner of those lips.

Putting the lady out of mind, he finally arrived once more at the public house. Taking a look at the shingle over the entrance, though, he discovered he'd come to the wrong place to begin with. He was supposed to meet Slee at The Fox and Hare; this was The Fox and Hound.

A frustrated growl rumbled in his chest. Too many foxes, hares, and hounds—not to mention stags, crowns, and kings—littered the names of establishments. Brandon vowed that if he ever had occasion to own a public house, he would call it The Purple Tortoise.

He stepped inside anyway, intending to ask the direction of The Fox and Hare. The stifling air was thick with tallow smoke, as well as the pungent smells of alcohol and unwashed humanity. Heads swiveled his way as he entered, and speculative murmuring began at once. Only one table in the corner, populated with five merrymakers, paid him no heed. Brandon was uncomfortably aware of how out of place he looked.

Distrustful glares followed him to the bar. Every step of the way, the soles of his boots adhered slightly to the filthy floor. He raised a hand to get the attention of the barkeeper, a rotund woman with scraggly hair falling from an untidy knot. "I beg your pardon, can you tell me how to get to The Fox and Hare?"

The woman wiped the inside of a pewter mug with a grease-stained apron. "This 'ere's The Fox 'n' 'ound." She snorted loudly and spat on the floor.

"And a fine place it is, too," Brandon replied. "But may I have the direction of The Fox and Hare?"

She sucked on her teeth. "Naw, I don' send custom elsewhere. What kind o' sense is that?" She plunked down the mug, selected another from the bar top, and gave it the same treatment with her apron. "Ken I get you summat?"

Brandon dug in a pocket and withdrew a coin, which he set in front of her. "Directions, please."

The woman sniffed and spat again. At last she deigned to acknowledge the offering. "Get outta 'ere and make a left. Then another one, an' a right. There you'll be." She swiped the coin behind the counter and shambled off to respond to a thirsty patron.

As he started to leave, the table in the corner caught his attention with their raucous laughter. One of the men rose, swaying as he stood. He hoisted a mug into the air. "To rum days ahead, me lads. Crib Cross forever!"

"Forever an' ever," came the happy reply from another.

Brandon halted, stunned. Here before him was the very gang causing him so much trouble. They didn't look more capable than any other resurrection men. Indeed, the entire breed seemed cut from the same cloth. Dirty and stooped from constant digging, eyes that squinted in the light, because they worked so much in the dark. One of the men at the table put the lie to Brandon's notions when he stood to offer another toast. Soft, golden curls framed a clean, handsome face. He looked like he'd just stepped out of a Botticelli canvas. Then a barmaid passed by, and he slapped her rump and made a bawdy compliment, shattering the angelic illusion. The woman fell, laughing, into his arms.

Brandon took a step toward the group, then stopped. With no plan, what could he accomplish? But perhaps the clean young man was a hint. Of what, Brandon couldn't say. The woman in black floated to the forefront of his mind. It could be no coincidence that a lady in deepest mourning was present in the same location as a gang of body snatchers, could it?

Mulling over the implications of this discovery, Brandon went in search of Slee.

Chapter Four

Lorna plucked glumly through her wardrobe. Never abundant to begin with, her selection of dresses slowly dwindled as, one by one, she handed them over to Mrs. Lynch and her dye vat. Her clothes, once so familiar, had become an uncomfortable uniform—a symbol both of familial obligation and of her ghastly activities.

Finally deciding that one black monstrosity was much the same as the next, she quickly dressed for breakfast. The previous night's overabundance of ale left her innards tender, but a cup of tea and a nibble of toast should put her to rights.

Before she made it out of her room, her brother scratched at the door and poked his head in. Worry furrowed his brow until his eyes settled on her, then his face relaxed. "Sissy!" He stepped into her waiting arms and clamped around her middle. "I had a nightmare last night."

Lorna cooed and smoothed one hand over his head, while the other patted his back. His shirttails, she noted, hung loose from his breeches. "Poor darling! Was it very terrible?"

Daniel squirmed out of her grasp. Dark circles bruised the delicate skin beneath his brown eyes. "It was Thomas. He screamed and yelled at me. I was trapped in his room, and I couldn't find the door." A shudder rocked his small frame.

She flinched at his words. Though she'd kept Daniel away from Thomas as much as possible, there had been no way to shield the boy entirely from their eldest sibling. No wonder those horrors haunted his dreams.

Crouching down, she took Daniel's hands. "That's all over now," she assured him.

He tensed as he continued. "He got out of bed and chased me around the room, all the time laughing and screaming. I ran, but

I couldn't get away. I called out, but you never came." He ducked his head to hide a trembling lip.

Gently, Lorna tipped his chin up. "I will always come for you, Daniel. I will always be here for you."

His jaw firmed; his gaze accused. "You weren't last night."

She breathed a nervous laugh. "What do you mean, darling? Of course I was—"

"No, you weren't." He took an obstinate stance, arms crossed, legs planted wide. "I woke up and I…I was frightened." She could tell how much it cost him to admit as much. "I came here. I thought I might…" His posture wilted.

Lorna knew what he would not say. Daniel used to come to her room at night after a bad dream. Snuggled at her side, he would sleep peacefully until morning. He'd needed her last night, and she'd failed him. Her heart sank.

"Where were you?" he demanded.

As though a puppeteer pulled her strings, her arms jerked up and her nails dug into her scalp, raking the skin. "I couldn't sleep." She covered the agitated habit by patting her unruly hair before clamping both hands in her skirts. "I went for a walk."

Daniel's eyes narrowed. "You give me warm milk when I have trouble sleeping."

Lorna's chin raised a notch. "Warm milk has no effect on adults, Daniel. Exercise is a better soporific, I find."

He remained unconvinced, she saw. Guilt stabbed through her, but admitting the truth behind her absence was quite out of the question. "Come now," she said, "you must eat."

She studiously avoided young Lord Chorley's pointed frown during breakfast, instead feigning deep interest in the contents of the marmalade pot.

Humphrey, his voice coming from the entrance hall, broke the silence. "Oh, no you don't. Get out! Out, I say! Oscar," he called, summoning the footman, "come at once!"

Alarmed by the commotion, Lorna sprang to her feet. She ordered Daniel to stay put and hurried into the corridor.

In the foyer, Humphrey made slow, arthritic attempts at shooing away the large tan and black bloodhound eagerly sniffing her way around the perimeter of the space. The dog paid the old retainer no mind, but her head snapped up when Lorna entered. With a happy woof, she trotted, jowls swinging and tail wagging, to Lorna's side. Red-rimmed eyes buried in folds of fur gazed at her adoringly, while drool dangled from a lip.

Lorna groaned. The last she'd seen of Bluebell, the dog had been gnawing on a beef bone in the mews that housed the gang's wagon and mules. The animal must have followed Lorna home last night after she retrieved her mare.

"Oscar, seize the cur," Humphrey ordered. The footman started for Bluebell, but Lorna stayed him with a hand.

"Just a moment, Oscar." She turned to the butler. "Where did you find her?"

Daniel whooped behind Lorna. "A dog!"

"I told you to stay in the breakfast room," Lorna scolded.

Ignoring his sister, Daniel bounded over, rubbed Bluebell's large ears, and was rewarded with sloppy licks all over his face. Daniel fell over on the yellow marble floor, giggling wildly, while Bluebell laved him with attention.

"Daniel," Lorna started. With a sigh, she left him to his fun and raised a brow at Humphrey.

"When I opened the door to sweep the portico, there it was." He pointed an accusing finger at his adversary. "The great lummox waltzed right in."

On the floor, Daniel now lay on top of Bluebell, his lithe body running the length of her back. The boy's arms wrapped around the dog's neck; his cheek rested on her withers. For her part, Bluebell panted contentedly.

"Get off of the dog," Lorna said.

Daniel's arms gripped Bluebell tighter. "Can we keep it, Sissy?" Boy and dog both gazed at her with liquid brown eyes.

Lorna squeezed the balls of her hands against her throbbing temples. Last night's overindulgence would not be forgotten anytime soon. With the headache came memories of the man who'd chased her down. Was he truly just a good Samaritan who'd gone to extraordinary lengths to return her money, or was he something else?

A chill washed over her. Whoever the man might be, he served as a pointed reminder of the risk Lorna took by working with the Crib Cross Gang. The sooner she repaid Wiggins, the safer she and Daniel would be. Another thought intruded—if Bluebell could follow her home, who else might do so?

"We can't keep the dog."

Her brother's face fell and he let out a disappointed whine. "But why? Oh, please! I promise I'll take care of it myself. You won't have to do a thing. I'll walk it and feed it and—"

"Daniel, no," she said firmly. "She must belong to someone." Truthfully, Lorna didn't know which gang member claimed ownership of Bluebell, but all the men considered her part of the team. "I have to go into the city for a few days. I'll take the dog with me and try to find her owner along the way. When I come home, we can discuss getting a dog of your own."

"I don't want *a* dog," Daniel protested. "I want *this* dog." He burst into tears and buried his face in Bluebell's fur. The animal rested her head on her paws and whimpered.

At the sight of his young master's outburst, Oscar discreetly withdrew. Humphrey gave a firm nod of approval at Lorna, then tottered away.

Lorna crouched and rubbed her brother's back. As he cried, her tired eyes took in the entrance hall. The marble tile showed scuff marks, and the tapestry wall hanging had faded in the sun. A fanlight above the door hosted a thick layer of dust, while one of the sidelights needed the glazier's attention.

It wasn't much, but it was home. It was hers and Daniel's, and she intended to keep it that way. Staying in London for a while would allow her to concentrate on her work with the gang, and keep anyone more undesirable than a dog from tailing her home.

"Darling, listen," she murmured. "I have to go see Thomas's solicitor in Town and settle some of his affairs. You be a good boy for Humphrey and Mrs. Lynch. Remember the Bonds, our tenants?"

He made a watery sound that may or may not have been an affirmative.

"Well, their bitch recently whelped. Maybe you'd like to have one of the puppies? If I get a good report about your behavior after I'm home, we'll go choose one."

Daniel lifted his face. Fur clung to the moisture on his cheeks. "What kind of pups?"

"Schnauzer, or perhaps Scottie—one of the little bearded terriers." She tickled his chin. "I hear they're great fun to play with."

The boy's lower lip pushed out. "I don't want a little dog."

Lorna's patience wore thin. "I won't force one upon you, but you cannot keep this dog, and that's the end of it. Now stop wallowing on the poor beast and go finish your breakfast." Her tone was testier than she liked; too many late nights were beginning to take their toll.

She rang for Oscar to return, and handed Daniel off to the footman. Her brother gave Bluebell a final hug. His head hung low as Oscar steered him back to his interrupted meal.

Bluebell's plaintive expression only further annoyed Lorna. "Don't look at me like that," she snapped. "This is your doing. Why did you come traipsing after me? You had no business turning up on my doorstep."

The dog rolled onto her back, tongue lolling to the side and tail thumping against the floor.

"Don't get comfortable," Lorna warned. "It's back to Town for both of us."

• • •

An hour later, a carriage rolled up the drive, bearing Lorna, Bluebell, and Oscar to London. With the servant seated outside with the driver, there was no room for the big dog except in the passenger compartment.

Despite Lorna's repeated order of *down*, Bluebell sprawled across one of the seats. The dog snored and her feet twitched. Lorna wondered whether Bluebell dreamed of cemeteries and corpses, or if she envisioned more pleasant things, like chasing rabbits and squirrels.

Whatever the case, she envied the canine's nap. She'd hoped Thomas's passing would give her a chance to rest and recuperate from the strain of tending him, but it hadn't happened. Would she ever get a decent night's sleep again? After the things she'd seen of late—the things she'd done—she doubted it.

The carriage stopped in front of Chorley House, the humble London abode of the Barons Chorley. Unlike the estate, Chorley House was entailed, a fact for which Lorna had never felt more grateful. However, should she lose Elmwood, Lorna would have no way to finance the upkeep of this place.

It was a simple town house situated between the fashionable squares that housed the truly elite. Cracks and bare patches marred the stucco exterior, while the adjacent homes stood in good repair. The eye tended to slide past Chorley House in favor of prettier sights. It was homely and easily overlooked, much like Lorna herself.

At the moment, the ordinariness of both the house and her own person suited her purposes. She wished to draw no attention of any sort. Not that she was in much danger of being noticed. There had been no London Season for her, no introduction to polite society. She had been too young for it while her father lived, and Thomas wasn't willing to put out for dresses and dancing slippers when the money could be better used on gambling and whoring.

She had no regrets on that front. Raising Daniel had been her duty and joy, and she wouldn't trade their little family for all the balls in the world.

A maid opened the door. Lorna stepped into a foyer marginally better kept than the one at Elmwood. Gray and black marble tiled the floor. Portraits flanked by gilded sconces were impressive enough, provided one did not closely examine the chipped frames and peeling gold leaf. Still, Lorna was impressed with the condition, given Thomas's propensity for violent outbursts. The interior might reveal a darker story, but at least the entryway didn't look like a house of horrors.

"Welcome back, Miss Robbins," the servant said as she bobbed a curtsy. "We haven't seen you since before...Well, not since..." Her voice trailed off in awkward silence.

"I've not been here in two years. Not since before my brother went mad," Lorna drawled. She'd long since run out of patience with decorum when it came to Thomas. She had no intention of shouting his shame and insanity from the rooftops, but neither did she have the energy to maintain a polite façade of genteel tragedy.

The maid's thin face blanched at her mistress's bluntness.

Lorna handed off Bluebell's lead. "Charity, please do something with the dog," she said, closing the subject of her brother. "I expect she needs food, water, and some time in the grass."

"I didn't know you have a dog, miss. What's her name?" Bluebell, seeming to sense the presence of an ally, lapped at Charity's hand.

"Oh, isn't she just the sweetest thing? We'll take good care of you, yes we will," the maid said in a sing-song voice. "Cook will give you all the best scraps and the juiciest bones and—"

"Charity," Lorna interrupted, "this is not my dog, we will not be keeping her, and I intend to reunite her with her owner as soon as possible. This very day, in fact."

Charity's face fell. "Oh. All right, miss. Come along, girl." The dog moped behind the dejected maid.

"What is it about that dog?" Lorna muttered. She still hadn't quite forgiven the animal for nearly crushing her that first night with the gang, but Bluebell seemed to have the rest of the world wrapped around her little dewclaw.

Lorna attempted to nap before the evening's activities, but nervous energy coursed through her veins, eradicating any possibility of rest. She might as well hunt down Coop straightaway, she decided, and have a word of prayer with him about finding better-paying jobs. His daytime whereabouts were unknown, but she would bet good money that if he wasn't in the public house, someone there could point her in his direction.

Lorna dressed and collected Bluebell from Charity, who reluctantly handed over the dog.

Outside, dense, gray clouds hung low, threatening rain. She shivered and decided a hackney was wiser than walking. "Come on, then," she said, tugging lightly at Bluebell's lead. "One last carriage ride for you, then it's back to the wagon."

Despite the inclement weather, a few intrepid pedestrians wrapped in heavy coats and fur muffs still managed to look fashionably turned out. There were more carriages, expensive equipages with liveried grooms perched on the back.

These people were all strangers, and she was glad of it. Not a single face turned in her direction. Anonymity was safety, Lorna decided. She descended the front steps and stepped onto the walk.

"Yoo-hoo!" called a cheery voice. "Miss Robbins, is that you?"

Startled, Lorna turned to see a young woman with an open, pleasant face waving from the neighboring stoop. Lorna gaped in horror as the lady approached.

The woman was of a height with Lorna, but possessed a rounder figure. A wide, lilac bandeau restrained chestnut curls; a cashmere shawl draped her shoulders. "It is you, isn't it, Miss Robbins?"

Lorna nodded mutely.

The woman's full cheeks dimpled with her answering smile. "I thought it must be. Oh, what a sweet dog." The unfamiliar person reached a gloved hand down to pat Bluebell. "Lord Chorley spoke of you so fondly. We looked forward to meeting you, when he finally brought you to Town." Frown lines marred the pretty face. "We were so sorry about his illness, and his passing. Please accept my sincerest condolences." The woman gripped Lorna's forearm and gave a gentle squeeze. "When I saw you arrive today, dressed as you are, well, I knew it must be our dear Miss Robbins, come at last."

Lorna was speechless. Thomas had spoken fondly of her? That could not be. Not the man who had cursed her and said those hateful, awful things. "I'm sorry," she said, bewildered. "I'm afraid you have the better of me."

"Oh, forgive me! Where are my manners? I'm your neighbor, Mrs. Freedman. You must come to dinner tonight. In fact, come for tea now and spend the evening with me. Please say you will."

Lorna shook her head. "Thank you, but I cannot."

"I won't take no for an answer," Mrs. Freedman said, gently scolding. "I know you can't really be out and about," she said, nodding to Lorna's mourning, "but a quiet evening with neighbors is perfectly acceptable. Your manservant can walk your dog while you join me for a lovely, warm cup."

"This isn't my…" Lorna glanced down at Bluebell, who wagged her tail.

With the appearance of neighborly neighbors, Lorna's hopes for anonymity crumbled to dust. Her mind grasped for excuses, but came up empty. Still stunned, she heard herself accepting the invitation. "I would be delighted," she said, feeling faint. How would she work now?

Mrs. Freedman smiled broadly. "Wonderful! I just know we shall be great friends."

A new friend. Just what Lorna didn't need.

Chapter Five

A hackney delivered Brandon to the day's last appointment. He was admitted to the house and led to the study, where his patient sat in a wingback chair, a book in his lap. The man looked up at Brandon's entrance and, with clumsy hands, set the book aside. His arms shook with the considerable effort of pushing to his feet.

"Don't get up on my account, Freedman," Brandon said.

Niall Freedman smirked, and for a moment he looked just like the boy Brandon had met at Eton fifteen years ago. "You always make me stand and walk about eventually, Dewhurst. I thought to get a head start." His smile slipped, and his slim face showed the difficulty of finding his balance.

Mindful of his old friend's pride, Brandon resisted his impulse to offer assistance. "Very well then, take a trot about the room for me."

He studied the man's awkward gait. Niall's feet hung loose from his ankles and landed all at once on the outside edge, instead of on the heel. There was a tremor in the right foot as it swung forward, which hadn't been there a few months ago.

After one circuit around the study, Brandon had Niall return to his seat. He knelt and removed his friend's shoes and stockings to examine the atrophied feet and ankles. "Have you had any new difficulties since I saw you last?" he asked, as he tested the range of motion in each joint.

"Since the park last Thursday, you mean?"

"Right, since then," Brandon said dryly.

He didn't like to attend his own family and friends. It became difficult to delineate where his interest as a practitioner ended, and his personal interest began. But when Niall first noticed the weakening of his hands and feet, he'd come to Brandon, insisting he'd consult no one else. The two saw each other socially, in addition to the quarterly visits Brandon paid as a surgeon.

Niall turned his hands palm up on his thighs. "My pen keeps slipping from my fingers. My handwriting has become…" Brandon glanced at his friend in time to see a flush spread toward his short yellow hair. "Nelly takes dictation for me now. I told her I'd hire a secretary, but she insists."

Brandon admired and envied his friend's marriage. Their devotion to one another was obvious, and Niall's condition did not discomfit his wife, as it would many women. "Mrs. Freedman is the very best of ladies," he said sincerely. "You're a fortunate man."

Niall smiled. "And don't I know it."

Brandon replaced Niall's footwear, then turned his attention to the hands. "Squeeze my fists as tightly as you can," he instructed. The responding grip was steady, but infirm. He extended his index finger. "Hold it as you would a pen." Niall's pinch grip was nearly nonexistent. The fingers had almost no strength.

"That bad?"

Brandon raised a brow.

"You nearly scowled your mouth right off your face," Niall explained. "What about exercises? Isn't there anything I can do to make my hands strong again?"

Here it was, the hard part—the reason Brandon hated being surgeon to a friend. His innards squirmed, even as he stood and squared his shoulders. "I'm afraid not, Freedman. This kind of atrophy is progressive, as we've discussed." The glimmer of hope in his friend's eyes faded. "Thankfully," Brandon continued, "yours is slow-moving. It's been several years since the first complaint, and the degeneration is still limited to your hands and feet."

Niall's shoulders slumped. In his lap, his fingers feebly closed and opened like the wings of a dying butterfly. "But it is spreading. It's in my ankles and wrists now, and my fingers are almost worthless." His words became more fervent. "You say my condition is slow to progress, but for God's sake, Dewhurst, I'm only thirty. What will I be like in five years? In ten? What will happen when I can no longer walk, when I cannot take myself to the privy? What will—" He drew a breath, visibly struggling to calm himself. His pained gaze met Brandon's. "Will my wife have to wipe me clean? Will we be able to be intimate, to have children? One day, I will wake up and lack the strength to hold her hand. Another day, I will no longer be able to embrace her. What kind of life is that?"

"I'm sorry, Niall."

And he was. Truly, deeply, terribly sorry. If Brandon had learned anything in his years of study and practice, it was that there was no rhyme or reason to the ravages of ailment and disease. He could disassemble the human body and name every fiber of it, down to the tiniest structures inside the ear, but he could not tell his friend why his muscles wasted away. It maddened him. Drove him. The answers were there, he was certain, if only he knew where to look.

"Are we done, then?" At Brandon's nod, Niall stood. "Join us for dinner?"

Brandon hesitated, uncertain whether the tense examination would carry into the dining room.

"It would be a kindness to Mrs. Freedman," Niall said. "Our neighbor—a lady—is joining us, as well. You'll keep the numbers even."

He groaned. "Not another matchmaking attempt. You know I think the world of your wife, but the ladies she puts in my way always dash for high ground. Mrs. Freedman should spare herself the trouble."

Few women found the idea of marriage to a surgeon the least bit appealing. The hours were grueling and the work distasteful to female sensibilities. McGully wasn't married, and neither were most of the surgeons Brandon knew. He'd long since accepted that marriage and family weren't meant for him. His brothers gave him nephews and nieces to dote upon, and the occasional liaison with a willing lady kept the edge off his physical needs. Students, patients, and research occupied his mind and time. Loneliness was only a problem at night, when he slid into a cold bed with thoughts tumbling through his mind and no one with whom to share them. But he could live with that. He'd chosen this course, and the sacrifice of having his own family wasn't too much to be able to do the work he loved.

His friend chuckled. "Nothing like that, I swear. It's just coincidence you're both here tonight. You won't be obligated to dance with this lady anytime soon, either. She's in mourning."

• • •

Lorna spent the afternoon tucked into a cozy sitting room with Mrs. Freedman. Mr. Freedman had joined them for tea. He was handsome, she thought, with a blade of a nose and kind eyes. At first, Lorna pitied his strange walk and his difficulty with the teacup. But his wife's tenderness in assisting him soon made Lorna feel quite a different emotion: longing. Her practical nature regarded marriage as something for other women. Daniel was her primary obligation. But seeing the affection between her neighbors stirred up girlhood fantasies she'd put aside the day her father died. She ruthlessly tamped them down. Perhaps she would find a husband someday, when Daniel was older and didn't need her quite so much.

After tea, Mr. Freedman withdrew to his study to await a visitor of his own. Mrs. Freedman retrieved an embroidery hoop from a sewing basket. "It's some sort of atrophy, we're told." She picked her thumbnail across a row of stitches. "There's nothing to be done. It will only grow worse with time."

Had Lorna stared? Heat crept up her neck. "I'm sorry, Mrs. Freedman. I hope I didn't—"

"You didn't," her neighbor assured her. "And, please, call me Nelly. I'm determined that we shall be good friends." She set her work in her lap. "He's been accused of public drunkenness before. The way he walks, dropping things…I just like for people to know, so there's no confusion."

"I understand."

Nelly's neck drooped. "He tripped over his own feet during our wedding waltz two years ago. It was the last time we danced."

A moment of heavy silence followed until Nelly rallied, once again the charming young hostess. "You must tell me all about Elmwood. The little the late Lord Chorley described to us sounded delightful."

Lorna spoke about Daniel and their home, and then Nelly contributed memories of her own childhood. Time slipped by unnoticed. Lorna even forgot to worry about missing her meeting with the gang.

Nelly was describing her debut ball when they heard male voices coming down the hall. A moment later, Mr. Freedman entered, followed by another gentleman.

The newcomer spotted Lorna and stopped, eyes wide. A half-second later she returned the favor when recognition clapped her over the head. It was the man who had chased her.

That night, she thought she hadn't really gotten a good look at him, but he was instantly familiar. He stood six feet tall with tousled dark brown hair, lightly silvered at the temples. Fine lines touched the corners of intense, gray eyes. He had a solid, healthy physique, though his face was a touch pale, as if he didn't get enough sun.

What was he doing here? Her skin prickled all over as sweat popped out.

She must have risen, for suddenly she was staring at a wall of broad chest as Nelly introduced them. "Miss Robbins, allow me to make you known to our dear friend, Mr. Dewhurst."

Mr. Dewhurst stood as still as he had that night in the alley, waiting. Her rational mind knew she was supposed to acknowledge the introduction first, but apprehension paralyzed her. How had he found her? Was he really a Bow Street Runner?

She turned an accusing glare on Nelly. "You promised a quiet evening with neighbors," she said in a rush. She risked a glance at Mr. Dewhurst, who watched her intently. Lorna flinched at his scrutiny. "I can't…That is, it wouldn't be proper…"

"Forgive me," Mr. Freedman interjected. "I invited Mr. Dewhurst to dinner but a moment ago, without speaking to Nelly first. It was thoughtless on my part."

"I'll take my leave." Mr. Dewhurst bowed curtly and turned.

Oh, no. A hot wave of mortification washed over Lorna. She was the newcomer to this house, and here she was causing a dreadful scene. "No, wait. Mr. Dewhurst, is it? Please."

He stopped, but remained facing the door. She supposed she deserved that bit of rudeness. "I'm pleased to make your acquaintance, sir."

At that, he turned back around and gave her a terse nod. "I'm sure the pleasure is all mine." An icy smile gave lie to his words.

Lorna felt two inches tall, shamed to her core. Nelly would never invite her back after tonight, but perhaps that was for the best. She reminded herself she didn't want people nosing into her affairs.

When dinner was announced, Nelly assisted her husband, leaving Lorna to place her hand on Mr. Dewhurst's arm as they followed. The firm muscle inside his dark sleeve flexed and released in time with their steps.

"Why do you keep running away from me, Miss Robbins?" he murmured.

Because I'm afraid you'll arrest me. Lorna firmed her lips and stared straight ahead.

"This is only the second time I have laid eyes upon you, yet you've attempted to distance yourself on both occasions. Have I offended you in some fashion?"

She shook her head.

He grunted. "I *am* glad to know you have a name. When you wouldn't give it to me at our first meeting, I wondered if you were perhaps some nameless, nocturnal nymph."

Lorna released an exasperated sigh.

"That's not the case, but still you begrudge me the knowledge of it." His voice was warm honey against her ear. "Does having your name give me power over you, like Rumpelstiltskin? Can I summon you in the night to spin straw into gold? Now that I know you, Miss Robbins, will you give me your firstborn?"

She stopped, stunned. "What a vulgar insinuation," she hissed. "And that isn't how the story goes." Her arms crossed under her bust as she glared at him, momentarily forgetting he might be a threat.

Mr. Dewhurst glared right back. "My apologies," he said at last. "I should have better command of nursery tales."

Lorna rolled her eyes and turned, only to see the Freedmans both standing at the dining room entrance, watching them. Mr. Freedman seemed amused, while poor Nelly looked scandalized.

"Bother," Lorna muttered under her breath. What an excellent impression she'd made on the neighbors.

After a meal featuring leg of lamb and herbed potatoes, she and Nelly returned to the sitting room while the gentlemen took their port. The ladies, who had passed the afternoon so companionably, now sat in awkward silence.

Lorna cleared her throat. "I'm so sorry, Nelly—Mrs. Freedman," she corrected herself, certain her neighbor wouldn't want to be on intimate terms with her after this disaster. "I had no right to behave as I did." Her voice hitched in her throat, forcing her to clear it again. "Since Thomas died, I have found myself doing things I never thought I would—"

"Oh, my dear!" Nelly took Lorna's hand in both of hers. "Please think nothing of it. I was so delighted to meet you at last that I selfishly imposed. It was wrong to force you into company before you were ready."

Nelly's sweet face held real sorrow, and Lorna wondered if it was possible for a person to feel more wretched than she. "Thank you kindly for having me," Lorna said as she rose. "I enjoyed our afternoon."

"As did I," Nelly hurried to reply. "Must you go?"

"Dinner was wonderful," Lorna prevaricated.

The gentlemen entered before she could escape. Lorna took leave of her host and nodded to Mr. Dewhurst. A hint of color touched the taller gentleman's cheeks—from the port, perhaps. It suited him. *He really should get more sun*, Lorna thought.

His eyes captured hers, communicating a slow, steady burn of interest. Her stomach flipped.

Finally, he broke the connection, only to allow his gaze to slide down her figure. She felt his appraisal like a feather brushed over her skin. Her cheeks flared. No man had ever looked at her like that. It was uncomfortable and embarrassing. Perhaps if she had a figure worth appreciating she wouldn't mind the attention, but Mr. Dewhurst must find her quite disappointing.

His gray eyes snapped back to hers. "Allow me to see you home, Miss Robbins."

"That isn't necessary, sir. It's not twenty paces from the Freedmans' door to mine." She was tempted to sprint every one of them to flee his scrutiny.

His lips twitched. "Still, it's dark out. We'd all feel better knowing you had a safe escort."

Lorna wasn't at all sure that Mr. Dewhurst constituted a safe escort. But the declarations of agreement from her host and hostess compelled her to accept his offer.

With farewells exchanged and the front door closed behind them, they stood for a moment on the stoop. The clouds had broken and the rising moon peeked through the rooftops. He was watching her, waiting, as he always did.

Well, he could spend eternity waiting for whatever it was he wanted. Struggling to regain her composure after his inspection of her, she ignored his proffered arm and marched down the walk. Lorna hadn't taken five steps before he was at her side. His hand wrapped around her elbow as she mounted her own front steps. Despite her annoyance at his forwardness, the slight pressure sent a pleasurable sensation through her arm and into her chest.

"Would you mind telling me something, Miss Robbins?"

Lorna tugged out of his grasp. Though a gas streetlamp gleamed nearby, the face peering at her was inscrutable, shadowed by the brim of his tall hat. "Indeed I would mind, sir. Thank you for the escort."

Realizing she'd left without a key, she raised her hand to knock. Mr. Dewhurst met her hand in the air, palm to palm. His fingers closed around hers. Before she could voice a protest, he drew her close. Mere inches separated them. Heat pulsed through Lorna, driving away any chill inflicted by the autumn night.

"Please tell me who it is you've lost," he said, "so I might offer proper condolences."

The sudden closeness to this large male stunned her. With considerable effort, she formulated a response. "My brother, Lord Chorley."

He exhaled a heavy sigh. "Of course. I'm so sorry. I should have known. Some time ago, Mrs. Freedman told me their neighbor was ailing and asked me to check in on him, but he left Town before I had a chance to come 'round."

Prickles crawled up Lorna's neck. "What do you mean, *check in on him?*"

His head cocked to the side. "In my capacity as a surgeon, of course."

"A surgeon? You, Mr. Dewhurst, are a surgeon?"

He dropped her hand. "Correct."

She felt lightheaded with relief. He wasn't an investigator come to haul her off to Newgate, after all.

Emboldened by the revelation that he posed no immediate danger, she couldn't resist broaching the subject of their—unbeknownst to him—common professional interest. "Do you practice your skills on the dead, Mr. Dewhurst?"

"I do," he pronounced in a defensive tone. "Distasteful as it is to the public, such work is necessary for the training of new surgeons, for deepening our understanding of disease, for the development of new treatments—"

"My brother's body was stolen."

His speech stuttered to a halt. "That must have been difficult for you," he said at last.

"It was an unexpected turn of events, to be sure."

"I would imagine."

Lorna sensed him grappling with his thoughts. "That's why I was in the public house that night," she said, answering the question she knew Mr. Dewhurst wanted to ask. Inspiration struck, and she elaborated, injecting her voice with a note of distress. "I caught them in the act, you see, but I was so shocked, I couldn't…I couldn't…"

His hands tightened around her upper arms. "There's nothing you could have done, Miss Robbins. You must in no way blame yourself. My God, if they'd seen you there, who knows what could have happened."

A grim smile curved Lorna's lips before she quickly schooled her features. "When I came to Town," she said in a small voice,

"I went looking for them, still hoping there might be a chance to return Thomas to his resting place."

His thumbs worked soothing circles on her arms. She took a tiny step closer. "It had been a week, but I was so distraught, I wasn't thinking clearly. Of course he was gone. Sold. One of the men gave me some money to buy my silence and sent me on my way."

Mr. Dewhurst tipped her chin up, allowing the light of the streetlamp to wash over her features. "That was courageous of you," he said, his voice husky, "but foolish, as well. Those criminals are not to be dealt with lightly."

With one strong hand on her arm and another cradling her face, Lorna almost felt embraced. No one but Daniel had wrapped arms around her in years—not since her father's death. And while her brother's sweet hugs never failed to warm her heart, the sensations coursing through her now were completely new. She shivered in response to a delicate tendril of pleasure snaking up her spine.

"You're cold," Mr. Dewhurst said, misinterpreting. He reached past her to the knocker.

The instant it struck the brass plate, a barrage of barking sounded on the other side of the door. Lorna startled, having forgotten her unwanted guest.

"Oh, you have a dog," Mr. Dewhurst said pleasantly. "My brothers and I had several while we were growing up."

From the entry hall, Lorna heard Oscar commanding Bluebell to sit. The door opened and the ill-mannered hound shoved past the footman and barreled into Lorna's thighs. She yelped and grappled Mr. Dewhurst's arm to keep her footing.

Mr. Dewhurst scratched Bluebell behind the ears. "Happy his mistress is home. What's his name?"

"*Her* name is Bluebell and I'm not her mistress." Lorna used her knee to prod the dog back to the door. "I'm minding her for a friend, but she's going home tomorrow."

She made several aborted attempts to politely wish Mr. Dewhurst a good night, but the infernal dog refused to behave in a civilized fashion, continuing to lean against her legs and trample her feet. Exasperated, Lorna shooed Oscar away so she could step into the house and order, "In!"

Bluebell followed at once, sat at Lorna's side, and gazed serenely at Mr. Dewhurst as if *she* were the hostess seeing a guest off.

Mr. Dewhurst laughed at the animal's antics. The smile utterly transformed his face. What had been a serious, forbidding set of features became very appealing, indeed. With amusement still tugging at his lips, he bowed. "Good evening, Miss Robbins, Miss Bluebell."

"Good evening, Mr. Dewhurst." Lorna closed the door and leaned against it, dazed. She glanced down at Bluebell, who watched the door as if he might yet walk through. The dog licked her chops and met Lorna's eyes. "It doesn't matter if he has a nice smile," Lorna informed the animal. "Why was *he* at that tavern?" Surgeons didn't meet the Crib Cross Gang on their territory; it was always the other way around.

"I'll ask Coop tomorrow," she decided. "And I shall be rid of you, as well." Bluebell woofed and followed Lorna to her bedchamber.

Chapter Six

Dingy fog lay heavy on the city, like an old quilt overdue for a beating. Through the cold mist, Lorna made her way along the streets, Bluebell at her side. The hound's usual cheerfulness was subdued this morning; instead, the dog stayed close to Lorna, nose to the ground.

The long, black veil Lorna wore had gone limp with moisture. It clung to her nostrils and mouth.

Laborers headed to legitimate employment streamed out of tenements. Some passersby gaped at Lorna. She heard "Blackbird" muttered more than once. A woman standing in a doorway crossed herself as Lorna passed.

At The Fox and Hound, she pounded on the door until the bleary-eyed proprietress opened up. She didn't know Coop's whereabouts, but gave Lorna directions to Pretty Lem's place.

Lorna followed them to a row of rundown stone structures stuffed cheek by jowl. Low, slate roofs ended in eaves only a foot above Lorna's head. Doors opened directly onto the street, and alongside the row, a sewage ditch carried steaming, noxious waste and refuse to the river.

Bluebell shook her head and pawed her snout. "Poor nose," Lorna said. "This is bad for me; I can't imagine how dreadful the smell is for you." Eager to escape the nasty air, she knocked at number eight.

Lem, barefoot and clad in breeches and a loose shirt, opened the door. "Blackbird!" He flashed one of his winning grins—the same one she'd seen him imbue upon every serving girl at The Fox and Hound. "Oh, hey, girl." Lem patted Bluebell. "What're you two doing here?"

"Does Bluebell belong to Coop?" Lorna asked. "She followed me home the other night."

"As much to him as anyone, I s'pose," he said with a shrug. "He found her as a pup an' she mostly sticks with 'im."

"Sounds to me like he owns the dog," Lorna said.

"Bluebell earns her keep," he explained. "She's not much of a lap dog, yeah? All Coop cares is that she pulls her weight. He was in a fine state last night when neither of you showed for work."

She shifted her weight from one foot to another. "I was detained by the neighbors." The horrid sewage smell was beginning to make her nauseous. "Do you know where Coop lives, Lem? I need to speak with him and return Bluebell."

"Yeah, of course. Give me a minute and I'll take you."

Lorna gestured to a nearby intersection. "I'll be at the corner."

Bluebell needed no encouragement to quickly relocate. The standard, filthy East End stink was like ambrosia after the stomach-churning aroma by Lem's.

He appeared in short order, having donned stockings, shoes, and the same threadbare coat he wore at night. A floppy hat covered the tops of his ears. Hands stuffed in pockets, Lem huffed a cloud of breath and tilted his head. "This way."

Finally, Lem led her around back of a pawn shop and up a flight of rickety stairs clinging to the building's brick exterior. He knocked on a door covered with chipped green paint.

When the door opened, Lorna was surprised to see Coop up and dressed at this early hour. He ignored the humans entirely, focusing on the canine. "How kind of you to grace me with your presence," he said with a mocking bow. "This one"—he pointed at Lorna—"I don't much need on a regular night, but you damned well should've been at work."

Bluebell butted her head against Coop's hand.

"Don't show up here after a night of carousing and try to make nice," he scolded. "I suppose you had a fine time, and now you expect me to give you breakfast."

The dog's tail wagged.

"Forget it!" Coop snapped. "There's no spongin' in Crib Cross. You want to eat, you work."

Lorna restrained the urge to roll her eyes. "She's been with me. I fed her this morning."

Coop finally deigned to acknowledge her presence. "Yeah, an' what were you doin' with her?"

"She followed me home. I brought her back, and here we are." Lorna thrust Bluebell's lead at Coop. He ignored it. "Look, Coop, I need to speak with you. I'm grateful that you've given me work, but I need more pay, and fast."

"Don't we all?" Coop said. "What's the problem? We're 'aving a good season, makin' more'n ever. Resurrectionist pay suddenly not good enough for yer ladyship?" he jeered.

Her chin worked back and forth. So far, Coop hadn't asked Lorna too many questions. Comments he'd dropped here and there indicated he thought this was all a bored, rich girl's lark. Obviously, he knew Lorna was the sister of a deceased baron, but she hadn't told him about the money she owed Wiggins. It seemed cruel to make keeping her estate a cause of concern for people who lived in squalor. Still, her home was threatened. Maybe he could understand that.

She pulled a deep breath. "My brother died with a mountain of debt. I'm going to lose my home if I can't pay it off."

"Sad tale." Coop sounded bored. "Happens I'm jus' heading out to see our best buyer. He sent a note 'round, said somethin' 'bout a special job."

It was then Lorna noticed Coop seemed to have taken pains with his appearance. His graying hair was carefully slicked back, his ivory shirt and blue trousers clean.

"Speaking of buyers, Coop, do you sell to a man named Dewhurst?"

He shook his head. "Dewhurst's one of Harty Choke's." He slipped his hands into his pants pockets. "Wish he was one of ours. That Scot he works for buys 'em up fast as Harty Choke can dig 'em. Why?"

A scrap of memory from the night she met the gang floated to the surface. *"Harty Choke Boys won't be none pleased when they find we've picked their garden,"* Coop had said. The sick feeling crept back into Lorna's stomach. Mr. Dewhurst bought from a rival gang, yet he'd appeared at Crib Cross's regular tavern. She couldn't shake the feeling that he was a threat.

"I'll come with you," she blurted, suddenly anxious to work hard and fast and get out of this dark underworld while she still could. "I'd like to meet our client. Maybe I can persuade him—"

"Hell no!" Coop interrupted. "You, Blackbird, are the ace up my sleeve. No one knows you're working with us."

Lorna tried to puzzle that out. Near as she could tell, *everyone* knew with whom she worked. "I regret having to tell you this," she said gently, "but I don't think my involvement is a secret—at least on this side of the city."

Pretty Lem snorted. "Yeah, Coop, you've done a good job makin' sure Blackbird's known to everyone at The Fox and Hound. But," he said, eyeing Lorna, "they don't know *who* you are."

Coop tapped his nose. "It's all about the mystique," he said with a wink. "The other gangs think I'm bloody crazy, but they don't know what you do for us. Our clients may catch wind of our lady in black, but they've never seen you an' they never will. Fly back to your nest and we'll see you tonight, yeah?"

Lorna dug her heels into the bare wood landing. "No. I'm coming with you. I want to know what's happening."

A brief shouting match later, Lorna strode beside Coop and Lem, trying to exude bravado she didn't have. She felt downright naked in the clothes Coop had lent her for a disguise. For the first time in her life, Lorna wore breeches. Her legs were encased in two thin sheaths of material, rather than properly concealed beneath layers of petticoats and skirts.

Her breath caught in her throat as she recalled how Mr. Dewhurst looked in his trousers, all long, lean muscle. Lorna's slim legs didn't look like *that* in Coop's old, loose breeches, thank goodness, but they were still indecently exposed. She tugged the brim of Lem's hat farther down over her face, hoping her unruly curls stayed put under there.

Lem glanced at her, his own hair gleaming like a burnished halo in the sun that had finally appeared to burn off the fog. He grinned and stooped to speak in a low voice. "Pull that hat low as you like, your pretty chin will never pass for a boy's, Miss Lorna."

"My chin?" she said, dismayed. As if concealing her admittedly unremarkable figure wasn't enough, she had to worry about her jawline giving her away?

"Here." Lem snatched Coop's scarf and passed it to Lorna. "And mind how you walk. Your hips sway too much."

Heat flooded her cheeks. She knew these breeches showed too much! She'd lived twenty-one years without hearing a single remark about her hips. Five minutes in men's attire and suddenly her body was an object of public commentary. "If you'd slow down, I could work on my stride."

"Both of you shut it," Coop snapped.

The rest of the walk passed in silence, with Lorna concentrating hard on appearing male, and Lem enjoying her struggle.

The two of them waited outside the Cheapside anatomy school while Coop went in to talk with their client, Mr. Manning. Lem lounged against the side of the building, one foot crossed over the other. Lorna tried to imitate his lazy posture. Her spine, governess-trained to maintain a straight bearing, protested the awkward curvature.

"Ow! How can you tolerate the brick digging into your shoulder blades?" She adjusted her arms and tried again, with no better success.

"You get callouses after a while."

"Really?"

Lem's face split into his heartbreaking grin. "Naw. Lord, you're easy to tease, Miss—"

She let out a sharp hiss and elbowed his ribs as she spotted two men approaching. "Hush, hush, hush," Lorna breathed. Her eyes widened in horror as Mr. Dewhurst strode straight toward her.

He was engrossed in conversation with an older man. Had he seen her? Surely not. Please God, no.

Lorna cringed against Lem's side, hiding her face.

"What are you doing?" He tried to nudge her off. "I don't want nobody thinkin' I'm a bugger."

"That man," she whispered in a rush, "I know him. Tell me when he's passed."

"Christ, Miss—ow!" he exclaimed as she jabbed him. "Well, he's lookin' now, frowning at us. Oh, hullo, sir," he muttered under his breath, "just your friendly neighborhood sodomites. Oi! Stop hitting me!"

"Don't look at him!"

"How'm I s'posed to tell you when he's gone?" After a few seconds, Lem said, "They went in."

Blood pounded in her ears. She lifted her head, gasping for air. "Too close. Much too close."

Coop appeared in the alley behind them. He clapped Lorna on the shoulder, as though she really was a boy. He beamed at her.

"Good news?" she asked.

"The best." Coop pressed his hands together and shook them, like a victory celebration, or maybe a prayer of thanks. "You're a gift, my little bird. We pull this job, an' it'll be caviar and champagne for us all." Coop moved with a newfound spring in his step. Lorna leaped to follow, eager to put distance between Mr. Dewhurst and herself.

"What's the job?" Lem demanded.

"Viscountess Fenton is expecting." He shot them a smug look. "Triplets. She's a dead woman walking and everyone knows it. Manning wants her."

Ice shot through Lorna's veins. "That's monstrous!"

"That's ten thousand pounds," Coop corrected. "If she passes with all three still inside and we get her, we'll be divvying up. Ten. Thousand. Pounds. That enough to suit you?"

Lorna nodded, her face numb. She gulped. "But why...why did you say I was a gift?"

Coop smirked. "Because you're a right proper lady, yeah? You can get into all them nice parties and dinners and dances and put an eye on her for me. Soon as she's in a bad way, we'll be there."

"I can't," Lorna protested. Her heart galloped at the thought of trying to make her way through the alien *haut ton*—a world she'd never known or desired—and for such a cold-hearted purpose. She relaxed a fraction as a perfectly good reason to avoid her duty sprang to mind. "I can't go out in company. I'm still in mourning."

Coop's smile slipped and his eyes hardened. "Not anymore."

Chapter Seven

"Not anymore," McGully repeated.

So Brandon hadn't misheard. With the exception of an upcoming address which would be open to the public, the eminent surgeon had relieved him of all regular lecturing and dissection duties for the foreseeable future. Instead, his employer had assigned a task straight out of Brandon's personal hell.

The floor of McGully's study must have suddenly pitched askew. It was the only explanation for the vertigo assailing him. He grabbed the back of a chair and held tight while his mind reeled. "I am not the man for this job," he ground out.

McGully reclined on a tufted sofa with a cigar. "On the contrary, lad, you're the only man for the job. I haven't the patience for the social hoo-ha—"

"And you think I have?" Brandon snapped.

The older man's eyebrows raised infinitesimally. "Who else is there? Who would you have me send in your place to watch the woman?"

A growl caught in Brandon's throat. He commenced an agitated pacing of the room. There was no one else. With the exception of himself, none of McGully's associates possessed the social connections needed to keep close watch on Lady Fenton.

McGully's lined cheeks collapsed as he drew on his clay pipe. "Come now, Dewhurst," he said in a cloud of blue-white smoke, "you won't have to trot about with the dandies and bucks very long. She's almost seven months gone, according to Manning, and Fenton hasn't taken her to the country."

Brandon turned on his heel. "Of course not. Lady Fenton requires constant care. She must remain in London. That goes without saying."

"Does it?" McGully cast him a shrewd look. "If my wife carried triplets, I'd bundle her off to rusticate for the duration, and pay a surgeon to accompany her. I certainly wouldn't let her gallivant about Town. What is the fool thinking? She'll perish in a month, mark my words."

His stomach soured at the cool detachment with which McGully spoke of Lady Fenton's death. Brandon was acquainted with Lord and Lady Fenton. She was a lively, happy sort, loved the social whirl. What could Fenton do? Force her to the country to spend whatever remained of her life in gloomy solitude? Of course he let her attend all the balls and parties she liked. Soon enough, something dreadful was going to happen.

Any pregnancy was difficult. Twin pregnancies could be harrowing. More than two? Almost impossible. It was inconceivable that Lady Fenton would deliver three live infants, and the chance of her surviving the ordeal was slimmer yet. Of course Fenton indulged her now.

"Lucky Manning, to be her surgeon!" McGully said. "Proud as a damned peacock to have discovered she's carrying three. I must have her, Dewhurst!" His fist thudded into a soft cushion. "A womb filled with late-term triplets would be the jewel of my book." His eyes glazed as he gazed at nothing. "To document such a pregnancy...How many placentas? How many bags of water? How are they configured?" His lips twitched in a faint smile. "It will be spectacular."

Brandon felt he might vomit. "I cannot dissuade you, sir?"

McGully's smile snapped to a frown. "Not for anything. This will make your career, and immortalize mine. A body like this one is worth any price. Make sure you tell your resurrection men so. I'll pay thousands for it, Dewhurst."

Brandon took leave of his employer and retreated to his small apartment. He paced again, too agitated to stop moving. Another pregnant woman. And he was supposed to feign interest in vapid *ton* affairs, all the while watching and waiting for her to die? He bellowed and kicked one of his two dining chairs. A leg snapped off and spun across the floor.

And how in the bloody blazes was he to get close to Lady Fenton? Though he was acquainted with her, he didn't move in her circles. So long had Brandon eschewed Society, hostesses no longer bothered sending him invitations. The Little Season was underway, but with his mother in Kent, he hadn't any way of knowing—

"Jeremiah," he blurted. He'd forgotten one of his four older brothers was in Town and staying at Marcel House with his wife, Alice, and their two young daughters. He jotted off a note, and received a reply inviting him to join Jeremiah and Alice that very evening.

• • •

Hours later, Brandon, along with his brother and sister-in-law, mingled among a crowd of finely dressed opera-goers. A few inches shorter than Brandon and thicker through the waist, with a blunt nose and fierce, blue-gray eyes, Jeremiah gave the impression of something only mildly more affable than a rabid bull. In startling contrast, his wife, Alice, looked like a porcelain doll, with gleaming yellow ringlets and a peaches-and-cream complexion.

As the trio greeted acquaintances, Brandon kept a surreptitious eye out for Lady Fenton. He spotted the woman a short distance away. Her red dress split below the bust to reveal a black slip covering her bulging abdomen. Beside her, Lord Fenton looked understandably anxious as his lady chatted with—

"Good lord," he breathed. It was Niall and Nelly Freedman, in the company of one Miss Robbins. What on earth was she doing here? Women in deep mourning did not engage in frivolous entertainments.

The feisty woman in black he'd twice encountered now glanced about nervously while her gloved hands pressed into her middle. She wore an ill-fitting lavender dress with a gray shawl draped over her arms—half mourning colors. The auburn curls he remembered in the wild disarray of their first meeting now erupted from the back of her head, the sides of her hair having been scraped back and held in place with silver combs.

Nothing about the ensemble suited her. The dress was obviously borrowed—from Nelly, most likely, judging by the excess fabric obliterating Miss Robbins's slight frame. There was something unintentionally alluring about her appearance, though, as if she had just risen from bed and swathed herself in a voluminous sheet. Under the mountain of fabric was a body ripe for discovery. He wanted to pluck the combs from her head and run his fingers through her hair, completing the illusion of dishabille.

His groin tightened in response to the erotic thought just as her bright, blue-green eyes met his. The space between them charged with awareness. Suddenly, Brandon felt as though a silken cord connected the two of them, and it shortened, drawing him closer. Lady Fenton and her ill-fated abdomen were all but forgotten as he made his way to Miss Robbins's party.

"Lady Fenton." He bowed. "Mrs. Freedman." Another nod. "Miss Robbins," he murmured.

Some of the tightness around her eyes and lips softened. "Mr. Dewhurst, I'm surprised to see you here."

"Not as surprised as I am to see you," he said, pointedly looking at her dress.

Fear clouded her lovely eyes. Miss Robbins raised a hand to her head then snatched it down again.

"Brandon, it's time to take our seats." Alice laid a hand on his forearm. She greeted the Fentons and Freedmans, and looked curiously at Miss Robbins.

"Alice, Jeremiah," Brandon said, "this is Miss Robbins. Miss Robbins, these are my brother and sister-in-law, Mr. and Mrs. Jeremiah Dewhurst."

Jeremiah gave a curt bow. His sister-in-law took Miss Robbins's hand. "There are already two other Missus Dewhursts in our family. Please call me Alice."

"Then you must call me Lorna," she replied.

Lorna. It suited her, he decided, straightforward and unpretentious like the woman herself.

After the Fentons made for their box, the Freedmans and Lorna started toward the doors for the floor seating.

"Won't you join us in our box?" Alice offered.

The trio accepted the invitation. They made their way upstairs, moving slowly to accommodate Niall's pace. Brandon was glad to see his friend in good spirits after their interview a few nights ago had dealt such a blow to Niall's hopes of recovery.

The married couples sat together, leaving Brandon and Lorna—he found he could no longer think of her by a more formal name—to sit beside one another.

When the orchestra launched into the prelude, Brandon tuned out the production. Opera bored him to tears. Lady Fenton's condition having been observed, he had nothing to do but focus on the woman at his side. She plucked the hem of her shawl and fidgeted in her seat. She worried her bottom lip, rolling it side to side between her teeth.

Brandon felt, but didn't voice, a lust-filled groan. How he wanted to do precisely that to her lip himself. He watched her mouth as intently as the others in the box watched the stage. Her eyes flicked his way, then quickly darted back. She was aware of his attention now and flushed, despite her attempt to appear enraptured by the performance.

Studying Lorna's mouth was doing uncomfortable things to the fit of his breeches. At last, he dragged his gaze to the stage, where a mezzo-soprano and a baritone bellowed unintelligible Italian at one another. Unfortunately, feigning interest in the theatrical wasn't nearly as interesting an occupation as examining Lorna Robbins.

Chapter Eight

Lord, what she'd do to escape this company.

It wasn't the particular people she minded. Everyone she'd met this evening had been most congenial, in fact.

Rather, Lorna minded that she must expose herself to people at all. After years of living a quiet, country life with Daniel— followed by the harrowing months of tending Thomas, and then dark nights filled with dark work—she felt like a subterranean creature shoved into the light for the first time. She was blinded by the sight of so many human beings in one space. The performance on stage was the ostensible attraction, but Lorna couldn't stop herself from scanning the crowd instead.

She knew the opera had ended only when the audience burst into applause. Even as the clapping ceased, the roar continued as the entire assembly erupted into conversation at once.

Boxes emptied and the audience on the floor funneled through the doors. By unspoken assent, the residents of their box made no move to depart. Given Mr. Freedman's condition, the group needed extra time to make their way downstairs.

"How did you like it?"

The male voice rumbling directly into her ear startled her. Whipping her head to the side, she found Mr. Brandon Dewhurst leaning toward her, his face not half a foot from her own. He braced himself with a hand on the back of her chair. His proximity did strange things to her body, tingly things.

"I, ah," she stammered. He turned her mind to pudding, too.

His mouth tipped in a half-cocked smile. He lightly tugged one of her curls. "I don't care for it, either."

They shared a silent exchange of kinship found in mutual disinterest until the Freedmans and Jeremiah Dewhursts made to leave.

As they filed out, Lorna was acutely aware of the large man looming at her back. Heat filled the space between them, tickling her nape.

Across the lobby, Lord and Lady Fenton were just making their way through a door. They must have similarly waited for the crush to pass. And no wonder, Lorna thought, taking in the impressive heft of Lady Fenton's abdomen. She couldn't imagine trying to navigate a throng with such a belly preceding her.

A laughing couple cut in front of Lady Fenton. She stepped aside, clapping protective arms across her pregnancy.

Some answering, yearning instinct echoed in Lorna's womb.

Before she had a chance to examine the sensation, the two parties converged in the center of the lobby. Alice, Nelly, and Lady Fenton bent their heads together, while the men clapped each other on the shoulder, spoke loudly, and generally stood about taking up entirely too much space.

Attempting to look purposeful, Lorna hefted her borrowed shawl to her shoulders and wrapped it tightly across her torso. She busied herself with tying and retying a knot in the ends, hoping no one noticed how awkwardly out of place she was on the fringe of the group.

"Where are you off to next?" she heard Mr. Jeremiah Dewhurst ask.

"Heapbys' ball," answered Lord Fenton.

"As are we," said Mr. Dewhurst. "Brandon, you'll join us, I hope?"

How lowering to overhear plans which did not include her! Lorna kept her eyes steadfastly fixed on the ends of her shawl while she picked at imaginary lint.

One of the ladies said, "Yes, you must! And you as well, Miss Robbins."

Startled, Lorna blinked up at Lady Fenton's warm expression. The gentlemen all looked her way, but Brandon's gaze was especially intense.

Throughout the opera, she'd caught him scrutinizing her. Or perhaps he'd caught her out staring at him. In any event, his attention unnerved her. She was as used to the male gaze as she was to handling herself in a crowd, which is to say, not at all.

"I couldn't possibly. I'm not dressed for it." She gestured to her borrowed, too-large gown.

Alice Dewhurst gave her hand a reassuring squeeze. "You look lovely. Doesn't she?" she called over her shoulder.

The men issued hasty, mumbled compliments, which did more to embarrass Lorna than settle her nerves.

She was on the verge of refusing, when she recalled her whole purpose in being here this evening. Coop would have her hide if he learned she'd shirked her duty over a dress. That duty, Lady Fenton, gave her an encouraging nod. "Very well," Lorna said. "I accept."

"Mr. Freedman has exerted himself enough today," Nelly said when Lorna asked if they would accompany the group. "But you'll have a marvelous time! You must tell me all about it tomorrow."

A few moments of discussion separated the women into one carriage and the men into the other.

"I take up one whole side by myself," Lady Fenton informed Lorna. The pregnant lady stroked her bulging middle and settled into the squabs with a moan.

A frisson of alarm tightened Lorna's back. "Is everything all right?"

"Gracious, yes. My slippers are just a bit snug."

Alice Dewhurst nudged Lorna into turning sideways. She'd offered to rearrange Lorna's hair for the ball. Nimble fingers withdrew her combs and sifted through the tight curls. Rhythmic, gentle tugs indicated braiding.

"You must not strain yourself," Alice said to Lady Fenton. "By six months with each of my girls, I gave up my daily rambles. I can't believe you're still going to balls."

"Might as well make hay while the sun shines," the other lady said in a chipper tone.

Did she so casually refer to her own probable death?

"With three babies in the house, when do you suppose I'll next see the inside of a ballroom?" Lady Fenton continued. Her fingers trailed loops across the surface of her belly. "It could be years."

Lord, she was deluded. Worry ate at Lorna while Alice's clever fingers worked in her hair. Lady Fenton seemed a friendly sort. Lorna hated to think she was fooling herself into believing in a future that couldn't possibly transpire. Except—what else could she do? Plan to die? Plan for one or more of her children to die?

The sensation of her combs snugly nestling into her hair stirred Lorna from her morbid reverie.

"There now," Alice said. "Not a lady in there will look prettier."

The carriage drew to a halt before a grand house on St. James Square. Lorna gaped at the imposing neoclassical façade, all aglow with the light of gas lamps, and arrived at a conclusion.

"I can't do this."

She, Lorna Robbins, was on the verge of stepping into her first London ball wearing borrowed half-mourning, with people she had only a passing acquaintance, for the purpose of waiting for a pregnant woman to die.

It was wrong, every bit of it.

A hand grasped her elbow. Before she knew what he was about, Brandon pulled her out of the carriage and to his side. "Your head has never looked so civilized."

With a gulp, Lorna summoned her courage and laid her hand on his forearm. "Shall I take that as a compliment, Mr. Dewhurst?"

His jaw worked back and forth as he guided her into the house. "No," he said at last, "you shouldn't."

The bottom of her stomach dropped out at his callous remark. How could she have thought his attention might have indicated some degree of preference? How could she have been so stupid?

He was handsome and connected and intelligent, while she was utterly ordinary. Except for the bit about stealing bodies.

Her scalp prickled. She wanted to scratch it, to tear loose the braids Alice had woven. The urge to flee was so potent she could taste it, a burning acid at the back of her throat. She slipped her hand loose, but he snatched it back and held her in place.

Then they stood on a landing, overlooking yet another sea of strangers. A servant bellowed her name. In a daze, she wondered how he knew it.

Lorna floated at Brandon's side down a flight of stairs and into the nightmare of her very first Society ball.

• • •

As balls went, this one was blander than most. Being the Little Season, most of the *ton* was flung about the countryside. Those in Town were engaged in the fall session of Parliament, acting as government advisers and ministers, or carrying out other legitimate business. They were a much more staid bunch than the spring flood of high-spirited debutantes and rutting young bucks.

Lord Sheridan Zouche was a welcome sight, and Brandon was glad to catch up with his old friend. They'd met at Oxford, where Brandon, Sheri, and the three other men in their set had gathered regularly at their favorite tavern to enjoy free-flowing ale and good conversation. One drunken night, the youngest of them, Henry De Vere, had suggested the group needed a name. After some spirited debate, they'd settled on The Honorables, based on the one thing all five men had in common: None of them stood to inherit their noble families' titles. As younger sons, each man was styled Honorable, as in The Honorable Mr. Brandon Dewhurst.

All of them except Sheri, that is, who, as the younger son of a marquess, enjoyed the courtesy title Lord Sheridan. He'd been quick to point out that *he* wasn't Honorable, which caused an immediate uproar of laughter. Chagrined, Sheri had gone along with the suggestion, and the friends had been The Honorables ever since.

These days, the five men were rarely all together at once. Norman Wynford-Scott lived in London, just as Sheri and Brandon did, but his legal studies at the Inns of Court kept him much occupied. Henry split his time between Town, where he worked at his family's shipping business, and his brother's estate in Wiltshire. Finally, Harrison Dyer spent a good deal of time in the country engaged in quiet pursuits. Last Brandon had heard, Harrison was trying to raise funds to start a breeding stable.

Brandon should have known he'd see Sheri here, as the fellow socialized with the same focused determination Brandon brought to his surgical career. Sheri's brown hair was a study of carefully deployed disorder, and his clothes were exquisitely tailored. Brandon wondered how long it took his friend to achieve such a state of formal splendor. There wasn't much time for the men to talk, however, as Sheri considered it his sacred duty to dance every set.

"My worth to Society is measured by how much the women around me enjoy my company," he explained. "I'm not a desirable match—thank God—but I do an excellent job of occupying a space at the dining table and filling out dancing formations. Should I allow my performance of these crucial functions to flag, matrons will drop me from their lists faster than a hot brick."

"So let them drop you," Brandon answered. "Isn't there something you'd rather do with your life than live on your allowance?"

"Is that Russian you're speaking, Brandon? I'm sorry, I don't comprehend a word." Sheri lifted his quizzing glass to his brown eye and frowned. "Who is that lurking behind the tree?"

Brandon looked in the direction his friend indicated. "That," he said, "is Miss Robbins."

Lorna stood against the wall, halfway behind a potted orange tree. Alice and some of her friends chatted nearby. His sister-in-law attempted to draw the young lady into conversation.

Lorna would not be drawn. If anything, she crept farther into her hiding place. Brandon had seen plenty of wallflowers in his time, but this was really beyond enough. If the female didn't wish to move about in Society, why on earth had she relinquished her mourning and accepted invitations to the opera and a ball?

When they first arrived, Alice had tucked Lorna under her wing and introduced her to a number of respectable persons. A few gentlemen expressed polite interest in the newcomer. That was when she made her strategic retreat to the forest.

"I can't make out much of her face," said Sheri, "but she has nice limbs."

Lines began forming up for a reel, so Sheri went to claim his partner. Brandon glanced over the floor and groaned. There, in the center of the ladies' line, was Lady Fenton.

Brandon cursed and plowed through the crowd. What was the woman thinking? Performing a sedate waltz was one thing, but a country dance? All the jouncing and capering about were sure to do her ill. She'd overtire herself, if she didn't put herself into premature labor.

No matter McGully's desire for a one-of-a-kind specimen, Brandon would do everything in his power to ensure Lady Fenton's well-being while he watched over her. Granted, she didn't know he was watching over her. And she'd likely run screaming if she knew of his task. There really was no delicate way to tell a woman your employer hoped to slice her open soon after her untimely demise. If she perished, then yes, Brandon would take her body for the good of science. In the meantime, he would stay close and pray it never came to that.

Reaching behind the orange tree, he fished out a dancing partner.

"What are you doing?" Lorna demanded. She wrenched out of his grasp and tried to edge back to her shelter.

He couldn't suppress a grin, even as he prevented her escape. Finally, here was a glimpse of the firebrand he was used to. "You haven't danced."

"I don't want to dance."

"Of course you do. Ladies love to dance."

"I don't."

"I'm sure that isn't true." He tugged her hand, but she mulishly dug her feet in. He let out an exasperated noise. "Miss Robbins," he said loudly, "may I have the honor?" He gave a florid bow, drawing the attention of Alice's group.

If she wished to save face in front of the ladies, Lorna had no choice but to accept. Her turquoise eyes shot daggers as she took her place in the line across from him.

Seconds later, the music began. Brandon knew the steps by rote, and only paid the dance enough attention to ensure he didn't collide with his neighbors. He kept glancing at Lady Fenton, fearing that at any instant a baby might fall from beneath her skirts. He and Lorna had moved up to the head of the formation before he looked at her.

And that was when the crisis struck.

All the hopping and skipping he worried would do Lady Fenton harm instead wreaked havoc on Lorna. Each jostling step worked the neckline of her baggy dress closer to her shoulders, exposing more and more décolletage. She was watching his feet and counting in time with the music, obviously concentrating too hard on the footwork to notice her gown's wayward progress.

Another hop. Another inch. With her hair trussed up in those braids, the entirety of her neck was bare. It was long and slim and milky as a swan's. The cinnamon sprinkle of freckles on her shoulders sent pangs to his groin. "Miss Robbins," he called.

She didn't hear him.

They clapped palms together. The bodice gaped. "Lorna."

She flashed him a quick smile and twirled to make her way back to the bottom of the formation. Brandon hustled to take his place in the column. They clapped again. This time he grabbed her hands. "Lorna!"

She startled at her name and dropped her hands to her side.

Fwomp. The dress slipped from her shoulders and fell.

White chemise. Ivory stays. A fraction of a second of bliss before horror kicked in.

Frantically, she grabbed for the dress.

He beat her to it.

He yanked the fabric up, spun her around, and whisked her through the nearest exit. *Away* was the only sense of direction he currently possessed. Down one corridor, around a corner, up a half flight of stairs, and through a door, which he closed and locked.

His forehead thumped against the door. He drew a deep breath and waited for his galloping pulse to subside. "Are you all right?" he asked. She didn't answer. "Lorna?"

He turned and saw her back. Not just in the orientation sense, but her actual, anatomical back. The blighted dress had come open all the way to her waist. Creamy skin gleamed in the moonlight filtering through the windows of the small parlor in which they were ensconced. Neat laces crisscrossed her spine, holding her stays in place. He'd never seen anything as erotic as the simple laces of Lorna's stays. It would be nothing but a few tugs to have them off, to see more, to touch. The thought had him hard in seconds. He closed the distance, halting just a few inches behind her.

Lorna's slender shoulders shook silently.

God, he was a cad. A flash of skin had him mentally stripping her, while she had just suffered public humiliation. "It's all right," he murmured. His hands hovered over her shoulders for a second before he wrapped his fingers around them. "Lorna? I'm sure no one noticed."

He lowered his head and inhaled. A hint of citrus wafted to his nose. He thought of mulled wine, and wondered if she tasted as sweet as she smelled.

Her shoulders, so delicate and slim beneath his large hands, kept trembling. His heart gave a funny kick. The urge to shelter and protect the fragile female was intense. Almost as intense as the other, potent urges she incited.

She let out a muffled sound. It grew louder. And then she snorted.

Lorna wasn't crying at all; she was laughing, the minx. Something inside him snapped, letting loose a flood of relief. On its heels came desire, hot and thick.

Her head shook from side to side. Brandon scowled at the dratted, prim braids. Those glorious curls shouldn't be contained. She let out great whoops of laughter, and he pulled the offending combs from her hair. Lorna grasped her sides and Brandon grabbed her waist. Trim and firm, her figure fit neatly in his hands. Lorna's head fell back against his shoulder, tears leaking from the corners of her eyes. She was so lovely in her mirthful abandon, so infectiously free. With her delicate scent filling his head and her laughter ringing in his ears, Brandon was caught in a moment of convivial arousal. He wanted to laugh with her and hold her and just *be* with her. Her hair tickled his lip and nose. He responded by rubbing the tip of his nose against her shoulder. She was right there, and he was right there, and before he could check himself, he leaned forward and ran his tongue up her neck.

Lorna's laughter died in her throat. She went stiff.

Brandon was stiff, too. She was sweet, and the slightest bit salty, like the very best dessert. He wanted another taste. But her utter stillness persisted, her air of confusion finally penetrating his addled brain.

"Christ, Lorna, I'm sorry. That shouldn't have happened. Just… Christ." He crouched behind her. "Let me fix your dress and get you back to the ballroom."

She grabbed at the curls springing free of her unraveling braids. "What did you do?" She swung around, slapping him in the face with frumpy satin. "Where are my combs?"

"Here," he said, retrieving them. "Turn around and let me do up your hooks."

"I most certainly will not." One hand clasped her dress to her bosom, the other covered her neck. "You licked me!"

"I'm sorry," he repeated. "You were crying and—well, I thought you were crying and—"

"So you licked me?" Lorna backed away slowly, as though fearful he might pounce. "I suppose it's good for shocking a person out of a weeping fit, but surely there are better ways, Mr. Dewhurst."

His hand raked through his hair; he cursed. He'd behaved as though he was a roe deer, and she a block of salt. They hadn't kissed, hadn't made it through so much as a single dance together, and he'd skipped right ahead to tongue-swabbing.

Brandon never lost control of himself like this. His profession demanded constant discipline, and he was well practiced with keeping himself under tight rein. It had to be the extraordinary situation that derailed him. Gowns didn't usually fall off of women in his presence quite so easily. There was typically some bit of effort on his part to bring about such a result.

"Would you please leave!"

"But your dress—"

"Devil take my dress," she snapped. "I can see to it. Alone," she added when he started to protest.

The wisdom of her words finally cracked his thick skull. Touching her velvet skin, when his cock was still convinced the main event was just around the corner, would be imprudent. "I'll just wait in the corridor, shall I?"

She huffed. "I came half undressed in front of…" Her hand waved in the direction of the ballroom. "You whisked me out—with your hands upon my denuded person, need I remind you—and you want to, what? Make a grand re-entry together?"

He stifled a groan. He'd been so long out of Society that he'd become fuzzy on some of the salient points. Such as not being caught with an unclothed woman in his arms. But what was he supposed to have done? Left her exposed to every leering male?

"It was something of an emergency," he reasoned. "People will understand."

"I'm not going back into that ballroom," she said. "You, however, must return. Otherwise, people will assume I came to one ball and fell into ruin with my first dancing partner."

Fine. Let the stubborn woman have her way.

Brandon slipped back into the ballroom and scanned it for Lady Fenton. There was no sign of her.

A short distance away, he spotted Jeremiah and Alice. Her arms crossed her midsection, one hand fiddling with the pendant in the hollow of her throat.

"Everything all right?" he asked when he reached them.

Alice's lips pursed. "It's Lady Fenton. She had some pains, so I accompanied her to the withdrawing room." Moisture glistened in her eyes. "Oh, Brandon, there was blood."

His face drained. How foolish he'd been to let Miss Robbins distract him from his duty! "Where is she now?"

"Lord Fenton took her home." She gripped his sleeve. "Will she be all right?"

"Her ladyship must be attended," he said. "I'll go see to her at once."

Chapter Nine

Lorna may not have taken London by storm, but she *had* taken it by surprise. This fact was brought to Lorna's attention when two posies were delivered that morning. The first, a sweet bouquet of freesia and baby's breath, came from Lord Everston. The second, yellow chrysanthemums bound with a white ribbon, carried a kind note.

"For livening up an otherwise dull affair. Compliments, from Lord Sheridan Zouche," Lorna read. "Goodness! I've never had hot-house flowers before, and here are two bunches in one morning."

For a Society debut she didn't want, last night had certainly been…interesting. When her dress fell from her shoulders in the middle of a set, she'd wanted the floor to open and swallow her up. Humiliated and shocked, she could scarcely string a thought together as Mr. Dewhurst evacuated her from the scene.

There was nothing for it but to laugh. After the things she'd endured with Thomas and her gruesome work with the Crib Cross Gang, losing her bodice in front of a ballroom full of strangers didn't seem such a catastrophe, after all.

What followed, well, she still wasn't quite sure what to think. It should not have happened. His hands had no business on her underthings, and his tongue most assuredly ought not to have touched her neck.

Touch wasn't even the right word for what happened. He'd tasted her. Exhaled hot breath against her. Enveloped her with his warm scent. At the feel of his tongue, her pulse jumped and her arms went to gooseflesh. Even after she escaped his embrace, the cooling trail of dampness on her skin continued the sensual assault.

Getting rid of him was harder than she'd anticipated. He took considerable convincing, and she'd been tempted to step back into his arms and request a repeat performance, please and thank you.

Finally alone, she'd put her clothes to rights, waited a few minutes, then returned to the ball. Running away would only cause more speculation, she feared.

Mr. Dewhurst had quit the ball, in any event. Alice explained Lady Fenton's crisis, and that Brandon had hurried to check on the lady.

Lorna was on the verge of insisting they do the same, when she was introduced to Lord Sheridan, who invited her to dance. Amazingly, her mishap had proved comedic, rather than scandalous. The fact that she'd brazened through the embarrassment showed her to be a good sport, Lord Sheridan said with a good-natured chuckle.

Lord Everston asked her to dance the following set, but Alice and her husband were ready to leave. Lady Fenton's situation had Alice on tenterhooks.

Thinking of Lady Fenton had Lorna anxious to call on the woman and see how she fared. To carry out her visit, however, she needed a companion to accompany her in public, a bothersome standard of propriety if ever she had heard one. But if Lorna was going to play the part of a genteel miss, she had to observe all the niceties. And so, after breakfast, Lorna informed the housemaid, Charity, she'd been promoted to lady's maid.

"Lord, Miss Robbins!" The servant knotted her fingers at her chest. "I've never dressed a lady's hair."

"That's all right," Lorna reassured her. "If you would, please sort through my wardrobe. I've some old dresses in my room which might still be serviceable."

A short time later, as the maid helped her into a sprig muslin dress and green, quilted spencer, Lorna felt the same spike of anxiety she'd experienced last night while donning the lavender satin. As much as she loathed her black mourning, she'd felt safe in it.

Descending to the foyer, Oscar approached. "A letter for you, Miss Robbins."

"Not another admirer, I hope," she teased.

No such luck. In a coarse, barely literate scrawl, she read: *F & H. Four o'clock.—C*

"Bother," she muttered. Allowing for all the travel to and from her destinations today left little time to visit with Lady Fenton. "Find me a hackney at once, please," she instructed Oscar.

Then she squared her shoulders and prepared to pay a call, take some tea, and steal a few bodies.

• • •

She was shown to a drawing room, where Lady Fenton lay on a récamier. Her skin had a wan appearance. Bluish circles bruised the skin beneath her eyes. Her belly, covered with the white muslin of her dress, reached skyward like a snowy mountain.

How heavy it must be, Lorna thought.

She experienced a moment of disconnect as she regarded the woman's abdomen. It was like an entity unto itself. Lorna had no trouble following the line of Lady Fenton's figure and picturing her without the protrusion. Almost, she thought she could lift the bulge, take a peek at the babies within, and cover them up again. How odd.

"Miss Robbins, how kind of you to call." Lady Fenton struggled to rise.

"Stay where you are!" snapped a masculine voice.

From the corner, Lord Fenton scowled at his wife. His red hair and brows framed an expression of doting exasperation. "Dearest, Doctor Possons says you are not to rise for anything."

Lady Fenton frowned right back. "Mr. Manning says light exercise is perfectly safe."

"Why you insist on consulting a sawbones when you have one of the finest physicians in London looking after you is quite beyond my ken, madam. I don't trust the man. I tell you, Marjorie…"

While his lordship rattled on, Lady Fenton rolled her eyes at Lorna. "Don't mind him, Miss Robbins. A more managing nursemaid could not be had for love or money. Do have a seat."

Lord Fenton huffed. He crossed to the sofa and ran a hand across his wife's dark hair. "Be careful, love." A tender look passed between the couple. Lord Fenton bowed to Lorna and left, quietly closing the door behind him.

The reclining lady glanced past Lorna. "Has Mrs. Freedman not accompanied you?"

Lorna perched on the edge of a chair, her spine held erect by nerves. "No, I'm afraid not. I won't stay but a moment, my lady. I only wondered how you were getting on today."

"I confess I may have overdone the dancing last night. My feet can barely squeeze into my slippers today." She waggled her blue brocade-shod feet. "Otherwise, I'm quite all right." Her head flopped to the side on the bolster pillow. "Besides my swollen toes and that bit of excitement last night, I haven't had a spot of trouble this whole time. But according to that fusty old physic, I'm due to expire at any moment." She chuckled. "Have you ever heard such nonsense?"

Lorna forced a humorless laugh. The poor woman had no idea of her danger. "Your husband seems to value the doctor's opinion."

The other woman's face screwed up petulantly. "Only because the man feeds Archibald's worries. My surgeon, Mr. Manning, is not afraid to speak contrary to the good doctor. And," she said, "he deigns to actually examine me by touch, rather than from a socially polite distance. It was Mr. Manning who discovered I'm carrying three."

"He sounds very competent," Lorna agreed.

A maid arrived with tea. The servant propped Lady Fenton into a sitting position by means of a great many pillows wedged behind her back.

Lorna served her hostess a cup of the aromatic beverage with a biscuit on the side.

Lady Fenton carefully balanced the saucer and cup on top of her belly. She smirked at Lorna's startled expression. "You see, it isn't all bad. I carry my own tray with me wherever I go."

The silly sight charmed Lorna.

Having never had a close friend as an adult, her heart jumped at the chance to embrace Lady Fenton as one. Sternly, she reminded herself that Lady Fenton could not be—must not be—her friend. Not only was Lorna's situation too dire to allow confidantes, becoming close to Lady Fenton was fruitless. The woman's days were numbered. Why invest emotions in a friendship doomed to end in tragedy?

The drawing room door opened, admitting Alice Dewhurst. Worry lines around her eyes eased when they settled on Lady Fenton. "Oh, Marjorie, I've been beside myself."

The small, fair woman leaned over to press cheeks with the raven-haired lady. "I told you not to fret, Alice," Lady Fenton chided. "I feel fine, and Miss Robbins has been good enough to keep me company this morning."

Alice turned to greet Lorna, then she scowled. "I told you to stay outside."

"Not that I don't trust your observational skills, sister, but I had to see Lady Fenton for myself."

Mr. Brandon Dewhurst crossed the threshold into the room. He wore a brown frock coat and trousers, with a quilted waistcoat and a pristine cravat knotted under his chin. The wave of dark hair flopped over his forehead softened his otherwise grave demeanor. Hard gray eyes swept over Lady Fenton, heavy and assessing, then slid to Lorna. A small, private smile tugged at the corner of his mouth.

A residue of embarrassment caused her to squirm. Recalling the previous evening's debacle made the place where he'd licked her tingle. She glowered with renewed disapproval.

Lady Fenton draped an arm across her eyes. "Mr. Dewhurst, as I told you last night, I have my own surgeon. You are kindness itself, but pray do not trouble yourself further." Her words were all politeness, but Lady Fenton's cool tone left no doubt as to her true feelings.

"Mr. Manning is a fine surgeon," stated Mr. Dewhurst, "but it cannot hurt to have another professional opinion."

"We have two, already." Lady Fenton settled an unwelcoming glare on Mr. Dewhurst. One of her hands spread over her belly. "A third only creates confusion."

Mr. Dewhurst's jaw worked, but he did not argue. He bowed. "Your servant, ma'am."

"I must be going," Lorna said.

"Allow me to see you home," said Mr. Dewhurst.

Her spencer suddenly felt too tight across her breasts. She had to keep her distance, she reminded herself. "Thank you, sir, but that won't be necessary."

The refusal seemed to please Lady Fenton. Her face once again radiated kindness. "Thank you so much for your call, Miss Robbins. I do hope I shall see you again soon."

Chapter Ten

"I don't believe this," Lorna murmured the following morning as she flipped through the post.

Invitations. Scads of them.

To be sure, the stack was smaller than what would arrive in a fashionable home, but for a nobody like Lorna, it was an impressive sight. Dinners, teas, musicales, and even balls celebrating the upcoming Christmas season.

She looked at Nelly, who was helping herself to cinnamon toast. "Has there been some sort of error? Why have these invitations come here?"

Her neighbor took a bite of toast before answering. "Lorna, my dear, do you not keep up with the papers?"

Lorna brushed an unruly curl out of her face. "What papers?"

"The Society pages are all abuzz. Everyone wants to know about you."

Lorna drew back. "Why?"

"Because you're an Original, of course." Nelly wiped her fingers on her napkin and settled back in her chair with her teacup. "The mishap at the ball the other night could have started a scandal. For any young lady of the Polite World, it would have. But you're different, you see. You could be *ton*, but you aren't quite. The episode was seen as comical, rather than scandalous. The fact that you remained at the ball worked in your favor, too."

It seemed silly to be admired for putting her clothes to rights and returning to the ball. Although, she conceded, her perspective might not be on balance with other women of her age and station. After a grueling half-year of nursing her violent and ill brother, followed by nearly a fortnight of bodysnatching, Lorna had no room left for typical, feminine sensibilities. What did she care if a few dozen people caught a glimpse of her stays? No real harm done.

In any event, she had no interest in cultivating connections within the *haut ton*. Her birth gave her the right to this world, but the possibility of it had been snatched away when she was fourteen years old and became mother, father, and sister to Daniel.

She couldn't say this to Nelly, naturally, but Lorna decided neither the invitations nor the curiosity they represented mattered. She'd attended the ball the other night only because Lady Fenton did. The sole reason she would have for attending *any* of these functions would be to keep an eye on her ladyship. And since the woman was presently confined—possibly to remain so for the duration of her pregnancy—Lorna saw no reason to accept any of them.

• • •

Coop, when he heard of this new development, did not share her opinion. "Kee-rist, what a stroke of luck!" he bellowed.

The Crib Cross Gang was assembled at the mews, loading up for another night of plucking bodies from the ground.

"What's lucky about it?" During normal nights like this, Lorna's official role within the gang was to act as lookout. Coop insisted she still dress in full mourning regalia. He believed Lorna's appearance scared away potential troublemakers who might otherwise try to infringe on Crib Cross's territory. As Blackbird, Lorna was gaining a second reputation, wholly different from the one forming in polite society. Here, in the East End, the lady resurrectionist was feared as an unnatural creature.

"Because, you goosecap," Coop rejoined, "this is the perfect opportunity for us to really make our mark. With you in good with all those nobs, we'll have first pick of the very best bodies. Toffs fetch a higher price than any old Jack or Jill." He helped

Daft Jemmy load the shovels into the bed of the wagon, then handed Lorna up into the seat at the front.

"You go to all the parties of pleasure you can," he said. "Find out who's ailin' and who's dyin' and who just done died. Then you bring that information to me, see, and soon we'll own this town. Am I right, me lads?" he called over his shoulder.

"Crib Cross forever!" chorused the men.

Lorna didn't like it, but she saw Coop's point. The faster the gang made money, the sooner she'd be free of that dreadful Wiggins. "All right," she reluctantly agreed. "I'll do it." Then she thought of her scant wardrobe, and while she was sure Nelly would loan her whatever Lorna required, she didn't relish the thought of habitually exposing herself to the general population. "I don't have anything to wear to a ball, or even a dinner," she complained. "I had to borrow a dress the other night."

He snorted. "God, if you ain't a female clean through. You wouldn't hear a man crying 'bout having naught to wear of a night."

If he was to attend the kind of events to which Lorna had been invited, she expected any man with a grain of sense would, in fact, worry about being properly turned out.

"If I may be so bold as to remind Mr. Cooper," she said, taking pains to emphasize his formal address, "this scheme is of your own design. I'm just a simple, countrified girl, but I do know that if one wishes to catch a fish, one must properly bait the hook. If I'm to be your worm, sir, then I must look like one."

They arrived at the cemetery adjacent to a hospital. Before the mules' hooves settled into the ground, Bluebell hopped out of the back and went to work, nose to the ground. Behind her, Pretty Lem, Fartleberry, and Bob streamed out silently, bearing shovels and covered lanterns as they followed the dog to fresh graves.

Coop and Lorna climbed off the bench, while Daft Jemmy tended the mules.

"Right, listen girl," Coop hissed. "Havin' you aboard has let me get creative in my work. Ain't no other gang got a lady—an' a real lady, at that." He held up a finger. "For that reason alone, I'm gonna make an investment. You're my own little six per cents, eh?" He chucked her on the chin, then took some paper bills out of his coat pocket.

From the depths of the graveyard, one of the men whistled.

Coop handed the money to Lorna. "Make it count. You'd best be the comeliest worm in London Town."

• • •

The ballroom was entirely white. Never had Lorna seen such a thing. From ceiling to floor, the grand chamber hosting the ball celebrating Lady Spencer's birthday was pure alabaster. The opulent moldings and pillars were also white, as were the window casings and the draperies. It was simple and stark, but bespoke a certain, arrogant wealth. Every speck of dust or smudge of mud would show in this room. Only someone with the means to maintain it in pristine condition would dare flaunt such a space.

Around the perimeter, gilded furnishings sparkled. A rococo console table supported a tray of champagne flutes, while, above it, a chaperon mirror in an ostentatious frame glimmered like a gaudy bauble, its convex surface reflecting the entire room at a glance. Swags of fragrant greenery woven with strands of white and gold beads offered a nod to the season.

"I've always loved this room," Lady Fenton declared on a happy sigh. Really, the woman should've been home in bed, but it was heartening to see a familiar face in the crowd. "Lady Spencer's birthday ball is the only time it's opened to the *ton*. Those who come to Town only in the spring don't know what they're missing. I'd take Lady Spencer's smaller affair over any great crush in May."

Twisting her neck to admire the vaulted arches framed in egg-and-dart, which divided the room into halves, Lorna added her thoughts. "It is lovely, though rather intimidating."

"This place does have a way of overwhelming the senses, doesn't it?" her ladyship agreed. "The white does that. It gives the room a quality of boundlessness."

Lorna's gaze took in the company. Each gentleman and lady was clearly delineated. Colorful silks and rich velvets were all the more vivid for their austere backdrop. "I feel so very exposed," she said, attempting to articulate the vague, unsettled feeling in her middle. "Almost as though I'm on display."

Lady Fenton's lips twitched. "But you are, of course. We all are."

True. Lady Spencer's elegant, white room provided nowhere to hide. One *must* see and be seen here. This was no ballroom for blushing debutantes. The décor was too sophisticated, too adult, for untried girls fresh from the schoolroom.

And though she sat off to the side, Lorna felt a surge of unfamiliar confidence. With Coop's money, she had purchased, secondhand, a gown with a skirt of heavy, olive satin and a bodice of Forester's green velvet. Ribbons of the olive satin were worked into a winged design on the bodice and provided simple banding around the sleeve cuffs.

In her green dress, white gloves, and simple gold earrings, she coordinated with the ballroom. She felt clever, as though she'd planned it just so. The boost which came from feeling good about her appearance for a change lent her a forwardness to which she was unaccustomed.

Soon, Lorna was chatting with many older ladies who had been strangers at the beginning of the night. "I trust the evening finds you well, ma'am," she said to one neighbor, Lady Dane.

The woman harrumphed. "Your trust is misplaced, missy."

Recalling how the butler at home, Humphrey, always responded well to her solicitous questions after his health, Lorna gently prodded the dowager for information.

Fifteen minutes later, the woman was still talking.

"… and that was the last time I let an apothecary talk me into administering medication *that* way. There's something indecent in having to take such care of how one sits. And it didn't do a thing for my hip, either, after all that! Of course my bad hip is nothing to poor Lord Weir," said Lorna's new bosom bow.

"What ails him?" Lorna politely inquired.

"Cancer of the bones."

Lorna's ears perked. "Is his health failing?" Later she'd jot down some notes to pass along to Coop.

"Tumors sprouted all over his spine," said the lady. "Great lumpy things." She seemed grimly satisfied with Lorna's unfeigned sound of distress.

"I'm terribly sorry," Lorna said. "My heartfelt wishes for his recovery."

"He won't make it. Only a matter of days," Lady Dane finished with a sniff.

She murmured all the right things, but inside Lorna thrilled. As her conversation with Lady Dane led to chats with other, older members of the *ton*, she experienced a sense of satisfaction at actually being good at something. She'd never be the darling of Society, or a popular wit, or even an eccentric bluestocking. Heretofore, Lorna had only displayed aptitude at holding Elmwood together by hook or by crook, and that just barely. But this, she thought, as she smiled around at her new, old friends, *this* she was good at.

Tonight, she was Blackbird. Secretly gathering information about the aristocracy's dead, dying, and disfigured—from behind her disguise of a simple miss in a festive gown.

If they only knew.

• • •

As Brandon scanned the white ballroom, he told himself he was looking for Lady Fenton. Upon his arrival, he'd heard the foolish woman was in attendance. Were she his patient, Brandon would order her home and to bed.

However, she was *not* his patient. And so he told himself he was anxious to find her to satisfy his curiosity, to see with his own eyes that she was well, and to keep track of her as McGully wished.

That his gaze arrested on Lorna Robbins he dismissed as mere happenstance, because she was seated at Lady Fenton's side. The easing of a knot in his chest—one he hadn't known he'd been carrying until he saw Lorna and it went away—was more difficult to explain. And so he tried not to think about it.

Steadily, Brandon worked his way through Lady Spencer's pristine ballroom. He came upon Sheri and Lord Fenton, who had their attention focused on the far end of the room. Suddenly, the two men burst into laughter and raised their glasses.

"Another point to Miss Robbins," Fenton said.

"What?" Brandon demanded. He strained his neck to find the source of their amusement.

"Miss Robbins lays waste to us all," drawled Sheri. "She's refused to dance a single set. Just keeps holding court with all the biddies."

Brandon now saw that Lorna was surrounded by an unusual set of company for a young lady. Besides Lady Fenton, who, thank merciful God, was not dancing, Lorna's companions were all aged well above fifty. Some of them had sailed past seventy, even.

It was the damnedest thing. She sat in the middle of her group and commanded attention, as though she was the belle of the ball. Her legion of followers, though, were the dowagers and spinsters, the wallflowers and the infirm. Now he spotted his friend, Niall Freedman, who hung onto Lorna's every word, just like all the rest. Altogether, the motley group appeared to be having a fine time.

As though she sensed his presence, Lorna looked from the old woman seated on her side, directly at Brandon. Their gazes locked. Slowly, her lips turned up in a shy smile. Brandon's chest constricted.

"Are you all having fun at her expense?" he snapped at his friend. "Miss Robbins must sense you're laughing at her. No wonder she turns you away." The thought of anyone making a mockery of Lorna sent something inside him snarling in her defense. She was so delicate and fragile in appearance, with her large eyes and unruly curls putting him in mind of one of the dolls in his nieces' nursery. And she was all alone in Chorley House, with only her servants for company.

And her younger brother, too, Brandon supposed. She must be responsible for the boy's care. Brandon wondered how old the lad was, whether he would be sent away to school or tutored at home. He thought of the large, happy dog that greeted him and Lorna at her door the evening they'd dined at the Freedmans', a cheerful beast with a bark deep enough to scare away most any miscreant. But it wasn't Lorna's dog, he recalled.

It should be.

Lorna needed a huge beast at her side, protecting her from the world.

Sheri punched him on the arm. "No, she's a fine girl. Seems to take us all in good stride. Playing along, you know?" Brandon's friend chuckled. "It's refreshing to have a lady present who hasn't set her cap after snaring a husband."

"How do you know she's not on the marriage mart?"

"Because," Sheri explained in a patient tone, "she wore the same dress to dinner last night. No husband-hunting miss would be caught dead in the same ensemble twice in a row."

Her gown was a fetching green, with some ribbon swooping around the front. Sheri had noticed what she wore last night, and he'd taken note of it again tonight. Well and good to say Lorna wasn't after a husband, but what if some marriage-minded man took interest in *her*?

Before he had time to think better of it, Brandon cut a path straight to her.

"Mister Dewhurst!" She sounded genuinely pleased to see him. "Good evening, sir." She stood and offered her hand. He drew her a little closer.

The color of her dress brought out the green in her turquoise eyes. He found himself lost in them, wondering where the blue bits had gone. There must be a biological mechanism at work, he decided. He thought he'd ask McGully about it, but the idea slipped away when a delicate blush spread beneath her freckled cheeks. "You look lovely," he blurted, though *lovely* didn't begin to do her justice. Enchanting, more like. "I hear you haven't danced."

Those mesmerizing eyes sparkled. "For once, Mr. Dewhurst, gossip does not lead one astray."

Her teasing banter encouraged him. "You will dance with me, though, won't you?" He leaned in and caught a whiff of her delicate scent. "I hope I can claim closer acquaintance with you than anyone else present."

"The last time we danced ended in travesty, you may recall." The shell of her ear pinkened. "Besides," she said, gesturing with her arm, "I'm having a lovely time getting to know some new friends."

Brandon glanced at the assemblage behind her and frowned. "You aren't in your dotage, Lorna."

She worried her plump bottom lip between her teeth and glanced over her shoulder. "I won't dance," she said. "It wouldn't be fair to the others I've refused."

As though Brandon cared about being fair to other men.

"However," she continued, "you may claim the set. I believe that is permissible?"

He answered in the affirmative. "I'd offer to stroll you through the garden, but the night's quite cold. Shall we promenade about the ballroom, instead?"

They made it halfway around the room before Lorna lifted on her toes to say near his ear, "It's too noisy to converse. Might we make use of the corridor, instead?"

The opportunity to have her more to himself was not to be wasted. Brandon quickly led her through a door.

From the hallway, they walked a short distance to a parlor. Though open to company, there were no others present. A fire glowed invitingly in the hearth.

Lorna sighed. "Much better. I'm still unused to so many people."

"You've lived a rather retired life to now, I take it?"

She nodded, a smile playing around her eyes. "It's just been Daniel and me for a long time." In front of the fire, she removed her gloves and extended her arms to the warmth.

"That's your younger brother?"

"Mmm." She nodded again. "And also Humphrey, of course. And Oscar."

"And they are?"

"Our butler and footman."

"What of your parents?" he inquired.

"Dead." She went on to explain about her father's three wives, each mother to one child, each buried young. Lorna's mother passed away when her daughter was four; Daniel's mother within hours of his birth. And then the old baron died. Though she didn't say so, Brandon sensed the responsibility of caring for her home had fallen to Lorna's young shoulders, rather than to her elder brother.

Her story made Brandon think of all the women like little Daniel's mother, who desperately needed the work he and McGully were doing.

But he didn't want to dwell on childbed deaths right now. He pushed work from his mind to focus on the fey woman beside him, so lovingly describing her strange little family comprised of old servants and a boy baron.

Considering how she'd literally bolted the first time he saw her, now being trusted with these confidences about the people she cared for made him feel ten feet tall. He *was* closer to her than any other man in that ballroom. And he wanted to be closer yet.

"Your hair is very pretty tonight." Her curls had been loosely pulled away from her face, rather than scraped back. The firelight gleamed over the reddish tint in her auburn locks, creating ribbons of flame twisting through mahogany. "I like it this way," he murmured, twining his index finger into one of the spirals.

Lorna self-consciously raised a hand to cover his. "My maid, Charity, is the first person who's ever known what to do with it. She told me she'd never done a lady's hair before, so I suppose my hair must not be very ladylike."

Brandon burrowed deeper into those glorious curls. They felt like living things vining around his fingers, snaring him.

Lorna's eyes fluttered. She pressed her cheek against his palm. Brandon's other hand came to her throat, where her pulse thrummed like a hummingbird's wings. He tilted her face up. The generous curve of her mouth beckoned him. Slowly, he lowered his head.

Before he made contact with her lips, Lorna stepped closer. She pressed against him, wrapped her arms around his waist. For a startled moment, his hands lingered in her hair, clasping her to his chest; then, he enveloped her in his arms. One held firm around her waist; the other hand stroked up and down her spine.

A shudder racked Lorna's body. Instinctively, he tightened his hold. This was intimate in a way he didn't expect. While his body registered all the ways she tucked neatly against him, his heart swelled at the show of trust. Again, the trust. He still wanted to kiss her—and would—but this…this was something new.

He rested his cheek on top of her head and stroked over her hair, loving the feel of it against his skin and the way it caught on his evening stubble. "Lorna," he murmured. "Sweet, sweet Lorna. Shh, sweet girl." They were dreamlike, his words, almost a lullaby. She needed holding. God, to be the man who held her all night. His body hardened.

She looked up at him, her eyes dark in shadow. "I've never been embraced before," she whispered. "It's marvelous."

He frowned. "Never?"

"Daniel gives me hugs," she corrected. "But never anyone closer in age to myself." She ducked her head, bashfully hiding her face against his waistcoat.

Brandon's mind reeled. He thought of his own family. His mother, so openly demonstrative with her affections; his brothers, whose good-natured slaps on the back became manly hugs when babies were born or times were hard. Hell, even his sisters-in-law kissed his cheek, and his nieces and nephews buried him under piles of hugs.

Lorna having lived her life without physical affection from anyone besides her young brother was just so bloody *sad*. No wonder she seemed like such an outsider. She wasn't just new to Town and new to the *ton*, she was new to interacting with anyone who wasn't a child or servant. In her long years of caring for everyone else, no one had bothered to care for her.

He just…he just wanted to be the one to care for her a little bit longer. Even in this small way. To know she could turn to him for a bit of affection, a modicum of comfort.

"Don't be embarrassed," he said, nuzzling her temple. "I'm honored you let me hold you. I would give you more, if you allowed it. I want to kiss you."

Wide eyes blinked up at him. "I don't know how," she said.

"Let me show you."

She drew her breath sharply, pressing the roundness of her small breasts into his chest. Brandon groaned as he covered her mouth with his. Her lips were soft and inviting, as luxurious as satin sheets and down pillows. He cupped her face, tilting her head to give him better access. His thumb stroked her cheekbone while he sipped her bottom lip between his.

In return, she drew his top lip into her mouth. Brandon smiled into the kiss and chuckled. Lorna giggled back. Her hands slid up his chest and around his shoulders; her fingers buried in the hair at his nape.

For another endless moment, he relished the feeling of the slender woman in his arms, her body warm and perfectly molded against his. He ached to deepen the kiss, to let loose the fire building between them. But they were sharing a moment of simple joy, and he was loathe to do anything to spook this creature who had, until a few minutes ago, never been embraced.

A clock struck the hour. Lorna pulled away. Her wonderful lips turned up in a smile and she stood on her toes to press one more kiss to the underside of his jaw. "Mmm, this is nice," she murmured. "But I must go."

"At the stroke of…" He consulted the clock. "Midnight? Will you turn into a pumpkin?"

Lorna laughed. "You make a terrible muck of fairy tales."

She tried to pull out of his arms. Brandon hated to let her go. "Perhaps I shall keep you here and see if you really do revert to a vegetable state."

Her teasing smile slipped. "Mr. Dewhurst, I must leave."

He released her at once, startled by her tone. "Brandon," he said. "My name is Brandon."

She pulled on her gloves and gave him a tight smile, all the while putting distance between them. "Brandon, then. Good night."

And she was gone, leaving him to wonder, yet again, why the hell Lorna Robbins kept running away from him.

Chapter Eleven

Cold rain splattered against filthy cobbles and ran in rivulets, slimy and smelly like the fluid leaking from a three-day-old quarron. Slee blew his nose into the crook of his elbow, then wiped his face on his sleeve. He moved with the flow of pedestrians, each one a variation on cold, wet, and miserable. An urchin brat darted in front of him, and Slee jabbed his foot out, tripping the kid. The child landed nose-first on the icy street.

"Watch where yer goin', ye little shit," Slee snapped. Lately, it seemed life did nothing but put obstacles in his path.

Only weren't nothing quite so esoteric as *life* that done him wrong. Slee knew who to blame. Crib Cross Gang. Those rotten nappers had caused him nothin' but grief for weeks now. And Mister high-and-mighty Dewhurst was getting right cantankerous with Slee, on account of not having the top-notch goods anymore.

"Nooo," he muttered as he edged past a slow old cow carrying a basket of garbage for the dust heap. "Crib Cross snatching up the best ones, easy as pissing the bed."

Moments later, he ducked into The Fox and Hare, the regular watering spot of the Artichoke Boys. The rain weren't falling on his head no longer, but the tavern was muggy from the close press of a couple dozen sodden bodies. It was warmer in than out, but 'twas a sickly kind of warmth, oozing 'round the dim establishment.

Slee spotted a pretty little piece by the bar. Her painted lips and the flesh spilling from her dress told him all he needed to know. Maybe a hot, wet rub would clear his head. She caught him staring at her teats and she stared right back, hate simmerin' in her eyes. Good. He liked an honest prostitute. The ones what played like they enjoyed a man…them's the ones he left with bruises. Teach 'em what lying to a hardworking fellow would earn.

He sidled up to the bar and knocked on the wood. Ordered a gin and poured it right down the hatch. Slammed his empty on the counter so the blighter with the bottle would hurry to refill it.

A whiff of vinegar alerted Slee to the doxy at his side. "Your cunny smells like pickled fish," he said without looking at her. At least she took pains not to get a belly full.

"A girl likes to be ready to take a chance when it comes."

The surprisingly soft voice reached down his pants and grabbed his attention all right. "Yeah, an' my cock gettin' brined, what's my chance of coming?"

She laughed, a breathy noise through her nostrils. "Name's Fanny. D'you want to buy me a drink?"

He lifted his glass and cracked a smile at his liquor. It tasted like shit, but did the job. "Hell no, I don't want to buy you a drink. Figure you can buy your own, after our business is done."

"What's your name?"

At last, he looked at her, glowered from under his heavy brow ridge. Took pains to inject a fierce tone, so she knew she'd better show some respect. "None o' Your Goddamned Business, me mam called me."

"Slee! All right, man?"

A jocular slap on his arm had him turning around to see one of his Boys, Pete. Fool chattered like a woman, but damn if he weren't the fastest digger Slee'd ever seen. Pete held a pint in one hand. The other he punched into his trouser pocket, then he rocked on his heels like he'd just won at the track. Idiot.

"Naw, an' I ain't all right, either," said Slee. His shoulder aimed at the bunter's face should've told her there was man business takin' place, and to get her arse out of the way, but the bitch stayed put, watching his exchange with Pete. "Dewhurst gone all glimflashy on me."

Pete took a long glug of his beer. "What's he mad about?"

"What d'ye think, fool? Told him it weren't our fault there was only hacked off limbs to be found behind the hospital, but he worked himself into a right snit, too. Said rancid amputations weren't no good to his *pupils*." He sneered out the last word, showin' just what he thought of anatomy students.

Anatomists liked to look down their noses at resurrectionists, but when it came right down to it, who was worse: the man who steals a body, or the man who buys it? The man who hands over an intact corpse, or the lout who lays it open and digs around in guts and shit and brains and loves every minute of it? What Slee did weren't even a real crime, strictly speaking, on account of corpses not really being no one's property, but that didn't stop the magistrates from bringing resurrection men down on whatever other charges they could. But even if Slee was strung up for theft, he'd never wind up in the hands of a monster like Dewhurst, on account of he weren't no murderer. That was the only ticket to the dissection table recognized by the Crown. The law gave the dissectors eight executions every year. 'Course, eight bodies weren't enough for the surgeon-anatomists. Like demons right out of hell, they were always hungry for more and more human flesh.

Looked at in the right light, what Slee did was downright noble. By satiating their appetite for the dead, he probably kept Dewhurst and McGully from snatching babies right out of their beds at night.

"They should give me a commendation," he muttered.

"Crib Cross puttin' the pinch on everyone," Pete offered.

In Slee's belly, the gin churned, all sick-like. "Damn that Crib Cross! I been in this game a dozen years, the best there is." His bony chest puffed with well-deserved esteem. "But then here come Nat Cooper and his gang o' nancies and an honest-to-God idiot, driving us an' all other honest men right off the road. He's up to no good."

"Crib Cross?" said Fanny the whore. "Ain't that the gang Blackbird works for?"

Slee's eyes rolled in his head. "What the hell is Blackbird, when he ain't flapping around the park, shittin' all over everything?"

"Lady resurrectionist," Fanny said.

Pete's eyes bugged. "You serious?"

Slee downed the remainder of his drink and ordered another. "No such thing. Resurrectin' is man work. What good's a woman?"

Fanny's mocking laughter rang in Slee's ears. "Not just a woman, fool, a lady. Seen Blackbird with my own eyes. And you better believe she's good for something, else why would you be in here moaning about Crib Cross being so much better than you?"

"I didn't say they were better," Slee spat. "Said they was up to no good." His nostrils flared. "Tell me about Blackbird."

A nasty smile spread across the prostitute's face. She still hated him. Good. He hated her right back.

"Guess you'll be buyin' me that drink now," she said.

Chapter Twelve

"It's so good of you to come."

"Thank you for having me, Lady Weir," Lorna said in a hushed tone. "Please accept my sympathies for your loss."

Two days after the memorable evening in the white ballroom, Lorna stood in the late Lord Weir's parlor with a handful of other guests.

She'd never met the man, but acquaintance was no requirement for attending a viewing. And the note from Lady Dane said that, since Miss Robbins had shown such Christian concern for the man's woes, perhaps she could extend her charity to condoling with the bereaved.

And so here she stood, meeting the new Lord and Lady Weir and feeling oddly conspicuous in her mourning. Having grown accustomed to wearing her Blackbird regalia only on the East End, standing in a Mayfair parlor dressed all in black was distinctly uncomfortable.

As she glanced around the parlor, she felt a pang of sorrow for her brother, Thomas, whose funeral had been embarrassingly unattended. Lord Weir's viewing, at least, had brought out his contemporaries, dowagers and dodderers who shook hands and said what a pity it was, what a shame. Wasn't he a good man? Oh, yes, the very best of them.

Lorna exchanged subdued greetings with some of her new acquaintances and looked at the clock. The hands had been stopped at one thirty-seven. *Damn and bother.* "Excuse me," she asked a gentleman standing in the corner sipping tea and looking bored, "might you have the time?"

He consulted his pocket watch. "Twenty past four."

Lorna thanked him for his assistance. Ten more minutes.

The butterflies did not contain themselves to her stomach. She felt nervousness fluttering all the way up her throat and feared it might escape in an inappropriate titter. She sucked her lips back between her teeth and clamped them tight in defense.

Lady Dane waved Lorna over. "Have you been in to see him?"

"Not yet," Lorna answered. "I'm working up my nerve. It seems strange for my first sight of the man to be his body."

The old woman twisted her hand around the ivory handle of her walking stick. "Prepare yourself to partake of the bread and wine in the room with Weir."

Lorna's nose wrinkled. "Why?"

Lady Dane leaned forward and gestured for Lorna to bend closer. "Sin-eating," the old woman hissed. "Some Scottish nonsense supposed to help the soul make it to heaven."

Blood drained from Lorna's face, leaving her cheeks cold. The thought of consuming anther man's sins in a mockery of Holy Communion did not seem the wisest course of action. She'd done quite enough to throw the state of her own soul into question, and was about to add yet another log to her eternal fire.

"Grotesque custom," continued Lady Dane. "Surprised Weir would have gone in for such hogwash, but, apparently, it's family tradition." Her pursed lips and sidelong glance communicated her opinion of this particular practice.

After she judged sufficient time to have passed, Lorna moved to the hallway outside the sitting room where Lord Weir was laid out. Hands gripped at her waist, she stood with her head bowed in an attitude of prayer. It wasn't with God she communed, however, but Daniel. She promised she was doing her best for him, that she was in this dreadful business only until she could ensure the security of their home.

A moment later, the sitting room door opened. Another woman dressed in black quit the chamber.

Drawing a fortifying breath, Lorna entered the room and shut the door behind her. Carnations, lilies, and rosemary filled vases and bowls on every available surface, eloquent displays of grief and discreet masks for the scent of the guest of honor.

Lord Weir lay in his open casket, dressed in a shroud of white linen that left only his face visible. His cheeks were sunken; his mouth pulled in a grim line. Marks like bruises stained his temple and eyelids.

Most of the corpses Lorna had seen the Crib Cross Gang retrieve were covered in winding sheets, reduced to oversized grubs. The face of the departed made her uneasy. Trepidation filled her middle as she stepped closer. The wine and bread Lady Dane had mentioned were on a small table at the foot of the casket.

Morbid fascination gripped her, and she found herself unable to look away from the unnaturally still face. Daft Jemmy had assured her the dead were only sleeping, but it wasn't true at all. She thought of Daniel as he slumbered, all rosy cheeks and plump lips pursed as he dreamed. Even in sleep, a person exhibited signs of life, breathing and turning and grumbling. While the dead... the dead waited.

Suddenly, a laugh burst from her lips. Poor old Lord Weir wasn't anything to be afraid of. Wherever his soul had gotten off to, what remained was just meat and bone and sinew, the same as any cow or sheep the butcher handled a dozen times a day. The coffin and the shroud and the heaps of flowers were a little bit absurd, she decided, like the fanciest presentation a Christmas goose could ever dream of having.

"And there's even a nice wine at the table," she murmured, pouring herself a small measure of the beverage. Lifting her glass, she silently toasted Lord Weir, rather than offering to drink up his sins. She'd let God sort those out.

After placing her glass on another stand for the used stemware, Lorna crossed to the window and opened it. In the street in front of the house stood a wagon loaded with pails, brushes, and canvas tarps—supplies for painters. The driver of the wagon glanced up at her and flashed his brilliant smile. Lorna waved at Pretty Lem.

In a matter of seconds, Bob had a ladder propped against the wall and scaled it, hauling himself into the room with a huge sheet of canvas folded and draped over his shoulder. Working as quietly now as he did at night, the burly man shifted chairs and tables to the sides of the room and spread the canvas on the floor.

Lorna took Lord Weir's feet while Bob grasped his shoulders. After a quiet count of three, they hefted the man from his casket to the center of the tarp. Lorna grunted with the exertion. Panting softly, she pulled the shroud back down to Weir's ankles.

Her companion methodically covered Weir in the canvas, folding and tucking as though swaddling an infant. Foisting the corpse over his shoulder, Bob worked his way out the window and down the ladder. Pretty Lem hopped off the driver's bench and loaded up the ladder while Bob got the body situated. He climbed into the back and covered Weir with another heap of canvas, so it looked as though the painters had carelessly piled their drop-cloths into the wagon after a day's work.

We actually did it, Lorna marveled as the wagon pulled away. Coop's plan was so audacious, so impossible, she'd thought surely the entire Crib Cross Gang was doomed. But their leader's brazenness had proved brilliant, and now a peer of the realm was destined for the dissection table and Lorna that much closer to repaying Wiggins.

A little thrill shot through her. Blackbird had successfully winnowed her way into the unsuspecting *ton*. She repressed giddiness, sternly reminding herself she still had to make an exit, hope the theft was not discovered until she was long gone, and pray suspicion did not fall on her.

She returned the room to its previous state—except for the notable absence of the body. On silent hinges, she lowered the casket lid, then placed several of the flower arrangements on top. Hopefully, the next person into the room would assume the casket had been closed the whole time.

Schooling her features, she let herself into the corridor. No one would be so gauche as to peek into the casket, she assured herself. The ruse would be a success, so long as she played her part and departed the house without incident. Her eyes remained decorously downcast as she passed the next mourner.

A warm hand took her arm. "Lorna?"

She blinked up into the gray eyes of the one person who could ruin everything. "Hello, Brandon."

• • •

She was clearly as surprised to see him as he was to see her. But why the surprise, Brandon mused, when more and more he saw Lorna frequenting the same places as he.

And wasn't that just a delight?

"Did you know Lord Weir?" he asked.

Her mouth pulled to the side, and he thought she was trying to stop herself from smiling. She shook her head. "Lady Dane asked me to attend, on account of my polite conversation the other night."

The other night. Since their embrace that night, he couldn't stop thinking about her. Never would he have imagined a chaste hug and a teasing kiss could send him into a frenzy of desire, but something about her stirred his blood. He wanted her in his arms again. Thinking of it made his palms itch to touch her.

"Mister…Brandon," she corrected herself, "I must be going, but I dread having you accuse me of running away again. Please, take note: I am departing in a perfectly civilized fashion, not fleeing before you."

He took her hands, wishing he could pull her closer. "Duly noted. May I have your carriage called?"

"Oh no, I'll walk," she said. "It isn't but a half mile or so. Not worth bothering with a carriage."

"It's cold and raining," he protested, appalled at the idea of her tromping through such conditions. "The weather's unfit for anyone, much less a lady. Please, Lorna, allow me to escort you."

"How kind," she said at last. "Thank you."

Warmth spread through Brandon's chest. He dipped his head. "I'll just be a moment paying my respects to Lord Weir, and then we'll away."

Lorna's eyes tightened at the corners. "Should you need to stay, then please don't worry about me. I really must be off at once." She pulled free and took a step.

"Wait." His hand shot out to snatch hers back.

"It was kind of you to offer," she said, tugging once more, "but you needn't inconvenience yourself."

Exasperating woman. With a guilty glance into the viewing room, he placed his hand on the small of Lorna's back. "Very well. I cannot like sending you off into this weather by yourself."

In the entrance hall, a footman helped Brandon into his greatcoat, while Lorna was presented with a black wool cloak. Brandon frowned at the thin garment. She should have a good, heavy redingote. One lined in fur, preferably.

Tucked into a hackney coach, Lorna wrapped her cloak about herself and huddled in the corner. "Come here." Brandon pulled her to his side. Even without blankets or warming bricks, the carriage was almost cozy, pressed together like this. The cold seeped through the floor and into Brandon's booted feet, but from the knees up, he was quite content.

There was something about the dreary, overcast day and this warm woman at his side that made Brandon feel a bit reckless. He brought Lorna into his lap and wrapped his arms around her. She tucked right beneath his chin. He grunted his approval. "Better?"

He felt her nod against his throat. "I wondered, if, after the other night…" She sat up and met his gaze. Her cheeks and the tip of her adorably freckled nose were pink with chill.

"What did you wonder?" he asked. His gloved fingers stroked her cheek.

"Whether it would happen again," she whispered.

"This, you mean?" He kissed her softly. Lorna hummed; the vibration traveled down his throat and into his heart. Pulling back, he rested his forehead against hers.

"Yes, that," Lorna answered with a smile. Delicate fingers curled around his ear. She tugged him to her face and brushed her mouth across his. Coolness tinged the edges of her lips, while the core of her mouth beckoned to him with tantalizing warmth.

The first time they'd kissed, he hadn't wanted to frighten her. But today, he sensed wildness in the way Lorna hunched her shoulders, pulling herself harder into the kiss. Brandon cupped her nape and ran his tongue across her lower lip. He swept back across the crease between her lips and slipped inside.

Lorna stiffened in his arms for a second. Then she relaxed and opened to the new experience. He showed her the tender caress of mouths moving together, a wordless conversation that communicated all sorts of things to Brandon's body. Things like *Yes* and *Want* and *More* and *Forget want—need*.

Long, drugging kisses swept away the exhaustion of endless days and late nights. For several minutes, he didn't think once about Lady Fenton's alarming condition. There was only Lorna in his arms. With her, he felt a sense of kinship he'd rarely experienced. She knew what it was to be an outsider. But together they created a place of belonging.

She shifted on his thighs, bringing Brandon's attention to the hardened state of his lower portions. Parting her cloak, he brought a hand to her stomach. Lorna inhaled and arched her neck. Brandon's lips drifted across her jaw and down her throat while his hand roamed upward. Her breast was small and firm. There were no stays beneath her dress. The sudden knowledge that only a few flimsy layers of fabric separated him from her flesh made him harder yet. His thumb stroked over a nipple, delightfully taut and responsive to his touch. She gave a little sigh of pleasure. Through the material of her dress, he tormented her other nipple until she clung to him, wordlessly pleading.

God, if she was this sweet bundled up in a carriage, what would it be to have her in bed? He groaned, wishing he could satisfy his curiosity.

The carriage jolted to a stop, and the jarvey clambered down from his perch, rocking the coach.

Lorna scooted off his lap just as the door swung open. She gave him an uncertain smile.

"I'll see you soon," Brandon assured her as he helped her down.

"I know," she said, and he wondered at her tone of regret.

Chapter Thirteen

"Mr. Dewhurst, get ye up here!"

In the upstairs parlor, Brandon set aside his cup of coffee and newspaper. The Scottish brogue summoning him was broader than usual, a sure sign McGully was worked up over something.

He found the surgeon in the office adjoining McGully's dissection room. The Scotsman clutched a letter in a tight fist. The instant Brandon stepped into the room he waved the paper. "Did ye hear, lad? Weir was taken! Snatched."

Brandon drew back. "Startling news, sir. I thought he was to be buried this morning. Was he interred last evening?" He would have expected a man with the resources of Weir's family to have hired guards for the old man's grave. But perhaps the foul weather had made it difficult to find help.

"Ha!" McGully slapped his palm against his desk. "No, an' he never was buried. Taken from his own viewing was Weir."

"From his viewing?" Brandon blurted, astonished. "How is such a thing possible? I was there! I saw..."

His mind raced through his memory of the event. He *hadn't* seen the corpse. The casket was closed. Lorna Robbins had been in the room, but she certainly hadn't smuggled a body out beneath her skirt. Had she, he would have discovered it during the ride to her home. His jaw muscles clenched and he cleared his throat.

The older surgeon plucked a skeletal foot from his shelf and tinkered with the joints. The bones had been carefully cleaned, bleached, and pinned together to replicate natural movement.

"Nooobody knooows when the body was taken." McGully sounded like he was weaving a ghost story to scare children. The older man waggled the foot at Brandon. "The family saw it at the start of the viewin', but it was gone by the end. In between, visitors came and went for hours, each spendin' their time alooone with the corpse."

Brandon crossed his arms, grabbing opposite elbows. "But one cannot just steal a body from a viewing. How…?" He rocked on his heels. "A fine mystery for Bow Street, I suppose."

McGully slashed the foot through the air and scoffed. "Ye'll not be seeing a Runner on the case. The family does no want word of this to get out." He replaced the foot on the shelf and flicked the letter. "Manning is crowing about a special delivery he received last night."

Sinking into a chair, Brandon's mind raced. If he'd been presented with the body of a nobleman last night, what would he have done? "Involving the authorities would make no difference," he concluded. "The dissection is long since over with, and the flesh already stripped from the bones. There's nothing left for the family to claim."

"Aye." McGully slumped into his seat and leaned back, hands behind his head. "Oh, but what I'd have given for those bones," he said wistfully. "His hips were always bad, and they say the cancer had tied his spine in knots."

"Perhaps Manning would show them to you, if you ask nicely," Brandon drawled.

His colleague snorted. "Nay, lad, those bones will be under lock and key for years, on the off chance the family decides to pursue the matter."

They were silent for a moment, and Brandon was about to take his leave, when McGully thumped his fists on the desk. "God, the audacity of it!" he bellowed. Jabbing a finger at Brandon, he went on, "That's the kind of work you're supposed to be doing for me."

"You want me to steal bodies right out from under the noses of their families? May I remind you, sir, that I do not steal anything? That's work for resurrection men."

"Yeah, an' if you had a thought for either of our careers, you'd be hirin' the sort of snatchers that got hold o' Weir."

Brandon's hands clenched around the arms of the chair. "I'm not interested in making my career via sensational corpse theft, sir. I'm interested in advancing the fields of anatomy and surgery. I thought you felt the same."

McGully's cheeks went ruddy. "An easier time I'd be havin' advancing those fields if the bodies you've brought me of late weren't so piss-poor."

It was on the tip of Brandon's tongue to protest that the failure lay with the Artichoke Boys, but he stopped himself. He wasn't the sort of man to pass the blame elsewhere. One of his duties was to procure bodies for dissection. The last couple of weeks, he'd done abysmally in that regard. If the source from which he purchased dissection materials had dried up, then it was time to look elsewhere.

Later that night, when he was woken from a dream about Lorna Robbins—a dream that had him aching with need—to open the door for Slee, his mood had not improved.

"More half-rotted trimmings from the amputation bench?" he snapped. Cold air gusted in from the alley and swirled around Brandon. He would feel pity for the gang of resurrectionists if he weren't mad as fire at them for their shoddy work, which had, in turn, landed him on McGully's bad side.

Slee gave Brandon a calculating look from over the muffler wrapped around the lower half of his face. "Pete," he called. "Bring it in."

One of the Artichoke Boys hefted a body over his shoulder and carried it into a room off the hallway where Brandon inspected the deliveries. The only furniture in the small space was a heavy farmhouse table, the wood dark with a patina of age and unsavory stains. Wrapping sheets concealed the body, but a long, steady slice of Slee's knife parted the covering.

Before Brandon had time to fully register what lay in front of him, his body was already reacting. Violent tremors shook his hands. Sweat beaded on his temple and ran to his jaw, down his neck, tickling like flies on his skin.

Flies and sweat and heat and the moans and begging and the stench. The unbearable, incessant smell of the surgery tents that clogged his throat and choked him, kept him from being able to eat a proper meal for months. How could he? How could he ever eat again, with the things he saw and did, day after day?

And into that hell of dying, shattered men, she came. He'd never expected to see her there...never expected to see her again, at all. But there she was, having birth pains in the back of a cart stinking of manure. From a glance, he saw the labor wasn't going well. Lathered in sweat, her sternum rose and fell too quickly; air scraped in and out of her throat in a harsh pant. When he glanced below her waist, he wanted to howl and weep and rage. Blood ran freely from beneath her skirt, staining the cart and dripping onto earth that had already seen too much death.

The older man who drove her pleaded with Brandon to save his daughter. From the cart, dark eyes that had once flashed at him with laughter now met his gaze with grim resignation. Her lips moved and he leaned over. *"You must care for him. Please,"* she whispered in Portuguese.

But he was an apprentice field surgeon, not a man-midwife. And in the end—after she'd slipped into her dying delirium and they'd performed a caesarian surgery to try to save the baby— there had been nothing. Nothing but two lives lost and the blood on his hands of a woman who'd trusted him.

Drowning now, gasping for air, he looked down and saw his fingers were curled around the edges of the receiving room table. Slowly, he began to detect sensation again. Fingernails digging into the wood grain on the underside of the table. Throbbing in his neck and between his shoulder blades where the muscles were knotted. Aching in his face, from clenching his jaw so hard.

By degrees, Brandon forced himself to relax. He was not in that long-ago army camp. He was in London, at the anatomy school where he'd worked alongside McGully for several years. The woman on the table was a stranger, not Florbela. The dead child inside her was just another sad case, not an infant he'd sworn to protect.

"Fine," he managed. "Perfect." McGully would be pleased. Another womb to explore. Another entry for his book. Another woman for Culpepper to reduce to lines and light and shadow rendered in ink, neat little marks in his sketchpad.

But from their work…hope. Progress. If this woman's death and dissection could help another woman live, then it wasn't entirely meaningless. It was meager consolation, but Brandon took what he could.

Slee watched from the door, eyes narrowed shrewdly. "I want a hundred for this one."

The outrageous sum was the slap on the face Brandon needed to snap him out of his head. "Fifteen. That's half again as much as usual."

"You ain't the only 'natomist likes the pregnant ones, you know," Slee groused.

Brandon blew out his cheeks. "I'll give you fifty," he finally said. Slee opened his mouth, but Brandon cut off negotiations with a pointed look. "And I warn you now, Slee, I won't keep dealing with you any longer if things don't improve. This is the first decent body I've had from you in weeks. I'm not sure you're up to the task of securing Lady Fenton when the time comes."

"Hey now!" Slee reached out imploringly. "It ain't my fault business's so dried up."

"Crib Cross again?" Brandon snapped. He drew himself upright and looked down the nose that had always been a little too large for his face. "I don't think much of a man blaming his failings on others."

"Yeah, well, now I know, sir," Slee said, brightening. "I know what Crib Cross's up to. They've got a woman, see—Blackbird. That's why they nabbin' all the good quarrons."

"What do you mean, a woman?"

"A lady resurrection man," Slee explained. "She's part of the gang."

Brandon tried to wrap his mind around a female taking any part of the grisly work of bodysnatching—and failed. "Her name is Blackbird?"

"That's what they call her on the street, yeah. Don't nobody know her real name."

Brandon huffed. Tonight's buy would appease Douglas McGully for the time being, but the dressing down Brandon got earlier still rang in his ears. "Regardless, *you* are the failure here, not Crib Cross Gang and not this Blackbird. If they're in your way, find a way around them. Be smarter than they are, tougher. Deal with the problem, Slee. Do better."

"That I will, sir, that I will. You'll have your Lady Fenton, sir, I swear it." Slee's words were all obsequiousness, but there was a nasty edge to his tone. Cap clutched in his hands, the resurrectionist theatrically bowed himself out of the room. A few seconds later, the alley door closed.

Brandon had to wake McGully and summon Culpepper so the dissection could begin as soon as possible, but he felt glued in place. For a long moment, he looked at the dead woman, fighting against the panic trying to once again rise in his throat. *Pull yourself together*, he commanded, grasping for the detachment he so desperately needed.

Even though the woman's abdomen was large, the baby inside her would be small. He lifted his hands, pictured an infant in them. *So small. No larger than…* No. Jerking his hands to his sides, he slammed the mental door. Then he turned and slammed the physical one behind him.

Chapter Fourteen

"What are we doing, Miss Robbins?" Charity asked. The maid's eyes were tight with worry as the hackney coach carried them into a seedy part of the city.

"*We* aren't doing anything," Lorna said, glancing past Charity to the gaming hells and taverns packed cheek by jowl with brothels and opium dens. Every vice she could imagine—and some she'd never thought to imagine—had a place here. "I have to meet with a man."

The maid's gaze turned suspicious. "What sort of a man?"

"A moneylender," Lorna explained. "My brother died deeply in debt. I'm attempting to make good on his notes."

Charity's lips pursed. "This about your blacks, isn't it? When you leave at night, wearing your mourning, that's when you make money."

Lorna gripped the cord of her reticule and mulishly stared straight ahead.

"Just tell me, miss, are you earning it on your back?"

"Charity!"

"It's just," the maid rushed on, "if you were, I'd want to make sure you were bein' safe, that's all." She raised her chin a notch. "I wasn't brought up in Mayfair, you know. I know how it can be. A woman's got to survive." Charity patted her hand.

The carriage stopped. Before she exited the vehicle, Lorna said, "You needn't worry, Charity. I'm not doing *that*."

She meant to leave the maid in the hack, but Charity scrambled down after her. "I'm not lettin' you go in there alone." Her voice only trembled a little.

Lorna knocked on the door in a spot where the blue paint had been worn down to the wood; many other knuckles had come before her. "I don't think you've quite grasped all that being a lady's maid entails. Generally speaking, she does her mistress's bidding."

"What if her mistress is all alone in the world?" Charity asked. "What if she takes off during the night, thinking nobody notices her coming and going, leaving the rest of the house to worry after her? What then?" The doughty servant looked Lorna right in the eye, challenging her employer.

Lorna was saved from the sudden feelings of guilt and gratitude by a shouted demand from the other side of the door. "Who's there?"

"Miss Robbins," she called back, "to see Mr. Wiggins. I've payment for him."

The door swung inward to reveal an enormous man. A shock of bright red hair fell over his broad brow. His jaw was square, as were his shoulders—and his hands, for that matter, she saw when he gestured her into the lender's office.

"Sit there." A finger as large as a sausage pointed Lorna to a rickety wooden chair against the wall of a small antechamber. The man opened another door and closed it behind him. His deep voice rumbled indistinctly.

"Lord, Miss Robbins!" Charity stood in the corner, her eyes gone round as wagon wheels. "That fella must be the muscle, you think? I bet he goes 'round thumping money out of people, and here you've walked right into this place."

Lorna didn't care to admit she shared Charity's trepidation. That beast who'd opened the door definitely wasn't here to take coats and offer tea. On the other hand, Lorna hoped that coming to see Wiggins of her own volition would keep him and his minions from ever again approaching Elmwood. She didn't want that enormous man and his ham-sized fists anywhere near Daniel.

Wiggins strutted through the inner door, one hand on the pocket of his waistcoat, toying with a gold watch fob. "Well, bless me, it *is* Miss Robbins," the moneylender said. "When Gareth"—he gestured to the hulk who'd followed him out—"told me the name of my visitor, I thought he must be mistaken. What a nice surprise." His face stretched into something she supposed was meant to be a smile. His front tooth was brown, dying. Lorna protectively tucked her lips around her own teeth.

She brushed past Wiggins and his brute and into the man's office, as though she had every right in the world to be there.

Not missing a stride, Wiggins circled the desk and took his seat without first offering her a chair. "Out of mourning already, are you? Chorley was a forgettable sort, poor old blighter. Still, would've thought his own dear sister would remember him."

Her cheeks flared with ire and she was glad for the modicum of shade her bonnet provided. "It's difficult to think of anything *but* my brother," she said. "Or his debts, at any rate."

The short man chuckled. "We're of a like mind, then," he said, "'cause I've been thinking about my friend Lord Chorley and his debts, too."

"I've come to make payment," Lorna stated, lifting her reticule.

Wiggins' eyebrows rose. "Fifteen hundred already? Color me impressed, madam. A man wants what he wants, though, and they say there's someone out there for everyone. Good for you, Miss Robbins." He winked.

Her cheeks burned hotter. "I'm not…" It didn't matter, she reminded herself. Didn't matter what the vile Wiggins thought of her. "I don't yet have the full amount," she said. "I have a few hundred, though. I wanted to buy some of Thomas's notes."

The moneylender kept playing with his watch. Now he pulled it out and, without looking at it, opened and shut the case. "All right." He rummaged in a drawer and produced a familiar stack of notes bundled together with twine. "What've you got?"

With shaking fingers, Lorna pulled bills and coins from her reticule. One at a time, she laid them in a row on the desk.

Wiggins flipped through the promissory notes, peeled out two, and laid them on top of the money.

Satisfaction warmed her belly when she picked them up. Thomas' signature was scrawled across each. She tore the notes into neat squares and tossed the bits onto the nearby grate, where the coals quickly reduced this small portion of Thomas' folly to ash.

"There," she said, feeling calmer than she had in a long time. "I'll be back with another payment in a couple of weeks."

"As to that," Wiggins said, a genuine grin spreading on his lips, "I'm afraid I shall require payment in full at the end of the month."

"What?" Lorna screeched, shooting to her feet. "That's half the time you told me I had."

"Is it?" Wiggins stood and sauntered around to stand far too close. "That was before you put your whore hands on me, remember? I warned you you'd regret doing that. And you with a little brother at home." He tutted. "I wonder what folks will make of a baron livin' in the workhouse."

A vision, one she'd tried so hard—for years—to keep at bay flooded her mind. Daniel in tattered clothes, his rounded cheeks gaunt with hunger.

Wiggins brought his face to her ear. Breath smelling of fish and sour wine gagged her. "So tell me, Miss Robbins, do you regret it yet?"

Chapter Fifteen

This one isn't getting away.

Brandon's mouth set in a grim line as he watched pallbearers trudge across Cross Bones Graveyard, their booted feet slipping on dead leaves and mud. The grave was a black gash in the earth. Around it stood the deceased's compatriots, performers in a traveling show spending the cold season in London.

Inside the casket was one of the show's human exhibitions. Known as The Great White Scot, Cam Kinley had been as huge as the brawniest Highlander. At six-and-a-half feet tall, The Great White Scot was made even more notable by a complete lack of pigmentation in his skin, hair, and eyes. Ironically, the strapping man had fallen ill and succumbed to fever.

On a rise a short distance away, a flutter of black caught Brandon's notice. A woman, swathed in mourning, overlooked the funeral proceedings. A thick veil concealed her face, but Brandon felt her gaze on him. Pulling his eyes away from her felt nigh impossible.

As the service drew to its conclusion, pallbearers lowered The Great White Scot to his not-quite-final resting place. One in particular caught Brandon's eye.

Physically imposing, with black tattoos across his swarthy face, Brandon recognized The Cannibal from an article which had breathlessly described an exhibition match between the Scot and the Māori warrior. Now, though, the large man's exotic visage bore none of the foreign ferocity that had drawn audiences to the troupe's shows, only deep lines of sorrow as he helped ease his sparring partner into the ground.

The Artichoke Boys were due to arrive in an hour. Brandon would guard the grave until then, playing the part of a mourner while the undertaker's men filled the grave. The resurrectionists would have Cam Kinley out again in no time. And Brandon would have an astonishing specimen to study. What caused Kinley's abnormality? Why were his eyes red? Brandon could scarce wait to see what answers the body would yield.

Movement from the mysterious woman once more grabbed his attention. She trudged one row of graves closer. She slumped against an obelisk marker, clinging to the memorial for support.

As mourners began dispersing, Brandon huffed. The woman might wish time to grieve at the graveside before the burial was completed. She would want privacy. Well, she couldn't have it. Brandon couldn't risk taking his eyes off Kinley's remains. He wouldn't be the only anatomist hoping to lay hands on this particular body.

A muffled sob carried through the chill air. His eye twitched.

The undertaker and two men carrying shovels entered the cemetery by a nearby gate.

The woman extended a black-gloved hand. Her head lolled while her shoulders heaved.

He tried to steel himself against her distress, to no avail. With a groan, he turned and strode to the gate, nodding at the undertaker as he passed. Let the woman have her time, he decided. Though the sky was overcast, a couple hours of daylight remained. No one would attempt to take Kinley's body before sundown.

Except for the Artichoke Boys. Brandon allowed himself a moment of satisfaction. The Crib Cross Gang weren't the only ones capable of daring exploits.

A quarter of an hour later, he was tucked into a corner table of a nearby tavern with a hot cup of spiced wine. Drawing the pungent fumes deep into his lungs, Brandon felt the icicles in his veins start to thaw. A cautious first sip was followed by a larger swallow. Warmth seeped down his throat and through his belly.

"Bliss," he said.

Around him, a clientele of respectable merchants and other professionals bent over steaming cups and plates. The taproom resounded with the sounds of convivial laughter.

Brandon wasn't immune to the general good humor. Under his breath, he hummed an off-key melody and thought about Lorna. He wanted to see her again, to get her in his arms and kiss her senseless. His hands, long used to remembering their way around a human body, perfectly recalled the feel of her breasts against his palms, her tight little nipples at his fingertips. And that was through her clothes. He tortured himself imagining how her skin would feel. Did the freckles he'd spied on her shoulders dust her breasts, as well? The thought had him half-hard in a matter of seconds. Surreptitiously, he changed position, easing the discomfort between his legs.

"Dewhurst!"

Brandon startled. Beside him, Slee stood with arms crossed, a thunderous expression on his red face. Behind him, two more Artichoke Boys looked like overgrown schoolboys watching their instructor scold a fellow pupil.

"What're you doin' here?" demanded the resurrectionist. "You're s'posed to be standing guard."

The rough appearance of Slee and his companions drew notice of the tavern's patrons. Brandon's mouth tightened. "I don't care for your tone, Slee," he said. Brandon stalked outside, leaving the criminals to follow.

"Now see here, sir," Slee huffed, when he'd rejoined Brandon, "we had a plan." He jabbed a soil-stained forefinger into the opposite palm. "You was gonna go to the service, then keep watch 'til we got there, so no one else would poach our goods. But here we come down the road and see you sittin' in the window having tea, pretty as you please."

"I did attend the service," Brandon said as he once more drew on his gloves and buttoned his greatcoat against the cold. "I left the grave only to give the man's widow a few moments of privacy. The undertaker had arrived, so it isn't as though anyone else could make a move."

Slee's nostrils flared. "Great White Scot weren't married."

Brandon waved a hand. "His mistress, then. Or daughter. Sister. Whoever she is, the poor woman was weeping buckets. The least I could do was give her a little time with the man before we snatch him back out of his grave."

One of the other men nudged Slee aside. "She wearin' black?" the man asked.

Brandon nodded. "Of course."

"Head to toe? Did you see 'er face?"

Dread trickled down Brandon's nape. "She was in full mourning, including a veil. I did not see her face."

The man groaned and kicked a pebble into the street.

Slee slapped his forehead and cursed.

"What?" Brandon demanded.

"You cully," Slee spat. "You've gone and handed our quarron over to Blackbird."

Brandon felt the blood drain from his face. Slee was right; Brandon was sure of it. How, he couldn't say, but there had been something about the woman that unsettled him. He'd been taken in by her performance. Such a pretty show of grief had trapped him in the rules of his upbringing, forcing him to accede to the wishes of a lady.

He barked an oath and took off down the street at a determined pace.

"Hey, now, what're you doin'?" Slee swiped at his sleeve, but Brandon brushed the man aside. "It's too late. Crib Cross's already got it."

"Good," Brandon snapped. "That's what I'm counting on." He stopped in front of a wooden booth on the corner and banged on the door.

A member of the Watch opened the door. Behind him, Brandon heard Slee yelp and run off.

The watchman's annoyed expression gave way to one of deference when he took in Brandon's aristocratic hauteur. "What can I do for you, sir?"

"I'd like to report a crime." The corners of Brandon's eyes tightened. "Grave robbery. Taking place at Cross Bones, even as we speak."

• • •

From across the cemetery, she'd known him. Her heart accelerated as she drank in the sight of him; each beat produced a twinge of desire and regret. Acres of graves and mounds of wool could not conceal Brandon's posture, the way he held his spine straight and his shoulders relaxed. It was a little different from the bearing of any other gentleman she knew—not quite the precise, rigid lines of the *ton*'s men, but centered slightly lower, as though to keep the feet rooted and allow the upper body to move freely while he worked. It was the posture of a man who could stand in the same place for hours.

But he couldn't stand there for hours. As much as she might wish she could run to him and bask in the smile he seemed to reserve just for her, she had to get rid of him.

"Why must you be here?" she whispered, her words whipped away from her lips by a biting wind.

"Well?" Coop said behind her. "What's the word?"

"It's a small gathering," Lorna reported. She glanced over her shoulder, through the tumbledown place in the wall, to the gang assembled on Union Street, a quiet road that bordered the south side of Cross Bones Graveyard. "Ten mourners. No undertaker yet." She struggled with her thoughts before imparting the next bit of information. "But I think we should let this one go, Coop."

"Why the hell would we do that?" asked her boss.

"There's a man over there I recognize, a surgeon. I think he's already laid claim."

Fartleberry snorted. "Has he got his 'ands on the body? Is he swimming in them innards? No? Then he ain't got no claim."

"He's right, Miss Lorna," piped up Pretty Lem. "'Sides, we know you can take care of it. After the viewing parlor, I bet you could smuggle the body right off a man's soul and sell it before he missed it."

She rolled her eyes, but couldn't help the frisson of pride she felt at Lem's compliment. Lorna detested this work, but the part of her that was Blackbird felt her confidence grow with every successful heist. The more creative, the more daring, the better. So different from her staid life of tending Daniel and Elmwood, this brief stint in the criminal underworld would remain the greatest adventure of Lorna's life. A terrifying and gruesome experience, to be sure, but indebted country spinsters couldn't be choosy about such matters. Years from now, these weeks as Blackbird would be the only memories Lorna would have to prove she was capable of more than just teaching her brother to tie his bootlaces and settling tenant disputes.

"All right," she said on a sigh. "Here I go."

The rest of the Crib Cross Gang wished her luck. Lorna drew her veil, blanketing herself in twilight. Carefully, she made her way to a rise overlooking the service.

Safe behind the concealment of her mourning, Lorna was free to indulge in watching Brandon. He spotted her at once. She drew a sharp breath and cringed, sure he would somehow know her. After all, hadn't she known him?

"He doesn't know," she reassured herself. "Why would I be here? He wouldn't dream of finding me here."

She was a ghost without face or name, given form only by her clothing. She was Blackbird, concealed by shadow, even as she stood starkly in the open. Brandon would not know her.

Gradually, Lorna's heart retreated from her throat back to its proper location in her chest. Her breath came a little easier. She turned her mind to the problem of shooing Brandon away. She'd come here prepared to deal with an undertaker, not a man whose kisses Lorna craved.

As the casket was lowered into the earth, Lorna made her move, hoping her intuition led her aright. Staggering forward wasn't a mummery; the mud, weight of her clothes, and cold toes truly made movement difficult.

Previously, she and Coop had decided Lorna would play the part of a grieving widow for the benefit of the undertaker. She was merely beginning her performance earlier than planned.

A marble obelisk propped her up while she started crying. At first, she only meant to mimic a weeping fit, but a strange thing happened after the first wail. She lifted her arm as though reaching out for the deceased Great White Scot, but Lorna's heart yearned toward Brandon. As surely as the dead man, Brandon was beyond her grasp.

He came from the finest family and held a respectable place in Society. Lorna was a criminal. Blackbird might be confident enough to lure a man away from a viewing room with an empty casket, but Lorna Robbins was poor and plain, and made hard choices to save her home and keep her little brother safe. A man like Brandon wasn't meant for a woman like her, even if he seemed to enjoy their kisses as much as she did.

It wasn't fair.

It wasn't fair that Lorna Robbins—poor and plain and never expecting to capture a man's notice—would discover mutual interest with a gentleman at the very time she was absolutely forbidden to do anything about it. She couldn't indulge in Brandon's kisses while she spent her nights stealing bodies. How could she allow him close, when she harbored secrets that would earn her a ride to the gallows, should they ever come to light?

Soon tears, real ones, poured from her eyes. All her life, she'd cared for her brothers, her home, her tenants, her servants. When had Lorna ever had any happiness of her own? Where was *her* Season, her carefree youth? At a time of life when other women of her age and station were already married and having babies of their own, Lorna was wallowing on the frozen ground of a cemetery, hoping she appeared unhinged enough to scare away the man she desired, so she could steal a corpse before he got to it first.

What sort of nightmare was she living?

Her performance, shameful as it was, did the trick. While Lorna hiccuped and struggled to regain her composure, Brandon departed, passing the undertaker and his two assistants on their way in.

Lorna stumbled through the rows of headstones to the open grave. The men with tools were already shoveling earth into the hole.

"Sir, please," she gasped. "Please wait."

The undertaker drew back at her appearance. "Madam," he said, "are you all right?"

Lorna gripped his arm. "Please just give me time to say goodbye to my husband. I'm not ready yet. You can't cover him up. Make them stop digging. Please, let me say goodbyyyye." Her voice melted into fresh weeping jags.

The two gravediggers slowed their work, then stopped, both of them held rapt by Lorna's performance.

The undertaker seemed likewise unnerved. "My dear madam," he said in a rush, "accept my condolences for your loss. If you'd like to remain here while my men work—"

"No!" she shrieked. "Please, just leave me alone for a little while. Let me be with him one last time." As she spoke, Lorna pressed a crown into the man's palm.

The undertaker's eyes widened. The money quickly disappeared into a pocket. "Half an hour." With a jerk of his head, he collected his men. They trundled toward a storage shed in a far corner of the cemetery.

For ten minutes, Lorna knelt beside the grave. Dampness seeped through her skirts to her knees. Her lower back ached.

"All clear," Coop's voice rumbled. "Good work."

"Twenty minutes," Lorna said.

Coop blew his lips in a sound of derision. "We'll be finished in five. Got time for a game of All Fours."

Before Lorna had risen to her feet, Bob and Fartleberry were already in the grave, while Pretty Lem stood at the ready with tools for prying open the casket lid, a hammer and chisel with a rag wrapped around the handle to muffle the noise. Fartleberry made quick work of clearing the soil off the casket. Then he clambered out while Pretty Lem handed the tools down to Bob. A moment later, a sound somewhere between a scrape and a chop filled the air. Nervous, Lorna kept swiveling her head around, watching for the undertaker to return, or for a visitor to happen upon them.

"G'on back to the cart now." Coop jerked his head toward the rear of the cemetery. "You done your part. Make sure Daft Jemmy is ready to go soon's we're there. We'll be right behind you."

A few minutes later, she and Jemmy were checking the mules' tack and rubbing their legs, preparing them for a hasty departure.

"Nice to be out in the daytime some, eh, pretty lady?" said Jemmy. His face broke into a beatific grin. "Nice to see so many people."

Lorna choked back the hysterical yelp that wanted to escape. No need to share her anxieties with Jemmy.

A small eternity passed, wherein Lorna was certain the gang had been caught. *Shouldn't they be here by now?* She only just restrained herself from yanking off her veiled bonnet and digging into her scalp.

"You all right, pretty lady? I help you." Gently, Jemmy lifted her to the seat.

Another minute passed before the remainder of the gang appeared at the break in the wall. Bob, Fartleberry, and Pretty Lem struggled under the weight of the immense, wrapped corpse, while Coop wrangled all the tools. Jemmy hustled around back and helped the men hoist their prize into the bed. He sang a lullaby while they covered The Great White Scot with dirty tools and other bric-a-brac.

With the body concealed, Pretty Lem took the reins, while Coop sat on his other side. They reached Redcross Street, but before Lem guided the cart into traffic, Coop stayed him with a hand. "Blackbird, this is where you get off."

Behind her veil, Lorna frowned. "Why?"

"'Cause you stick out like a sore thumb is why," he snapped. "In a cemetery, havin' you decked in black is right as rum. But not here. Me an' the boys are just a labor crew, but you'll have th' whole damned city cutty-eye at us." He passed a few coins across Lem's lap. "Take a hack. Get on, now."

Lorna grumbled while she hoisted her skirts in preparation to descend.

"You there, in the cart! Stop!"

She whipped around and saw two watchmen running their way. Her breath froze in her chest.

"Bugger it all t'hell!" Coop roared. "Go, Lem, go!"

Lem slapped the reins against the mules' haunches, and the cart lurched forward. Lorna, still poised to disembark, tumbled gracelessly onto the street, landing on her back. She heard Lem shout and Coop yell for him to keep going.

It was Bob, hunched in the rear of the cart with his hands braced on the side rails, who snapped Lorna back to her senses. "Get up, Bird," he called. "Fly! Fly!"

The charlies were bearing down on her, while the cart carrying The Great White Scot trundled away. She scrambled to hands and knees, pushed to her feet, and ran.

Her veil snagged, caught in a hand. Lorna's head snapped back. "I got her," called one of the charlies. "I got the thievin' bitch."

Chapter Sixteen

"Cork-brained!" Pete pronounced.

Slee hawked up a wad of phlegm and spit it onto the tavern wall. At the next table, a couple of swells eyed him all disapproving-like. A mean curl of Slee's lip showed them his ivories, letting the bastards know he weren't no rank coward who could be intimidated by fancy togs and a clean face. Didn't he have as much right to a pint as any honest man?

"Y'damn right," he said, turning back to Pete. "Dewhurst is plain dicked in the nob, falling for Blackbird's tricks."

Blackbird. He'd never yet seen her, but Slee pictured her: A dress of shimmery black feathers flashing blue and green, barely concealing showy tits and hips. She'd have the kind of figure what turned honest men mutton-headed. Beady black eyes, yellow claws, and a sharp little beak for plucking at the dead. God, how he hated her.

"And then going straight to the Watch!" Pete bleated. "A charley coulda nabbed you quicker'n they'd get to Crib Cross. We ain't exactly unknown to the Watch."

Slee swiped a weathered hand across his jaw. "He shoulda let us handle it. We'd've got the quarron and be livin' easy for the winter. One like the Scot don't come along every day, now does it?"

He didn't tell the Boys he'd been to see the show and had been well and truly dumbfounded by The Great White Scot. That such a man existed! A great strapper, all bulging muscles and skin as white as bleached bones. And his eyes! Red like a demon from hell. Never would Slee forget their ferocious gleam when the Scot roared at the crowd.

Nabbing that corpse would've been a feat to crow about to the end of his days. And that idiot sawbones took it from him—not to mention the bang-up pay he'd promised Slee for acquiring this special body.

"Goddamn!" Slee snatched the cap from his head and flung it onto the table. "There's gotta be something we can do."

Pete eyeballed him like he was empty in the upper story. "You still want that body?"

Slee huffed. "Naw, Great White Scot's gone. And there ain't another like him. He was one of a kind, God bless 'im."

The other Boys watched him dubiously.

Pete nodded. "There ain't another Great White Scot," he said, casting Slee a shrewd look, "but there is a Cannibal."

Slee sucked his teeth, remembering the Scot's opponent. Next to the Scotsman, The Cannibal had looked like something half-formed, a hulking mass of muddy skin and hair, with heathen marks all over his ugly heathen face. But he *was* huge, almost as tall and even wider than Cam Kinley. That made him a good catch, right?

Now, Slee hadn't ever manufactured his own wares. An honest resurrection man had more to fear from an outraged mob than from the magistrate. If he was nabbed for murder, though, he'd be dancing at the end of a rope for certain—and then turned over to the anatomists for dissection. Thinking of Dewhurst cutting him open and rooting around his insides sent a shudder up Slee's spine.

But wouldn't it be just grand to see the look on Dewhurst's face when he opened up those wrappings and saw The Cannibal grinning at him? And they'd get their big payday, after all, for delivering a one-of-a-kind body.

Plus, it weren't like *real* murder, what with The Cannibal being a savage, and all. He grinned at Pete. "It'd be a public service."

"Yeah, an' it would," his man agreed.

Slee slapped the table. "What say you, Harty Choke?" he asked the gang, putting the matter to a vote. He was nothing if not an honest man.

Chapter Seventeen

Lorna frantically knocked on the servant's entrance, and after what felt an eternity but was likely only minutes, Charity opened the door. Lorna stumbled through and grabbed onto the surprised maid's shoulders. Choked sobs of relief clawed up her throat.

"Lord have mercy!" Charity drew her mistress to the servant's hall. "Here now, Miss Robbins, what's the matter?" Utilizing her foot, she hooked a chair around the leg, pulled it away from the long table, and urged Lorna to sit.

With numb fingers, Lorna pulled the black ruin from her head and dropped it, the tattered remains of the veil fluttering like the battlefield flag of a defeated army.

The maid tutted. "Don't you look a fright. Are you hurt, miss? Sick?"

Lorna shook her head, despite a terrible ache throbbing in her temples. Hours of running and hiding, not daring to return to Chorley House until after dark, had taken their toll. Her eyes were gritty, and her lungs burned like they'd been scoured with pumice.

Charity briskly strode to the kitchen and returned a few minutes later with a steaming cup and a biscuit. "There we are, miss. Whatever happened, it's nothing a spot of tea can't put to rights."

Grateful for the maid's reassurance, Lorna took a swallow; the hot liquid stung her raw throat. She suspected the burn was caused by a drop of something more potent added to the tea. "Thank you, Charity," she managed.

"Do you want to tell me about it?"

Lorna shook her head slowly. Her wits started to dull around the edges. "Please tell me you did not dose me with laudanum."

"Just a tot of Cook's kitchen brandy," Charity replied. The maid plucked at her skirt. "You need a bath and bed, you do, but you've company that's been waiting over an hour for you to arrive."

The pleasant drowsiness fell away. Lorna snapped upright. "Who?" Visions of being hauled before the magistrate filled her mind. She thought the watchmen hadn't seen her face, but maybe they had.

From upstairs, a throaty baying echoed through the house.

• • •

Lorna flew up the servants' stairs to her room, stripped out of her clothes, scrubbed her face, hands, and underarms at the basin, struggled into a clean frock, and yanked a brush through her hair. Charity made a sound of despair at the resultant halo of frizz.

"Let me do something with that," begged the maid. She reached for the box containing Lorna's ribbons.

"No time," she snapped, giving herself a final going-over. In the mirror, her cheeks shone bright pink. The scrubbing to which she'd subjected her skin didn't seem adequate to wash away the horrible things she'd done this day. Something would show and give her up. Her scrutiny revealed no tell-tale smudges of dirt, but she feared she was missing something. How could she conceal the truth of her actions?

In the parlor, her guests had made themselves right at home. Lady Fenton played a merry tune on the pianoforte, while Nelly Freedman and Alice Dewhurst crouched on the floor and rubbed Bluebell's belly. The animal's tail wagged madly; her tongue lolled onto the rug. Lorna couldn't repress a surge of resentment toward the dog. While she'd sprinted through London, cowered on the floorboards of a hackney cab, and finally hid amongst crates and rubbish behind a coffee shop, the dratted hound had, yet again, trotted into Lorna's house and made herself at home.

Marjorie's sable head lifted; her fingers stilled on the keys. The silence drew the attention of the other women. "There you are." Lady Fenton let out a soft groan as she hoisted herself out from behind the instrument. "That was quite a walk you took, Miss Robbins."

Her dry tone told Lorna she didn't believe the story they'd heard from Charity regarding her whereabouts.

"I didn't just take a walk, of course," Lorna explained. "I had to see my brother's solicitor regarding some matters."

Alice and Marjorie exchanged a look. Nelly took Lorna's hands and led her to a seat. "What a busy day," she said. "I'm afraid it's not over yet, because we must speak with you."

The trio wore grim expressions that made Lorna feel she was being drawn into a council of war. If her hair hadn't already been standing on end, the sudden spike of alarm in her blood would have done the trick. "What about?" she asked, cautious.

"Your behavior." Marjorie accepted Alice's assistance in lowering onto the sofa beside Lorna.

Lorna's throat clenched. *They know.* Something *had* given her away. Had they witnessed her acting as Blackbird? *Or perhaps it's the dog.* Bluebell sat on the edge of the rug and blinked somber brown eyes. The drapes of loose skin adorning her jowls and neck lent her a stately air. Lorna's gaze narrowed on that affected visage of canine piety. *What did you do?*

Dipping her head, Lorna dug fingers into her scalp. Nails torn against cobbles and bricks during the evening's harrowing race across the city lacerated the skin. Blood collected around two of her cuticles. Shoving her fingers under her thighs, Lorna raised her chin a notch. "What about my behavior?"

"We're concerned you might be impeding your chances at finding a husband," Alice said.

Heat crept up Lorna's neck. "You've gossiped about me?"

Marjorie patted her knee. "We're your friends, Lorna; we want to help."

Nelly helped herself to a tray of cakes, then passed them around to the others. Lorna did not partake.

"You don't dance at balls," Nelly stated. Pretty brown curls bobbed around her face in agitation.

"And you go everywhere without a chaperon," Marjorie added. "You live alone—"

"I'm not alone," Lorna interjected. "I have servants, and my maid accompanies me when I go out."

"Yes, but she isn't a proper chaperon, dear," Alice said. Her eyes held nothing but concern. "To whom should a gentleman apply if he wishes an introduction, or to come calling? Not to your maid."

"To me, of course," Lorna muttered, feeling petulant.

Marjorie nibbled on a cake, and delicately wiped crumbs off the top of her enormous abdomen. A topaz ring on her fourth finger twinkled. "Don't be absurd," she said. "No one can call on you here. It isn't done. And believe me, there are gentlemen who wish to do just that."

"Call on me?" Lorna asked, incredulous. She'd never had a single suitor in her life.

Marjorie nodded. "You created quite the sensation with that unfortunate mishap at the Heapbys' ball, but let us be frank: The only thing that has saved your reputation from disaster is the fact that, for the moment, you are entertaining. Society loves an Original, until it doesn't. Eventually, they'll turn on you, and the very things they find amusing now will become fodder for viscous gossip."

Despite telling herself that her foray into Society was just part of her job as Blackbird, Lorna was dismayed by Marjorie's words. It shouldn't matter what the *ton* thought of her—and it didn't really—but a small part of her recognized the importance of keeping up appearances.

After all, wasn't this all about Daniel? What was the use of working so hard to keep Elmwood—of blackening her very soul to settle Thomas's debts—if she ruined Daniel's chances of ever being accepted by Society in his turn? What was the point of anything, if she couldn't give her brother the life he deserved?

She let out a weary sigh. "Thank you all for bringing my transgressions to my notice," she said, her voice glum. "Withdrawing from Society *would* be for the best."

"That's not what we mean," Alice protested. Sarcenet ribbons wove a harlequin pattern across the bodice of her dress. Lorna stared at the little diamonds instead of meeting her friend's eyes, until she realized she might be suspected of bosom-gazing. "We don't want you to withdraw from Society, dear; rather, we wish you to shine in it."

"To what end?" Lorna said. "I'm a dowdy spinster without fortune or recommendations."

Marjorie's behemoth abdomen bobbed with her sigh. "You're a lovely woman of impeccable lineage, and you've got the *ton*'s attention."

"Only for the sake of their laughter," Lorna pointed out. "They noticed me because I made a fool of myself."

Alice leaned forward, her expression intense. "Be that as it may, Lorna, the attention will not merely fade away. It will transform, either into goodwill or disdain. We must take control now, while we still have the opportunity to do so."

A tight chill stole up the back of Lorna's neck and she felt her heart in her throat. "Just how would we do that?" she asked, cautious.

"Well, we thought—I thought," Nelly said, "you might come stay with me."

Lorna drew back. "Move next door?"

Nelly's hopeful smile faded at Lorna's obvious skepticism.

"So you'll be properly chaperoned, of course," Marjorie explained. "Even better—no offense, Nelly, dear—would be to stay with Alice. I would offer you my home, but with multiple infants looming on the horizon, I don't expect to partake in the coming Season's entertainments. Alice is an excellent choice of sponsor."

"Sponsor? Season?" Lorna heard herself echoing single words like a gibbering fool.

Alice reached across the little sitting area to pat Lorna's fisted hands. "The winter in Town is a good start for finding your footing. By spring, you'll be poised to set Society on its ear. You'll have your pick of beaux, just you wait and see."

Lorna could scarcely believe what she was hearing. To be taken under the wings of such ladies, to be shepherded through her entree to London Society.... It was all she could have ever hoped for.

A year ago.

Now, it was too late. It was far too late for anything resembling a conventional Season. Lorna would never be a blushing debutante, or a blushing bride, or a blushing anything else. Thomas had robbed her of life's blushing moments. Instead, he'd condemned her cheeks to burn. With shame. With cold. With upset at the sight of yet another grave defiled. With the knowledge that she was a fraud. Even in her own home, Lorna could not have a peaceable conversation with her friends; not when she was waiting for one of them to die so she could set a gang of resurrectionists on the body. If the ladies in her parlor knew what Lorna truly was, they would set the law upon her themselves.

As though sensible of her gnawing despair, Bluebell laid her heavy head on Lorna's lap and looked up at her with those keen brown eyes. For once, Lorna was glad of the infernal beast's presence. Bluebell was a fraud, too. As much as she wanted to be a pampered pet, the animal was as deep in the underworld as Lorna. She drew a trembling hand down one long, silky ear. The hound groaned.

Mustering a smile, Lorna looked at her little circle of friends. "Thank you all for your generous concern, but I have no plans at present to relocate. Nor do I intend to marry in the foreseeable future. Once I have Thomas's affairs settled, I shall return to Elmwood. Daniel needs me."

The women exchanged another telling glance. Lorna was developing an immense dislike for this way females seemed to have of wordlessly communicating with one another. It was yet another example of her own deficiencies as a lady; she had never learned the feminine mysteries which came so easily to her friends. She'd had no governess past the age of fourteen, no one to see her finished and polished and prepared to get on in Society.

Marjorie broke the tense silence. "As to that, I wonder if it might not be time for Lord Chorley's guardian to step in and take charge of the boy."

Lorna suddenly felt as though her ears had been boxed. She heard a hollow ringing, through which she barely discerned Alice's question:

"Who *is* his guardian, by the by?"

"Me." She pressed a hand to her chest. "I'm Daniel's guardian, of course." But even as she asserted the claim, her innards twisted on themselves. She *was* Daniel's guardian, wasn't she?

"You couldn't be," said Marjorie. "He's a baron, after all. Another peer will have been named in your elder brother's will. You might not have known the man's identity prior to your brother's death, but surely your solicitor has informed you. Or the gentleman himself, hasn't he stepped forward?"

A guardian. A strange man appointed to take charge of Daniel. To take him away from her.

Something happened in Lorna's chest, constricting her lungs. Her heart stopped, then convulsed in rapid, irregular beats. Around her, the three women faded at the edges. Bluebell whined.

From far away, Nelly cried, "Lorna! Are you all right? Someone fetch my reticule. I've a vinaigrette."

No, I'm not all right! Lorna wanted to shout. But her throat would let out nothing but a choked gargle. It was impossible to conceive of some man she'd never laid eyes upon stealing her brother away from her. That was a nightmare Lorna would never allow to come to pass—never! She had not willingly committed her soul to perdition only to lose the only family she had left.

Pain crushed her chest. She had to get away, needed to escape, but hands held her down. Sharp fumes forced a gasp from her lungs, but nothing could penetrate the fear gripping her in an iron fist. Her head swam and numbness began to spread through her hands and feet.

At some point, Oscar lifted her from the couch and conveyed her to her room. Lorna was dimly aware of Charity tucking her into bed and of the worried note to the murmurs being exchanged just beyond her bedchamber door.

Chapter Eighteen

What had come over him? Brandon still wasn't sure what had compelled him to send watchmen after the Crib Cross Gang. The question occupied his mind as he ate a simple meal of soup and filet of turbot at his small table.

After all, it wasn't as though they'd stolen Brandon's rightful property. Incensed that Blackbird had duped him out of The Great White Scot, he'd experienced something like a childish fit of pique and gone running to tittle-tattle. Not his proudest moment. Still, being done in by his gentlemanly instincts toward a woman proved the criminal work was best left in the hands of the criminals. Slee wouldn't have abandoned his graveside post, not for anything.

Drained by hours of cold and frustration, Brandon prepared for a well-deserved evening spent in front of the fire with a book and a glass of whiskey. He made his ablutions, wrapped in his heavy dressing gown, donned his fleece-lined slippers, and with a grateful sigh, sank into a plush chair. Leaning his head back, he let his eyelids slide shut.

A knock on the alley door pulled them open again.

With a muttered curse, Brandon abandoned his quiet haven to answer the call.

Slee stood on the stoop. A sly smile plowed furrows in his gaunt, stubbled cheeks. "Evenin', Mr. Dewhurst, sir."

"Slee," Brandon returned with a curt nod. "What is it?" He glanced past the gang boss. The cart and the rest of the gang crowded the mouth of the alley. "Awfully early, aren't you?" he said with a touch of scold in his voice. "You might have been seen."

Slee's eyes gleamed. Strangely, the man's expression reminded Brandon of the cat Lorna had used as a weapon the night he'd first seen her. Feral and dangerous and poised to attack.

"Oh, aye, we's early, indeed," the grave robber said. "But you'll be glad of it when you see what we got. Bring it in, Harty Choke," he called.

When the gang pulled a massive corpse from the wagon, Brandon felt a flash of elation. The Great White Scot! He laughed. Slee, grinning, nodded and tapped the side of his nose. What an incredible turn of events.

His buoyed mood lasted only as long as it took for the men to deposit the wrapped body on the receiving room table. Blood, red and wet, soaked the material around the head.

"What is this?" he demanded.

With a flourish, Slee yanked the fabric covering the face. "Take a peep."

Floating on the surface of skin that had been full of healthy color only hours ago, The Cannibal's intricate black tattoos now adorned a face unnaturally sallow. Drained of vital blood, the large man's lips were tinged white.

Brandon reached a trembling hand to the wrapping, exposing the viciously laid-open throat. "What have you done?" he rasped, his own throat constricting in sympathy.

Slee's jocular tone set Brandon's teeth on edge. "Why, we've brought you a right plum specimen, is all."

Rounding on the smaller man, Brandon roared, *"What have you done?"* He pointed a finger to the fresh body on his table. "Did you do this?"

Slee cut his eyes to the shadowy figures of his gang lurking in the doorway. Drawing himself to his full height, he sniffed. "You seem to be implyin' I done wrong, sir. I didn't do nothin' but bring a quarron, same's I do every—"

Brandon's forearm slammed into Slee's chest, driving him into the wall. Savage fury pulsed through Brandon, unlike anything he'd ever felt before. He brought his face within inches of the resurrectionist's. "You murdered him."

Fear splashed across Slee's features, but was quickly replaced by anger of his own. "I ain't no murderer. Murder is for a man, and *that* thing," he said, pointing his own finger now, "ain't no man. Brown and heathen, and it *eats* good Christian people," he said. "Ain't that right, Pete?" he called to the door.

"It's true," said one of the Artichoke Boys. "A cannibal eats human folk."

Brandon wanted to laugh and scream and pummel and vomit, all at once. He released his hold on Slee and wiped a hand down his face. "It was a stage name, you fools." Despair welled in his gut. "But you knew that. Not even you could be that brainless, Slee. Nor am I the imbecile you want me to be. Your flimsy justification does not excuse murder, which is exactly what you've done." Through his mind tumbled the idea of an impromptu lecture. He could show the Artichoke Boys how the poor soul on the table was exactly the same on the inside as any one of them, proving that he was, indeed, a human being. But it wouldn't be of any use, he knew. They didn't want education; they wanted money. "How could you think I would pay you for this? I will not reward you for taking the life of an innocent man."

"Hey, now," Slee countered. "You promised us good pay for The Great White Scot."

"Which you did not deliver."

Slee threw his arms wide. His ratty jacket gaped, revealing the filthy shirt beneath. "Yeah, an' whose fault is that? Who skipped away with Blackbird perched in front of his face?"

Brandon needed no reminder that he, himself, was to blame for losing Cam Kinley. "I'm the one who lost out. I'll compensate you for your time, but I cannot pay for a body you didn't deliver, and I *will not* pay you for murder."

"You will, too," piped up Pete. "You wanted a freak and we brunged you one."

A chorus of agreement rumbled through the group.

Brandon's hands flexed and curled into fists. "No," he snarled. "Get out."

Slee planted his hands on his hips and ran his tongue around the inside of his lips. "Fine. There's plenty more like you, Dewhurst. We'll take our savage elsewhere." He pulled the fabric back over the murdered man's face.

"The hell you will," Brandon snapped, wresting Slee's hand away from the corpse. "You will not profit from murder." What the Artichoke Boys deserved was the gibbet, the whole lot of them. But Brandon was sorely outnumbered. He had no way to apprehend the entire gang at this moment. Justice would have to wait until he could get to the magistrate.

"Well, I ain't leaving that body here," Slee insisted. "You got no right to keep it, if you ain't buyin'."

The other gang members pressed threateningly into the room. Not only couldn't he bring these men to justice, he couldn't even give The Cannibal a proper burial. "Take it and be damned."

In tense silence, the Artichoke Boys collected their victim and left.

When they were gone, Brandon found himself back in his chair, where, a short time ago, he'd sat down with the expectation of nursing nothing worse than bruised pride. At his elbow sat the glass of liquor he'd poured for himself. He raised it to his lips.

The front bell rang.

"Damnation!"

He replaced the beverage. Bracing elbows on his knees, he waited. Two minutes later, Mrs. Moore let herself in after a soft knock on his apartment door. "A man is upstairs with a summons for you, Mr. Dewhurst. You're needed."

• • •

In the hackney, Brandon tried to shake his mind free of the disturbing visit from the Artichoke Boys. Morning would be soon enough to consult with McGully and take steps toward reporting the gang for murder. For now, though, Niall Freedman needed him at his best. Nelly's note hadn't detailed the nature of the crisis, but the hasty scrawl of her writing conveyed the need for urgency.

When the carriage stopped, he grabbed his bag and opened the door, then started when he saw they'd drawn up in front of Chorley House. His questioning gaze met the eyes of the manservant, who was waving him toward Lorna's door.

Apprehension stole over him as he stepped into the small entrance hall. Even if Niall had taken ill here, in Lorna's house, he would have been carried next door to his own bed.

"Thank goodness you're here," said a familiar, but unexpected, voice. Alice appeared at the bottom of the stairs and scurried across the foyer. "Marjorie wanted to call for her surgeon, but Nelly and I outvoted her." A crease between her delicately arched brows conveyed concern. "I do hope you'll tell us at once if it would be prudent to summon a physician. We wasted a good ten minutes dithering over who to call."

In all of his sister-in-law's speech, he heard no mention of her hostess. "Where is Miss Robbins?" he asked.

Alice stopped. "In her room. The footman carried her. I thought it unwise to move her during the spell, but it seemed to go on and on—"

"A spell?" he blurted. "You mean *Lorna* is the one I'm here to see?" The sudden sense of alarm rendered him incautious with her name. He bit his tongue half a second too late.

Thankfully, Alice seemed not to have noticed the slip. She led him to the upstairs parlor, where Mrs. Freedman and Lady Fenton huddled together on a couch. "Mr. Dewhurst," Nelly cried, leaping to her feet. "You must help our dear Miss Robbins." At his prompting, the three women launched into a recitation of the events leading up to Lorna suddenly taking ill. They talked over one another and argued and corrected each other like a bunch of clucking hens.

The thought of Lorna being sick or hurt chilled his bones. Brandon's palm issued cold perspiration around the calfskin handle of his surgery bag. "I think," he said, silencing the clutch of frightened females, "I'd like to see her for myself. Alice?"

With a nod, the petite blonde led him up another flight of stairs and down a corridor before tapping on a door. A maid opened it and bobbed a curtsey. "Here, sir," the servant said with a gesture.

Brandon spared the chamber a cursory glance. The small room contained only a narrow bed, clothespress, and washstand by way of furnishings. A chair too large for the space had been brought to the bedside. The maid seemed to have been nursing Lorna from it, if the water basin and cloth on the floor were any indication.

"She's gone back and forth between tossing off the covers and taking chill, sir," the maid explained. "I hope I've done right."

"I'm sure you've done just fine," he said.

Bluebell, the dog Lorna said belonged to a friend, was lying on the foot of the bed. Doleful brown eyes followed Brandon as he set down his bag.

Lorna's own eyes were tightly closed, as if she were consciously squeezing them. Damp curls clung to her temples. Brandon brushed them away and called for more light. While the maid fetched candles, he lifted Lorna's hand. The fingers were clenched into her palm.

"Miss Robbins," he said in a voice remarkably free of the choking dismay he felt. "Lorna, can you hear me?"

Her head shook back and forth; her lips made soundless words. Tears oozed from beneath her eyelids. Under his fingertips, the pulse at her wrist fluttered wildly.

A hand pressed first to her forehead and then her cheek registered a normal degree of warmth. *No fever. Thank God.*

The maid returned and made quick work of setting more candlesticks around the room. With better lighting, Brandon detected pallor beneath Lorna's freckles. Suddenly, the image of The Cannibal, gruesomely bled of color, filled his mind's eye. Fear clawed at his throat.

He straightened and took a couple steps away, drawing deep breaths and fighting to create clinical distance between himself and Lorna Robbins. *Lorna will not die*, he mentally assured himself in his best surgeon voice. It didn't help. God, this was why he couldn't bear to treat his family and friends. Watching those he cared for suffer was trial enough. Being responsible for their very lives was sheer torment.

On the bed, Lorna thrashed and whimpered.

He would indulge in a mope later. Right now, Lorna needed him. "Please remove her gown," he instructed the maid. "I'll wait in the corridor."

When he returned, Lorna's dress was draped over the top of the clothespress. The blanket was drawn to her chin.

Brandon sat on the edge of the bed and, under the maid's hawkish supervision, pulled the coverlet back to Lorna's waist. She still wore her shift, but it wouldn't have mattered if she was naked as Lady Godiva; lustful thoughts were the furthest thing from his mind. Though his nerves were still in disarray, he'd mastered himself enough to observe Lorna as a body in need of his surgical skill.

Reaching into his bag, Brandon fished out his ear trumpet. Gleaming silver with his initials inscribed on the tube, it had been a gift from his mother. He set the bell of the device upon Lorna's chest and brought his ear to the earpiece. His eyes closed; he held his breath. The reassuring sound of Lorna's heartbeat carried through the tube. Faster than he'd like, but steady. Moving the bell to another location, he listened to the workings of her lungs, and then her belly.

Everything sounded as though functioning properly. The ear trumpet went back into the bag.

He felt along her throat for swelling. Nothing unusual there. His fingers easily closed about a wrist. Her bones were delicate, her musculature graceful beneath his palms as he examined one arm, and then the other. He'd not previously had the chance to observe her so closely, but he drank in the sight of more freckles scattered down her arms. Another time, he thought abstractedly, he would uncover them all and kiss every one.

"Has she recently complained of any pains?" he asked the maid.

"No, sir." The woman hovered on her toes. "Miss Robbins doesn't get enough rest, if you care to hear my opinion, but otherwise, she's healthy as can be."

Abruptly, Lorna seized Brandon's arm. Her eyes flew open, revealing pupils constricted to pinpoints. "Don't let them take him," she panted.

At once, Brandon was in Portugal again, tending a soldier. The man suffered no physical complaint, but his mind had been shattered by the horrors he'd witnessed.

The dog lifted her head and whimpered.

Moving quickly, the maid scooped up the damp flannel and daubed Lorna's face, making shushing noises as she worked. She cast a frightened glance at Brandon.

With his fingertips, he dug lightly into Lorna's shoulders. A little of her tension eased. As Lorna's body began to relax, Brandon's own anxiety ebbed. The problem was becoming clear. "Would you please excuse us, Miss…?"

"Charity, sir," the maid supplied.

"Thank you, Charity," Brandon said. "Please give me fifteen minutes, then bring your mistress a cup of broth and some bread."

The maid eyed him warily, but did as she was told.

After the door closed behind Charity, Brandon chaffed the inside of his patient's wrist. "Lorna? Can you hear me?" She moaned a little as he repeated the action on the other arm. "Come now, my dear, I know you're awake. You're home, in your own bed. Your friends are here, and they're worried about you, Lorna."

Behind the lids, her eyes rolled about before they opened a fraction. Just that tiny peek of aquamarine let another knot loosen in Brandon's chest.

In the Army, he'd discovered that using a dazed soldier's name helped keep the patient focused on the present. "Lorna," he repeated, "do you recognize me?" His breath hitched in his throat as he awaited her response.

Her eyes opened more, settled on his face. Slowly, the muscles in her jaw unclenched. Her pupils widened a fraction. "Brandon," she whispered. "You're Brandon."

He stroked her cheek with a knuckle. "That I am. And you've given me a fright. Can you tell me what happened?"

Her eyes clamped shut once more, and she pressed her thumb and forefinger into them. "I can't quite remember," she said. "The ladies were here—Nelly, Alice, and Lady Fenton."

"They're still here," he told her.

At this, Lorna brought her other hand to her face and groaned. "They all saw me like this?"

A wry smile hitched one side of Brandon's mouth. "Not quite so unclothed," he assured her. Then added in a low tone, "I kept that just for me."

Giggles cascaded from behind her hands. Brandon felt further at ease.

A dull thumping from the bottom of the bed caught their attention. "Hullo, Bluebell," Lorna said. "I see you've made yourself comfortable."

The attention set the hound's tail into a blurred frenzy of joy. She dipped her head and woofed, then rolled onto her back, tail still swishing.

Brandon reached down and scratched the animal's belly. A heavy, pink tongue lolled out of the jowly mouth. "You said, 'Don't let them take him.' Were you referring to your brother?"

She nodded. "One of the ladies mentioned his guardian. I never thought of it. I don't know who it is." Fingers plucked at the coverlet. He saw her pulse leap in her throat. "What if he takes Daniel away from me? He's all I have, Brandon, my only family."

With her voice rising in pitch and speed, Brandon feared her setting off another spell. "Hush now," he said, taking hold of both shoulders. "You're making yourself sick. No one is going to take Daniel from you, I swear."

A draft set the flames of several candles to flickering. The shadows of her nose and lips jounced across the side of her face. Her eyes looked hollow of everything but despair. "You can't swear that; you don't know. And now I'm ill. Do you think it's serious?"

"Listen to me: You've suffered a shock. I saw similar in Portugal."

"I'm no soldier." Her voice was thin, reedy.

"I beg to differ," he said. "Just one of a different sort." Obviously, the woman would sacrifice anything, even her own well-being, for her brother's sake. If that didn't make her a warrior, what did? "The battlefield can traumatize the nerves, but the condition isn't exclusive to the military. Other situations cause it, as well."

She wrinkled her nose. "So, you aren't going to tell me I'm merely an overwrought female?"

"Overwrought you may be," he said. He stood and helped her sit up in the bed. "And most certainly female. But this spell did not result from any complaint particular to your sex. Nervous disorders afflict men and women alike." He poured a glass of water and watched her take a sip.

She grimaced. "*Nervous disorder* sounds ominous."

"It may be an isolated incident that will never repeat. Has anything like this ever happened to you before?"

Her lips parted on an inhale, as though to speak. But then she ducked her head. The welter of her auburn curls hid her face.

Brandon bit back an oath of frustration. "I can't help you if you don't tell me."

When she lifted her head, tears glistened on her eyelashes. "Once. Right after Thomas died. I had just…spit on his grave. I thought God must have punished my blasphemy."

Brandon's eyes widened. Lorna certainly was full of surprises. "Some people," he said, careful not to comment on her supposed sin, "are prone to such episodes. They can be brought on by upsetting events, or prolonged emotional strain."

"This one was worse than the first," she whispered. "I've never been so scared in my life. It felt like my heart was being squeezed in a vise. Truly, I thought I was going to die."

Her confession sent the practitioner packing, and brought Brandon's emotional responses back to the fore. He set aside her drink, then collected her in his arms. "I know, sweet girl," he murmured against her ear. "But you're safe, Lorna. I won't let anything happen to you." They weren't idle words of comfort; they carried the weight of a vow.

Something heavy shifted on the mattress. Hot, damp breath panted over the side of his face. Bluebell butted against his shoulder, as if she wanted to participate in their embrace. She lapped at the salty tracks on Lorna's face.

Lorna grimaced and pushed the dog's snout away. "Having you here, Brandon …" She wiped her cheek with a corner of the coverlet. "I *feel* safe. Isn't that silly? I was perfectly safe before, but I didn't believe it until you were here."

Inside his ribs, Brandon's heart gave a funny kick. If he could, he'd stay with her all night, and make damned sure she felt safe.

*Just a minute…*A devious idea slithered into being. He *was* acting as her surgeon, after all. And she *had* suffered a rather serious bout of nervous delirium. The surgeon had a duty to his patient.

He kissed her temple. "Your maid will be in shortly with a little supper. Try your best to take it all. I'll see you again soon."

"You're leaving?" Her pleading expression unmanned him.

Shaking his head, he let the tip of his nose graze the sensitive skin below her ear. "I'm not leaving. But you need nourishment and rest. I'll be close by." He patted his thigh. "Bluebell, down."

In the corridor, Charity headed his way, carrying a tray bearing a steaming bowl and two slices of bread, just as he'd requested.

"How is she, sir?"

"Improving," Brandon said. "Ready to take some supper, if she'll heed my advice."

The maid's lips firmed. "I'll see to it, Mr. Dewhurst," she said, her voice resolved. "Anything else, sir?"

For just an instant, Brandon hesitated, fearing the servant would see through his request. *I'm the surgeon*, he reminded himself. "Yes, in fact. Miss Robbins needs supervision until she's past any danger. I intend to see her through the night. Would you have a room made ready for me?"

Charity sputtered. "But ... but, sir, I can tend her myself."

Unsure whether the maid protested out of moral outrage or a feeling of professional insult, Brandon offered further explanation. "If Miss Robbins only needed convalescence, I would have no qualms about leaving her in your capable hands. Unfortunately," he said in a grave tone, "while I spoke with her she gave signs of continued distress. I fear she might suffer another attack like the one for which I was summoned. Should that happen, I would much rather be just down the hall, rather than in Covent Garden."

"Very well, sir," Charity said at last. "It will have to be his lordship's room. That's the only one I can have made ready on such short notice."

Brandon thanked the woman and continued to the parlor, where his flock of nervous hens were still gathered.

Nelly cried out when he entered the room.

He raised his hands in a calming gesture. "Please, Mrs. Freedman, I shouldn't care to have another patient to tend tonight."

Alice crossed the room and laid a hand on his arm. Fine lines creased the delicate skin around her eyes and between her golden brows. "How is she, Brandon?"

"I'm afraid I cannot yet say."

Nelly let out another sound of dismay.

Brandon didn't wish to increase the ladies' anxiety, but neither would he do anything to cast aspersions on Lorna's reputation in any way whatsoever. Let them, instead, believe she was a little worse than she truly was.

"Fear not," he said, "Miss Robbins's maid and I shall keep watch over her tonight. If there are no problems by morning, then I see no reason why Miss Robbins won't make a full recovery."

"What *is* the problem?" asked Lady Fenton. "Is she sick?"

The pregnant woman looked as affected as Nelly and Alice. While her gaze bore into Brandon, her arms wrapped her abdomen in a protective gesture.

"Not sick, no," he said. "Suffering from the strain of seeing to her older brother's affairs, while caring for the younger." With a tone of admonishment, he added, "She mentioned a conversation she had with the three of you, which was greatly upsetting. I would ask you to refrain from introducing distressing topics when next you speak to Miss Robbins."

The women exchanged guilty expressions.

"We were only trying to help," Lady Fenton protested. "Many ladies in her situation would be glad for some advice about finding a husband."

"A husband?" Brandon's brows shot into his hairline. "You're attempting to marry her off *and* frightening her over her younger brother all in one sitting? No wonder she's been laid low. Rather than judge her for delicate nerves, I must now admire her resilience. Your meddling would have sent a lesser mind screaming into madness."

"Perhaps it was a bit much for a single evening," said Nelly.

The trio took their leave, but not before extracting a promise from Brandon to keep them appraised of Lorna's condition.

The footman showed Brandon to his room. A fire had been lit, but it had not yet driven either the chill or the mustiness of disuse from the air. On the hearth, a brass bed warmer gleamed invitingly. He could almost feel the delicious warmth of freshly heated sheets seeping into his bones, relaxing him into a peaceful slumber.

But there would be no sleep for him yet. Not with Lorna so close.

He peeled out of his coat and waistcoat, then clumsily untied his cravat and pulled off his shirt. Brandon's hands trembled as he quickly washed at the basin, trying to counter the skin-pebbling cold water with a brisk scrubbing.

There was no chance of him donning any article of clothing belonging to Lorna's dead brother, so he put his own shirt back on. Opening his door an inch, he kept an eye on the corridor until Charity left Lorna's bedchamber, once again burdened with the supper tray. Like a thief slinking through a marked house, Brandon crept down the hall. Slowly, he turned the knob of Lorna's door and slipped into her room.

Chapter Nineteen

An unidentified sound woke her up. Before opening her eyes, Lorna spent a moment trying to place it. It wasn't a frightening noise, just unexpected. Then she heard it again: snoring.

The previous day and night returned to her in a rush. The cemetery, Brandon, the body, nearly being nabbed by the authorities. And home at last, thinking she was safe, only to find herself besieged by harbingers of social doom. A ruined reputation and her brother snatched from her arms ... these dire events awaited Lorna if she did not fall in line with the plan set forth by Marjorie, Alice, and Nelly.

A third—and obnoxiously loud—snore teased her eyelids apart. She blinked bleariness from her vision, allowing the dearest sight to come into focus.

An armchair had been brought to her bedside, and Brandon was asleep in it. In a manner of speaking, that is. His rump was firmly planted on the seat, but his torso was slumped onto the mattress. He lay with his face toward her. His left hand was on top of her stomach, clasping her right hand.

She took advantage of his continued slumber to examine him. Weak light slipped through the cracks in the draperies to highlight his features. In sleep, the lines around his eyes were softened. Lax muscles gentled the sharp angle of his cheekbone. His nose, she decided, was exquisite. Prominent, but not overlarge, it perfectly balanced the strong sweep of his brows. Dark stubble shadowed his jaw. She couldn't resist brushing her fingers along it to his sideburns, and from there to his temple, where silver frosted the edge of his hairline. It looked dignified, she thought; it lent him the air of experience one wants in a surgeon.

Another snore, but this time she noticed the sound wasn't coming from Brandon. On the floor, a certain bloodhound lay with her haunches beneath the bed and her head at Brandon's feet.

Lorna sighed. *That dog.* What was she to do with her? In spite of her long-standing grudge toward the beast, Lorna felt herself softening. Bluebell had, after all, remained at her side throughout last night's terrifying episode. Not once had the hound advised her to move house, or told Lorna that her chance for a respectable marriage was slipping away. Nor had the animal spoken horrible words about a guardian taking Daniel from her.

When she looked back to Brandon, his gray eyes were open, studying her. He held himself still in that particular way of his, waiting for her.

She continued stroking the silky hair at his temple. "You should return to your own room before Charity finds you here."

"Don't want to," he groused in a morning-rough voice. "That feels like heaven." His eyes drifted shut again. He groaned and nuzzled his head into her side. "How are you?"

"Just fine, I think." In fact, Lorna felt quite well. She'd slept better than she had in ages, although she was still tired and worried about Daniel. "That position cannot be comfortable."

A sleepy smile made him look younger than his years. "It's deuced painful, truth be told. My back is screaming."

She nudged his shoulder. "Go on, then. Be a good surgeon and put yourself to rights."

He grimaced as he stood. His fists dug into his lower back. Blinking, he gazed down at her. "You seem better."

"I feel fine." At his doubting scowl, she corrected herself. "I feel a great deal better than I did last night. How's that?"

A soft chuckle filled the small room. "Honest. We'll talk more in just a bit." He pulled the bell cord beside her headboard. "Tell Charity you feel up to something a little more substantial for breakfast."

She raised her brows. "Do I?"

Brandon leaned over, his hands bracketing her face. "You do." He kissed her forehead. "I'll be back in shortly."

True to his word, Brandon reappeared after no more than a half hour. To her surprise, he carried the breakfast tray. "I intercepted your maid in the corridor."

Bluebell had sauntered out with Charity to stretch her canine legs and break her own fast. Even though Lorna might feel a little more kindly about the dog, she was glad the animal did not accompany Brandon.

Though he'd made an effort with his appearance, he still looked tousled as a rogue after a night of carousing. The stubbled jaw, limp cravat, and rumpled hair, combined with the breakfast tray in his hands and the heavy-lidded gaze those gray eyes cast her way, all sent a cascade of warm sensations through her.

Glad of the bed jacket Charity had insisted she don, Lorna combed her fingers through her hair and nervously twisted it. Of course, it sprang back to its unruly state the instant she released it.

He set up the tray and sat on the edge of the bed, where he poured her tea. "Sugar and cream?" he asked.

"Just lemon, thank you."

"Butter for your toast?" he asked after passing her the cup.

"A touch of jam."

"No wonder you weigh no more than a sparrow," he exclaimed. "You should have chocolates and cakes and custards. Rolls slathered with butter. Crumpets swimming in honey. Roasts dripping with sauces. Yorkshire puddings floating in a pond of gravy."

The thought of so much rich excess made her stomach turn. "Stop!" she said with a laugh. "You'll put me off my breakfast."

"I think I've made myself ravenous."

"Here." Lorna thrust a slice of bacon toward him. "I should not like to have an irritable surgeon on my hands."

Brandon lifted her hand to his mouth and took a bite of her offering. Then he plucked the slice and held it to her lips. "Now you."

Lord, she thought, as she accepted a nibble of smoky, salted pork, she never would have imagined that sharing a meal could feel so intimate. Nerves skated all over her skin. She retreated into her teacup.

As the meal progressed, Brandon continued to feed her by hand. Between bites of toast and soft-cooked egg, he stroked her arm. While she sipped her tea, he played with her hair. As he leaned over to bring a slice of apple to her mouth, he rested his other hand on the coverlet over her thigh. All his little touches and caresses kept her happy and soothed, and distracted her from the troubles that had weighed so heavily on her last night.

"I know what you're doing," she said.

"Oh?" he said around another slice of bacon. "What's that?"

"Occupying me. Are you afraid I'll succumb to another fit unless you distract me with constant contact?"

His gray eyes cut to the window, where heavy clouds threatened more precipitation. Then he glanced back to her. "Does my touch bother you?"

"No," she whispered. "It's nice."

And it was. Oh, it was. If she had a tail like Bluebell's, she'd thump it every time he handled her. She wondered if it was possible to become drunk on caresses, because Brandon's clever fingers intoxicated her senses. She was overwhelmed with contentment, but yearned for something else, too. Something more. Like the Crib Cross Gang at the tavern. One drink made them feel so good, they wanted another, and another.

"Good." He flipped her hand and traced the lines of her palm with his one, calloused fingertip. "Lorna," he said. His brows drew together, though he kept giving her those light, delicious caresses. "I think we should discuss something about last night."

A hard lump formed in her throat. She forced a dry laugh. "Have you changed your mind and decided I'm hysterical, after all?"

He winced; his hand tightened around hers. "Of course not. What you suffered is exactly what I saw in men on the Peninsula who had been through the strain of war."

"Then what did you wish to speak about?"

Brandon collected the various dishes of their meal onto the tray and set it aside. Returning to his seat on the bed, he held both of her hands. "If you'll talk to me about it, I think we should discuss your fears regarding Daniel."

A chill froze her blood. "What about him?"

"The issue of his guardian. I am given to understand you do not know the man's identity. Is that correct?"

She nodded.

"Haven't you spoken to your elder brother's solicitor?"

Lorna felt herself shrinking away from Brandon. She sank back into her pillows and drew her hands out of his grasp.

"Don't hide from me." Brandon retrieved her hands and gave them a little shake.

Hot prickles of shame crawled up her chest. How could she explain this without having Brandon question her actions? "Not long after Thomas came home," she started, "when he was sick, I took over his correspondence. Because he was…" She cleared her throat. Brandon squeezed her hands encouragingly. "There were so many bills from merchants in London. I couldn't pay them all with the estate's meager profits. So I came to Town to see Mr. Gordon, Thomas's solicitor."

"Very wise."

His somber nod of approval prompted a little smile. She couldn't go so far as laughter. Not with the dread welling in her gut. "He's a good man, Mr. Gordon. He met with me for more than an hour, and very patiently explained just how ruined we were."

Brandon drew a sharp breath. Lorna found herself rushing to make the situation sound less dire. "We aren't penniless. Don't think Daniel and I are in danger of going hungry."

At this, he paled.

"It's just, there's not enough to go around, you see. Elmwood is a small estate, smaller than it used to be. Evidently, my father broke the entail so he could sell some land. The money the estate makes goes right back into sustaining itself, with just enough left over for basic expenses."

His mouth drew a grim line. "How basic?"

Lorna gave an uncomfortable shrug. She didn't care to discuss how she'd sold off the few pieces of jewelry left by her father's wives, or how faded the parlor's furnishings had become. Nor did she wish to detail how many years it had been since she'd had a new dress, or how the few servants remaining in her employ did so on half wages.

"We make do," she finally said. "That's all beside the point, in any event. Since I saw Mr. Gordon so recently, I didn't think it necessary to see him again. Daniel was Thomas's heir, so everything belongs to him. Simple enough."

Brandon nodded slowly. "Except for the guardianship question, of course."

Her fingers plunged into her hair; the nails pressed against her scalp to the point of pain. She quickly pulled them away before Brandon knew what she was doing.

"Ordinarily," he said, "I would recommend you recuperate for a day or two." He twirled his finger into one of her curls. "But in this case," he said, tucking the strand behind her ear, "I believe meeting with Mr. Gordon would go a long way toward easing the distress behind yesterday's episode. I'll come with you."

Lorna frowned. "Why would you do that?"

Brandon blinked. "Because I care about you."

She considered that a moment. Something very much like happiness, or maybe hope, started filling her up where the cold dread had been. "Oh," she said at last. Lorna bit her lip in an effort to hide the smile trying to overtake her face. "That's the loveliest thing anyone has ever said to me."

• • •

Under orders from her surgeon, Lorna jotted a note to Thomas's solicitor. About an hour later, Mr. Gordon replied that he would be happy to discuss with Miss Robbins the particulars of the late Baron Chorley's will.

True to his word, Brandon joined her. Despite the somber nature of her errand, Lorna enjoyed a light mood. Bundled together in a hired carriage, the outing felt almost like a holiday. The clouds delivered their contents to the earth in the form of a light drizzle.

Brandon removed her glove and his, the better to hold her hand tucked inside his coat, against his stomach. His thumb drew lazy circles on her palm. For a few minutes, it was easy to ignore her troubles and just enjoy the pleasure of Brandon's company.

As it was on the way to Mr. Gordon's office, they stopped at the Covent Garden School of Anatomical Studies, where Brandon lived and worked. He left Lorna in the care of the housekeeper, Mrs. Moore, while he went for a fresh change of clothes.

Mrs. Moore made a fuss over Lorna, keeping her in a steady stream of tea and almond biscuits. Brandon reappeared just as Lorna was fending off yet another sweet.

"Now, now, Mrs. Moore," Brandon said with a teasing smile. He tugged the cuff of his dark blue coat. "Miss Robbins has just arisen from the sickbed. I would thank you not to place her right back in it with a stomachache."

The servant sniffed. "What am I to do, Mr. Dewhurst, when you bring me a young lady so clearly in need of tending?" She nodded at Lorna and spoke about her as if she couldn't understand this embarrassing discussion. "She can't weigh more than a wisp of smoke. You'll have to take better care of her, if you don't want my intervention, sir."

Lorna's cheeks flamed, but Brandon just threw her a wink. "Right you are, Mrs. Moore. Perhaps I can tempt Miss Robbins with a house made of confectionery, like in 'Hansel and Gretel.'"

Back in the carriage, Lorna said dryly, "You realize, do you not, that tempting me with a house built of sweets makes you the witch of the story."

He drew back. "Does it?" At her affirmative reply, he grabbed her around the waist and dipped her low, so that her back almost touched the squabs. "I shall gladly be the villainous sorcerer, if it means I can lure you into my sweet-house and lock you away in a tower with all the apples and toffees you can eat."

She squealed with laughter. "In one fell swoop, you have demolished at least three stories."

He grinned, then bent his head and kissed her, instantly bringing tingling awareness to her most private areas. Brandon carried her away to a marvelous place of happiness and light, if only for a moment. Lorna never imagined she'd catch the notice of someone as remarkable as Brandon.

The hackney stopped and jostled as the driver climbed down from his box. Brandon gave Lorna a reassuring smile as he handed her down from the conveyance.

Despite the solid male presence at her side, the sight of the solicitor's name engraved on a gleaming brass plate beside the door made Lorna's breath catch in her throat.

"It will be all right," Brandon murmured as he rang the bell.

Middling in both years and height, Mr. Gordon looked every inch the respectable solicitor. His thinning hair was a nondescript brown at the crown of his head, but quickly transitioned to stately gray. His eyes and mouth turned down at the outer corners, as though drooping beneath the weight of his somber occupation. He wore an ocher waistcoat; against the black of his neckcloth and coat, the earthy color nearly shone.

"Miss Robbins," he said, greeting her in a small antechamber. "How good it is to see you. I wish it could be under pleasanter circumstances."

She introduced the man to Brandon and asked, "Is there a pleasant circumstance under which one would have occasion to visit one's solicitor?"

The man gave a half-smile. "Not many, it's true, although there are a few. Marriage contracts, for instance, can mark happy occasions." Here, he glanced at Brandon.

Realizing the direction of the man's thoughts, Lorna quickly said, "May we go into your office, Mr. Gordon? I fear the anticipation of Thomas's final wishes has me on tenterhooks." At the solicitor's nod, she took Brandon's arm.

Mr. Gordon raised a staying hand. "Forgive me, Miss Robbins, but is Mr. Dewhurst your husband?"

"No," she quickly answered.

"Affianced, perhaps?"

Heat flushed her neck. "Mr. Dewhurst is a friend," she clarified.

Mr. Gordon smiled apologetically. "I'm afraid I cannot speak freely of your family's affairs in Mr. Dewhurst's presence. It would be a violation of my professional ethics."

"Oh." Lorna looked uncertainly to Brandon.

He nodded once. "I'll just step out for a paper and read it here."

The solicitor sat Lorna down in a chair in his office. Watching him settle behind his desk, she was unhappily reminded of her last similar meeting, that one with Wiggins, the moneylender. Would she never be free of her brother's troubles?

"Thank you for seeing me on such short notice," she said.

"Not at all," replied Mr. Gordon. "I'd have contacted you soon if you'd not come here, in fact. There are issues which must be addressed."

Anxiety writhed in her gut like a pit of vipers, nearly stealing her breath. She wished Brandon could be beside her, holding her hand. Not that he would do so in front of Mr. Gordon. Knowing he was nearby, lending her moral support, helped a little.

"The matter I wished to see you about today concerns my younger brother, Daniel. Does Thomas's will appoint a guardian?"

Mr. Gordon flipped through some papers—the will, Lorna assumed. He tapped his forefinger against some text. "Yes, in fact, Lord Chorley did name a guardian."

Lorna's heart sank.

"Lionel Pelham, Viscount Huffemall is the gentleman your brother appointed."

She shook her head. "I don't recognize the name. Where does he live?" With a guardian for Daniel now a certainty, Lorna could only hope he wouldn't be taken too far away from Elmwood.

"Nowhere," the solicitor said, his tone bland. "His lordship passed away some two years ago."

"Then..." Her mind reeled. "What does that mean? Is there no guardian?"

Mr. Gordon sighed. "It's a little complicated." He rubbed blunt fingers across his forehead. "It all depends on the contents of Lord Huffemall's will, you see. Had he assumed guardianship before his death, then his heir would fill the role. When Huffemall died, Lord Chorley should have revised his own will, naming a new guardian."

"But he didn't."

"Precisely."

Lorna scratched under the edge of her bonnet ribbon. "What now?"

The solicitor waved his hands in an agitated gesture. "I shall have to track down Huffemall's will. If he died with no male heirs, then young Daniel may, in fact, have no guardian."

"But what if there *is* a male heir?" Lorna asked.

"Then, that gentleman might be Daniel's guardian. We can't know anything for certain until I uncover that will."

What a muddle! There had to be a way to keep Daniel with her. "Could an heir refuse guardianship?"

"Conceivably. And if he does, then the case will have to be decided by the court at Chancery. It could be tied up there for a long time."

Her ears perked. "How long?"

"Months." Mr. Gordon shrugged. "Years, even, depending on a number of things."

"Couldn't we just ignore the matter of a guardian? It seems like such an awful lot of trouble. Daniel is perfectly happy at home, with me."

"Certainly not!" Mr. Gordon seemed affronted by the suggestion. "Forgive me, Miss Robbins," he said, moderating his tone. "I'm sure you have given your brother a wonderful childhood home, but as an unmarried woman, you cannot make decisions vital for his upbringing. Now that Daniel is Baron Chorley, there is no question but that he must have a proper education. He must be prepared to, eventually, take up his seat in the House of Lords. Not to mention, you cannot manage the boy's finances."

"I have so far," she protested. "Elmwood has gotten along under my management."

Mr. Gordon exhaled a long sigh. "Miss Robbins, when I spoke with you some months ago, I appraised you of certain truths regarding your elder brother's situation."

"Money," she said dryly. "There is none."

"As you say." Mr. Gordon swiped his tongue across his lower lip. "Chorley House is entailed, but Elmwood is not, and it is struggling. Daniel's guardian may decide it's in the boy's best interest to sell the estate."

Lorna could not allow Elmwood to be taken away from her and Daniel. It was his birthright, and she would save it for him. "No," she said with a firm cut of her hand. "I won't let that happen."

The solicitor's droopy lips raised in a sad smile. "It isn't your decision, Miss Robbins. This is precisely why a guardian is needed, to make sound judgments for Daniel's well-being."

The implication that Lorna was not fit to care for her brother in all ways left her cold.

Mr. Gordon cleared his throat. "Now, things might be different if you married a nobleman."

Lorna raised her brows.

"In that case," the solicitor continued, "the court might see fit to appoint your husband as guardian." His fingers drummed the desk and his eyes cut to the door. "I don't suppose Mr. Dewhurst...?"

A sharp pang went through her. Oh, how she wished...But not now, not with so many secrets hanging over her like the heavy blade of a guillotine. "No."

He raised his hands, palms out. "Very well. No harm in asking. The man did accompany you, after all. And if he's a Dewhurst of Lord Marcel's family, as I suppose him to be...Well, there's no point in pursuing that line of thought, since the matter is moot."

There was little else to say. Mr. Gordon promised he'd begin tracking down Lord Huffemall's will and heir at once, then he escorted Lorna back to the waiting area.

Brandon glanced up from behind his broadsheet. With a quick economy of motion, he folded and tucked it beneath his arm while he rose to meet her. "All right?" he asked near her ear.

With few answers and a surplus of questions, no, things were not *all right*. But she pasted on a smile for his benefit.

Back in the hackney coach, Brandon, naturally, wanted to know the outcome of her meeting.

"There are still some things to be settled," she prevaricated. She couldn't bear to tell him the truth, that some stranger was going to be named her brother's guardian. Speaking it aloud would make it real.

To distract herself, she took Brandon's paper and opened it. Full of the usual boring politics, Lorna was about to close it again when an article caught her eye. Reading through the brief text, she gasped.

"Oh, did you spot the bit regarding Lord Weir?" Brandon said.

Lorna glanced up to see his steady gaze trained on her.

"Stolen right out of his own funeral—the very one you and I both attended." Quietly, he mused aloud, "Isn't that the damnedest thing?"

Chapter Twenty

The first issue that kept Brandon from enjoying the soiree was the foot he'd amputated several hours ago. His mind kept drifting to the operation, which had left a watchmaker with a superfluous shoe. He'd done good work, but there was always the possibility of infection and fever developing, and worry nagged at his thoughts.

The second matter that Brandon found to be detrimental to his pleasure was the sight of two men flirting with Lorna across the Blessingtons' salon.

It had been two days since he'd accompanied her to her solicitor's office. Brandon had been delighted to see her among the assortment of guests at dinner, but he hadn't yet had the opportunity to speak with her. He had, however, observed her whenever he could unobtrusively do so during the meal.

Once again, she wore her green satin and velvet. It seemed to be the only evening gown she owned. Had he the resources—and the right—Brandon would fill her wardrobe with new dresses. No matter how pretty her green gown might be, she'd never survive the spring Season wearing the same ensemble time and again. The tabbies would tear her to shreds, and delight in doing it. But her attire didn't seem to matter a whit to Lord Sheridan and Mr. Jonson, who regaled her with some highly amusing conversation. Lorna clapped a hand over her mouth and laughed—*laughed!*—at whatever the men said. Brandon's back teeth ground almost to nubs at the sight of other men—even one of his best friends—basking in her smile. Silently, Brandon cursed Sheri to perdition. Couldn't he exercise his wiles on another female?

A moment later, Mr. Jonson moved on to chatting with a peaked-looking Lady Fenton. Not even the glow of candlelight flattered the pregnant woman's wan complexion. In her precarious condition, she tempted fate every time she exposed herself to the excitement of entertainments or the changeable elements out-of-doors.

Brandon strode across the ballroom with determined intent toward the woman's husband. "Fenton," he said with a slight bow, "might I have a word?"

"Dewhurst," Lord Fenton said, nodding in return. "Of course."

Dressed in a burgundy coat stretched tight over his shoulders, elegant breeches, elaborately clocked stockings, and black velvet slippers—and with his faintly vulpine features registering an expression of aristocratic boredom—Lord Fenton looked every inch the sophisticated gentleman of fashion as he led Brandon to a small room just off the salon.

"What the hell are you doing, Fenton?" Brandon scolded. "I know it isn't my place, but I would be a disgrace to my profession if I did not advise you, in the strongest terms possible, to take your wife home, put her to bed, and keep her there for the duration of her pregnancy, even if you have to tie her down to accomplish it."

Lord Fenton raked a hand through his red hair, sending wayward strands jutting out every which way. "I know! Damn it all to hell, Dewhurst, *I know.*" With one hand on his hip, the other gesticulated in huge, dramatic motions. "Doctor Possons issued those same orders a full month ago! But Manning, that damned surgeon of hers, insists she's well enough to continue going about as long as she pleases."

Brandon blinked, shocked that his colleague would offer such unsound—even dangerous—guidance. "At the risk of creating greater confusion in the matter, I must respectfully disagree with Mr. Manning's opinion."

"There is no confusion here," Fenton stated. "*I* disagree with Mr. Manning. Doctor Possons disagrees with Mr. Manning."

"Forbid him from entering your house!" Brandon's voice boomed in the small chamber. He took a breath and reined in his frustration. "If he is giving your wife unsound care, then you must not allow him to treat her."

Fenton let out a bitter laugh. "Do you think I've not threatened that very thing? But Marjorie refuses to consult Doctor Possons any longer. She says his prognostications of doom and gloom are upsetting, and therefore, dangerous for her to hear. She only minds Manning, because he tells her all is well, and that she may do as she pleases."

Why would Manning say such a thing? Brandon wondered. Manning knew as well as he did what a dangerous situation Lady Fenton was in. The likelihood of her safely making it through the birth of three babies was already infinitesimal. Every outing she made, she put her very life at risk.

Fenton's eyes gleamed, wild and desperate. "What should I do, Dewhurst? Isn't Manning's care better than none?"

Other eyes appeared in his mind, equally desperate, begging him for a miracle. Brown eyes. Portuguese. Filled with pain and refusal to accept the inevitable.

Brandon bit back a growl. When McGully tasked him with keeping watch over Lady Fenton, he knew his fortitude would be tried. But this had become excruciating. He couldn't just stand by and wait for her to die, so McGully could have his anatomical prize.

"*His prize...*" he whispered.

Manning sought acclaim in their field, just like every other surgeon in London. He'd wound up with Weir's body, and if Brandon were to put money on it, he'd wager Manning was also behind the highway robbery that claimed the corpse of Lady Dawton, an outrage that had been much discussed this evening. Was a man so hell-bent on outdoing his rivals really the best one to care for a delicate patient like Lady Fenton? Might he not willfully give her bad advice, making her death a certainty, and thereby granting him the chance to take her body for his own anatomical work?

"Holy Christ."

"What's that?" Fenton asked.

"Listen to me," Brandon snapped. "If there's any chance of Lady Fenton surviving her ordeal, you must strictly limit her activity. She should not leave her home for the remainder of the pregnancy. If she were my patient, I would insist upon confinement to her bed, rising only as nature requires. And for God's sake, man, no matter what else, keep Manning away from her."

Lord Fenton drew a shaky breath. "You're right. Of course you are. Thank you for your counsel, Dewhurst."

The men shook hands. Brandon clapped Fenton on the shoulder and wished him well. He waited a couple of minutes after that gentlemen departed—hopefully to spirit his wife home at once—before emerging from the little room.

He stepped out just in time to see Lord and Lady Fenton headed for the exit. Once more the picture of composure, Fenton sent a cool nod in Brandon's direction.

Lorna was no longer where he'd last seen her. He caught a glimpse of rich, green satin swishing between some nearby guests. Before he could work his way through the group, she appeared at his side, a mischievous smile playing across her lips. She clasped her gloved hands behind her back and rocked on her heels.

He bowed, taking her offered hand in his own, unable to resist brushing her palm with his fingertips. "You look for all the world like the cat who got the cream. Good evening, Lorna."

Now that she was close enough to examine, he saw a delicate gold chain woven into a braid that circled the crown of her head. She was as natural as a milkmaid, he thought, the antithesis of the tonnish women he was accustomed to meeting, all traces of genuine sentiment trained out of them before they left the schoolroom.

It was no wonder she was beginning to attract admirers, though it galled him to have any other man lay claim to her attentions.

"Not as decadent as cream, but I do feel as though I have been given something equally pleasant."

The blush he'd come to crave the sight of made an appearance over the apples of her cheeks. Her eyes gleamed with warmth. Simply enchanting.

"Whatever it is you find so gratifying, my dear Miss Robbins, I'm sure one of your suitors will make sure you have it in endless supply."

She gave him an arch look. "What suitors would those be?"

"Lord Sheridan and Mr. Jonson, of course. You positively thrived in the warm sphere of their attentions."

He detested how churlish he sounded, how juvenile, as though Lorna was a toy he didn't want to share with the other lads. It was undignified.

Her smile widened. "Alas, Mr. Dewhurst, though I did enjoy the society of those gentlemen, they cannot give me that which makes me gladder than anything else."

"And what would that be?"

"A moment spent in your company, sir."

He was slain. Such simple sweetness laid him to waste and left him speechless. An unfamiliar lump rose in his throat.

"I heard the most extraordinary tale at the table," Lorna said, "regarding the fate of Lady Dawton."

"I'm sorry you had to hear such an unsavory topic over your meal," he said abstractedly. After what she'd just said about being made happy by spending time with him, he wanted nothing more than to whisk her away from this place.

Her lush mouth twisted. "It was all the talk at the bottom of the table, where I was seated. No one had a word for anything but the sudden rash of body theft." She cast a look to the left and right, then leaned forward and said, sotto voce, "Confess, Brandon, you are the highwayman who absconded with Lady Dawton's body, aren't you?"

That snapped him out of his romantic reverie. "For God's sake, of course not!"

Lorna laughed. Chagrined, Brandon realized she'd been teasing him. No woman had ever joked with him on this grim topic. Lorna was so…unexpected.

"Not I," he said gamely, "though I do wonder how our intrepid highwayman managed to secret a purloined corpse about his own person."

"Perhaps he has very deep pockets," she suggested with a chuckle.

"Doesn't it bother you?" he asked with a tone of wonder. He realized he'd swayed closer to her, but he couldn't have stopped himself from getting closer, even if he cared to try—which he did not.

Not pretending to misunderstand him, Lorna tilted her head thoughtfully. "I've had a bit of time to think about this, since Thomas was taken," she said. "And while I cannot like what happened, there is no use expending energy on anger or regret. What was done cannot be undone. So I am left with the hope that his body proved genuinely useful to some surgeon or anatomist, somewhere."

At that instant, Brandon could have been felled by the lightest touch of a feather, so dumbfounded was he. "What a remarkably generous attitude."

In just the few minutes he'd actually spent with her tonight, Lorna had turned Brandon inside out with jealousy, lust, and humility. Of all the women he'd ever known, she was utterly unique in every way. Suddenly, not having her seemed an impossibility not to be considered.

Feeling reckless, he leaned down to whisper in her ear, "I want to be alone with you, Lorna."

She softened, brushing her ear against his chin. Sparks flew through Brandon's veins, and desire swirled around them. He couldn't wait to slowly undress her, to send that green velvet and satin slithering to the floor. She would feel soft and feminine when he pulled her beneath his hard body.

When she turned her face to him, banked heat smoldered in those turquoise irises. "How?" she whispered back.

He considered and discarded a dozen ideas. The most obvious answer was to bring her home with him, but *home* was an anatomy school. On his way to bed tonight, he'd pass a room containing two dead bodies. He couldn't bring Lorna to such a place. Neither would he insult her by taking her virginity in a carriage, or in some out-of-the-way inn.

"I'll come to you," he finally murmured. "If there's no vine I can climb to get into your window, you can let down your hair after your maid goes to bed." Need be, he would batter down the door.

Lorna nodded to Lady Dane as the older woman passed. "I think you finally got a story right."

"All I needed was the proper motivation," he answered with a lecherous waggle of his brow.

Lorna bit her bottom lip, considering.

Brandon groaned low in his throat at the unintentionally erotic display.

"All right," she said.

He drew a sharp breath and quelled the urge to raise his arms in a victorious display. "Marvelous," he drawled, instead. "I'll have a carriage summoned, shall I?"

A footman entered the salon; Brandon raised a hand to draw his notice. But when the servant reached them, he held out a note. Brandon's name and the word *URGENT* were scrawled across the parchment.

"This came for you, Mr. Dewhurst."

With a sinking sense of inevitable defeat, Brandon read the missive. Already, he felt pangs of frustrated arousal.

"I'm so sorry," he said, meeting Lorna's questioning gaze. "I must go see a watchmaker about a foot."

Chapter Twenty-One

Lorna let herself into the house, closed the door, and slumped with her back against it. Burning eyes and temples testified to the restless night she'd passed. For hours, she'd tossed and turned, wondering whether Brandon would somehow materialize at her window. He hadn't, naturally. The welfare of his patient took precedence over an assignation, and there wasn't really a vine for him to climb to her window, in any event.

Nevertheless, nervous anticipation made proper sleep impossible. She'd fallen into a fitful doze just as the sky began to lighten, only to be roused a few hours later by an invitation to breakfast with the Freedmans next door.

Idly, she rubbed a hand over her stomach, uncomfortably stuffed with kippered herring, poached apples, and omelet. Brandon would be proud of the meal she'd tucked away, she thought, recalling how he'd fussed over her the morning after her episode. A tired smile nudged one side of her mouth. Those pleasant memories would occupy her mind while she sank into a much-needed rest.

Aiming for the haven of her bed, she trudged up several stairs. Behind her, quick, heavy steps crossed the entryway.

"Miss Robbins," called Oscar, "a letter came for you while you were out."

It was from Mr. Gordon, requesting a meeting at his office. Her stomach flipped. What had he learned? "Send Charity to my room, please, Oscar."

Moments later, Lorna sat at the vanity while the maid worked a wide-toothed comb through her hair. The woman clucked in disapproval. "Look what you've gone and done to yourself," she said, parting the curls and prodding at Lorna's scalp. "So scratched up. Why do you do this?"

Lorna gave an awkward shrug, her ears burning at having been caught out. "It's a nervous habit."

"And what're you so nervous about, Miss Robbins?"

Her lips drawn inward, Lorna stared into the mirror. There was no satisfactory answer she could give. Entrusting her maid with the secret of her body-thieving was out of the question. Neither would she share her troubles regarding Daniel, and the possibility of him being taken away from her.

Charity's voice turned smug. "It's that Mr. Dewhurst has you all in knots, just as I reckoned." She twisted Lorna's curls around to pin them up. "If you want him to come up to scratch, miss, you'll heed me and not permit him liberties such as the other night."

"What on earth do you mean?" Lorna demanded.

"He spent the night right here in this very room," the maid asserted. "Every time I came in to check on you, there he was."

And here Lorna thought shooing him out before breakfast had been enough to preserve their secret. Her fingers twitched; she laced them together in her lap. "I was sick. Mr. Dewhurst was tending me."

Charity snorted. "No surgeon I've ever seen holds the hand of his patient all through the night." She jabbed a hairpin in with too much enthusiasm. Lorna yelped. "The fact you were ailing is the only reason I didn't say nothing sooner." Sure fingers worked steadily while Charity continued, "What you do is your own affair, Miss Robbins. But you've got no man here to protect your honor. I don't want to see you taken advantage of."

The large meal she'd eaten felt like a ball of lead in Lorna's stomach. Brandon didn't mean to take advantage of her, she was sure. But how could she trust her own judgment, when she had no experience with men to draw from?

With a flourish, the maid drove a final pin into the mass atop Lorna's head. "There," she said with a nod. "You'll do."

Not precisely a ringing endorsement for Lorna's appearance, but then the drab, Manilla-brown walking dress, the hated freckles, and the tight coils all over her head didn't exactly inspire rhapsodies, either. *Oh, well*, she thought. *This is why the good Lord gave us bonnets, is it not?*

• • •

When next Lorna passed over the threshold of Chorley House, it was with a handkerchief pressed to her mouth and tears burning the backs of her eyes.

Mr. Gordon had wasted no time discovering the identity of Lord Huffemall's London solicitor, and had appraised that man, Mr. Page, of the guardianship question. Mr. Page could not give Mr. Gordon a definitive answer, so the two men of law were setting off the following morning to meet with his lordship at his home in Wales.

Gordon had gone on to relate Mr. Page's description of Lord Huffemall. The incumbent was named Marcus Pelham. Forty years of age, he lived a quiet life above reproach, passing most of the year in Wales, but coming to London for the spring Season. His wife had never borne a child, and was unlikely to do so at this point in time. By all accounts, Lord Huffemall was a pillar of his community, a patron of many worthy causes, moderate in his consumption of spirits, and faithful in observing the Sabbath.

In short, he was perfect.

Why couldn't he have been a reprobate? She despaired. If only he was a self-centered voluptuary, with no inclination to serve anything but his own desires.

"He'll take Daniel," she murmured to herself, dabbing her eyes with the soggy linen. "He'll take him away and give him a wonderful life and Daniel will forget all about me."

In her room, she tore off her bonnet and flung herself onto the bed. Exhausted and distraught, she wondered how, exactly, one went about having a fit of the vapors. She didn't want another attack such as the one she'd experienced three days ago, but Lorna supposed she was entitled to a minor tantrum.

Below, someone employed the knocker on the front door. "Brandon?" she wondered, hopeful. She dragged the heel of her hand across her eyes and sniffed. Scrambling off the bed, she bent to look in the vanity mirror. She slapped lightly at her cheeks to bring color to the skin and tucked back a few loose strands of hair.

Charity opened the door. "A Mr. Allen is asking for you."

She frowned. "I don't know a Mr. Allen."

The maid scowled. "I knew it! I told Oscar not to let him in, but the fool stuck him in the parlor. You don't have to see him, miss. I'll get rid of him. I don't trust him. Too flash by half."

The cant term tickled something in Lorna's mind. "Just a moment. Can you describe Mr. Allen?"

Charity's hip cocked to the side; she reached up a hand over her head. "About *yea* tall. Trim, with broad shoulders. Gold hair all in curls, white teeth he shows in a big smile, like everything's a lark…" The maid's voice drifted off for a moment before she recalled herself. She cleared her throat and wiped her hands on her apron, an embarrassed flush pinking her ears.

Lorna shook her head. "It's all right, Charity, he has that effect on most women."

When she walked into the parlor, Pretty Lem sprang to his feet. "Miss Lorna!" He flashed his expansive grin, displaying his chipped front tooth in the otherwise neat row of white. "Not too bad, eh? Getting in your front door. Bob and Fartleberry bet half a crown I couldn't do it."

"You nearly didn't," Lorna informed him. "If my maid had her way, you'd have been tossed on your ear."

Lem's youthful brow creased in a frown. "Don't I look the part?"

With arms held wide, he spun in a circle for Lorna's inspection. He wore the suit Lorna had insisted upon the time they masqueraded as siblings to take the body of a pregnant woman from her tenement house. Since then, the clothes had clearly been crammed into a corner. The coat was badly creased, and his neck cloth sported the same knot the gang used to secure bodies in the wagon.

"You look fine, Lem," she said diplomatically, taking a seat. "What brings you?"

"Coop sent me." Lem fished in his pockets. "First, to give you this." He handed over a roll of notes. "Your take from the last job."

A quick count of the banknotes showed she'd be able to repay another small measure of Thomas's debt. In her life, Lorna had never held so much money in her hands as she had this month. It went to Wiggins almost as soon as she touched it, but it still wasn't fast enough.

"Since you're here, Lem," she said, "I'll tell you what else I've heard. Pass this along, so Coop can make a plan. A Mr. Kenrick, second cousin to a duke, broke his back the other day. He isn't expected to live much longer. Perhaps we can—"

"Listen, Miss Lorna," Lem interrupted, waving his hands. "Coop don't want to pull any more risky jobs right now."

Lorna sputtered. "Wh-what? But I need the money, Lem."

If she couldn't secure Elmwood for Daniel, there was no possibility of keeping him with her. It was the only chance she had to show this Lord Huffemall that she could give her brother a good home.

He shrugged. "We'll still work—just normal things, you know? No more big stuff until it's time to get Lady Fenton." The toe of one scuffed shoe traced back and forth in a U. "Speaking of, Coop wants the word on her. She 'bout done?"

Lorna flinched. "That's my friend. Have some respect."

Lem held up his hands. "Sorry." Those work-roughened fingers combed through his angelic curls. "Coop wants you to know we've got competition, so keep close to Lady F."

"What competition?"

He chuffed. "We ain't the only ones aiming to have that body. Coop's the one in the know; he just told me to tell you. You better stick to her like a tick on a dog."

"And how am I to do that?" Lorna asked, exasperated. "I see her almost every day as it is. It's not as though I can move in with—"

An idea stopped her in her tracks. Only the seed of an idea, really. It warranted more contemplation than she could devote to it at the moment.

"For the sake of argument," she said, "let's assume I can stick to Lady Fenton like a tick, as you so artfully stated. What about Blackbird?"

Lem shifted his weight from one foot to the other. His eyes cut downward. "Coop says Blackbird's grounded for now. It was a close thing with The Great White Scot."

Her eyes widened. Lorna hopped to her feet. "Are you referring to my near-apprehension? Which happened—in no small part, I might add—thanks to your mad driving." She jabbed a finger into his chest. "The rest of you louts left me to the Watch while you made good your escape."

"Aw, Miss Lorna." Lem's voice took on a wheedling tone, once again betraying his youth. "It weren't like I meant for you to fall out of the wagon. Besides," he said, flashing his cocky grin, "you made it out right and tight, just like the plum cove you're turning out to be."

Something inside Lorna snapped. "Though you might find this the incarnation of amazing, believe me when I tell you that never in my life have I aspired to the compliment of *plum cove*. I do this only because I must, and only for as long as I must.

Blackbird has given Crib Cross Gang an advantage over all other resurrectionists, yes?"

The wide-eyed youth nodded warily.

"You owe me more than to strand me in the street, Lem. You treated me very shabbily, indeed."

"Sorry, Miss Lorna, but the Watch—"

"To hell with the Watch, as you lot would say! I thought there was honor among thieves, but perhaps that trait does not extend to the practitioners of corpse theft. Am I being cut loose, Lem? Does Coop want me out?"

"No!" he cried. "Lord, Miss Lorna, we've never made so much as we have since you been here. Coop just needs you to lay low and keep an eye on Lady Fenton. None of the rest of us can do that, Miss Lorna. Just our Blackbird."

He reached out and ruffled her hair. She scowled, earning another of his smiles.

"I don't like this, Lem," she said, giving him a little shove toward the parlor door. "Tell Coop I want to see him."

• • •

28 November 1816
Elmwood

Dear Sissy,

I asked Mrs. Lynch if I might send you a letter. She said I may, and that I should tell you about the things I have been doing. The trouble is that I can't think of anything. I've been very dull without you here. Mrs. Lynch doesn't make my lessons exciting like you do. Yesterday, she made me practice my penmanship by copying verses from the Bible. I told her that you let me write whatever I please, and even make up stories if I want, but she said Scripture eddyflies the soul, AND it's good practice for my hand, AND that this house needs to invite the

Spirit more than ever since our Recent Troubles. At least she let me copy out the verses in Joshua about the war between him and a lot of kings with strange names.

You said you'd be gone for a few days, but it's been weeks. Why are you gone so long? I miss you. Please come home. I promise I'll eat my turnips without any complaint from now on, if that's the trouble.

Love,
From your brother,
Daniel August Robbins, Baron Chorley (Did I say it right?)

P.S.—Did you find the dog's owner? If not, I still promise to take good care of her. Humphrey says a big beast like her would eat us out of house and home, but don't those mean the same thing? I could take her hunting and she could eat whatever we catch, so she wouldn't be any trouble at all.

Another P.S.—I miss you very much!

Lorna read Daniel's letter again. Each reading stole her breath. The poor little dear blamed himself for her being away from home so long. She yearned to put her arms around him and hold him on her lap, as they always did. She missed his baby-soft cheeks and the mischievous sparkle in his eyes. No one else in the world called her Sissy, or thought she made anything exciting. Daniel needed her, and she needed him, too.

Missing him was a painful, sucking wound in her chest.

And if it hurt so much now, how much worse would it be when Lord Huffemall separated them for good?

Sitting at a table, with a blank sheet of parchment beside Daniel's letter, Lorna attempted to compose a reply. She wanted to assure him he was not to blame for her absence. She wanted to promise she'd be home any day now.

But the words wouldn't come. Nothing was right. A dozen times she picked up her quill, and a dozen times she dropped it again. She scratched and scratched her head until her fingers came away stained with blood and tangled in loose hairs.

I have to get out of here, she decided. A walk would be just the thing to clear her mind.

Ignoring Charity's inquiries as to her destination, she wrapped in Thomas's cloak and set out into the cold afternoon, begging the vastness of London to subsume the bleakness eating at her heart.

Chapter Twenty-Two

The fresh air worked wonders to ease her aching heart and troubled mind, and some time later, Lorna found herself on a familiar corner. Looking at the anatomy school where Brandon lived and worked, she blinked, confused by the sight before her.

A group of about thirty men congregated outside the Covent Garden School of Anatomical Studies. For the most part, they were a reputable-looking bunch, wearing neatly tailored, if not fine, clothing. The gentlemen stood in smaller bunches, heads bent together in conversation. Several clutched a pamphlet in their hands, and she spotted what looked to be the same printing sticking from the pockets of a few coats.

"What is this?" she murmured. Curious, but cautious, she approached the edge of the group.

"Oh, good, here's another one," said a female voice to Lorna's left. "Miss. Miss! Over here."

Startled, Lorna looked for the owner of the voice. Two women stood against the neighboring building, away from the male congregation. The taller of the two waved her over.

"You're so brave to come alone," the tall woman said. "I'd never have had the nerve to come without Hetty." She nudged the second woman with her elbow and gave that female a little smile. "I'm Doris," she said to Lorna, nodding. "Doris Watling. And this is Mrs. Fisher."

Doris looked about thirty, judging by the fine lines in her forehead and around her eyes and mouth, while the smaller Mrs. Fisher looked older, perhaps forty. Both women wore plain, serviceable dresses and coats, with gloves and hats fashioned with an eye on warmth, not style. There was an air of kindness around both ladies, while Mrs. Fisher, who had yet to speak a word, exuded a certain competence, as well. Lorna liked them both at once, and felt her despondence over Daniel's letter begin to lift.

"Pleased to meet you, Miss Watling, Mrs. Fisher." She nodded to each of the women in turn. "I'm Lorna Robbins."

Mrs. Fisher had a rolled copy of the pamphlet peeking out of her flannel reticule.

"May I?" Lorna asked.

As she handed over the paper, Mrs. Fisher spoke. "Are you a midwife, too, dearie?"

Frowning, Lorna unrolled the pamphlet. "A what? No. I'm…" Her voice trailed off as she read the notice, advertising a public lecture on advances in the field of obstetrics, delivered by Mr. D. McGully, with accompanying anatomical demonstrations by McGully and Mr. B. Dewhurst, and a display of never-before-seen artistic renderings by the renowned illustrator Mr. A. Culpepper.

"Oh, good, they've opened the door," Doris said. "We'll just slip in and sit at the back." She looped both of her arms through the other women's. "Hmph. Look at that man raising his brows at us," she said under her breath.

Indeed, one of the men moving with the flow of bodies into the school gave the three women a stern look of disapproval.

"Never mind him," Mrs. Fisher said. She raised her chin and shoved her spectacles up the bridge of her nose. "Remember, Doris, we're doing this for the mothers and babes in our care, not to win the approval of the Royal College of Surgeons."

"Quite right," Doris said stoutly. She squeezed Lorna's arm. "You see, I couldn't have come without her! Mrs. Fisher is our champion."

Together, Lorna and her new companions made their way to the entrance, where they were intercepted by Mr. Disapproving. He must have been waiting just inside to ambush them, for he stepped in their path the moment their toes crossed the threshold.

"My dear ladies," the man said, "you seem to have misplaced yourselves. Allow me to escort you to the hackney stand on the corner."

"Well, I don't know about you, sir," Doris said in a low rush, "but I'm just where I mean to be." She pursed her lips and gave a little *hmph*, then added, "Though I do thank you for your kind concern."

The man looked down his nose at Doris, who wilted under the force of his condescending glare. Lorna, too, felt distinctly uncomfortable. She had come in the hopes of seeing Brandon, not a lecture. Perhaps she should leave.

"This event is a serious gathering of professional surgeons," he informed them, "not a tea social."

"The notice says it's a public lecture," Mrs. Fisher said. "Are we not members of the community?"

"As good, Christian women," he said, "I should hope you'd take care not to offend public morals."

Doris and Mrs. Fisher exchanged a look. Lorna felt Doris's arm start tugging her backwards.

"No," Lorna declared, mulishly standing her ground. Even though this wasn't her fight, she resented the man's bullying. She'd been pushed around by too many men in the last year: Thomas, Wiggins, Coop. She wasn't about to be pushed around by yet another obstinate male.

"The notice says the lecture is open to the public, with no exceptions given. As Mrs. Fisher has rightly pointed out, we *are* the public. Instead of policing, you should welcome newcomers. You, sir, will not stand in the way of my scientific curiosity," she finished with a flourish.

Behind her, someone broke into applause. "I say, Miss Robbins, well done."

She turned and found herself looking up into a laughing, handsome face. "Lord Sheridan," she said. "What are you doing here?"

"Now, now," he tutted, waving a finger. "Having vanquished your foe, are you the new gatekeeper?"

Not waiting for her response, Lord Sheridan took Lorna's hand, tucked it into his arm, and strolled into the building. "Run along with you," he told the ladies' tormentor. "These ladies may be good Christians, but I assure you I am not." From his waistcoat pocket, he produced a quizzing glass, through which he gave the man an imperious stare. "If you're so inclined, we can step outside so I can demonstrate the commandments with which I particularly struggle." He delivered an icy smile.

Intimidation and doubt shadowed the surgeon's features. At last, he muttered his excuses and hurried away.

On Lorna's other side, Doris released a breathy sigh. Lorna sympathized. With his devastating good looks, fashionable attire, and aristocratic manners, Lord Sheridan positively oozed wealth and charm. Had Brandon not already addled her emotions, Lorna might be tempted to throw her heart at Lord Sheridan's feet, herself.

The gentleman squired them into the lecture hall, where he procured seats in the top tier. Lord Sheridan took the seat beside Lorna.

To her questioning look, the gentleman shrugged. "It's a dull week. Positively *nothing* amusing is happening before Thursday. Why not?"

"Why not, indeed," Lorna said. "Does Mr. Dewhurst know you're here?"

"No. You?"

"No."

An awkward silence followed, which neither seemed willing to fill. Lorna wasn't prepared to tell Lord Sheridan her reasons for coming—especially when she wasn't entirely certainly of her motivation herself—and he, apparently, was just as reticent with his own thoughts.

Lorna peered around the chamber, which was unlike any room she'd been in before. Large windows were placed to collect ample sunshine, but at the current hour and inclement weather conditions, they merely gleamed a dull, watery gray. Lamplight flooded the round center of the room like a stage, leaving the audience in shadow. The walls were lined with shelves, which boasted an array of specimen jars and other anatomical bric-a-brac. A covered body rested on a table in the center of the lit area, while numerous easels on the right side showcased the promised display of artwork. To the left stood a cherry lectern.

The squeak of door hinges silenced all the murmuring in the room. A hush descended as an older gentleman stepped to the lectern. The man (Mr. McGully, Lorna surmised) paused for a moment to polish his spectacles before stuffing a handkerchief back into his pocket and settling the eyewear on his face.

"Gentlemen, we have a problem." McGully's rich brogue easily carried around the room, collecting all ears and holding them rapt. "The problem, sirs, is that the act of childbirth is frequently fatal for the mother, the infant, or both. I do not think it is a stretch to say that, in fact, the human female can undertake no greater challenge than to carry and deliver a child. We men would not be so glib about undertaking what we are told is a natural human process if we knew that one per cent of all participants in this process will assuredly die. And yet, this is precisely the sacrifice we demand from the mothers of our children."

Lorna had never heard the risk of childbirth put in quite such stark, startling terms.

To her left, Doris watched Mr. McGully like a hawk eyeing a rodent. At his last comment, she quietly chuffed and nodded her agreement. Meanwhile, Mrs. Fisher had produced a pencil and bit of foolscap, and scribbled down every word of the lecture. Lorna admired these midwives for thrusting themselves into an inhospitable crowd in the pursuit of knowledge.

Behind McGully the door swung, and Brandon moved silently into the theatre to arrange tools and other items on a table beside the corpse. Lorna tracked Brandon's every movement, her eyes drinking in the careful precision with which he maneuvered the equipment. Recalling the feeling of those strong, capable hands on her fevered body had her flushing, and grateful for the dimness concealing her reaction.

"… childbed fever being the most egregious culprit, of course, but we also lose many females to hemorrhages, as well as obstructed labor. All surgeons should possess a basic understanding of the processes of pregnancy and birth. My recent and ongoing studies on the anatomy of the gravid uterus and pelvic girdle will, I believe, provide illumination on this most critical of physical undertakings."

On her other side, Lord Sheridan sat with legs crossed at the knee, an elbow resting on the top knee and his fist propping up his chin. He seemed to have slipped into something of a stupor, and Lorna wondered yet again why the man had even deigned to attend.

"… useful tools to keep at hand," McGully was saying. "There are the forceps, of course"—here, he gestured and Brandon stepped forward, holding the instrument aloft—"used to assist the infant through the birth canal."

Lorna cringed at the thought of having such an implement put into her body, but it only got worse from there. After the forceps, Brandon showcased a variety of scissors, hooks, awls, and saws. One cranking device, meant to force the pelvic bones apart—its efficacy demonstrated on a skeleton—caused Lorna to make a sound of distress, barely muffled by her hand covering her mouth. A man in front of her swung around to give her a disapproving glare.

Brandon's sharp gaze swept the shadowed audience, seeking the source of the feminine gasp. Lorna slid down in her chair and turned her head, praying Brandon could not identify her.

In a straightforward manner, Mr. McGully explained the circumstances in which one tool was preferable over another. "In some sad cases," he intoned, "you may be faced with choosing whether to preserve the life of the mother, or that of the infant. This heavy duty must be carried out with all due somber consideration, but once you've chosen your course, you must not hesitate to act. Time is often your greatest enemy."

Because she was so attuned to him, Lorna noticed Brandon pale. His lips drew taut.

"If it has become clear that the mother will not survive the birth, it is best to dispense with niceties such as the forceps and instead retrieve the infant by the most expeditious means possible."

Naturally, her thoughts turned to Marjorie. Would these torturous-looking devices be used to pry her babies from her dying body? To be forced to endure such horrors in the last moments of life was a dreadful fate. Too well could Lorna imagine the pain and indignity. Her lower portions twitched with phantom sympathy, while her arms reflexively clamped over her middle.

A sheen of sweat collected on Brandon's upper lip, while his pallor intensified. He turned his head and gulped. But still he remained at his station, demonstrating every piece of equipment, pointing out the illustrations that corresponded to various portions of McGully's lecture.

After what felt like a week, McGully stepped away from the podium and it was over. Lorna exhaled, her shoulders slumping in relief.

By contrast, Brandon licked his lips and drew a deep breath, every line of his posture growing more tense by the second. He removed his coat and rolled his shirtsleeves up his forearms.

"The body," she whispered, her heart once again hammering.

Lord Sheridan's eyes flicked to her. "You don't suppose that's really a…"

"Absolutely, it is."

With his surgical apron secured over his clothing, Brandon whipped the cover from the corpse, revealing the body of a pregnant female.

It was a fine specimen. How had Crib Cross missed it?

Shame raced through her. After the harrowing lecture she'd just endured, how could her first thought upon seeing this poor woman's dead body be professional envy? Her molars ground together.

Mr. McGully stood at the head of the dissection table, while Brandon moved to the middle.

"For this evening's highlight event," McGully boomed like the master of ceremonies at a spectacle, "my colleague Mr. Dewhurst will perform a dissection, revealing the female reproductive organs in full bloom." He gestured grandly. "Mr. Dewhurst, if you please."

The audience collectively held its breath and leaned forward in its seats; Lorna cringed and pulled away.

With measured calm, Brandon made a long incision across the woman's abdomen, then methodically made his way through layers of tissue, narrating as he went.

Now the audience grew excited; men murmured to one another and even the midwives exchanged whispers while they watched.

In spite of all her personal unease with the topic, Lorna couldn't help but admire and appreciate the work Brandon and McGully were doing. When audience members asked questions, Brandon spoke with as much knowledge and conviction as McGully. Obviously, he had a passion not only for gaining knowledge, but for sharing it, as well.

"Now we've arrived at the womb," Brandon said. Only Lorna's close acquaintance with him allowed her to sense the unease edging his tone. And yet he worked on, never permitting his discomfort to impede his task.

At a request from the audience, Brandon plunged his hands right into the abdomen and pried the uterus free of the surrounding viscera. There was an awful squelching sound.

"Good God," Lord Sheridan croaked. Lorna glanced at the man in time to see his handsome features take on a faintly green cast. "I take back every disparaging remark I've ever made about the opera." He looked at Lorna, his nose wrinkled. "Are you enjoying this?"

Hastily, she shook her head in the negative. "I only came to speak with Brandon. I had no idea all this would be going on."

"Shall I escort you away from this gruesome entertainment?" Sheridan flashed an impish smile. "I swear I will not hold it against you if I am deprived of any more of this demonstration."

Lorna cast a longing look at the door. Brandon didn't know she was here. If she slipped out unnoticed, he'd never know she'd come and gone. Why did she feel like she'd be abandoning him?

"I'll stay," she said, "but please don't feel obligated to remain on my account."

Lord Sheridan clicked his tongue. "Never let it be said that I am not manful enough to passively endure a performance, no matter how disgusting it may be. Never fear, Miss Robbins. I shall perse—merciful heavens, what is that *smell*?" The gentleman clapped a handkerchief to his face and offered another to Lorna, which she gladly employed.

A moment later, men started swarming around the dissection table for a closer look. Lorna was glad to have her own view obstructed.

"What d'you think, Mrs. Fisher?" asked Doris. She pointed to the hub of activity. "Would it be all right for us to go down there?"

The older woman stood, straightening her shawl with the grim determination of a soldier headed into battle. "I don't know whether it's all right, but we're doing it."

Doris let out a whoop and jumped to her feet. "How about you, Miss Robbins?"

"None for me, thank you," Lorna replied. "You're welcome to my portion of viewing."

"Mine, as well," Lord Sheridan called behind them.

Finally, the dreadful ordeal ended. Surgeons, students, and the morbidly curious milled about for a while, closely examining the displayed illustrations and conversing with one another while assistants cleared away the body and implements. The midwives spoke with Brandon for a few minutes then departed, exultant at having successfully breached the male domain. Lord Sheridan took his leave not long after, leaving Lorna alone in the back row. He shook Brandon's hand and clapped the other man on the shoulder.

At last, Lorna collected her reticule and her courage, then made her way down the steps to the floor. Brandon's back was to her; he'd just taken off his surgical apron and was re-donning his coat. She watched the play of his shoulders as he settled the garment into place and buttoned it. There was a little, vulnerable slice of bare neck between his collar and hair; she longed to press her lips there.

Though she might have left home with no destination in mind, in her heart, Lorna knew she'd wind up here. Where else could she have gone? She'd come with Brandon's words from the other night in mind: *I want to be alone with you.* She'd come seeking what he offered, an escape from the guilt and pain that had threatened to swallow her. Instead, she'd caught a glimpse of an echoing torment inside this man who had so captivated her, a suffering he ignored for the sake of his work, and she found herself even more helplessly drawn to him. Could they not, perhaps, offer that escape to one another?

Brandon turned. His eyes landed upon her; he blinked, surprised. "You're here."

Their gazes locked, she scarcely felt her feet move as she closed the short distance. "You did a wonderful job."

"You watched it? All of it?"

"Lord Sheridan sat with me." She smiled ruefully. "I'm afraid we didn't make a very good account of ourselves. We cowered in the back with handkerchiefs to our faces while those splendid midwives came to the fore to see everything."

One hand took hers, while his other skimmed over her jawline. Lorna leaned into his touch, unable to resist seeking more contact.

He peered from a frame of dark lashes, his gray eyes piercing the shadows and causing her breath to catch. "I'm sorry you were distressed by what you heard and saw."

If only it were just a surgical procedure that caused her distress.

His index finger twirled into one of the curls at her temple. "This isn't the sort of thing I'd have wished you to attend. Although," he continued, with a touch of humor tugging at his lips, "you seem to have fared better than Sheri. Poor devil was heaving on his way out the door."

"And you?" Lorna reached out to return his caresses. Brandon sighed, resting his cheek against her palm as though it was the softest pillow. "This was terrible for you, I can tell. Why do you do it?"

"Because it must be done," he answered simply. "I once lost..." A pained expression crossed his features. "We're going to make sure more women and children come through childbirth healthy and whole. I hate this particular subject of work, Lorna. It rips my heart out every time, but I believe in it. I have to do it."

There was something personal underlying his words. Curiosity had her tongue itching to ask, but she clamped down on the impulse. His profession might be deemed unsavory by society, but Brandon Dewhurst was committed to his cause, striving to change lives for the better. She admired him so much, his knowledge and skill, his bravery and determination.

No, she realized, she didn't just admire Brandon; she loved him. She loved him, and she wanted him. The goodness of who he was, the sweet oblivion of his passionate kisses.

She needed him. Right now.

"You live downstairs, do you not?"

"Yes." His head canted, as though he was trying to puzzle something out. "There's an alleyway beside the building," he said in a low tone. "The door to my apartment is at the end of it. I can meet you there in five minutes."

A thrill shot through her. She bit her lip and smiled, then spun away and headed for the door.

Outside, she turned her face to the sky. Night had fallen, offering its familiar, comforting cloak of concealment.

As Brandon had said, a dark alleyway ran between the school and the neighboring building. It could have been a tunnel into the abyss, for all she could see.

Drawing a deep breath, Lorna screwed up her courage. The alley pitched downward, exposing the back half of the basement level. At the bottom of the incline stood a simple wooden door. Before she could talk herself out of it, Lorna raised a fist and rapped three times.

After a moment, the door opened. Lorna blinked in the sudden pool of lantern light.

Brandon was dressed in black trews and waistcoat, coat already discarded, the collar of his white shirt open, exposing a tantalizing bit of upper chest. His lips parted, but she never knew what it was he meant to say.

Lorna stumbled forward, flung her arms about his neck, and kissed him.

Chapter Twenty-Three

His lips felt like something warm and comforting she could sink into. Lorna knew a second of bliss before she realized he was stiff with shock. What in heaven's name was she thinking, literally throwing herself at the man? Her forwardness would disgust him; he would think her unnatural. After a heartbeat of panic, she started to pull away.

With a growl of denial, Brandon clamped his free arm around her waist and swung her inside, keeping his mouth firmly anchored to hers. Fumbling a little, he deposited the lantern on a table in the entryway and kicked the door closed. Fingers drove into her hair and held her fast while his tongue thrust into her mouth.

Lorna moaned, welcoming the invasion. Sensation speared down her throat and darted to her breasts. The points puckered, eager for his touch.

Their tongues writhed, mouths angled to allow deeper contact. The stubble on his chin rasped her skin, scouring away the despair that had driven her here, and Brandon lifted his face. His arms still held her tight, safe and warm—exactly what she needed.

Panting, he touched his forehead to hers. "What are you doing here?"

Lorna noticed her chest was heaving like his. "I wanted to see you. Is it all right?"

He gave her a crooked smile. "Of course. It's just a surprise. A very nice surprise."

She canted her hips and lifted on her toes, eliminating every particle of air between them. With a flick of her tongue, she licked the length of his throat, returning the first intimate touch he'd given her, what now felt like a lifetime ago.

A shudder passed through his neck and shoulders. Lorna reveled in the evidence of her feminine power.

Emboldened, she whispered, "Take me to bed, Brandon."

A groan came from deep in his chest.

For the first time, she glanced at her surroundings over his shoulder. The neat flagstone floors and clean white walls could have been the belowstairs of any respectable house. He lived somewhere in these dusky halls.

"Do you know what you're asking me, Lorna?"

She'd spent months listening to her raving brother describe the acts he wanted performed by a prostitute. Virgin she might be, but Lorna's knowledge of the bedroom was not, she thought, lacking. She gave him what she hoped was a seductive smile. Her hips swayed as she moved deeper into the house. Her hand alighted on the knob of a nearby door. "I know."

She opened the door, expecting a bedroom, or perhaps a sitting room, but found instead a wrapped body on a table. She gasped, hand flying to her throat.

Behind her, Brandon cursed. Gently, he pulled her back and closed the door. "Not here, Lorna. Let me take you somewhere nicer."

She gave him a reassuring pat on his chest. "I was just surprised. I'm not horrified or offended, Brandon. You won't frighten me away. I want to be here. With you."

A look of profound tenderness filled his eyes. He brushed the tip of his nose over hers. "You're sure?" he whispered.

"Yes."

The next instant, she was in his arms as he strode down the hall. He paused to open the door to a small sitting room, illuminated by an oil lamp on a little, round table. Brandon continued through the space to the next room.

Like the sitting room, the bedchamber was modest in size. She saw a narrow bed and a washstand, and through another door, slightly ajar, caught a glimpse of a wardrobe. A dressing room, she decided. Coals burned in the small fireplace set into one wall, with a kettle warming on the simple brick hearth. Compared to the lavish homes she'd visited of late, Brandon's apartment was refreshingly unassuming. It was cozy and comfortable, and suited Lorna perfectly.

With infinite care, Brandon set her on her feet, then removed her cloak. Lifting the garment to hang it on a wall hook, Brandon frowned. "This is much too large for you," he said, indicating a wide swath of material at the bottom, which had been dragged through wet and dirty streets.

Lorna didn't want to discuss her cloak, or anything else. If they started talking about trivial matters, she would lose her nerve and have to go home, humiliated. Her heart thudded in her throat, but she kept her gaze steady on Brandon as she unfastened the first button on the front of her dress.

The surgeon drew a sharp breath. "Let me."

She watched his face while he worked, the raw desire evident in his features echoing her own. Brandon's fingers slid beneath the material, parting it wide and pushing it off her shoulders. His mouth settled onto her neck. Kissing her with tongue and lips, he nudged her head back, exposing more of her throat to his sensual assault.

A tiny moan burst from her lips. Lorna's eyes drifted shut. Hot, tingling sensation poured through her bones, melting her joints. Brandon's lips drifted to her shoulder while he tugged her dress over her hips, leaving her in her shift. She wore no stays, and her tight nipples were tormented by the cool, thin cotton of her plain undergarment.

It was on the tip of her tongue to insist Brandon remove his waistcoat, but then his teeth closed lightly over her collarbone and words escaped her. Heavy fullness pulsed through her intimate flesh. "Ah!" she gasped. Her hands clasped either side of his head, but she didn't know whether to push him away or hold him close.

For a woman new even to embracing, such exquisite sensation was nearly beyond bearing.

"Are you all right?" Brandon's concern cut through the fog of lust. "We can stop. If you've changed your mind—"

"I don't want to stop."

She brought her mouth to his and gave a bold thrust of her tongue. While they kissed, Lorna unfastened his waistcoat buttons. Without the kiss to serve as distraction, she'd never have the gumption to touch him so brazenly, but Lorna's bravery deserted her when he was down to shirt and trews.

He squeezed her waist. "My turn again."

When he started lifting the hem of her shift, her throat tightened. "Bed!" she yelped. "When do we go to bed?"

The corners of his eyes crinkled in a smile, Brandon stepped around her to turn back the covers. Lorna dove for the protection of the wool blanket and pulled it to her neck. The bedding part she thought she comprehended and knew she desired, but somehow, she'd failed to imagine this step of the proceedings, this slow unveiling, intimately exposing themselves to one another.

With a husky chuckle, Brandon removed his braces and tugged his shirt free of his waistband. "Would you feel easier if I undressed first? I want you to be comfortable."

Lorna's lips pulled between her teeth and she wiggled her chin back and forth, considering.

Before she answered, Brandon pulled his shirt over his head, revealing a broad chest peppered with dark hair. Flat, brown nipples puckered in the cool air. Lean muscle created masculine angles on his abdomen, guiding her eyes to the undeniable bulge behind the placket of his trousers.

He was so handsome, she thought, despairing, while she was all sharp elbows, disobedient hair, and an alarming quantity of freckles.

Brandon didn't hesitate in moving on to the fall buttons. His gaze was steady on her; he evidenced none of the trembling anxiety she felt.

"Are you not afraid?" she asked, her voice scarcely more than a whisper.

His thumbs hooked into his waistband, he pushed his trousers and smalls down over lean hips. Her eyes went to the patch of dark hair at the apex of his thighs, from which his hard shaft rose, long and thick. The ache inside her grew more insistent.

"I'm only afraid you'll change your mind."

She shook her head. Lorna didn't think she'd ever wanted anything more. "I won't change my mind."

Brandon lifted one side of the blanket and slid into the bed. She scooted over to make room. He brushed a stray curl from her cheek and kissed her gently. "Are *you* afraid?"

She almost wasn't. With the weight of his long body against hers, and his hands touching her so softly, she couldn't remember ever feeling so secure—but still not entirely.

He nipped her earlobe; she gave a little gasp. Brandon seemed to like that. He surged against her, rubbing his hard length against her hip. She loved the feeling of his masculine body holding her tight. "I can't promise it won't hurt at first," he rasped, "but I swear I'll make it good for you, if you give me the chance."

His tongue swirled around the shell of her ear before dipping inside. Lorna prickled all over as she broke into a fine sheen of sweat.

"It's not that." She swallowed as his tongue found her heartbeat on her throat. The pace of that organ increased again, pulsing into his mouth. Beneath the covers, Lorna's legs grew restless, bending and flexing. The cotton shift felt like the most sensual silk against her heated skin. The confession tumbled out before she could restrain herself. "I'm only a little uncertain because…because I'm not as well-formed as you."

Brandon lifted his head. One dark brow arched over eyes hazy with desire. "I take leave to contradict that claim."

Lorna's hand reached for her head. Deliberately, she tangled her fingers into the curls and clenched her fist so she wouldn't scratch. "There isn't much to my bosom, I fear. And I'm too skinny. Ugly."

Unbidden, memories of Thomas in his final sickness filled her mind. *"You're too scrawny to fuck,"* he'd said. In the depths of his madness, he'd not recognized her as his sister, but simply as a woman. And as a woman, she'd been judged undesirable.

At the memory of those jeering words, Lorna shuddered. Brandon's jawline firmed. "Who told you that? It's a damned lie."

She released a ragged exhale. He was just being kind, but she appreciated the gesture. "It doesn't matter," she said, stroking his temple.

Brandon harrumphed and propped up on his elbows. A lock of chestnut hair fell over his forehead, giving him a rakish air. "Well, whomever leveled that insult against you is a fool. You'll allow, please, that I do possess a certain degree of expertise on the subject of anatomical fitness."

He was so stern, she couldn't help but giggle.

The callous of his right index finger traced the bridge of her nose, her cheekbones, the sweep of her jaw. His eyes followed, as though fascinated by what he saw. He slid down, dragging his erect shaft along the outside of her thigh, and pulling back the blanket as he went. Brandon performed the same careful inspection of her collarbones, shoulders, and arms. "The subject's skeleton is exquisite," he declared. "Fine-boned." He spread her hand out on his, palm to palm, and reverently kissed each finger. "Proportions skew just to the long, given the overall height, rendering the subject delicate and graceful."

Brandon rose on his knees and pulled her to sitting, putting her face level with his powerful thighs and male organ. Lorna had only a few seconds to admire the view before he perfunctorily worked her shift over her hips and pulled it off.

Lorna started to protest, but the flare of heat in his gray eyes stopped the words in her throat. Brandon cupped her breasts and pushed her back into the pillow. His hands kneaded and tugged, branding their possession into her flesh. "Silky and firm," he whispered. "Two perfect handfuls." The whiskers on his jaw rubbed over her collarbone. "How dare you insult these gorgeous tits?"

The coarse word prompted a laugh of surprise. Brandon flashed a cocky smile, then dipped his head. His hand was replaced by the tip of his nose tracing circles around her nipple, the delicate touch a whisper on her skin. She arched her back, wanting more.

"You smell like honey. And you taste ..." His mouth closed, drawing her flesh deep into his mouth.

Pleasure lanced through her body. Lorna cried out just as Brandon made an appreciative sound.

As he settled in to feast first at one breast, and then the other, the weight of Brandon's body slowly shifted onto hers. His skin was suede-soft and warmer than any blanket. She rubbed her belly against his chest and wrapped her arms about his neck. He found her hand and pinned it above her head. Their fingers laced and held tight.

With his mouth and other hand, Brandon set out to explore her like an undiscovered country. He kissed, licked, and stroked a path from sternum to navel, which he treated to a tongue kiss as passionate as those he'd given her mouth. Broad shoulders pinned her hips. Lorna squirmed from side to side, wanting her legs free.

"Look at you," he murmured into the curve of her hip. "Like cream dusted with cocoa."

Her freckles, she realized he meant. But he didn't seem to find them repugnant. Instead, he laved her as though she was a delectable treat. Some hard knot, buried deep inside her chest, released. Lorna's body undulated beneath Brandon's skillful ministrations. Here, in this small room, on this narrow bed, she felt womanly for the first time in her life. Not just accepted, but desired. Wanton. Beautiful.

Bolder now, Lorna allowed her hands to roam his shoulders and back, testing the firm muscles she found there. When she dragged her fingers up his spine, Brandon rose and covered her with his body. Lips parted and pupils wide, he brought his panting mouth to hers, treating her to a searing kiss.

One of her legs hooked around his. She dragged her foot up the back of his calf, the light fur there luxuriously soft.

Brandon's hips flexed. The bulging head of his member nudged her opening. With a hiss, he shifted and brought a hand between them. "Don't want to hurt you," he said, almost in a daze. His fingers parted her.

Now that he was touching her aching flesh, her desire became a thud she felt, and almost heard, in her ears. Her wetness eased the way for his fingers to press into her core, dipping in and out. Brandon's thumb flicked over her taut bundle of nerves, while two fingers stretched and filled her. She scrabbled at his neck and shoulders, anywhere she could gain purchase. A keening sound started low in her throat. With every thrust, he brushed over that swollen bud, tormenting her.

"Don't stop," she choked out on a sob. "Please, please, please."

"I'll never stop," he rasped, his wicked fingers driving her beyond reason. "Come on, sweet girl. Give it to me now. Just like that." His words were almost meaningless, just sounds of approval and encouragement. Somehow, pleasing her brought Brandon pleasure, knowledge which fed her own. Her mouth fell open wide. "God, yes," he continued. "So wet. So good. There?"

"There," Lorna cried. "Just there. Yes. Yes!"

Indescribable pleasure overwhelmed her senses. Her womb throbbed, and her inner muscles clamped tight around Brandon's fingers. He kissed her deeply, swallowing the sounds of her ecstasy.

Gradually, the flood began to recede, and she became aware of his thigh moving between hers. She gladly parted her legs. If he could bring her such pleasure with his hand, she could scarcely wait to fully join her body with his.

"You, too," she breathed. "I want you to feel this, too."

"I will, sweetheart." Brandon held himself on his forearms; his hands cradled her head. "You're so lovely."

Reaching down, Lorna took him in hand. His nostrils flared on a sharp inhale. He was thick, heavy, and so hard against her palm. Delicate, too, she thought. The skin was thin as gossamer. Easily bruised. She must take great care.

Her thumb swept over the tip, encountering a slick tear. "Come inside where it's safe."

Slowly, he pressed inward. He stretched and filled her like nothing she could have imagined. There was pain, but she welcomed it. It meant he was hers. If only for this one night, he trusted her to house his body in her own.

An enormous emotion she couldn't possibly contain pressed against her ribs. Tears leaked from the corners of her eyes. She let out a gasp.

Brandon's lust-hazed eyes snapped into focus. "Damnation, I'm sorry. Breathe, sweet girl. Be still a moment and accustom yourself."

She shook her head. "Not the pain. I'm just…happy," she sobbed.

A confused look creased his brow, but then his eyes rolled back in his head and he gave a lopsided smile. "God, you feel good." He gave an experimental roll of his hips. "So tight. I never thought… *Mmmm…*"

Seeing how well he liked being inside her made Lorna rock her hips in reply to his movement. The pain was already diminishing, and if she could help him experience pleasure like she had, then that's what she wanted to do.

"Like this?" she asked.

His weight shifted onto one arm. His right hand cupped the side of her face. "Perfect." He pulled back a little and moved forward, filling her again. Again, she canted to meet his thrust. "Bring your legs 'round me."

Lorna did as he asked. If possible, he was even deeper inside her than before. And it felt … good. The pain was gone.

"You like that?" Brandon asked.

But she didn't have to answer. He knew she did. He knew, and he gave her that exquisite stroke over and over. She was wet again; she could tell by the way he easily slipped in and out, and the lush sound of flesh clapping together. Brandon's thumb rubbed at her lips. Lorna sucked the tip into her mouth.

Another climax built deep in her belly. Brandon stoked the flames higher and higher until she couldn't breathe or see or be. Lorna didn't exist anymore. There was only Them, and this beautiful pleasure they created together.

Her body felt wrenched inside out as she came. Brandon moved with abandon, hips pumping, slapping against her bud with every thrust, keeping the climax going on and on. His hands clenched in her hair, pulling her head back as he strained against her, stilled, and groaned his own release.

For long moments, they lay in a heap of sweaty, tangled limbs. Panting and kissing, they clung together while their bodies recovered. Lorna felt Brandon soften inside her. She clenched her muscles, wanting to keep him there longer. It had been so lovely to hold him like this. So very lovely.

Brandon's growl rumbled at her ear. "Watch yourself, my dear, or you'll have me rutting on you all night long. I don't want to cause you injury."

Lorna grinned. Brandon lifted his head and met her smile with a questioning look.

"You mean we can do it again?"

•••

The knock woke him at once, as it always did. Brandon's eyes snapped open. In the split second before he lurched out of the bed, he felt the weight of the woman in his arms. Nestled together like spoons, his body curled protectively around Lorna.

Carefully, he slid his arm out from beneath her shoulders and swung his leg over her, hoping to reach the floor with a minimum of jostling the mattress. In her sleep, Lorna frowned and burrowed into the warm place he'd left behind. Brandon smoothed the pad of his thumb over the crease in her brow.

Something had driven her to his bed tonight. The desolation he'd read in her eyes told the story, though the details were still a mystery.

Morning would be soon enough to uncover the particulars, he decided as he pulled on his trousers and dressing robe. He'd let himself get caught up in the passion when Lorna arrived, welcoming the way her ardor diminished his own gloominess brought on by the lecture. She'd wanted him as a woman wants a man, but she'd needed him on a deeper, primal level, too. Her kisses tasted of loneliness and hurt.

Thank God she'd come to him, instead of another. The thought of Lorna giving herself to any other man made him insane.

He checked his watch lying atop the clothespress—one thirty—then retrieved the lantern and opened his chamber door. Looking back at the slight woman in his bed, he wasn't sure how he'd ever bring himself to let her out of it again.

Cold reality brought him down from his fantasies when he opened the alley door to find a grinning Slee on the stoop.

"Evenin', sir," the thief said, tugging his cap in a deferential gesture. "Harty Choke's done you proud tonight, Mr. Dewhurst, sir. We've got a brood mare for you. Seven months gone I'd say," he added with a wink.

Brandon's gut clenched. How he despised Slee, the murderous filth. But he couldn't interrupt the supply of bodies to the school in the middle of an anatomy term, and with McGully deep in his study of pregnancy, besides. As soon as possible, Brandon would find new resurrectionists to do business with. Maybe that Crib Cross Gang that had given Slee's Artichoke Boys such trouble these past weeks.

He stepped back to make way for the body to be carried in. He directed the men to deposit it on the table in the receiving room beside the other body, just long enough to verify the condition of the corpse.

"Upstairs, if you please," he requested, "to Mr. McGully's dissection room."

The master surgeon would be delighted with the specimen, and eager to perform the dissection at the earliest moment. That meant Brandon must take charge of tomorrow morning's student dissection.

With the new body situated, Brandon hustled Slee and his crew out the door. He breathed a sigh, relieved to have them out from under the same roof as Lorna.

A chill hung in the air when he returned to his bedchamber. He crouched beside the hearth to build the fire back up.

"Where were you?" asked a sleepy voice. "Come back to bed."

He smiled as he washed his hands at the basin before shucking his robe and trousers and nudging his bedmate aside. "I like the sound of that," he said. He placed his hand on her stomach.

Lorna squealed and batted at his wrist. "You're freezing!"

"The water was cold," he protested. "Help me get warm." Playfully, he grabbed the back of her neck with his other hand, then patted her all over while she yelped and tried to squirm away.

Her laughing face thrashed from side to side, sending the wild curls he loved whipping over her cheeks. Brandon gripped her face. The smile slipped from her wide, gorgeous mouth; desire kindled in her blue-green eyes.

There was no preamble to the kiss. One second their gazes met, the next their mouths were locked together. Intense need flashed to his groin. Brandon felt his cock twitch and thud as it quickly grew erect.

He petted her and found her eager body ready. Still, he didn't want to overtax her. After their intercourse, he'd loved her once more with his mouth and hands. She'd be sore come morning.

Lorna broke the kiss. "I want you." Her legs hitched around his thighs, drawing him closer to her center. Slim fingers dug into his buttocks, urging him.

"Greedy wench," he growled. "You make it deuced difficult for a man to be considerate of how you'll feel tomorrow."

The smile that curved her lips was pure sin. "Only consider how we feel right now."

How could he resist such a command?

• • •

They broke apart, gasping. The night had become a blur of love-making and dozing just long enough to recover their strength to explore one another more. Brandon had never felt so utterly sated. Lorna's delectable body had wrung every drop from him. An edgy sort of energy kept him returning to her, although a gathering exhaustion threatened to pull him into slumber for a week.

"Why can't we stop?" Lorna asked between panting breaths.

In the faint light from the fire, he studied her features. Her skin was flushed. Perspiration like delicate drops of dew mingled with the freckles scattered over her cheekbones. Her lips were plumper than usual, swollen by the good use to which they'd been put this night.

"It's the bed's fault," he rasped. Reaching for the pitcher of small beer on his nightstand, he poured some of the cool liquid into a mug and handed it to her. She gave him a questioning look over the rim as she took a swallow.

"Too narrow," he explained. "We have to pile on top of each other to prevent tumbling to the floor."

One side of her lips twitched in a smirk. She glanced about the room as she passed him the beverage. "I like your apartment."

Brandon drained the mug, then reached across her to deposit it on the table. "It's underground. Dark like a tomb."

"Cozy," she said with a reproving nod. "It's like a secret den tucked away from the world."

Did she need sanctuary so very much, then? A protective warmth filled him. He could keep her here and shield her from her troubles, never allowing anything bad to happen to her. The idea was madness, the result of too much sexual activity and exhaustion. He forced it away.

Propped on one elbow, he traced the bottom arc of her petal-pink areola. As it happened, most of her freckles were confined to her face, shoulders, upper chest and arms, but he had uncovered a few others, such as this lone dot on the underside of her left breast, accentuating the porcelain skin like a beauty mark. Reverently, he kissed the spot.

She hummed with pleasure. Lorna was so deliciously responsive to his touch. The desire he'd felt crackling between them from the beginning had erupted into an inferno. Everything about her body enticed him, from her pretty toes to her glorious hair. But it wasn't just the physical that called to him. Beneath her delicate surface, Lorna Robbins possessed a unique kind of strength. Life had caused her great pain, but Lorna absorbed the hurt and kept going for the sake of her young brother and the servants who depended upon her.

Far be it from him to complain about the soul-changing lovemaking they'd shared, but Brandon wished she'd confide what had happened to bring her here. He would face down her foes and wipe away her pain, if only she would let him.

His hand slid to her hip and he met her gaze. As much as he rued ending the night's magic, he had to ask her some difficult questions.

Fear flashed in her eyes. Faster than he'd have thought possible, Lorna twisted from beneath him and clambered onto his back. With a surprised "*Oof*," Brandon collapsed onto his stomach.

"What are you doing?" he asked in an exaggerated, strained voice. In truth, her slight weight felt pleasant.

Her arms snaked under his chest as she rested her cheek between his shoulder blades. "I can't do it again," she said, her tone apologetic. "I ache in places I didn't know I possessed."

"Lorna, I wasn't—"

"The look in your eyes—"

There was an awkward pause. "Oh," they said in unison.

Brandon chuckled. A lock of her hair tickled his nose, but he didn't brush it aside. Tonight was an anomaly, he knew; he would savor every moment of it—every moment of *her*.

Something large loomed just over the horizon of his thoughts. His heart flipped in his chest. Swallowing the sensation away, Brandon tried to distract himself. Perhaps if he confided in Lorna, she'd see he was trustworthy of her confidence in return.

"We're friends, aren't we?" he began.

On his back, he felt her shoulders shift. "I should hope so, after what we've done." He sensed her hesitate. "I've never had many friends. Nelly and Alice and Marjorie—Lady Fenton, that is—they're the first friends of my own sex I've had since Daniel was small."

"It must have been difficult to find the time to socialize with young ladies your own age, what with the responsibility of caring for a baby."

"Yes." The single word sounded small and forlorn.

"Generally, my childhood and youth was ideal in every way," Brandon said. "I hadn't a care in the world beyond trying to live up to the high standards set by my brothers. Or best them, if I could." He smiled against the sheets as he recalled being stranded at the top of an elm tree his brother Hubert dared him to climb. He'd been petrified when a wind kicked up, swaying his perch to and fro. Unwilling to cry out in fear, however, he'd stoically clung to whip-thin branches until the second eldest, Francis, had come to fetch him down.

"Besides my brothers, I have some excellent friends. But I know what it is to not have time for them. These days, my work keeps me much occupied."

Lorna sat up, her haunches bracketing his hips. Brandon felt a featherlight touch run down the column of his spine. "Your work is important. You help people every day. It must be very rewarding."

Her thumbs dug circles in his shoulder muscles, easing some of the soreness their exertions had generated.

He grunted when she hit a particularly tender spot. "Teaching is rewarding. And tending my patients, certainly. There are frustrations. Like the watchmaker, whose foot I amputated. He fell into a fever that night. After three days, he died."

Lorna's hands stilled. "Oh, Brandon. I'm sorry. You tried your best. I know you did."

"Of course I did," he said, a little too gruffly. Drawing a deep breath, he turned his face to exhale directly into the mattress. She didn't deserve to be lashed out at, just because he was frustrated by his inability to prevent infection from following operations. He kept his face planted until the need for air forced him to turn once more.

Tentatively, she started massaging again. Brandon sighed. A night of sexual repletion, followed by a back rub—a man could get used to this.

"Worst of all is getting the bodies," he said, his voice slurring as drowsiness firmly took hold. The rhythmic movements of her hands lulled him while the deep kneading of his muscles helped him to relax entirely. "Hate those thieves."

"The resurrection men, you mean?" She sounded amused.

"Yeah," he let out on a sigh. Too heavy to hold open any longer, his eyelids slid home. "Nasty criminals. Lowest part of this life."

She squeezed his biceps and curled over to kiss his cheek. "You do what must be done." Behind his lids, Lorna was talking to him in the too-large gown she'd worn to the Heapbys' ball. It dangled precariously off one shoulder. He needed to tug it up. He wanted to let it fall.

"You're a rare man, Brandon Dewhurst," she went on. "Not many could do your work. It's necessary, even the distasteful parts."

"Nice of you to say so." He clasped her hands as they lined up for the dance. As the music began, he leaned forward and licked her neck. God, she tasted good. Beside them, Lady Fenton laughed. Her belly shook dangerously. With a start, Brandon realized it wasn't Lorna's dress that would fall, but Lady Fenton's belly. It would rip free of her body and then—

"Dead. Her and all three babies. And I have to watch it happen."

Then the music began and he led Lorna into the dance.

Chapter Twenty-Four

For the first time in the week since Lorna had come to stay with Marjorie, they were not hosting company for tea. As much as Marjorie adored being surrounded by people, Lorna was grateful for a peaceful afternoon.

"How was your visit with Mr. Manning?" she asked her hostess.

Marjorie glanced up from where she was pouring three cups of tea; she expected her husband to join them momentarily. "I didn't see Mr. Manning. Doctor Possons came. Fenton has insisted I consult a physician all along, and has now forbid Manning from continuing with me." Her tone was decidedly acid. "The children all seem to be healthy, though Possons would never know, since he'd never lower himself to touch a patient. They flop around each other like a pile of puppies from morning to night. Pesky babies." She huffed. Gradually, her vexed expression gave way to a warm smile. "I cannot wait to hold them in my arms, Lorna. I pray they will remain as good of friends on the outside as they have been on the inside."

Despite Marjorie's grave peril, Lorna couldn't help envying her just a bit. To have so much joy to anticipate—an entire family, all at once.

Lord Fenton strode into the room. He bent over the back of the chaise to kiss his wife's cheek. The burnished copper of his hair was an attractive contrast to her ladyship's sable. He murmured something into her ear. Marjorie's eyes widened and shot to Lorna.

"Miss Robbins," said Lord Fenton, "if you would be so kind." He gestured to the hallway.

Puzzled, Lorna preceded her host into the corridor.

Lord Fenton tucked her hand into the crook of his elbow and strolled toward the central stairway. "Mr. Dewhurst has come to see you," he said as they descended one flight. "He awaits you in the library."

Lorna's heart stuttered. A seed of light pulsed in her belly, but Lorna fought to quash it. "I cannot speak for Lady Fenton, but I'm sure it would be no trouble if Mr. Dewhurst joined us for tea," she said, gesturing over her shoulder toward the parlor.

"He asked to speak with you in private." Lord Fenton stepped off the landing and, with fingertips light on the small of her back, guided her to the nearby library. He stopped just outside the door and regarded her kindly. "I am not your male relative, but you are staying under my roof, and are therefore under my protection. Do not hesitate to call upon that protection, should you have need of it, Miss Robbins."

"Thank you, my lord, I shall."

The viscount pointed with his chin. "Will you see him, or shall I show him the door? I consider Dewhurst a friend, but if his presence is unwelcome, I'll just make sure he knows there are no hard feelings involved as I pitch him into the street."

Lorna stifled an indelicate snort. "For the moment, that won't be necessary, my lord. Should I change my mind, I'll be sure to alert you."

Lord Fenton patted her hand and left Lorna to her fate.

Inside the library, she closed the door and took the space of a breath to compose herself before turning.

Brandon faced the door, his back to the fireplace, with legs braced and hands clasped behind his back, a soldier at ease. She hadn't seen him in a week and now, with a lover's knowledge, she feasted on the sight of him. The long lines of his legs were displayed in snug gray-blue breeches and brown top boots. Lorna recalled the feel of those powerful limbs tangled with her own. She swallowed.

Broad shoulders filled his darker blue coat. Lorna remembered clutching those shoulders and arms for all she was worth as she came apart in his bed, as though only they were strong enough to keep her tethered to the mortal plane.

Gray eyes, which had held such heat and tenderness when they lay together, were now the focal points of a portrait of anxiety. Lines bracketed a mouth that had joined with hers in such melting sweetness. Her heart compelled her to race across the room and kiss away whatever it was that troubled him; fear rooted her to the spot.

His steady, appraising gaze never faltered. He was waiting, as he'd done from the first. Lorna gathered her fortitude and wits, hoping she'd find the words to—

"Where the devil have you been?"

Lorna's mouth popped open.

Brandon waited again for her to speak—for perhaps half a second. "You haven't answered my notes. You've avoided my calls." He advanced at a measured pace as he spoke. "Of course, I just learned from Alice you were not even home for my notes or calls, as you'd decamped to another house entirely." As he drew nearer, Lorna discovered she'd been mistaken in her initial assessment. His gray eyes were anything but anxious. Embers crackled deep in his irises, ready to burst into a conflagration, but for the restraint holding them in check, evident in the tense lines at the corners of his eyes and the hard set to his jaw.

His height bested hers by more than half a foot; she felt every inch of his advantage as he drew closer. Her back touched the door. Still he advanced, squeezing the space between them like a cheese press, forcing out the air like so much whey.

An unfamiliar aroma drifted from his clothes. It burned the back of her nose ever so slightly, like the faintest fume of vinegar. It was a surgical smell, she decided. Some sort of chemical. Beneath that unpleasantness, though, she detected his own, warm scent, steady and sure. The queer combination unsettled her further.

"Why did you leave, Lorna?"

This time, he did give her time to respond, but her head was swimming. Every excuse she'd thought of for this eventuality vanished in a wisp of smoke. Of a certain, she couldn't tell him the truth: that they were at odds, battling for the corpse of a still-living woman who, at this moment, sipped tea in her boudoir.

Squeezing her eyes to try to clear her head, she said, "I'm not... Please, just give me a moment."

"You've had a week," he snapped. "Are you ashamed of what we did?" A trace of hurt colored his words.

"Shouldn't I be?" She'd asked herself that question countless times over the past seven days. She *should* feel shame for what they'd done. Lorna had thrown herself at Brandon and demanded he take her to bed. But, God help her, she wasn't ashamed—which didn't say much of her character. "I've cheapened myself, have I not?"

Brandon's nostrils flared. He grabbed her forearm; Lorna felt cold waves of rage pumping through his body. "If I'd wanted to degrade a woman in my bed, I'd have employed the services of an experienced whore."

Her elbow caught his chest as she shoved her way past him. She reached the middle of the room and rounded. "As opposed to an inexperienced one, such as myself?"

"I didn't say that." Brandon followed and jabbed a finger at her chest. "Don't you dare twist my words. I'm not the one who ran away, Lorna. I asked you to stay."

True. When she awoke in his bed, she'd found a note on the nightstand:

Teaching upstairs. Back in two hours. Please don't go. Yours, B.

"Had you done so, you'd have received an honorable offer of marriage as soon as my class ended. Instead, I've spent a week knocking on the wrong blasted door."

His stubborn chin still registering annoyance, Brandon snatched her hands and dropped to a knee. "Miss Robbins," he said in a testy tone, "will you do me the very great honor of becoming my wife?"

For a minute, her resolve wavered. He was vexed just now, but Lorna knew Brandon genuinely cared for her. They'd become friends. And when they came together in bed he'd made her feel desirable for the first time in her life. To be able to feel that way again and again was temptation, indeed.

And Lorna knew Brandon was lonely. His work isolated him from his social peers. He spent his days with students and patients, and his nights with resurrectionists. For one beautiful evening, she'd been able to cherish him, to ease his loneliness just as he'd eased hers. Lorna had always thought caring for Daniel was enough, but she'd found a special satisfaction in caring for this stalwart man.

If they married, Lorna and Brandon could give that gift of companionship and caring to one another. They could, and they would. She knew it. For a few, shining seconds, she saw it all so clearly: years passing gently with Brandon at her side; she supporting him in his work; Daniel, safe from the threat of a guardian; children of her own, raised in a home free of madness and despair.

In her bleaker moments, Lorna had thought of the life she presently lived as a nightmare. How wonderful it would be if all of this—the poverty, the corpse stealing, Daniel's guardian—were, in fact, a bad dream. Maybe she was trapped in a cursed sleep, like the princess in one of the fairy tales Brandon was always botching. His proposal was her opportunity to awaken from her bleak existence and embrace a beautiful future.

But reality squelched her rosy vision with hard truths. Lorna wasn't cursed by a malevolent fairy, but with the carelessness of her forebears. And as dear as Brandon was to her, he was no prince capable of sweeping her away from all of this. If they married, he would insist upon assuming Thomas's debts. Lorna couldn't allow Brandon to take on that responsibility. He was a surgeon, not a wealthy, entitled lord. Marrying her might very well ruin him.

If they wed, he would eventually find out she was a member of a resurrection gang. Even if she never again engaged in her dismal profession, having to conceal this secret for the rest of her life seemed too great a task. He'd voiced his distaste for the criminals his profession necessitated he engage with in commerce; what would he say if he found out he'd bedded one? How much more would he despise her if he learned he'd married her under false pretenses?

Oh, unfair, unfair.

Gently, she laid a palm on top of his head, as though offering a blessing. "Thank you for the compliment of your offer, Brandon."

"That was not a yes."

"I'm sorry."

Rising, he tugged the bottom of his goldenrod waistcoat. All of his previous anger seemed to have melted away. "May I ask why not?"

Fair question. "I promised Lady Fenton I'd stay with her through her confinement."

"We don't have to marry at once," he said. "Unless you find you're increasing, of course. That would change matters." A hint of a smile ghosted across his lips. "Most likely, Lady Fenton will be taken to childbed before you know anything certain about your own condition."

Lorna's stomach lurched at the reminder of her recklessness. She sat in a chair to cover her agitation. "There is no worry there. My…" Heat flooded her cheeks. She cleared her throat. "Two days ago."

"Ah." Brandon rocked back on his heels. "Good. Well, then, you can stay on with Lady Fenton, and we'll be married sometime after her confinement. It will take time for the banns to be called, after all."

Why must he argue? His persistence was cruel, forcing her to suppress her own desires and try to shoo him away. She blurted out the first thing that came to mind. "Alice has offered to sponsor me for the spring Season. She has hopes of making a fine match for me."

Brandon crossed to the window. A bleak, dribbling rain fell. Everything, from sky to earth and all between, was awash in shades of gray and brown. His fingertip traced a rivulet down the pane. Then his hand curled into a fist and he lightly knuckled the glass.

"Is that what you want?" he inquired of the window. "A *ton* marriage?"

Lorna shrugged, even though his back was to her. "Isn't that what all young ladies are taught to want?" she prevaricated. No matter that she could not accept his suit, she couldn't bring herself to lie to him outright. Still, he must be made to abandon this impossible dream of their being together.

He pivoted, his eyes once more bright with emotion. Lorna steeled herself for another show of temper. Instead, he crouched before her; his hands curled around the arms of the chair, caging her.

"Is my work the problem, Lorna? The fact that I'm in trade? I'm not a wealthy man, but my income is sufficient to support both you and Daniel."

She wanted to weep. "What you do is so important, Brandon. You help people. You save lives."

"But it isn't enough," he said grimly. "I'll never have a title. I'll never be more than The Honorable Mr. Brandon Dewhurst."

"Do you think that matters to me?" she demanded.

"Why would you want a Season," he countered, "if not to be showcased on the great marriage mart? If it's only a matter of wishing to attend balls and parties, I'd be happy to squire you about—as your husband."

Lorna took his face in her hands. "Dear Brandon," she said sadly, "we won't be marrying at all. I'm sorry."

His nostrils flared and he shoved to his feet. "Is there someone else?"

"There's no one else."

He pulled his hands through his hair. "Why are you being so difficult? I took your virtue, Lorna. We must marry."

She stood, drawing herself to her full, unimpressive height. "No."

Brandon grabbed her arms and pulled her against his chest. His fingers drove into her hair, scattering pins and releasing her curls. "Have you forgotten this?" he hissed, then crushed his mouth to hers.

Of course she hadn't forgotten. She would remember him always, and was glad to have the memory of one more kiss. Her blood sang as she melted against him; she hummed in the back of her throat. But when he tried to deepen the kiss, she pulled away, even though the action felt like tearing out her own heart.

"It would be best if you leave now."

He wiped a hand down his jaw. "I know you aren't indifferent to me. Marriage between us makes sense. This isn't over, Lorna."

Her hands were shaking badly, but her voice was remarkably steady. "I'm sorry, but it is. And I cannot see you again."

"I *will* win your hand."

"Please don't try."

Chapter Twenty-Five

"I must say," said Lord Sheridan Zouche, dropping his head against the back of his horsehair armchair, "this is certainly an improvement by several degrees over our days at The Hog's Teeth."

He drew deeply from the cigar in his hand, rolled the smoke in his mouth, then exhaled three precise rings.

"But any time we gather," Sheri went on, "I can't help but remember the many nights we whiled away in that worthy establishment."

Brandon took a pull of his own cigar. He tried to imitate the way Sheri savored the tobacco, but, to him, the smoke tasted of burnt dirt. He blew it out in an inelegant huff, then cleared the flavor from his tongue with a sip of Madeira, which he could unreservedly endorse as excellent.

The furnishings and refreshments were far superior to the plank tables and benches of their youthful watering spot in Oxford. Indeed, Brandon suspected their corner of this room easily rivaled the finest gentleman's club in London.

Alas, a corner was all the erudite surroundings they had. Across the room, Henry De Vere sat at his desk, poring over the ledgers for the family shipping business, De Vere and Sons. In fact, the company had been started as a joint venture by Henry and his elder brother, Baron De Vere. As yet, there were no sons to take up the family trade, but Brandon supposed one must keep an optimistic eye to the future in these matters.

Beyond the walls of Henry's office, the company's warehouse bustled with the activity of workmen moving barrels of wine and crates of cigars, the cargo having just arrived from Charleston, by way of the Dutch Antilles.

Henry growled as he made slashes of ink through several lines in his books. His flaxen hair stood up on one side where he had clutched it with a fist.

"I wager you don't view our Madeira and cigars a step above the old days, do you?" Brandon inquired.

Henry snorted. "Like hell. At least I got to enjoy myself back then. While you two drink up my profits, I must do battle with these wretched numbers. This entire trip to Town has been nothing but one headache after another, dealing with this shipment." He glumly regarded his mathematical nemeses, who seemed to be winning the battle.

Sheri's eyebrow shot up. Somehow, he seemed to invoke the sense of staring one down through his quizzing glass without actually reaching for it. "I beg your pardon, but I seem to recall we had quite a bit of sport the other night at the expense of our favorite poet."

Henry snorted. "That *was* fun," he admitted. "You should have been there, Bran. Lady Fay helped us pull one over on stupid old Prick-ring."

Brandon chuckled at Henry's unflattering moniker for their old rival from university, Sir Godwin Prickering, a self-important jackanapes with delusions of literary grandeur.

"She got him all wound up, and then left him hanging. Literally," Sheri added cryptically. "Elsa was magnificent." A gleam of admiration shone in his eyes.

"Why don't you marry her already?" Brandon asked. "I can't imagine any woman more suited to be your wife."

Sheri took another puff of his cigar. "Nor can I." His legs crossed at the ankle, one elegant Hessian bounced over the other. "However, I don't intend to take any wife, no matter how well-suited one female may be. Why should I, when there are so many marvelous women in the world?"

Henry made a sound of disgust. "Not that I don't admire your zeal for the cause, Sheri, but how can you stand to sleep with so many different women?"

"I managed a different one every night last week," Sheri announced proudly. "And there isn't usually any standing involved. Well…" He thoughtfully puffed on his cigar. "… sometimes."

"Don't you worry about disease?" Brandon asked. "I could show you some specimens that may put you off bed sport altogether. Penises all over with warts and ulcers, testicles swollen with gonorrhea…"

Sheri's aristocratic nose crinkled; his lips twisted in extreme distaste. "Good God, man! What the hell is wrong with you? I still can't believe you're actually serious about this surgery business. It gives me horripilation, just thinking of all the disgusting things you do on a daily basis. That dissection I witnessed haunted me for days."

"Thank you," Brandon drawled. "It's always cheering to know my chosen work is revolting to my nearest and dearest. I'll be sure to remind you of that when you come crying to me about the yellow pus oozing from your—"

"Please stop." Henry looked a little queasy, too. "Bran, you know we all admire your accomplishments. But from afar." He closed his ledger and started straightening the stacks of paperwork on his desk. "How did we get on this subject, anyway?"

"We were discussing Sheri's inveterate womanizing."

"No, the two of you were lecturing me; we weren't discussing anything." Sheri scowled at each of them in turn. "It's the same lecture you've been delivering for years. You're like a couple of parson's wives. Not even Norman gives me as much grief as you two, and Harrison never has a bad word to say."

"Norman has the patience of a saint," Brandon pointed out, "and Harrison is as accepting as they come."

As ever, Brandon felt the absence of the missing Honorables. Of course, they all kept in touch and got together when they could, but it had been two years since the entire group of five had been seated together at the same table. Even in Henry's cramped office, there was a sense of emptiness where their other friends should have been.

"But not you two?" Sheri asked.

"No, not us," Henry agreed with a cheeky grin.

"Well, enough of that," said Sheri. "What of you gents? If you're so keen on marriage, why haven't either of you done it yet?"

Henry stood and retrieved his frock coat from a hook on the wall. Following his lead, the other men likewise made ready to depart.

"I'd like to marry someday," Henry said. "Business is going well. Hopefully, it won't be too much longer before I'm in a position to support a family."

"Have anyone in mind?" Sheri asked. "What about that girl you're always chumming around with out in the country? The one with dozens of siblings?"

"You mean Miss Baxter," Henry said. "And there aren't dozens of them, only nine."

"Nine!" Sheridan shuddered. "Gads, that's a line too far, even for me. There's something obscene about that many children."

"Two of them are twins," Henry protested, as though eight pregnancies were significantly less shocking than nine.

"Too much domestic bliss for my taste," Sheri said.

The men descended the narrow stairway to the warehouse floor, boots clunking on treads worn smooth from use. The warehouse was a hive of activity, with sacks and crates being moved hither and yon, sorted by some system Brandon didn't comprehend. The foreman called out Henry's name. While their friend dealt with some administrative concern, Sheri lifted his quizzing glass and turned his piercing gaze on Brandon.

"What's that about?" Brandon pointed to the ridiculous object. "I've done nothing to earn the famed Lord Sheridan stare-down."

Sheri pursed his lips. "Don't think I haven't noticed how you've maneuvered this conversation, Dewhurst. All this talk of marriage makes a man think it must be on your mind. Have you something you wish to tell me?"

Brandon bit back a groan. He lifted his hat with one hand and raked the other through his hair before settling the garment back atop his head. "Believe it or not, Sheri, I wish I did have news to tell." He took a breath and met his friend's steady gaze. "She said no."

Sheridan winced. "I'm sorry." He clapped a hand on Brandon's arm. "The good news is, you're still a free man."

"Free of what?" Henry asked as he rejoined them. The group exited the warehouse and bundled into Sheri's coach.

Sheri answered once they settled. "Brandon had a close call with the parson's mousetrap."

Henry cast a startled look at the surgeon. "Who?"

"Lorna Robbins." Saying her name provoked a twisting pain in his gut. How could she have refused him? It didn't make any sense. She was the perfect woman for him, Brandon was certain. Why couldn't Lorna see it, too?

"Lots of ladies refuse the first offer," Henry helpfully supplied, "or so I hear. Just try again in a week or so."

"I don't think she's being coy," Brandon said. "The ways of high society are totally alien to Miss Robbins. It wouldn't cross her mind to play those games with a man. She told me she wouldn't see me again. I think she must mean it."

"You can't give up," Henry said with more vehemence than Brandon would have expected. "If you care for her—you do care for her, don't you?"

"Of course I do," Brandon answered gruffly.

"Good choice, Brandon," Sheri interjected. "I can't fault you for being besotted with that one. There's a certain spunk about Miss Robbins that appeals, isn't there?" His admiring smile was a little too warm for Brandon's liking. "Obviously, she's a sensible woman. Her refusal makes me admire her all the more. Do as she suggests and move on. There are a million women in this city to choose from, Brandon. Don't let one chit discombobulate you."

Too late, Brandon thought.

The others wanted to go on to a coffee shop to continue the outing, but Brandon's heart was no longer in spending time with his friends. Sheri and Henry had put voice to the very same debate Brandon had with himself every moment of the day. Did he take Lorna at her word and keep his distance, or did he follow his desires and keep attempting to court her? The thought of not marrying a woman whose virtue he'd taken was anathema to everything he'd been taught about gentlemanly conduct; of course, had he been minding his lessons, he'd never have allowed things with Lorna to go as far as they had. But neither could he stand the thought of forcing her into a marriage she didn't want.

"Sorry, I've patients to attend this afternoon," he lied.

When Brandon stoically withstood their protests, Sheri finally called to his driver to head for Covent Garden.

Upon arriving at the school, Brandon stepped down from the coach. He turned to bid his friends farewell.

"Brandon!"

As one, the three men turned to the source of the feminine cry. Lorna scurried over from the alley that sloped down to his own basement door, a now-familiar hound loping at her side.

"Is that her?" Henry asked in a low voice. "The one you're having fits over?"

Brandon's jaw clenched and he shot his friend a warning look.

Glancing back to Lorna, he saw her face was paler than usual, her cheeks damp.

Forgetting the interested stares of his friends, Brandon hurried to take her hands. "Lorna, what's wrong?"

She shook her head and swallowed hard. "I need you. It's Daniel."

Chapter Twenty-Six

Lorna stared through the coach window, at an incongruous patch of blue sky through which a lone starling wheeled, riding the currents high and swooping low. She craned her head to watch the bird as they passed, and kept her eyes riveted on it until the clouds obliterated the bit of blue, swallowing the little animal.

"Lorna?"

Startled, she turned to Brandon; vertical lines pleated his brow.

"It was very kind of Lord Sheridan to offer his coach," she said.

"Sheri's a good sort, in his way," Brandon answered.

He looked past her to the window. Lorna wondered, strangely, if the starling had made a re-appearance, but she wouldn't allow herself to turn and look. What if it hadn't? What if the clouds had devoured the hapless little bird? She didn't think she could bear it.

"Will you please tell me now what's wrong with Daniel?" Brandon asked.

"I'm not entirely sure." She swiped her tongue over her bottom lip. "I had a letter from Mrs. Lynch, our housekeeper at Elmwood, saying that Daniel fell and is gravely injured and to come at once. That's all I know."

On the seat across from them, Bluebell whined. Her tail thumped against the velvet upholstery. It only now occurred to Lorna that Lord Sheridan might not wish to have an enormous hound lounging in his fine carriage, but at the time when they'd loaded into the vehicle, she hadn't thought of anything but bringing the dog to see her brother. He would need the cheering and company. Bluebell had stayed with Lorna when she was unwell; having the dog with her little brother seemed somehow right. Surely, with the dog at his side, Daniel would recover. He had to.

"What is the nature of his injury?"

"I don't know."

"From where did he fall?"

The anxiety in her chest rose to her throat and wound fingers around her neck, choking her. What if that dreadful moneylender, Wiggins, was somehow involved in Daniel's injury? He had that enormous lackey, after all, and had already made vague threats. What if he'd decided to be less vague?

"I don't know! She didn't say, I tell you! Stop asking me questions I can't answer. I've told you everything. Here." She dug into the pocket of her cloak and pulled out the housekeeper's letter, now crumpled and stained. She thrust it at Brandon's chest. "Read it for yourself, if you don't believe me. There's nothing, nothing ..."

Somehow—she wasn't sure how—she was buried against Brandon's neck. His arms were around her; he made shushing sounds while rubbing her back. "It's all right, Lorna. He'll be all right. I swear."

She wanted desperately for his words to be true. And she trusted him, didn't she? When she read Mrs. Lynch's note, she only wasted enough time to fetch Bluebell from Chorley House before heading straight for Brandon. No matter that she'd vowed to stay away from him, there was no one else she trusted with seeing to Daniel's care.

A little piece of her heart suggested that Lorna had, perhaps, needed Brandon for herself, as well. She resolutely ignored it.

Sniffing loudly, she drew back and wiped her hand over the wrinkles she'd made in his attire. "Sorry."

"Hush. Come here." He settled her so her head rested on his shoulder; his arm wrapped around her waist and held her close. Solid and warm, he felt strong enough to carry the weight of the world. Her own insignificant mass was nothing.

"Tell me more about Daniel," he said.

Lorna squeezed her eyes shut against a sudden vision of her brother's frail body, broken and bloody. Of resurrectionists clawing through dirt for his small corpse. *He has to get better.*

"I would rather hear about your family," she said, her voice thin and reedy.

After a pause, Brandon started speaking, but it wasn't of his family he told her. "Did I ever tell you about my group of friends from university, The Honorables?"

She shook her head.

"There are five of us. Besides myself, you've met two."

"Lord Sheridan," she said. "And the other fellow. I didn't catch his name. He seemed very kind, though. Concerned."

"That's Henry De Vere," Brandon said. "And he is kind. They all are, except for when they're getting into scrapes."

Lorna noted his choice of words. "They? Don't you include yourself in the group?"

She felt his smile against the top of her head before he answered. "Naturally. The Honorables are like a second band of brothers to me. In some ways, I'm closer to them than to my blood brothers. But we're all very different. I'd like to think I've outgrown my days of pranks, but Sheri and Henry, in particular, keep the flames burning on an ongoing rivalry with a miserable twit of a poet."

Brandon related anecdotes of his friends' antics, and soon, despite herself, she was laughing at his stories. After a while, he asked, "Feeling better?"

To her amazement, Lorna realized she was. "I'd been starting to feel like I did before those spells."

"I thought so."

"I'm still worried about Daniel, but it isn't quite so overwhelming." Without thinking, she turned her head and kissed his cheek. "Thank you."

He squeezed her waist. "My pleasure."

While they talked, Bluebell napped. Lorna watched the dog's ribs expand and contract as she breathed. She noted, then, the rhythm of Brandon's own inhales and exhales. Like gentle waves, each breath rocked her head up and down as she nestled against him.

Gentle rocking. Strong arm. Warm man.

. . .

When he was certain Lorna was asleep, Brandon let out a heavy sigh. She should be all right now. The poor thing had been near to another nervous fit. Thank God he'd been able to distract her.

The congestion outside the city gave way to fields of frost-tinged grasses, stands of bare trees, and ponds rimmed with ice. Upon arriving in Lorna's home village, they made a brief stop at the local tavern so the driver could get directions to Elmwood. Before much longer, they arrived at their destination.

The house was a haphazard jumble of architectural...well, *styles* might be stretching the word. It seemed to be more of a collection of architectural impulses. The main part of the house looked as though it started life as a glorified farm dwelling. As the family increased in prosperity, he supposed, subsequent generations added on bits and bobs. A stone wing here; a Tudor-style second story there. It would never be featured in a guidebook to England's loveliest manor homes, but Elmwood did possess a certain character other, more sanely constructed, houses lacked. And it was Lorna's home. That was all Brandon needed to know to find the place charming.

"Lorna." He jostled her lightly. "We're here."

She exhaled a sigh and blinked open her eyes. The bright turquoise orbs were so fuddled with sleepy confusion, he couldn't resist placing a smiling kiss on her mouth. If she didn't want to be with him, she would have to be the one to keep her distance. He couldn't pretend he hadn't enjoyed holding her while she slept.

A whiff of an answering smile flitted across her lips. Catching sight of the house, her spine straightened. Before his eyes, she transformed into a purposeful creature; gone were the visible signs of her distress. Had he not witnessed for himself those underpinnings of vulnerability, he might be tempted to believe Lorna was resolve personified. She had a mission, and nothing was going to keep her from it.

His observations were proven accurate when an elderly butler admitted them to the house. "Hello, Humphrey," she said in a clipped tone, removing her cloak even as she stepped over the threshold. "How is Daniel?"

The old man cast a curious glance at Brandon, and an appalled one at Bluebell, before answering. "I cannot lie, Miss Lorna. The young master has had a rough go of it. Poor little mite's been whimpering and tossing since the accident. If you hadn't come, Mrs. Lynch was determined to send for the blacksmith to see about the setting."

Brandon saw Lorna's face drain of the little color it possessed, but she firmed her jaw. "That won't be necessary. This is Mr. Dewhurst, a surgeon from London."

With pursed lips and a tilt of her head, she led Brandon toward a curved flight of stairs. Bluebell trotted at their heels, claws softly tapping against the marble floor. Beneath Brandon's palm, the dark wooden bannister was warm and smooth, gleaming with fresh wax. He stopped and turned. The old butler remained in the center of the foyer, clutching their coats in withered hands.

"It was the railing, wasn't it?"

Humphrey nodded. "Indeed, sir. He slid down twice, despite my scolding. Went back up for a third ride and slipped off the bannister. Fell from the top to the foyer floor."

When Brandon turned to resume his ascent, Lorna was staring at him. "How did you know?"

He shrugged. "It's what I'd have been doing on a cold, dreary day. A young boy's energy will find an outlet one way or another, even when cooped up indoors."

At the top of the stairs, Brandon leaned over to take a look at the fall his patient had suffered. It was a drop of about fifteen feet to the tile below. Far enough to prove fatal, should one land at the wrong angle. Fortunate thing Daniel hadn't snapped his neck.

They found the boy in the nursery, moaning plaintively in his bed while an older woman—the worthy Mrs. Lynch, Brandon assumed—stroked his head and tried to calm him.

Lorna let out a gasp of dismay and ran to the child's bedside. Brandon's long strides followed. At once, he saw the trouble and winced. Not one, but both of the boy's arms looked broken. The left bent at an unnatural angle in the middle, while the right was swollen from shoulder to wrist and curved in a way the human arm just shouldn't be.

"Daniel!" Lorna crouched at the head of the bed. "Sweetheart, it's Sissy. I'm home." She kissed her brother's forehead and ran her fingers through hair matted with sweat.

The boy opened his eyes. "Sissy?" When he saw his sister, he burst into tears. "It hurts."

Lorna's face crumpled. "I know, darling, I know." She turned her tear-bright eyes on Brandon, her expression full of pleading. "I've brought a special friend to see you, Daniel. This is Mr. Dewhurst. He's going to help you feel better."

The weight of Brandon's duty settled on his shoulders. Every patient had a loved one who looked at him like that, begging him to heal the afflicted. Each time, Brandon strove to do just that. He could never quite express the terror he felt when confronted with illness and injury. No matter how deftly he cut, no matter how much he studied, all his expertise was paltry in the face of human frailty. He was David to Death's Goliath. And all too often, Brandon's little arsenal of knowledge wasn't enough to defeat the enemy.

Lorna moved aside to make room for Brandon.

"Don't go!" Daniel cried.

"I'm not going anywhere," Lorna promised. "I'll be just over here. She turned and nearly tripped over the dog, who had sat just behind her. "Look, Daniel," she said, "look who else has come to see you."

The boy managed a wavering smile at the sight of the hound. "My dog! Sissy, did you decide I could keep her, after all? You never told me her name. What is it?"

While the boy was momentarily distracted, Brandon seized the opportunity to examine the injured limbs. The left arm, he discovered, was not broken, after all; the elbow was simply dislocated. The right arm, however, was a different story. He pressed into the upper arm and felt bone shift.

Daniel yowled and squirmed.

"Keep him still," Brandon said.

Lorna held her brother down. "Come now, Daniel, just a bit longer. You must let Mr. Dewhurst look, so he can help you."

"Stop, stop! It hurts!" Daniel cried.

"Almost done, my lord." Brandon's fingers worked down the length of the arm. "You're doing remarkably well. I know men with loftier titles than yours who wouldn't be half so brave."

In the forearm, he discovered that both the ulna and radius had snapped.

"How bad is it?" Lorna asked under her breath.

Brandon stood and looked down at his young patient. The boy's eyes were round with fear and pain.

"Daniel," Brandon started, not answering Lorna just yet, "I have formed a picture in my mind of your accident. Will you tell me whether my guess is correct?"

Daniel nodded.

"Humphrey told us you were sliding down the bannister. Is that true?"

Daniel cast a guilty look at Lorna and nodded. Clearly, this activity had been forbidden by his elder sibling.

"And then you slipped and fell to the side," Brandon said. He touched a fingertip to the dislocated elbow. "But you caught yourself with your left hand. You held on as long as you could, didn't you, my brave young man?"

The boy's lower lip trembled. "It hurt so much. I couldn't hold on any longer."

"I understand," Brandon said. "Your elbow is what we call *dislocated*. That means the end of the bone has come out of the joint. I'll have it put to rights in no time. Your arm will be sore for a few days, but no lasting harm done. The other arm, however, is a different story." Brandon kept his tone light while imparting the bad news. "You've managed to break every bone in your arm—a feat which bests anything I or my four older brothers ever managed. It's impressively thorough."

Lorna made a sound of distress. Brandon gave her shoulder a reassuring squeeze. Their gazes met and held; he felt something familial in their little tableau. There was a sense of rightness in he and Lorna being together with this child he'd only just met. It didn't matter that Brandon didn't know the boy. Lorna loved Daniel more than anything in the world; it only followed that Brandon would feel protective toward him, as well, for the sake of the woman he cared for and meant to marry.

Blast it all, why was she so stubborn?

Mentally, he gave himself a shake. There would be plenty of time for maudlin reflections later. Now was the time to get Daniel patched up.

He gestured for Lorna to follow him. Leaving the lad in Bluebell's capable care, the two stepped into the corridor.

Lorna rubbed her hands over opposite arms. "What must be done now?"

"The broken bones will have to be set, of course, and the dislocated elbow popped back into place. The elbow can be repaired in only a moment. The other arm will be trickier, since all three major bones are involved. I can do it, but it will take a bit longer and is likely to be quite painful for Daniel."

Lorna blew her cheeks out on a deep exhale. "Can anything be done to make it less painful for him?"

"I don't like giving laudanum to children as young as Daniel, but if you feel strongly that he should have some, we can try a tiny dose. A posset of whiskey in warm milk might be a better choice."

Her slender fingers went to her temples, and then into her hair, eyelids squeezed shut. She did that sometimes, he'd noticed, when she was vexed. It was like nail-biting or other nervous habits. The auburn curls shook from the agitation at the scalp.

"We'll use the whiskey," she said, blinking her eyes open. "I'll go make the drink. Please tell Mrs. Lynch what else you need." She turned to go.

"Lorna?" he called.

She looked back over her shoulder.

"I'm going to do my best for your brother."

She gave him a tight smile. "I know. That's why you're here."

• • •

It was done, and Brandon needed a drink. Not just the alcohol, for that could be had at Elmwood, but he needed a change of scenery and air, a tavern or public house where men gathered to relax over a pint after a long day.

And what a day it had been.

Brandon headed to the stable, where the lone groom saddled the one horse in the building and gave him directions. Before long, Brandon was on his way to the village, inhaling deep the air of a Middlesex twilight.

By any measure, his work on young Lord Chorley had been a success. Still, hot prickles like tiny bolts of lightning sparked his nerves, making his skin feel too tight. His mind raced; it was a good thing the horse, an amiable beast, seemed to know the way without his input, for Brandon could not focus on directing the animal.

A soft wind blew through the gloaming. Despite the chill temperature, the air had a plushness to it that reminded him of Portugal.

His business there had been with the Army, of course, but that didn't stop the locals from turning up at the surgery tents. Even though Brandon had been new to his vocation, he did what he could for the unfortunate souls whose villages, farms, and towns had been caught in a war not of their making. There had been children—lots of them. Mothers, clearly with ailments of their own, begged for help for their little ones, with no mention of their own afflictions. Children suffering the ravages of famine induced by hungry armies were more susceptible to illness. Too often, he could do no more for a juvenile patient than offer his own ration of bread and whatever had been stewed in the cook pot that night. On one particularly harrowing occasion, a mother and child, both stricken with smallpox, had been denied entry to the camp. Brandon offered to come out to them, but when he arrived at the perimeter, he learned the mother had been shot for attempting to force her way past the guards.

And then, of course, there had been Florbela and the baby. His greatest effort. His worst failure. The guilt he would carry for the rest of his days.

It was with these happy thoughts in his head that the Elmwood steed brought him to the establishment wherein he was given to believe he would find a dram of good ale and the company of stalwart men. Briefly, he wished he was arriving at The Hog's Teeth back in Oxford, to spend the evening with The Honorables. Back then, no matter what kind of day he'd had, the companionship of his friends never failed to raise his spirits.

The taproom hosted an array of local color. Laborers and merchants of every stripe seemed to have assembled for a pint, that great British equalizer. Someone wearing clothes marking him for local gentry shared a table and a laugh with a strapping man whose bulging forearms and ham-sized fists made him a likely candidate for the village blacksmith. Smoke from pipes and cheroots created a hazy, fragrant atmosphere, while a youth in the corner sawed out a merry tune on his fiddle.

Propping an elbow on the bar, Brandon allowed the scene to wash over him, carrying away a bit of the day's pressures. *Lorna should be here*, he suddenly thought. If anyone could use a respite, God knew it was her. Throughout the grueling process of setting Daniel's bones, Lorna had not only remained in the room for the boy's sake, but also assisted Brandon like the most capable apprentice. Only the occasional tiny gasp and the clenched set of her jaw betrayed that she was affected by the proceedings. When it was all over, he'd advised her to find some rest, but the stubborn woman wouldn't hear of leaving Daniel's side.

"What will you have, sir?"

"A pint of ale, if you please," he said over his shoulder. He heard the mug touch the bar behind his arm with a heavy *thunk*. Turning to retrieve the drink and offer his thanks, Brandon caught sight of the woman who'd served him.

Of average height with a pleasant figure and golden brown hair twisted into a knot atop her head, she might have been a pretty woman once. But her face was a ruin. Jagged, badly healed lines of purple-red marred both cheeks. One eye drooped at the corner where a shiny patch of scarred skin drew the surrounding flesh tight.

An animal attack, he concluded, as the scars seemed to consist of both claw and bite marks. Perhaps a feral dog, Brandon mused.

"I've not seen you 'round here before," the woman said, her voice pleasant. The kind smile she offered was the last vestige of beauty remaining to her. "Passing through, or will you be in the neighborhood for a while?"

"I'm staying a night or two at Elmwood," Brandon answered.

Her expression soured. "Can't say's I envy your accommodations."

Over the rim of his ceramic mug, Brandon raised a brow in question.

"I used to be in service there," the woman explained. "S'posed to be quite the honor to work in the house of a lord, right?" She barked a bitter laugh. "I've got my face to remind me of the honor."

"A person did that?" Brandon blurted.

He instantly regretted the words, but the matron only smiled wryly. She wiped the bar with a cloth as she moved down to refill another thirsty patron's beverage. When she returned, she propped her hip on the polished length of wood.

"Not just *a* person, *the* person. Lord Chorley himself."

Brandon gulped his beer to cover his grimace. He knew, of course, of Lorna's elder brother's madness, but he hadn't been made aware of the extent of his derangement. An unhinged, grown man capable of ravaging a woman's face like a wild animal could be strong enough to inflict any sort of violence on those around him. What had Lorna and Daniel suffered at the hands of their sibling?

"He's dead now. Elmwood is safe as can be," he said, feeling the need to defend the Robbins siblings.

The woman's good eye narrowed. The other stared at him dully. "Who are you, then? Courting Miss Lorna?"

Villages kept no secrets, Brandon knew. By morning, the whole neighborhood would know who he was and why he'd come, so he saw no harm in divulging the information himself. "I'm a surgeon. Young Lord Chorley suffered an injury and required my assistance."

At that, the woman softened. "Poor lamb. Is he all right?"

"He will be," Brandon answered with a nod. "Thankfully, young boys are made of rubber. He'll be good as new in no time. And his sister is as devoted as they come."

"Yeah, she's a good sort," the barkeeper allowed. "It was me who got the tooth and claw that time, but it could've been Miss Lorna just as easy. She spent more time with the baron than any of us. I was only in there that day because the housekeeper, Mrs. Lynch, had finally talked Miss Lorna into stepping out for a meal and a rest. She didn't like for us servants to have to deal with the lunatic. Took most of his abuse herself."

Brandon felt himself go still to his very core, where a cold stone settled in his chest. "Did he hurt her?"

The woman shrugged in obvious discomfort. "He yelled at her a lot. Cursed, you know? Filthy, vile things I never heard the likes of before, and never care to hear again. I don't know if he ever did more than that. After my accident, I left, of course. That was months before he died. Miss Lorna still gives me a pension to make up for what happened."

A pension Lorna couldn't afford, Brandon surmised. But she was determined to care for Daniel and her little family of servants. Determined enough to put herself physically between them and a source of potential harm, namely, Thomas.

Little wonder Lorna had spit on her brother's grave. It was the least the man deserved for the hell to which he'd subjected his sister.

He marveled that a woman of her relatively tender years could handle such heavy responsibilities, but then she'd taken on the burden of raising an orphaned infant when she was only fourteen. It was plain to see how devoted she was to Daniel. Having attended plenty of children in his time, Brandon was well-acquainted with parental desperation. Lorna clearly loved her brother every bit as much as any mother Brandon had encountered.

Until he met Lorna, Brandon had scarcely allowed himself to consider a family of his own. Now, he longed for that life, and not in a nebulous way. His dream looked like Lorna and Daniel.

I could care for them both. But Lorna didn't want him to.

After speaking with the former maid, Brandon could very well imagine that Lorna feared relinquishing any control of her situation to another. No doubt, she blamed herself for the attack on the servant, and felt it wouldn't have happened had she remained at her post.

Life had foisted plenty of hardship upon Lorna, and Brandon hated to think that his attentions could be just another unwelcome trial. But Brandon was certain in the very marrow of his bones that Lorna returned his affection. She had come to him for physical comfort, had she not? And she had turned to him today when her brother was in trouble. She accepted a relationship between them only in small doses. Somehow, Brandon had to make her see that partnering with him in marriage and life would be a good change for both her and Daniel.

The following morning, Brandon gave young Lord Chorley another going-over. He wrote out instructions for the boy's care, went over them with the housekeeper, and returned to London alone but determined to prove to Lorna that he was worthy of a place in her life.

Chapter Twenty-Seven

When Lorna returned to Fenton House three days after Daniel's accident, she was startled to find a crowd milling around in front of the house. Not sure what to expect, she left Bluebell in the carriage, and instructed the driver to deliver the dog to the mews with the horses. As she disembarked, a man in a ratty gray greatcoat yelled for her notice. "Who are you?" the man demanded. "What's happening in there? Is she dead?"

Startled, Lorna scurried inside and hurried upstairs. Lord Fenton admitted her to his wife's bedchamber, where the late afternoon's gloom was pushed back by ample candlelight. The air was thick with the pungent scent of camphor.

"Come in, Lorna, dear," Marjorie called in a weak voice.

As she approached the bed, Lorna saw how her friend had deteriorated in just the span of a few days. Her pallid skin had a waxen sheen. Her eyes, once so lively but now wreathed with dark circles and lines of strain, settled dully on Lorna.

"How is your brother?" After asking her question, Marjorie panted to catch her breath.

"Well, thanks to Mr. Dewhurst," Lorna replied. Her gaze fixated on Marjorie's forehead, where sweat-damp strands of hair clung to pale skin. "Who are all those people outside?"

She crossed to the window and pulled aside the brocade drapes to examine the throng milling about, blocking the street. Drivers hollered at men to step aside so their carriages could pass, while pedestrians were reduced to prodding with walking sticks and parasols to clear the path.

"Resurrection men," Lord Fenton spat.

A sickly feeling twisted Lorna's gut. Toward the back of the crowd, she spotted Bob and Fartleberry. One of the diggers nudged the other in the ribs and nodded toward the window. They waved at Lorna. Startled, she dropped the curtain.

"Waiting for me to die," Marjorie said, "so they can take me and my babies away. They'll give us to the anatomists for dissection. Oh, my babies. My poor babies!"

Her arms, looking emaciated against the immense girth of her middle, clamped feebly over her stomach. She rocked back and forth, as though cradling her children.

All those men out there, with dirty faces and work-roughened hands, stalking Lady Fenton, waiting for her to die, just as Lorna had been doing these past weeks. But she, Blackbird, had sailed past them all, had gained entrance to the inner sanctum, camouflaged by her birth, her sex. Her friendship.

"I'm so frightened." Marjorie's chin trembled. Her wide eyes held nothing back; raw fear and hopelessness were communicated in every glance. Gone was the carefree pregnant woman dancing quadrilles while Society matrons tutted behind their fans.

Lorna hurried to her side and clasped her friend's hand, which felt over-plump and clammy. Glancing over her shoulder, she saw that Lord Fenton had gone.

Guilt and shame had Lorna's innards twisting like a pail full of worms. How could she participate in something her friend feared and abhorred? She smoothed a trembling palm over the woman's forehead. "Everything will be well."

Marjorie shook her head. "I'm dying, Lorna. I can no longer feel my legs. You see how swollen I am. My feet are even worse. I'm going to burst like an overripe melon." She swiped at the tears leaking from the corners of her eyes. "I wanted children. I would have been a good mother. If only God hadn't given them to me all at once. What if they don't survive the birth? What if they do, and they're raised by nurses, or worse—a stepmother?"

Lorna barked a dry laugh. "There are worse fates. Still," she hastened to add, "the very best thing would be for your children to have their own mother."

Marjorie turned her face away. "But I can't give them that. I might not even be able to give them life. I pray that we're able to rest in peace together, but we won't have even that, if those butchers out there have their way."

Suddenly, the woman gasped. Her eyes rolled back in her head, and her hand slipped from Lorna's.

"Marjorie," Lorna cried. "Marjorie!" She lightly slapped the woman's face and chaffed the inside of her wrist. When that didn't bring her to, Lorna ran to the door and called for help.

Soon, Lord Fenton sprinted into the room, with an older man Lorna didn't know hard on his heels.

Lord Fenton grabbed Lorna's arm, while the other man scurried to the bed.

"What happened?" Lord Fenton demanded.

"We—we were speaking," Lorna stammered, "and she fainted."

The man felt Marjorie's neck and wrist. He placed a hand over her mouth and nose. "Her pulse is pounding and irregular," he reported. "The dropsy swelling her face may have spread to her heart."

"It isn't just her face," Lorna said. "Lady Fenton said she was swollen all over."

"I'm sure I wouldn't know," the doctor replied primly.

"Why did this happen?" Lord Fenton asked. "What's wrong? Will she wake up?"

"Are the babies coming?" Lorna chimed in.

The doctor sniffed. "I'm sure I wouldn't know about that, either."

Lord Fenton's face flushed beet red. "What the hell *would* you know?" he bellowed. "What am I paying you for, Possons?"

Straightening and smoothing his hands over his waistcoat, the doctor lifted his chin. "For my not inconsiderable expertise, my lord."

A muscle in Fenton's jaw twitched; his knuckles cracked as he balled his hands into fists. Lorna took a step back, certain she was about to witness an explosion of violence. He snatched the older man's lapel in a fist. "Then use that expertise," Fenton said between clenched teeth, "and *help Lady Fenton.*"

He shoved the physician, who wasted no time in scurrying from the room.

Fenton shot an anguished look at his wife. Marjorie still hadn't opened her eyes. Her chest rose and fell, though to Lorna's eyes it looked as though her body was struggling to draw breath under the immense weight of her womb.

The viscount let out an anguished moan. He dropped to his knees at his wife's bedside.

Recognizing his need for privacy, Lorna vacated the bedchamber.

The household went into a tizzy, with Possons rattling off orders to have water boiled and this poultice and that tincture fetched from the stillroom. Maids and footmen hopped to do his bidding.

The end for Lady Fenton was finally here, Lorna realized with a sickening certainty. In the chaos, no one paid any notice as she ghosted through the house, collected her cloak, and slipped out the front door and into the mob of resurrectionists slavering after a prize corpse.

• • •

As she slipped out the door, Lorna made eye contact with Fartleberry. Her compatriot started plowing his way toward her through the crowd, no doubt wishing to be appraised of the situation inside the house.

But what could she tell him? *This is it, boys, the moment we've been waiting for is here.* Only too clearly could she imagine the Crib Cross Gang whisking Marjorie's body out of Fenton House, just as they had Lord Weir during the man's funeral. Except, with Marjorie, there well may be violence as rival gangs fought over her friend's corpse like hungry dogs over a scrap of gristle. They would tear her apart, every man desperate for the fortune her body promised to bring the successful gang. Even if her body made it through that ordeal intact, Lady Fenton would never know the touch of the grave; these resurrectionists would make sure of it.

Lorna couldn't take part in this, not anymore. Marjorie was her friend, but even if she wasn't, no one deserved the terror to which the pregnant woman was being subjected.

Before Fartleberry could reach her, Lorna turned and ran.

As she had the night she met Brandon, she sprinted fast and hard, hoping to lose any pursuers. Glancing over her shoulder, she didn't see Fartleberry or any other member of the gang. But on she ran, arms pumping and cloak streaming behind her, cutting across stately squares and fashionable lanes, heedless of the curious looks she drew.

Mar-jo-rie-is-dy-ing-Mar-jo-rie-is-dy-ing. The thought looped through her mind, syllables synchronized to the rhythm of her feet hitting the pavement.

Lorna ran until her lungs ached and her throat burned. Finally, she slowed to a walk, gasping and clutching at a stitch in her side.

There was no question but that she was going for Brandon. Lord Fenton should have found a new surgeon for Marjorie after he'd dismissed Manning. If she were being charitable, Lorna could allow that perhaps Doctor Possons had offered good consultation during Marjorie's pregnancy, but most physicians coveted their social status as gentlemen and would never stoop to anything approaching manual labor—including physically examining their patients. If ever there was a patient in need of hands-on care, it was Marjorie.

Lorna didn't doubt that Lord Fenton had acted with his wife's best interests in mind, no matter how misguided his decisions might have been. Time and again, she'd witnessed his devotion to Marjorie, and Lorna didn't like to think what would become of the man if—when—his wife perished. *Devastated* didn't begin to encompass the grief he would experience.

In a moment of wistful envy, Lorna wished she'd had the chance to experience that kind of love. The only man she could imagine sharing that with was Brandon, and there were too many reasons why they could not marry.

Even now, she did not seek him out for herself—though God knew she longed to feel the comfort of his arms again—but for Marjorie. Brandon was the most competent man she knew. The lecture and dissection she'd attended might have made her woozy, but she'd seen for herself how dedicated Brandon was to improving childbirth for women and infants.

But what could he do for Marjorie now?

The thought stopped Lorna in her tracks. Up the road, the streetlamp lighter was making his round, but he'd not yet made it this far. Just ahead, the anatomy school loomed in shadow.

Lorna stood at the mouth of the alley and stared down the slope, as though into an inky abyss. Marjorie was going to die. Not even Brandon could prevent it. So what, exactly, was it Lorna thought he was going to do for her friend?

When the answer came to her, she inhaled sharply. Was she mad for thinking of this? Then she remembered something Mr. McGully had said during that lecture: *"… once you've chosen your course, you must not hesitate to act."*

In her heart, something important slid into place. For the first time in months, Lorna felt as though a weight had lifted from her shoulders. This was the right thing to do, she was certain. Now, if only she could convince everyone else involved to listen to cold, hard reason.

Fingertips trailing over the brick, she made her way down the alley to Brandon's door. She rapped three times, firm and decisive.

When he opened the door and saw her, he broke into a smile, but a worried expression quickly squelched it. "Daniel?"

Lorna shook her head. "Lady Fenton."

His jaw firmed. "I'll get my bag."

Soon, they were back on the street, waving down a hackney. As he helped her into the carriage, Lorna put a hand on his arm. "Brandon, I believe we're also going to need a solicitor."

Chapter Twenty-Eight

Even as he handed Lorna down from the hired carriage in front of Fenton House, Brandon couldn't believe what they were doing. All during the ride here, Lorna sat in his lap. While he'd idly stroked her back and waist, unable to keep his hands from her, she'd whispered in his ear, the warm, breathy rush of her voice tantalizing his body, even as her extraordinary words sent a thrill of terror through him. It would never work.

In the street, a veritable horde of resurrectionists kept their grim vigil. Oh, yes, Brandon knew them for what they were. No only did he spot a few faces from the Artichoke Boys, but the entire lot of men looked like trolls who had crawled out from beneath the nearest bridge—dirty and dank with the whiff of rot clinging to the air around them.

When the crowd saw that Brandon and Lorna were headed into the house, they surged forward, clamoring and grasping. Instinctively, Brandon tucked Lorna into his side and whisked her to the door. The footman stationed there slammed it behind them, locked it, and produced a stout crossbar that looked like it had been purloined from some medieval fortress.

Lorna trembled against Brandon. "Did they harm you?" he asked. If one of them had laid a hand on her, Brandon would have the offending limb on his dissection table before the night was out.

"No." She took his hand and led him to Lady Fenton's chambers. In that instant, with her cool palm pressed against his, Brandon didn't care whether or not her scheme succeeded. Having her, keeping her, was the only thing that mattered.

A maid opened the door. At once, Brandon surveyed the room. Lady Fenton lay on her side. Her chest made shallow, panting motions. Her eyes flicked to the door. Frankly, after what Lorna described to him on the journey here, Brandon was surprised the woman still lived.

At her bedside, Fenton sat in a chair, elbows braced on knees. His haunted eyes told the tale of a man staring into the abyss. "Dewhurst," Fenton said. "Are you here for Marge?"

"In a manner of speaking," Brandon said, bowing briefly to Fenton and his lady, then setting down his bag. "I am entirely at your disposal, should you wish my services. But the help we came to offer is not…" His voice faltered; he cleared his throat and cast a glance at Lorna.

As though reading his thoughts, she squeezed his hand and stepped forward. "Lord Fenton, Marjorie, Mr. Dewhurst and I would like to speak to you about a particular matter. This will not be an easy discussion, but it is one I fear we must have."

With her simple dress swishing about her trim hips and her spine straight, Lorna was both alluring and eminently competent. It was a combination that appealed to Brandon on a fundamental level. There was no fear in her as she sat beside her friend, only compassion and grace. Brandon wanted that for himself. Oh, he wanted.

He pulled another chair beside Lorna and sank into it, the two of them situated on one side of the bed, Fenton on the other, and poor Lady Fenton in the middle.

"What is it?" Fenton rasped. "There's nothing more serious than my wife's peril."

On his knee, Brandon rubbed the pad of his thumb over the side of his knuckle. Lorna scratched at her nape with one finger. It was her anxious tell, he knew, albeit much more restrained than he'd seen in the past. They were both in knots over this.

Brandon cleared his throat once more. "If I may speak plainly, there is a mob of resurrectionists on your doorstep. Should the worst occur, and Lady Fenton perish before the babies are delivered, one of them will get his hands on her."

Lady Fenton let out a quiet sob, while her husband blanched. "Not a chance."

Lorna furrowed her brow and pursed her lips.

For a moment, Brandon wrestled with what to reveal to the Fentons. At last, he decided these people needed as much honesty as he could give them.

"Fenton, my lady, speaking as a member of the surgeon-anatomist community, I happen to know that there is a great deal of interest in your case. I do not exaggerate when I tell you that every knifeman in the metropolis hopes to obtain your body."

"A group in which you must number yourself," Lord Fenton laughed bitterly. "And to think I trusted your advice over that of another surgeon, when the truth is none of you would lift a finger to help my family."

A muscle in Brandon's jaw ticked. Fenton was in hell and lashing out wherever he could. Brandon wouldn't take the bait and challenge the man.

Marjorie shook her head, her swollen face and long, dark braid giving her an almost childlike appearance. "Why?" she asked. Her lips, red and cracked, trembled.

"Because you are exceptional," Brandon answered. "You have successfully carried triplets nearly to term, which makes you a prized specimen."

"She isn't a specimen," Fenton spat, his cheeks flushing as red as his hair, "she's my wife. The mother of my children. Don't you dare speak of her like some frog in a jar." He didn't budge from his seat, but his fists balled on top of the coverlet, his knuckles bloodless.

Brandon sympathized with the man; truly, he did. He tried to imagine himself in Fenton's position. What if that was Lorna on the bed? Brandon would be crazed. He would go for the throat of anyone who spoke this way.

But having begun, he must persevere. "Unfortunately, my lady, the consensus among my peers is that you are not likely to survive the birth. Every one of those resurrection men out there has been promised the biggest pay of his life for bringing you in. They will stop at nothing to obtain your body, I'm sorry to say."

Across the bed, Lord Fenton's nostrils flared. His jaw clenched so tightly, Brandon wouldn't have been surprised to hear his teeth crack under the strain.

"Why are you telling me this?" Lady Fenton moaned. "If there's nothing we can do? All I want is for my sweet babies to be healthy and well. And if they cannot, then to be left in peace. Is that too much to ask?"

It was, but Brandon didn't say so.

"Marjorie," Lorna said, her voice a velvet caress. "I want to tell you about something." Gently, she ran a hand over the other woman's forehead and skimmed the top of her head, petting, soothing.

"I saw a woman anatomized a fortnight ago," she said in that tender voice. "It was the most dreadful thing I ever saw."

Brandon's heart stopped in his chest. This was not the way!

"But," Lorna continued, heedless of Brandon's frantic gestures, "you have never seen such dedication as I saw in Mr. Dewhurst." She turned a smile on him, and his heart sputtered back to life. "Though we find these methods unsavory, this is how science advances. Brandon has committed *his* life to improving the lives of others. How can he, and other surgeons, do that, if they aren't given the opportunity to learn?

"With all my heart, Marjorie," Lorna said, her lovely eyes shining, "I hope you and the babies survive, well and strong. But, should you not, wouldn't it be something of a balm to know that in your deaths, there is the possibility of discovery, which may in turn help other women facing difficult circumstances?"

Marjorie's brows drew together. Lord Fenton shot to his feet. "I've never heard such codswallop in my life. There could be no meaning in the deaths of my wife and children. Perhaps you two should go now."

"Lady Fenton," Brandon hastily interjected, "the plain truth is this: Should you perish with your babes still in your womb, you *will* be dissected." He pinned a hard look on Fenton. "Deny it all you wish. Post guards if you'd like. Commission a lead coffin. It won't matter. Someone will outwit you. For God's sake, did you not hear that Lord Weir was stolen from the parlor *during his own funeral*? What resurrectionists want, they will get."

Lorna's hands clasped in her lap, her thumbs tracing over each other. He caught the noise of her teeth clicking together as her chin jounced up and down. "Your body will be stolen, fought over, and sold to the highest bidder. The dissection will be a spectacle, like the one I saw."

"That wasn't a spectacle," Brandon defended. "It was instructive."

Lorna gave him a withering look that begged to disagree. "*Or*," she said, meaningfully, "this could be done respectfully. If you gift your remains to Mr. Dewhurst and Mr. McGully, I know they will ensure you are handled with the utmost decorum. And after their examination, you will be afforded a proper burial."

Lady Fenton whimpered and curled around her belly. Labor pains, or an anguished heart?

"Hush, darling," Fenton said, stroking his wife's back. "Don't listen to them. No matter what, I will protect you."

With a sigh, Lorna stood, pressing a hand to her chest. "My brother was stolen from his grave."

Lady Fenton's eyes widened. "I didn't know," she said weakly.

Lorna's voice never grew loud, but increased in fervor. "All the way out in Middlesex, London resurrection men come at night and take our dead. Thomas was a baron, safe in the hallowed ground of the churchyard." She exhaled a humorless laugh, flung her arm wide. "The only reason I know it was done is because I caught them in the act. But I wasn't able to stop them. Oh, no. They just tied me up and kept right on with their business."

Brandon grimaced. He hadn't known she was tied up by the lowlife scum who plundered her brother's grave.

Lord and Lady Fenton both exclaimed at this revelation. Lorna waved her hand. "After it was done, there was no way of telling what had happened. If I took you to my brother's grave this moment, you'd have no reason to suspect it was empty. But it is. Thomas isn't there, and I don't know what became of his remains."

She raised her brows at Brandon in question.

"Probably incinerated," he answered. "Or reburied in a mass grave."

Tears streamed down Lady Fenton's face, while his lordship sank to his knees.

"We tell you these things not for the pleasure of frightening or horrifying you," Lorna went on, "but to give you the chance to take control. Legal papers can be drawn up this very night, as a codicil to your will. Once it's known in the surgery community that you have legally assigned Mr. Dewhurst and Mr. McGully to carry out a postmortem operation, there will be no more cause for the other anatomists to pursue you. My lord, you will never have to wonder whether your wife's grave is empty. And you, my lady, will have given a beautiful gift to the world by sharing the knowledge you carry."

After a heavy silence, Lady Fenton wiped her face. "How long would the operation last?"

"An hour or two," Brandon answered.

"And…" She screwed up her face. "Could I stay here for it? At home?"

"Of course," he assured her. "In attendance would be myself, Mr. McGully, and Mr. Culpepper, an artist, who would help us record our findings."

The pregnant woman drew a deep breath—as deep as her abdomen would allow. "I should like to talk this over with my husband. Would you give us a few moments?"

He placed his hand on the small of Lorna's back and guided her into the corridor. She leaned against the wall and closed her eyes. Brandon took the opportunity to study her. There was something different about her, he thought. She'd changed, even in the short time he'd known her. When first they met, her back was always ramrod straight, *but look at her now*, he thought, slumped with her shoulders on the wall and hips thrust forward, unintentionally provocative. It suited her, he decided.

"Tired?" he asked when she rubbed her temples.

"Not really." She opened her eyes, treating him to a view of those stunning turquoise irises. "What we did in there…I feel a little queasy."

Gently, Brandon wrapped his arms about her waist and drew her close. "I know what you mean," he said, rocking her back and forth. "That was the most difficult conversation I've ever had in my life."

"Do you think it will work?"

Brandon frowned against her hair. "I don't know," he admitted. "We gave them the truth and a damned good option." Gratitude welled in his chest. He cupped the back of her neck and peered into her face. "Thank you, by the way, for coming to me with your idea. It's brilliant and beautiful. Just like you."

Before she could reply, he fit his mouth to hers. Those lush lips opened for him, and her sweet little tongue lapped at the corner of his mouth. Instantly, heat swamped his veins. He wanted to let it consume him, consume them both the way they needed. But he refrained from deepening the kiss.

Reluctantly, he pulled away, savoring the sweet torture of her nails digging past his sleeves and into his forearms. She hated the parting, too. The knowledge gave him hope.

The rattle of the knob was the only warning he had. He took another step back as the door opened.

Lord Fenton looked from Brandon to Lorna and back again. Fury crackled in his gaze. "Come in," he said, his words clipped. "We've made a decision."

Chapter Twenty-Nine

It was all settled, then. Lord Fenton summoned his solicitor. In the meantime, Brandon examined Marjorie. She was not in labor, he said, and with his ear trumpet he found the heartbeats of all three babies. Marjorie's maid had been taking a much-needed rest, but as Brandon went downstairs to his lordship's study, the servant returned to her mistress's bedside.

Lorna kissed Marjorie's cheek. "Good night, dear," she said gently, knowing in her heart she was saying goodbye.

"I'm so pleased we met," Marjorie said, voice thick and eyelids drooping. "If you'd come to Town earlier, we could've been friends for years. Wasted years. Pity." Her ladyship slipped into slumber.

There was no reason for Lorna to remain in Fenton House any longer. She could have had Charity pack her belongings, but the maid would undoubtedly try to cajole Lorna into putting off her departure until morning, like a sensible person. And Lorna just couldn't wait.

She needed the comfort of her own bed tonight. The queasiness she'd described to Brandon remained, a sort of hollow aching looking for an escape.

Returning to her room, Lorna wrote a note for Charity to find in the morning, explaining she'd returned to Chorley House and asking the maid to follow with her belongings. Then she wrapped herself against the cold and headed down the stairs.

When she reached the door, a strong hand gripped her elbow.

"Where are you going?" Brandon demanded. "It's freezing out, and the middle of the night, besides."

"Home. It wouldn't do for me to be here when…when Marjorie…"

Understanding softened his face. "Let me take you home."

Rain was falling, but Lorna stopped Brandon from summoning a carriage. Chorley House was only a few streets away. Besides, she thought as they walked, she was glad for his arm around her waist and the umbrella he held above their heads. Having this moment of closeness was a gift. He didn't know how much he supported her right now.

By ensuring Lady Fenton's body would go to Brandon, Lorna had sealed her own fate. There would be no way to earn enough money to repay Thomas's debts now; time was up. And when Coop found out what she'd done, she'd be lucky if she walked away from the encounter with all her teeth.

Without the funds to hand over to Wiggins, it would only be a matter of time before the moneylender came after Elmwood. The man made it clear he would delight in seeing her and Daniel turned out of their home, and she had no doubt he'd make good on his threats.

Losing her brother's birthright would prove her inability to properly care for him. There would be no way to stop Daniel's guardian, Lord Huffemall, from taking the boy away from her.

Yet, even with her entire world falling into disarray, Lorna couldn't regret what she'd done. She didn't know what life would look like tomorrow, or the next day, but she knew she'd done the right thing tonight.

At her doorstep, Brandon kept his arm around her middle. "I don't want to let you go," he murmured, pulling her tight against his chest. "I'm afraid that if I do, I'll never see you again."

A very real possibility. "Come inside," she said on an impulse. She wasn't ready to let him go, either. "Stay with me tonight."

His breath hitched. "Have you changed your mind?"

She winced. "I can't give you more than tonight. Please let that be enough." She didn't know if she was pleading with him, or herself. Could one night really be enough, when her heart yearned for more?

Rising on her toes, she brought her arms around his neck. "Please," she whispered, kissing a trail across his jaw.

He groaned in defeat and captured her chin between his thumb and forefinger, holding her still for a searing kiss. He plundered her mouth with a delicious, steady rhythm made all the more erotic because Lorna knew what that motion imitated. In no time, her mind sizzled with memories of their bodies straining together. Having him became a necessity of living through the night. If he turned her away now, Lorna would die as surely as she could perish from lack of air.

"Damn you, woman," he rasped against her ear. "As if I could ever deny you." His body was already hard, ready for her. How sweetly he fit against her softness. "Open the door before I drag you to the back garden." His needy growl thrilled her.

Fingers unsteady, Lorna fumbled the key. Impatient with her performance, Brandon thrust the umbrella into her hands, unlocked the door, then scooped her up.

She let out a squeal. "What are you doing?" In the entrance hall, she carelessly tossed the umbrella aside; it rattled as it struck the tile then spun across the floor. Lorna felt intoxicated, his kisses more potent than any ale she'd drunk with the gang.

His firm hand swatted her rump. "Hush," he warned. "Else you'll rouse the servants."

"There's only a few. They're probably asleep belowstairs."

"Let them stay that way." Brandon climbed the stairs in a few seconds, her weight in his arms no more than a trifle. Striding past her bedroom door, he made for the master's suite.

"That isn't my room," she said as they approached the portal.

"It is tonight. We'll need plenty of space for what I have in mind."

Good thing he already held her, for her bones melted at his words.

When Brandon stepped into the large bedroom, they were plunged into cold and darkness. He made his way slowly, feeling with his foot before committing to a step.

"I think the bed is over here," he muttered, then cursed when his shin struck an obstacle.

Smothering her laugh in the crook of his neck, Lorna directed him to the desired piece of furniture. He placed her in the center of the mattress and followed her down, blanketing her body with his own. His hands pinned hers overhead, their fingers bound together. Their mouths once more began a sensual duel.

Within the confines of her clothes, Lorna's body began to soften in some places, harden in others. She arched against him as they kissed, enjoying the delicious friction on her nipples. Her legs parted in wordless invitation.

The callous on his right index finger lightly abraded her skin, providing an arousing counterpoint to the silky glide of his other fingertips as he moved up her legs, rucking her skirts around her hips. No other hands in the world felt like Brandon's. Only he could give her these glorious sensations.

He surged over her, rocking his thick shaft against her core while he plucked her nipples through her bodice. This was madness, she thought.

"Clothes off," she said on a pant.

"No, sweetness, not yet." There was a pained edge to his words. "If you're only giving me tonight, then I'm going to have you every way I can. The second I'm out of my clothes I'll be in you. I want this to last."

Then he was working her throat with his mouth, laving her with warm, wet kisses while his whiskers lightly scratched her delicate skin, and any thought of protest flew from her head. This was perfect. *He* was perfect.

Her feet hooked around his hips. She rose to meet him, thrust for thrust. Every grind of his erection against her sensitive flesh sent her closer to the sweet oblivion she craved.

"Yes," she whimpered. "Oh, yes, please. That. *That.* More."

Hot breath whooshed over her face. "Is this what my woman needs?"

The possessive words slayed her. How she longed to be his woman in truth. When the sun rose, they must part forever. But for tonight…tonight she was his, one last time, and he was hers. Tomorrow was soon enough to think about her woes.

"Sufficient unto the day is the evil thereof."

A low chuckle rumbled in his chest. "Quoting verse won't deter me, you know."

And wasn't she glad?

One more thrust, two, and she came apart in his arms. Shattered into pieces, but somehow he held her together. He was the only thing that existed in her world, her only reason for existing.

At least for tonight.

•••

"It's like we're tucked away in a private little cave. In a mountain. The Pyrenees, I think," Lorna said as she recovered from that exquisite orgasm. Brandon regretted not seeing her as it happened. Or feeling it skin-to-skin. But maybe it was just as well. The sound of her—not to mention her heat and, Christ, her delectable scent—had nearly been enough to make him lose control with her.

He laughed softly. "Pleasure makes you fanciful, love. I like that." He kissed her, felt her smiling against his lips. Satisfaction curled in his chest like a cat purring in the sun, even though his body was strung tight with the need for release. Lorna didn't smile enough. Catching those lush lips turned up in joy, and knowing he was the cause of her happiness, filled him with pride.

More, perhaps, than most people, Lorna needed to laugh and smile every day. It was good for her health, kept the nervous disorder at bay. Unbeknownst to Lorna, Brandon had assigned himself the task of making sure she received her daily dose of happiness. All of his hesitations about tending his loved ones went out the window where Lorna was concerned. When he accompanied her to Elmwood, Brandon realized that he'd follow her anywhere. There was nothing more important to him than protecting the woman in his arms.

She might think she was only giving him one night, but Brandon would convince Lorna that she needed him as much as he needed her. They were ideal together.

He was humbled all over again when he thought of how valiantly she championed his cause. Lady Fenton would never have agreed to the postmortem operation without Lorna's heartfelt testimony on his behalf.

The nose she nuzzled into his jaw was cold at the tip. Her hand fluttered over his cock, the little featherlight touches causing it to twitch and tighten. Brandon clenched his jaw on a groan.

"Shall I get these clothes out of the way now?" she asked.

"Fire," he managed to croak. "Let me start one." The need to care for her, to provide, was like a primal compulsion. No more could Brandon stop it than he could order his heart to stop pumping blood through his veins.

While he made his way to the fireplace, he adjusted the steel rod in his breeches. Lord, he couldn't wait to drive into her hot, wet core over and over, wring pleasure from both their bodies until neither of them could see straight. He would spill inside her. She'd carry his child—

The fantasies were doused with that chilling bucket of water. As the coals caught, Brandon made a decision. He intended to marry Lorna, but she deserved to know she was getting a damaged article. And if tonight really was all they had, well, he would treat it like their forever. He would be as open with her tonight as he planned to be every day for the rest of his life.

Standing from his crouch, Brandon turned back to the bed. Lorna lay on her side, propped on one elbow. She still wore that monstrous cloak and her plain dress. Her skirts tangled about her thighs, giving him a view of her slim, shapely calves encased in stockings and the half boots on her feet.

He dispensed with his own coat and boots, then divested her of cloak and shoes. "There are so many layers," he said. "I could spend all night unwrapping you." He pressed their foreheads together. "My very favorite present."

"Please don't spend *all* night unwrapping me. A little time devoted to the project is acceptable, but I had a few other things in mind, as well." She bit her bottom lip and peered at him from beneath a fringe of lashes, looking every bit the coquette.

"We'll let the room warm a little before anyone is unwrapped." He swallowed around his heart, which was suddenly in his throat. "There's something I want to tell you, Lorna."

Her flirtatious smile was replaced by a creased brow. "All right." Sliding her feet over the edge of the bed, she sat up and took his hands. "What is it?"

"You asked…" Now that he'd begun, the memories he'd fought so hard and long to distance himself from rushed back in a flood. "You once asked why I consent to work with pregnant bodies, when doing so distresses me."

Bless her for noticing, even though he'd experienced a flash of shame when she mentioned it after the lecture. But he'd told her not to feel embarrassed about having had a nervous episode in front of him; he wouldn't be ashamed of showing his own weaknesses, either.

She nodded, urging him to continue.

"In my younger years, I was in the Army. My regiment was sent to Portugal."

"Alice told me about your war experience," she said. "That's where you began your career as a surgeon, correct?"

"Yes, that's right. In any event, during a week's leave, I met a woman. Florbela." Lorna stiffened, but Brandon didn't let himself stop. "She worked on her father's farm, outside of Lisbon. I met her on my first day of leave, when I was headed into the city and stopped at the farm to buy some bread and cheese."

For the first time in years, he remembered the woman as she looked when he'd met her—laughing brown eyes and a wicked smile that promised carnal delights that he, at twenty-two, was eager to experience. Bounteous curves on a tall frame, with an ocean of glossy, dark hair that spilled over the pillow.

"We spent the week together in the city," he said, lost to the memories now. Her English was spotty; his Portuguese sufficient only to ask directions to the nearest tavern. And yet, they'd managed to tease and laugh and strike up a friendship. In bed, he was overeager, his limited experience obvious. Patiently, she showed him the way of things.

And at the end of the week—"I asked her to marry me." Lorna's fingers tightened on his hands. "She told me no. Said my English morality was adorable, and sent me on my way. I never saw her again until…" Impressions flipped through his mind. Sun. Heat. That godawful smell of the surgery tents. The droning sound of flies and dying men. "It was nine months later, I suppose. Huh." A bitter laugh that sounded more like a punch in the gut. "Florbela's father brought her to me in the back of a cart. She was in labor, and it wasn't going well."

Lorna gasped. "Oh, Brandon. Oh, no."

He blinked against hot prickles stinging the backs of his eyes. "It was already too late, but I tried, I did." His voice was thick with pleading. He'd never spoken of this to another soul, never revealed what Florbela was to him to the other surgeons on duty that day.

"I know you did." Lorna stroked his thigh in a soothing gesture. He was surprised to hear tears in her voice. "I know you did, Brandon."

With a hard gulp, he summoned the wherewithal to finish the story. "The last thing she did was exact my promise to care for the child. When it became obvious that Florbela was beyond help, I operated. I cut her open to try to save the baby. My son. But it was no good. She—they—died."

It had been such a shock, seeing Florbela again, realizing she carried his child and that he was going to lose them both. In the frenzy of trying to save her and the babe, he'd had no time to think about what it meant to him.

Since then, he'd done his level best to forget. He told himself that if her father hadn't brought Florbela to the English surgeons, he would never have known about the baby. He'd never have felt the ache of loss that even now had him rubbing his chest. Ignorance would have been so much kinder. If only he'd never known at all—

All these years, he'd dreaded working with the bodies of pregnant women. His impotent anger at an unjust universe fueled his work. Every lecture was the best he could deliver. Every operation, every consultation, was performed to the utmost of his ability. The never-quite-healed wound on his heart compelled him to seek answers, better ways to mend the sick and afflicted.

But Florbela and the child were always there, somewhere in the back of his mind, ready to condemn his failures and remind him that nothing he did would ever atone for letting them die.

"What was his name?" Lorna's voice pulled him from the maelstrom of emotion.

Brandon blinked, surprised by the moisture he felt clinging to his lashes. "He had no name that I knew of. After they died, Florbela's father took them away. Maybe he was given a name before burial?" Brandon shook his head. "I don't know what Catholics do in that situation. He, my son, was already dead when I took him from his mother's womb. He was so small, just..." He showed her a distance between his hands. "Hardly larger than a loaf of bread. He never drew breath. He never cried. I never saw his eyes. They say babies have a particular, lovely smell, but mine smelled like blood and the brine of her waters. He never…"

A jagged sob tore from his chest.

"Oh, Brandon!" Lorna threw her arms around him. She scrambled onto his lap, straddled his thighs, and clutched his head to her chest. Before this moment, he'd never cried for his child. Told himself he didn't deserve the pain he felt, that he grieved something, someone, he'd never had to begin with. Tears were out of the question.

They flowed now, scalding his eyes. Lorna folded her body around him and held him close, riding out the emotional storm with him. Gradually, he became aware of motion. Lorna's fingers sifted through his hair as she moved side-to-side, swaying his body with hers. Rocking him. She sang softly, a tender, soothing ballad. Brandon squeezed her waist to let her know he was all right.

Without a word, Lorna slid out of his grasp. She removed his clothes and guided him into the bed. Lorna joined him a few minutes later, as bare as he. Cuddled into his side, she nestled her cheek in the hollow of his shoulder.

"I'm so sorry, Brandon. It doesn't matter how little time you had with him, you lost your son, and that's a terrible thing for any parent to endure."

"Thank you." His throat felt raw; his voice gravelly. "It's taken me a lot of time to acknowledge that I really did have a son. He was there. He was mine. I didn't mean to make him, but, by God, I'd have loved him."

Lorna covered his body with hers, as though shielding him with her flesh. "Of course you would have. Any child would be fortunate to have you for a father. You give yourself entirely to the people and causes you care about. You're clever and strong and hardworking. The only fault I've discerned is that you tell terrible fairy stories."

With a gruff noise, Brandon flipped their positions, pinning her beneath him. "I'll have you know I've been practicing reading stories with my nieces. Although one of them seems as hopeless with the subject as I am. She thought Princess Mayblossom was the ship those fanatics took over to the colonies."

Lorna snorted, and Brandon chuckled softly. "How did you do that?" he asked, stroking her cheek.

"Do what?"

"A few moments ago, I felt...But now, my heart feels like it's convalescing. Bruised, but whole."

The sweet lips he loved so well turned up in a sad smile while she returned the caresses to his face. "If I've helped you at all, I'm so glad. But I think, mostly, the work you've been involved with of late has brought the matter to the forefront of your mind, and you were finally ready to acknowledge what you went through." Her finger alighted on the end of his nose. "You healed yourself."

Tilting his head, Brandon took her finger between his lips and sucked gently on the tip.

Lorna hummed; then her breath caught. "I'm sorry, too, about Florbela. You must have loved her very much." He heard the tension behind her generous words, knew it cut her to think of him with another woman. Were their places reversed, Brandon would rather gouge out his own ears than hear about Lorna laying with someone else.

"No." Idly, he played with her curls. "I wish I could say I did. She was lovely and kind, but I only proposed because it's what I was taught was the correct thing to do."

"Like me," she whispered, so softly he almost didn't hear.

Brandon snatched her jaw, forcing her to meet his gaze. "Not like you. I want you, Lorna. It's true that I first proposed because we'd been together, but I would have done so, anyway. Even then, I knew that you were mine. There is no other woman for me. I love you."

He hadn't intended to blurt it out on the heels of so much emotional turmoil, but he was glad he'd said it. He would always be honest with Lorna, and loving her was the truth—perhaps *the* fundamental truth of his soul. He. Loved. Her.

At his declaration, Lorna's face transformed. Her eyes widened and her lips parted. She seemed to glow from the inside out with wonder and joy. "Do you truly love me?"

He took one of her hands, pressed a kiss into the palm. "You know I do." Emotion clouded his words again, but it wasn't painful this time. It was warm and hopeful and generous.

She raised her head for a kiss and he gladly obliged. With long, languorous strokes, their tongues glided back and forth, feeding the desire once again thrumming through his blood. He became aware that Lorna was delightfully naked beneath him. Her slim hips wriggled against his belly, sending a hot pulse of need straight to his groin.

He wanted her. He wanted *all* of her. He wanted her erotic-as-sin lips and her adorable freckles, her wild hair and lithe limbs. He wanted her forgiving spirit, her generous heart, her fierce loyalty, her quirks of humor and attitude toward life. He wanted the way she could turn this dark night of his soul into one of hope and peace. He wanted the instincts she aroused in him, to protect and nurture and bond with this—*his*—woman.

Propped on hands and knees, he kissed down the creamy pillar of her neck to the hollow where her collarbones winged outward. He swirled his tongue there, just as he planned to do to her navel, and to any other indentation he discovered.

Her nails dug into his shoulders, a delicious pleasure-pain that made him even harder. Shifting his weight to one forearm, his other hand covered her sweet breast, which fit perfectly in his palm, as though she'd been made for his touch—or he for hers. Taut nipples begged for his ministrations.

Lowering to her breast, he drew as much of the lovely mound into his mouth as he could. Her skin smelled like lavender and tasted like cream, a veritable feast for his senses. Brandon teased her nipple, flicking a circle around the needy flesh with the tip of his tongue, then using the flat of it to rasp over the sensitized bud. She moaned, her stomach hollowing as she arched into his caresses. Her fingers flexed in his hair, holding him captive. He worked her other nipple with his hand, rolling and tugging until it was as hard as the other. Then he shifted his mouth to that one, giving it the same treatment he'd delivered to the first.

She raked his back and haunches, her hips undulating, urging him closer to her core. Slick, female heat brushed over the head of his cock. "More, Brandon," she said. "I need you."

The way she responded to him made him desperate to sink into her body. It took all his restraint to resist the sweet entreaty. "Soon, sweetheart," he promised. "I want you ready for me."

"I am," she protested. "Now, please."

He raised his head from her breast. Their eyes locked, hers blazing with an intense desire that echoed his own. Her breath panted between lips red and swollen from his kisses; her tongue darted out to moisten them.

There was more he wanted to do. He wanted to roll her onto her stomach so he could palm and kiss and nibble the pert globes of her rump. He needed to continue his quest to tongue all her indentations, including the two dimples above the aforementioned derrière, as well as the long column of her spine. And the hollows behind her knees. And the insides of her elbows.

There would be time to indulge his longings later, he decided. He flipped their positions, settling her on his waist. "If you want me, take me." It was a challenge. A supplication. *Please want me as much as I want you.* It hadn't escaped him that Lorna had not returned his declaration of love. What if she still planned to walk away from him? He couldn't allow that. Before this night ended, every fiber of her being would be saturated with his touch and scent. There would never be any question that Lorna belonged with him.

Lorna scooted back to his thighs and cautiously enclosed his length in her fist, like she held a butterfly and was being careful not to crush she wings. She slid up and down, from root to tip and back again, while her other hand rested on his belly. The gossamer cocoon of her hand was a torment. His need developed a painful edge, cutting his insides to ribbons. Abdominal muscles twitched with the strain of holding back his release. His nostrils flared and he breathed in the musky tang of her arousal.

Reaching between them, Brandon parted the silky folds guarding her entrance. The springy curls on her mound tickled his palm as he worked one finger into her tight heat, and then another. He thumbed her swollen bud. Lorna gasped, bucked against his hand. Hers clenched tighter around his shaft, nearly obliterating his control. Brandon ground his teeth, determined to last.

"Brandon." His name was a plea on her breath.

"Ride me, love. Give us what we both need."

When, at last, she sank onto his length, Brandon's soul sighed in relief. *Here* was where he belonged, more than anywhere else in the world. One hand gripped her haunch as he surged into her downward glide, loving the way her tight sheath stretched to accommodate his body. The other reached into her hair; curls snaked around his fingers like living things, snaring him in a trap he never wanted to escape.

Lorna's eyes rolled back in her head as she let out an earthy moan. The sound flowed up his spine and caressed the insides of his ears, sending waves of satisfaction through his body.

"Nothing sounds sweeter than your pleasure."

Her head lolled forward and her eyes blinked open. For a moment, she tensed. Her mouth worked silently, then she let out a tiny sound of defeat. She bent down, crashing their lips together in an open-mouthed kiss. Teeth tapped together as their tongues sparred, darting and retreating.

With his hands still on her hip and the back of her head, Brandon guided her back and forth on his length. A quick study, his girl. In no time, Lorna caught his rhythm and took over. Their bodies undulated together on a liquid tide of passion, each time they connected taking Brandon closer to the breaking point. His hand slid from her hip to the small of her back. He splayed fingers over her firm buttocks and pulled her lower body tighter against him, so that every thrust hit her most sensitive spots, inside and out.

She tore her mouth away, but kept it close, hovering a couple of inches above his face. Their breath mingled, leaving them nothing to inhale but the air they created together. Lorna's eyes squeezed and her lips curled as she made the most decadent sounds, gasps and whimpers and croaks that caught in the back of her throat. Her breasts jounced with their movements. Brandon took one of those petal-pink nipples into his mouth and suckled hard.

In reaction, her entire body tensed. "Oh," she gasped, her eyes flying wide. "Oh, yes. Oh, Brandon. Brandon!" Her inner walls bore down on him, clenching and releasing in exquisite waves that set off the most intense climax of his life. Engorged to the point of pain, his cock drove home once more, then throbbed in time with her orgasm as every muscle in his body clenched around bone. Her sheath milked him of every drop, and still he came, shaft pulsing and hips jerking. He was being turned inside out, pulled out of his skin and into hers. Soon he'd be completely inside her and they'd be one. One. One.

Slowly, so slowly, his head cleared of the post-coital haze. After covering them with a blanket, he gathered Lorna into his arms. She nestled into his side with a contented sigh, all limber, replete femininity.

He tucked a curl behind her ear and kissed the corner of her mouth. "I love you, Lorna," he said, his thumb brushing across her cheekbone. He wanted to say more, wanted to insist she consent to marry him. But she'd refused to speak of the future tonight, and the guarded expression that met his words told him he was wise to hold his peace.

"It means everything to me that you do," she replied. She buried her face in the crook of his neck, hiding from his sight.

She cared for him, he was certain, and yet she continued to keep him at a distance. Brandon had bared a part of himself tonight that he'd never revealed to another person. And she had given him much of herself—but not all. Something still held her back.

Brandon turned them both on their sides, Lorna's back snug against his chest. He rested a hand over her stomach and focused on the feeling of her belly rising and falling. Long after she was asleep, Brandon lay awake, counting her inhalations. He coveted every one, because he had a bone-deep fear that no matter what he did, he couldn't keep this woman. At last, exhaustion from a taxing day pulled him unwillingly toward sleep. The last sensation he detected before unconsciousness claimed him was the tickle of one of her curls brushing over his nose.

In the morning, she was gone.

Chapter Thirty

The days spent in front of Fenton House had been a waste. Things had got exciting yesterday evening, when no other than Dewhurst showed up with a woman in tow. If the surgeon (and a midwife?) had been called, things must be happening. Slee hoped the presence of his best buyer meant he'd have an advantage when it came time to snatch the body. The sawbones may have got all high in the instep over The Cannibal, but surely the time had come to let bygones be bygones.

This cheering thought carried him through the next several hours, until disaster struck. A man who identified himself as Lord Fenton's solicitor stepped outside sometime after midnight. "It has come to the attention of his lordship that you *gentlemen*"—Slee could hear the phlegm dripping from the word—"are camped at his doorstep in the hopes of profiting from a private, family matter. His lordship has instructed me to inform you that in the event of her ladyship's untimely death, her body will be voluntarily given to an already-selected surgeon for the purposes of a postmortem examination, which will be carried out at this location."

A ripple of surprise carried through the assembled resurrectionists. Who'd ever heard of such a thing?

"Dewhurst." Slee ground the hated name out like a curse. "It's him that done it. He's cut us out."

Slee's insides roiled with acid. He felt gutted and betrayed. Wasn't he an honest man? Hadn't he always given that surgeon good service, keeping him in a steady supply of quality bodies? And *this* was how Dewhurst thanked him?

"To hell with that. Come on, Harty Choke. Let's move."

It had been a busy night, but Slee returned to Fenton House just before dawn with a grim smile on his face and a pocket full of money. He knew the surgeons who'd been hoping to have the cow's body to poke around in for themselves wouldn't be none too pleased with this unprecedented turn of events, and in a matter of a few hours, Slee found one only too willing to partner with him.

Manning, Crib Cross's regular buyer, was the man—a fact that pleased Slee to no end. Turned out he'd already been burned by Dewhurst. The meddler had convinced Lord Fenton to bar Manning from attending Lady Fenton, once again standing in the way of an honest man's labor.

God, how Slee despised Dewhurst. He'd have liked to stick him with the knife tucked into the waistband of his trousers, but he weren't no murderer. Thwarting Dewhurst would have to suffice. Manning seemed to relish the notion, too.

The surgeon seemed to hold with Slee on other matters, as well. It said right in the Good Book that women was below men. The law knew females wasn't the same as men, too, Manning pointed out. If they were, women would have the same rights as men. Only stood to reason, then, that women wasn't really people. Murder was a crime against people. And since women—much like dark-skinned heathens—didn't count...

"We're bringing her in like The Cannibal, Harty Choke."

One of the fellas shook his head and slipped off into the dark. Slee spat. Good riddance. More for him.

When they approached Fenton House, one of his boys split away to wait in the square across from the front of the house. A big hound dog was laying on a stone bench in the little green, somehow making it look even more abandoned. Pete and another man took up positions near the rear. Slee couldn't know yet how he'd be exiting the place, so he needed all possibilities covered.

Prepared to present himself as the surgeon's assistant, Slee shifted the leather bag Manning had provided him to his left hand. Smoothing a palm down the front of his borrowed waistcoat, he knocked on the servant's entrance. A kitchen boy opened the door. Slee paid him off easy enough to gain entry.

Slee strode confidently through the belowstairs, even stopping a maid to ask for directions to her ladyship's apartment. Fine clothes and a good story went a long way toward getting a man places.

Before he reached the lady's rooms, the door opened. A woman came into the corridor and softly closed the door behind her. Dressed better than the downstairs maid, her position of servitude was still made obvious by her careful demeanor. No keys at her waist, he noted—not the housekeeper. *Must be the lady's maid.* She turned, pausing when she saw Slee. "May I help you?" she asked in a quiet voice.

Arousal darted up Slee's legs, gathering in his groin. He bit back a smile. *Stupid whore.* He hefted his bag. "I'm the surgeon's assistant."

The woman shook her head. "There's no surgeon here."

"He's on the way," Slee assured her, trying his damndest to talk like a nob. "He asked me to get her ladyship's examination underway."

The maid clearly didn't accept his tale, or maybe his feigned accent didn't pass muster. "Who did you say you assist?" She was getting agitated, he saw, creeping toward her mistress's door.

"Let me show you my calling card," he said, setting down his bag. Fast as a snake, Slee struck. In one motion, he clamped his left hand over the woman's mouth and pulled her back against his chest. Retrieving the knife from his waistband, Slee held it to the woman's neck. At the touch of the blade, she panicked, and damn, how sweet it was. Slee's cock swelled against her arse as she struggled in his grasp.

"Know what's wrong with you?" he hissed against her ear. "You got no respect for man's authority. I tol' you to get outta my way. You didn't." With a quick swipe, he raked the blade across her throat. A spurt of blood splashed over the white door. The female's struggles soon grew weaker, then ceased. He lowered the body to the floor, taking a moment to wipe his blade on her skirt.

Then he retrieved his bag and opened the pregnant woman's door.

Inside the bedchamber, his prize lay on the bed, sleeping. A man, the viscount, one must assume, curled against her back. Soft snoring came from one of them.

"Can't do murder," Slee whispered under his breath. "God's own law says so." The male would have to be dealt with another way, since Slee would never sully his eternal soul by committing murder. Good thing whores and heathens didn't count.

From the bag, Slee fished out a short truncheon. He palmed the leather-wrapped weapon, testing its weight as he crept around the side of the bed. His blow landed on the back of the sleeping man's head with a satisfying *thwack*. Another shiver of arousal had him stiff as the club in his hand.

There was only the whelping doggess left to contend with. Slee tilted his head, considering her long, dark braid, pictured it wrapped around his fist while he fed her his manhood. His instrument gave an insistent twitch. He rubbed himself through the borrowed, close-fitting trousers and bit back a whimper. If he worked fast…It wouldn't take much, not hard as he was.

Hands shaking with excitement, Slee dragged the unconscious man off the bed and let him fall to the floor in a heap. He pulled back the covers and eagerly clambered onto the mattress behind the cow, who still lay on her side.

The woman shivered. "Archibald?" she murmured, voice thick. "Will you get the covers, please? I finally slept a bit." She started to move, as though to turn.

Slee grabbed her shoulders, flipped her onto her back, and pushed the point of the knife against the soft flesh beneath her jaw. "I'm afraid dear Archibald won't be gettin' you no blanket, nor nothing else."

She gasped. He grabbed her throat and applied pressure. "Not a sound, bitch. Not a single, bloody sound. Understand?" When she nodded frantically, he released her throat. Air wheezed into her lungs, lifting her breasts. He hadn't noticed them before, for the huge abdomen overshadowing everything else.

Roughly, he palmed one through the fancy material of her nightdress. She flinched, but didn't squeak. The flesh was hard and heavy in Slee's hand. "Nice dugs. Bet they're full o' milk, yeah, cow?"

She met his gaze, shook her head, silently begging. Slee inhaled, detected the fumes of her terror, heady like the whiff of the fine brandy he'd shared with Manning to seal their deal. She knew *he* was in charge. The power of it nearly had him spilling in his pants.

"Think I wanna see what all the fuss is about," he declared. A single, wrenching tug split the material of her nightdress at her neck. Her shivers increased in intensity as Slee ripped the garment down the length of her body, revealing her skin.

He sat back on his heels to admire his handiwork, the mattress shifting beneath him. He curled his lip at the sight of her abdomen. "*Yech.*" The sound of disgust was accompanied by his tongue protruding from his mouth. "It's like a dead fish," he jeered. "All pale and bloated."

A choked sob escaped her. Slee's gaze raked up her torso to the swollen dugs, each topped with a berry-brown nipple, just right for feeding her calves. Tears leaked from her eyes. Her nose and lips were bright pink.

Under his heated gaze, she raised an arm to cover her breasts. The other hand she tried to use to cover her twat, but she couldn't reach around her own damned belly to do it. Slee laughed, enjoying the spectacle of her discomfort.

"Please," she whispered. "We can pay you, whatever you want. Please, just go away."

Casually, he backhanded her across the face. "I told you not to talk."

Her hand flew to cover the already-reddening cheek, her expression stunned. Maybe she wasn't as sure of their positions as Slee had assumed, if she thought she had any say in what happened.

She licked her lips. "Jewels," she said, persisting in her foolishness. "I have lots. You can have them. All the money you could ever want. Lord Fenton will give you anything. A house, even. An estate. Whatever you—"

He jabbed the knife at one of the lumps moving around in her belly. "Which one shall I stab first, milady? *This* one?" He pressed, bringing a bead of blood to the surface of the skin.

"No!" she gasped. "No, no! Please, God, no, leave the babies alone. Please." Just like that she crumbled. Her face collapsed in anguish, her hands fell, defeated, to her sides.

Smiling, Slee reached for the front of his pants. "Now you see how it is, whore."

Chapter Thirty-One

As Lorna awoke, she became aware of an unfamiliar weight pinning her to the mattress.

Brandon.

He was still here with her, still sleeping soundly, his arm draped over her waist. Lightly, so as not to disturb him, she traced a fingertip over his whiskered jaw. "I love you," she whispered. "I love you with all my heart."

Last night, something had shifted between them. Or maybe it had just been Lorna who had changed. Brandon had trusted her with his darkest, secret pain. And what had she given him in return—her body? So what? He could get the same from countless others.

What they shared went beyond physical pleasure. She trusted Brandon like she'd never trusted another person in all her life. When Daniel needed aid, to whom had she turned? Brandon. When life overwhelmed her, to whom did she run? Brandon.

She owed him better than this. She owed him all of her, good and bad. Lorna had shucked herself of the scheme for Marjorie's body, and it had felt good. Right. She had to do right by Brandon, too. It was time to be honest with him, to tell him about her involvement with the Crib Cross Gang.

He might despise her for it. He might turn away. But she had to accept that possibility, because her heart could no longer bear to keep secrets from the man she loved.

And, oh, she did love him. There might not be any way for them to be together after she told him the truth, but if there was any man for her, it was Brandon. Only Brandon. Even though he didn't yet know everything about her, he understood her like no one else.

And she understood him, too. Last night, hearing about the loss of his infant son broke her heart. She'd felt his pain as if it were her own. The baby would always be part of Brandon, and therefore part of Lorna, as well.

She breathed deep of his scent, nuzzling her nose into his neck. His masculine beauty always took her breath away. She was so used to her own body that the hard lines of his face, the solid planes of his torso, always surprised her. She traced one thick, winged brow. With a smile on her lips, her eyes drifted shut.

Charity can't read.

The thought snapped her eyes open once more.

How could she have been so foolish as to leave a note for her maid? Charity probably couldn't write anything more than her own name, and almost certainly didn't read at all. When the maid entered Lorna's room at Fenton House, she would discover her mistress's bed had not been slept in and raise an alarm. Lorna couldn't permit that to happen. With poor Marjorie on death's door, Lord Fenton did not need to worry over a wayward house guest. Lorna would simply slip inside and tell Charity in person that they were relocating back to Chorley House. The errand would take no more than half an hour; she'd be back before Brandon awoke.

Gingerly, so as not to disturb the slumbering man, she crept out of the bed and into her own room, where she hastily donned her blacks. Not only did she have little else to wear, she was venturing into pre-dawn London. It felt safer to have the ability to blend into the shadows. After slipping into a black gown, she tugged on gloves, bonnet, and veil—all black. She half-expected to trip over Bluebell in the corridor, but it occurred to Lorna that she'd not seen the dog since they'd returned from the trip to Elmwood the previous day. Perhaps the animal was still at Fenton House, or had found her way back to Coop.

Out on the street, she drew a deep breath, then broke into a jog.

When she arrived at her destination, the house was still dark. She pulled her veil aside and turned to face the square. The crowd of resurrection men was gone. Had Lorna's and Brandon's plan worked, or had the worst befallen Marjorie overnight? Lorna rang the bell, praying the noise only sounded belowstairs, not where Marjorie and Lord Fenton might be disturbed by her intrusion.

A bleary-eyed footman admitted her after several minutes. Lorna glided up the stairs. At the landing, when she should have turned right to go to her own room, she glanced left, instead, toward Marjorie's.

That's where she saw the body in the hallway.

"Oh, God," Lorna blurted. "Marjorie!"

She darted down the hallway and vaulted the body—the maid, she thought. Her hand landed on the doorknob, which was slick with blood. Lorna tumbled into the room…

And found a man on the bed above Marjorie, his knees pinning her arms, his erect penis prodding at her lips.

Lorna shrieked. Before she had time to think better of it, she charged the assailant and shoved him off her friend. On the other side of the bed, the man tangled with Lord Fenton's body.

"Help," Lorna cried. She yanked the bell pull before running for the corridor. "Help!"

Alarmed voices sounded downstairs. Behind her, the man let out a sound of dismay. She looked over her shoulder, but he was already on her, tackling her to the ground.

"Goddamn you!" he shouted, his fist connecting with her jaw. "Stupid fucking bitch!"

The pregnant woman wailed, struggling to rise from the bed.

Marjorie should lie down, Lorna dazedly thought. Every day her friend rested was another day she and the babies lived.

A slap across the other side of her jaw snapped Lorna's head in the opposite direction. Her skull felt packed with wool. Over the ringing in her ears, she heard a woman screaming, realized it was her own voice.

"Shut up," her assailant yelled. His hand tightened around her throat, cutting her voice. Lorna blinked, struggled to focus. Everything was gauzy. Her veil, she thought. It had fallen back down over her face. "Blackbird," the man spat. "You fucking cunt. I've got you at last."

How did he know? Her head swimming, Lorna felt herself hauled to her feet. He released her throat and spun her around. Her knees felt like water; she stumbled against the doorjamb, caught herself with numb fingers. Something sharp poked her in the back, between her ribs.

"Move," the man snapped, "or I'll gut you like the wrinkle-bellied whore you are."

Another sharp prod in her back made her yelp. Of their own accord, Lorna's feet carried her forward. In the corridor, she nearly collided with two footmen.

"Not a move!" the man hollered, jerking Lorna back against his chest. "If a one of you's takes a step before we're out the door, the woman here gets a belly full of knife."

The footmen skidded to a halt. One of them caught Lorna's eyes.

"Marjorie," Lorna muttered, shaking her head, warning him off. "Help Marjorie."

The man forced her down the stairs and out the front door. When her heavy feet stumbled, he righted her by yanking on her hair. Halting just outside, the man whistled a signal. Two forms broke away from the shadows and descended on Lorna. Everything went dark.

Chapter Thirty-Two

No. Not again.

Brandon would not tolerate being left the morning after making love to Lorna, *again*. It wasn't just his pride, he told himself. Last night had been special, important. She'd felt it too, he was certain. They'd connected on a deeper level, and Brandon was sure he was close to finally breaking through the walls Lorna used to distance herself from him. For her to have left like this…

Was something wrong? Had she received word about Lady Fenton?

Hastily, he dressed in the clothes he'd worn last night, his activity illuminated by the newly risen sun just peeking through the window. He yanked the bell pull and waited for a servant to arrive while he tied his cravat.

Oscar, the footman, burst into the room, confusion scripted across his features. Brandon recalled that the servants didn't know he and Lorna had spent the night here.

"Good man," he stated, pretending there was nothing odd about his presence. "Miss Robbins is in need of fetching. If you've a horse available, I'd be most grateful for the loan."

He strongly suspected she'd returned to Fenton House—where else would she go? "Oh," he said as a thought occurred to him, "send someone next door to see whether she turned up at the Freedmans', just in case."

By the time the horse was saddled, Oscar had gone to the neighbors' house and confirmed that Lorna was not present.

Brandon didn't need the horse for the short walk to Fenton House, but Lorna's absence tugged painfully at his chest, and he was glad to have swifter transportation at his disposal.

When he arrived at Fenton House, the place was a scene of pandemonium. For a dreadful moment, he assumed Lady Fenton had reached her crisis. But when he stepped over the threshold, the butler was rattling off instructions to one of the footmen for summoning the magistrate and the coroner.

"What's going on?" Brandon asked.

"Murder, sir," the upper servant explained. "Her ladyship's maid. Lord and Lady Fenton were attacked, as well. And Miss Robbins—"

"Good God!" Brandon vaulted up the stairs to Lady Fenton's chamber. His worst fear was coming true: Yet again, he'd failed to protect the woman for whom he was responsible.

She's not Florbela, he reminded himself. *Lorna isn't dead. She can't be. I can't live without her.*

Two footmen crouched before Lady Fenton's door. In front of them lay the maid's body, lifeless eyes staring at the ceiling. Her throat gaped from being slashed. Blood stained the door and wainscoting, and collected in a puddle around the woman's shoulders.

One of the servants grabbed the body's ankles, while the other, grimacing, took position at the head. "Leave the body as it is," Brandon snapped. "The coroner needs to see exactly what transpired."

Without knocking, Brandon barreled into Lady Fenton's chamber, fear crushing the air from his lungs. "Lorna," he called.

"Not here," Fenton said. The man sat on the bed with Lady Fenton, cradling his wife. The pregnant woman's face was buried in his chest, her shoulders heaving as she cried.

Brandon swallowed past a lump of terror. "What happened? Where is she?"

"From what I've been able to piece together…" Lord Fenton hissed and raised a hand to the back of his head. "Sorry," he gritted out, then closed his eyes and drew several deep breaths. "About half an hour ago, a man entered the house under false pretenses, told the servants he was a surgeon's assistant. He struck while we were sleeping. Nearly brained me." He grimaced. "I never even woke up, during..." The viscount glanced at his wife, then his eyes darted to the window.

Images flashed through Brandon's mind of Lord and Lady Fenton and Lorna all accosted by a shadowy assailant. Heart hammering against his ribs, he raised a shaky hand to his brow. "My lady? What...? Lorna." Fear was making him stupid. He had to pull himself together.

With a considerable show of will, Lady Fenton raised her face. A large bruise discolored one cheek. Brandon's mind added contusions to his picture of Lorna. A bolt of nausea shot through his midsection.

"He was upon me when I woke up," Lady Fenton said. She stared past Brandon, not focused on anything in the room. "He was going to, to kill me. And the babies. But first he tried..." The woman shook uncontrollably.

Lord Fenton tightened his arms around her and murmured in her ear. She squeezed her eyes shut and nodded, her chin and lips trembling.

Rape. Merciful God. Had Lorna been beaten and forced against her will? Nausea returned, this time in an overwhelming wave that sent acid surging up the back of his throat. Brandon fought back the rising bile and managed to croak, "Lorna. Please."

Lady Fenton sniffled. "She came in just before he...She stopped him. Saved me without any thought for herself." Lady Fenton gasped on a sob. "So brave. He, he took her."

"Where?" Brandon shouted. Every muscle in his body tensed. He had to find her, had to save her. "Where?" he demanded again.

Lady Fenton shook her head. "I don't know. I'm sorry, I don't—" She cried out, clutching at her belly.

"Marge!" Lord Fenton yelled.

Lady Fenton groaned. Her spine curled over her abdomen.

Lord Fenton's gaze flashed to Brandon. "Is it…?"

Brandon put a hand to her stomach, felt the evidence. "Yes." He licked his lips. "Her pains have started." A frustrated huff escaped him. "Who is attending her?"

"I don't know. Doctor Possons doesn't attend births. With the resurrection men…" He jerked his chin to the window. "There wasn't time to find anyone. You'll help us, Dewhurst, won't you?"

Brandon squeezed the heels of his hands to his temples. He wanted to scream. Lorna was in danger. But she would want him to care for Lady Fenton. His soul felt rent in two.

"Save her," Lady Fenton gasped. Her contraction had ended, and now she slumped back on her pillows, sweating and panting. If her first pain was this intense, it would be a terrible labor. "Save her like she saved me."

Damn him to perdition for being a selfish bastard, but Brandon felt lightheaded with relief. He had to go after Lorna, couldn't live with himself if she was harmed and he'd done nothing.

He took Lady Fenton's hand and kissed it, silently sending up a prayer for her safety. "You need multiple attendants," he said. "One alone cannot care for you and all the babies, too." Quickly, he forced himself to think of good candidates. "I met two midwives," he recalled, thinking of the women who had attended the lecture. "Intelligent women, know their business. I'll send for them, then I'm going for McGully. You want the very best for her ladyship, and between the two of us, my mentor is the more skilled practitioner."

The couple agreed to Brandon's suggestions, so he quickly put his plan into action. After sending couriers in search of the midwives, he jotted off notes to The Honorables currently in London, summoning them to meet him at his rooms as soon as humanly possible. He needed their support, both material and moral.

After the midwives arrived, Brandon prepared to take his leave. "Lady Fenton, I know I have not always been your favorite person. But I wish you to know how much I admire you. Hold close to your optimistic spirit. If anyone can make it through this, it's you."

The woman favored him with a smile. "At least my death won't be the only exciting thing that happens today," she said, her eyes glinting with a touch of her old, irreverent humor. "I hope we meet again, Mr. Dewhurst. I'd like for you to have the opportunity to earn my grudging approval."

In spite of everything, Brandon chuckled. "I should like nothing better, my lady." He shook Lord Fenton's hand, then hurried to the horse waiting outside.

Time to get his woman.

• • •

When he arrived at the anatomy school, Mrs. Moore met him at the door.

"Mr. Dewhurst," she said, "You've visitors in your parlor. They said they must see you at once."

"Thank you," he said. "Is Mr. McGully in?"

His employer was in the lecture hall, setting up for the morning's dissection. When Brandon told him of the developments with Lady Fenton, the Scotsman wasted no time in posting a notice on the door, canceling the day's classes, then gathering his supplies and heading out.

"No matter the outcome, lad," he told Brandon as he shoved his arms into his greatcoat, "Lady Fenton will be one for the history books."

At last, Brandon felt he'd done all he could for Lady Fenton. Hopefully, Lorna would see things his way and not fault him for coming after her instead of attending her friend.

Downstairs, he found his small parlor bursting at the seams with four men who turned to look at him, concern etched into every face.

"Harry," Brandon said in amazement. "When did you get to Town?" For the first time in two years, all five of The Honorables were gathered together. There was no time to enjoy the reunion, however.

"Only last night." Harrison Dyer's toffee-colored gaze bored into Brandon. "I'm staying with Henry, so I was there when your note arrived."

Norman Wynford-Scott stood against the wall, trying to take up a minimum of space and failing. The man was enormous, six-and-a-half feet tall with broad shoulders and chest. His boyish features and gentle demeanor kept him from overwhelming the senses of everyone around him. A great paw clapped Brandon's shoulder. "Good to see you, Dewhurst," Norman said. "Wish it didn't take an emergency to pull me away from the Inns of Court. Your note worried us. Tell us what's happening."

Lord Sheridan lounged in one of Brandon's two armchairs, legs extended and booted feet stacked. "Where's the fire, Brandon?" he drawled. "I haven't made it to bed yet, so this had better be important."

"It's Lorna," he blurted. Quickly, he recounted the morning's events, while omitting some of the more personal details.

"Damnation!" Henry blurted from his position in the second chair. His fist clenched on his knee. "Miss Robbins is a fine girl. I hate to think of her at some scoundrel's mercy."

Sheri's demeanor darkened, his casual elegance replaced by a hard determination. "Fine girl, hell. Miss Robbins is spirited and strong and the best thing to liven up the *ton* in an age. I don't mind saying I adore the chit, and will gladly dismember the bastard who laid hands on her. Just point me in the right direction."

At once, Brandon's brothers-by-choice surrounded him. They gripped his arms and clapped his back, offering words of assurance and vows of assistance. For the first time since he woke that morning, Brandon felt the smallest bit easier.

He told his friends what he knew: that Lorna had been abducted at knife-point by a man purporting to be a surgeon's assistant. He supposed the villain could even actually *be* an assistant or apprentice surgeon. Every anatomist in London wanted Lady Fenton's body; it made a terrible kind of sense that one of them had snapped after word of her ladyship's gift had gotten out.

Norman stroked his chin. "I understand why the man used Miss Robbins as a shield to secure his own escape from the house, but why didn't he release her once he was free?"

"What more could he want with her?" Henry chimed in. "Ransom?"

"No," Brandon said, his tone bleak. "Miss Robbins has no family to apply to for a ransom."

For so long, Lorna had been alone. Oh, she had Daniel and the servants she cared for, but no one to care for her in return. It gutted Brandon to think that she could die without knowing that *he* was her family. And by extension, he thought, looking around himself, so were The Honorables. Lorna had inherited four new brothers who would always look out for her.

"He means to abuse her," Harrison said flatly. His mouth pulled into a grim line. "I don't like that we're still standing in this room, Bran. While we twirl our thumbs, Miss Robbins is suffering."

"We'll start with the surgeons," Brandon said. "Try the other anatomy schools and hospitals, see if we can get anyone to talk."

Sheri rose, his quizzing glass spinning rapidly back and forth between his thumb and first two fingers. "We should split up to cover ground more quickly."

The others agreed, so Brandon jotted two lists, then passed one to Sheri. "Take Norman," he said. "Henry and Harrison, with me, please."

They moved to the issue of weaponry. Harrison had a pair of pistols tucked about his person, one of which he passed off to Norman, while Henry retrieved a wicked-looking dagger from a sheath tucked down the side of his boot. At the surprised glance Sheri tossed him, the younger man shrugged. "The docks aren't the safest place to work."

Brandon supplemented their meager arsenal with an array of surgery knives. Once each man had several implements secreted about his person, the group made ready to depart.

Their preparations were interrupted by a knock on the alley door.

Frowning, Brandon opened it. A couple of Artichoke Boys stood on the stoop, a jarring sight at ten in the morning.

"Morning, Mr. Dewhurst, sir," said one of the men, doffing his cap. "Slee would like to offer you a special specimen."

Brandon huffed. "No," he said, shaking his head. "I'm not buying today. Something has come—"

"I really do think you want this one, sir," the man interrupted, his eyes glowing with an avaricious gleam. "Dig deep in your purse, because you're going to get to carve up a Blackbird."

Chapter Thirty-Three

With a gasp, Lorna returned to consciousness. Cold liquid dripped from her nose. Her eyes opened in time to watch a small puddle in her lap seep into the black fabric of her dress. Some of the fluid rolled into her eye; it stung. She blinked and tried to wipe her face, but her hands refused to budge. A flash of panic caused her to struggle. Something rough rubbed her wrists, holding them tight behind her. Lorna was in a chair, she realized. Her ankles were also bound, and a rope around her middle kept her upright.

"Rise and shine, little birdie." The blackguard who had taken Lorna from Fenton House bent in front of her, hands resting on knees. The man's lumpy nose hooked to the side, as though it had been broken many times. One of his fists clutched a mug. Lorna detected the acrid smell of cheap ale clinging to her skin and hair. That's what he'd thrown in her face.

Her temples throbbed painfully in time with her heart. Squinting, Lorna peered at her surroundings. One horizontal window, high in the wall, had a horn covering, rather than glass. The resulting light had a stagnant quality, yellow and stale. It allowed her to see that she was in the center of a small room, with casks stacked against the walls and burlap sacks haphazardly piled in the corners. A rough-hewn table supported a motley array of wooden trenchers and plates. The dirt floor smelled damp, and a chill oozed up through Lorna's feet. Overhead, she heard faint voices and scraping, the sounds reminiscent of the Crib Cross Gang at work, quietly talking while they pulled the dead from graves.

She couldn't locate a door, making her morbid associations even more alarming. She was sealed up in a veritable tomb with a lunatic. Behind her, someone coughed and spat. Another person?

Guarding the exit, she didn't doubt. There must be one, even if it wasn't in her line of sight.

While she examined her surroundings, her abductor studied her. "You ain't much to look at." He sounded almost disappointed. "Scrawny. So freckled you look like you fell in the dirt." Roughly, he fisted her hair. "And this mess on your head…I'd hate to see what's 'tween your legs." In the yellowy light, the man's eyes gleamed a sickly, pale green. He smiled coldly, displaying a mouth of brown teeth and the holes where many had gone missing. "Pretty lips, though. Bet they'd be good an' snug on my cock."

Lorna jerked in reaction, his words bringing back the image of him forcing himself on Marjorie. "Leave me alone," she spat. "I'm not afraid of you."

He laughed in her face, his fetid breath washing over her. Lorna's stomach churned.

"Naw, an' why would you be?" the man asked, almost convivial in tone. Straightening, he strolled to the table and filled his mug from a pitcher. "Drink, Pete?"

"No, thanks," said the man behind Lorna.

Pulling deep from his ale, the man smacked his lips in satisfaction, then leaned back against the table. "We's colleagues of a sort, ain't we, Blackbird?" He drained his mug and plunked it down beside his hip. "Both in the body business." The resurrection man picked up a knife, tapped the flat of the blade against his palm.

Lorna's limbs began to shake. The rope dug painfully into her wrists and ankles and squeezed her ribs.

"An' I don't mind introducing myself to another fellow in the trade. I'm Slee." He slapped a hand against his chest. "That there's Pete," he said, pointing over Lorna's shoulder.

"Hello," said the disembodied voice.

Slee bounced the blade against his hand again. "Thing is, though, you ain't another fellow." He took several slow, measured steps to stand before her. "You's a filching mort who takes work from honest men like me an' Pete."

Lorna shook her head. "We're all doing our best, just trying to make our way. There's plenty of business to go around."

Slee's pleasant demeanor collapsed into a feral snarl. "Lying whore. There *ain't* been plenty of work for me an' my boys. 'Cause of you, we've missed out on the best prizes to come 'round in years. That sow with a maggoty belly. The Great White Scot, bless 'im." Slee's voice hitched on this last remark.

He waggled the knife in her face, like a scolding finger. "I know it's you been the brains behind Crib Cross. Coop's never run so many daring jobs in all 'is life. Now, he's snatching nobles right out o' they's own bleedin' parlors!" The knife touched her jaw. Slee's eyes glittered dangerously. "Tell me that weren't your doin' so's I can cut out your lying tongue."

Lorna flinched at the press of cold steel against her skin. She might die here. Her heart lurched at the thought of never seeing Daniel again. The idea of never seeing Brandon again would have driven her to her knees, if she wasn't already seated. *Think, Lorna, think*, she commanded herself. If she was to make it out of this alive, she had to be smart.

"It was me, you're right." Swiping her tongue over her lips, she weighed the impact of her words.

Slee's nostrils flared; his chin lifted a notch. "I knowed it. Cunning baggage like you may be smarter than a fathead like Coop, but you'll never outwit me."

"You're very clever," she said weakly. "By far the best in the business. Everyone knows that." Maybe if she flattered him enough...

The fist that landed in her gut squelched those hopes.

Air rushed out of her middle. Black spots swam across her vision, while pain blossomed in her belly. Even though Slee had hit her before, Lorna was stunned by the sudden violence. Tears welled and quickly spilled. "Why?" she gasped. "Why?"

Slee took two steps, turned on a heel, paced back. "Are you hearing this stupid dodsey? Ain't I just told her why?"

"Yeah, you did," said Pete. "Sticking her bubbies where only cock-a-doodles belong."

Nodding, Slee clapped a hand on her shoulder, once again bending over to put himself on eye level with Lorna. "The only man who hates you more'n me is the surgeon you done also wronged. After I'm done with you, he'll have a nice, fresh soul case to play with."

He really meant to kill her. Lorna shook her head in vehement denial. "I haven't wronged anyone." A tickle on her lip indicated liquid trickling from her nose. She flushed, embarrassed in spite of herself. "Please, Mr. Slee, I have a family to care for. That's the only reason I started, not to take work from you or your buyer."

"But you did," called Pete from behind.

Slee huffed. "Yeah. You did."

Suffocating tightness claimed her chest. Numbness took hold of her hands and feet. *Not now!* But she couldn't control the panic. She was going to die; the knowledge crushed her beneath its inexorable weight. She couldn't protect Daniel. After she was dead, he'd lose Elmwood. His guardian would send him off to a school full of cruel bullies and indifferent masters. Or worse, Huffemall would abuse Daniel himself. What if he didn't feed her brother, or beat him? Daniel was going to suffer because of her, because she—

Liquid splashed her in the face again, jerking her out of the spiraling episode.

"You listen when I talk, bitch," Slee bellowed. Stepping back, he raked a hand through thin, oily hair. His chest puffed on an inhale. "I knows the order of things as set forth by Almighty God. Man is made to rule over Woman." Bending low, he sniffed Lorna's bodice, grazing his nose over the curve of her breast, lingering where the cold ale and air had puckered her nipples. "You stink of Eve's sin," he whispered.

Straightening, Slee adjusted himself. Lorna saw the evidence of his arousal and gagged.

"Wait outside, Pete," Slee said.

"No," Lorna croaked, panic clawing at her throat. "Please, Pete," she called to the man she hadn't seen. "Don't leave me alone with him. Help!"

The indifferent Pete abandoned her, pulling the door shut behind him. She didn't hear it catch, though, and Lorna wondered if she should chance shouting. But the instant they were alone, Slee stashed his knife at his waist and went for her breasts. Roughly, he squeezed and twisted the tender flesh until she cried out.

"You like that, don't you? Bet your madge is weepin' for me." He drove a hand between her legs and fondled her through her skirts. "Dripping wet, you nasty whore."

Hot anger drove away Lorna's anxiety. She pulled back her head then slammed forward, cracking Slee in the temple.

He stumbled back with a roar.

Lorna's own skull felt like it had split open, but she was too outraged to care. "My skirts are wet because you threw beer on me, you idiot!"

Once again, Slee unsheathed his knife. "Now, now, Blackbird, that ain't no way to talk to a man. You gots to learn to respect your betters, and *all* men are your betters. You been left to fly free too long. Time to clip your wings."

With two quick strokes, he sliced both of her upper arms, below the shoulders.

There was a shock of cold and then a rush of heat as blood flowed down her arms, soaking the sleeves of her dress and dripping off her fingertips behind her. For an instant, the hot liquid felt good on her cold skin; then the pain arrived. Groaning through clenched teeth, Lorna fought to keep her wits about her.

An insane gleam lit Slee's eyes. He tilted his head, considering. "Maybe more like this." Snatching the shorn material of her sleeves, he tore them loose and shoved them down to bunch around her elbows, exposing the wounds to his hungry gaze. "Oh yes," he said, his voice thickening. "That's a pretty sight."

He eased a hand to his erection, freeing himself from his clothes. The bulbous, purple head of his shaft bobbed in front of her. Slee straddled her thighs, grabbed the back of her head, and exerted pressure, trying to force her downward. She resisted. "Come on, Blackbird." His voice turned cajoling. "Serve a man like you should. God might forgive some of your sinful ways if you learn your proper place before the end."

Though she fought with all her strength, Lorna's neck muscles soon tired. Eventually, his tip brushed against her lip, smearing a slick drop on her skin. A sob choked in her throat. She didn't dare open her mouth to let it out.

"Take it like a good little whore."

A shout sounded outside the room, just before the door slammed open. An almighty row of yelling and baying immediately preceded a black-and-tan streak hurtling into Lorna. The chair tilted, spun crazily on one leg, and fell. Lorna landed heavy on her right side. Sharp pain issued from the wound on her arm down to her fingers and through her chest; the rail of the chair wrenched her shoulder.

Slee howled in frustration. Bluebell woofed in Lorna's ear, then yelped as she was pulled off, her front paws scrabbling at the dirt.

From her awkward vantage point, Lorna saw the dog twist out of Slee's grasp. Bluebell planted herself between Lorna and Slee, hackles raised, a menacing snarl rumbling in her throat.

Male voices thundered through the small space. Lorna could see just a sliver of the doorway. There seemed to be a great many people out there, but no one besides Bluebell had made it through the door.

"Lorna!" Brandon. The cacophony of skin smacking skin, grunting, and cursing seemed to form a wall he couldn't physically penetrate.

"Here," she called, but her voice was small in her abused throat and swallowed by the chaos of the brawl. Lorna strained against her bonds. One ankle worked a loop of rope down the chair leg and off. A thrill of victory rushed through her, until she realized one free foot did not lend itself to a cunning escape.

"No you don't!" Slee clutched his knife in his fist, his nakedness forgotten. Amazingly, he was still erect, his shaft pointing toward Lorna as he confronted Bluebell. He feinted to one side of the hound, then darted to the other.

But Bluebell was faster. The dog launched herself at Slee's groin. The resurrection man roared as the dog's teeth found their mark, then the two fell in a tangle of flailing arms and fur.

Bluebell kept Slee's privates locked in her powerful jaws, shaking her head back and forth. Fury and anguish contorted the man's face as he screamed. With a mighty effort, he hoisted an arm and plunged his knife into Bluebell's back.

The dog yowled, contorting as she rolled to the side.

"No!" Lorna screamed in concert with the animal's cry.

"Go to hell, Blackbird," Slee yelled. He struggled to his feet, murder blazing in his eyes. Blood cascaded from the mess of viscera where his genitals used to be. He pulled the knife from the now-still dog, and took a shambling step toward Lorna.

A clap-crack ricocheted through the air. A dark, wet bloom appeared on Slee's brown waistcoat, spread. He looked at Lorna, brow furrowed in confusion. Then he slumped to the floor.

Men poured into the small room. "Miss Lorna," shouted a familiar voice. "Miss Robbins," said another.

"Blue!" wailed a third.

Lorna's neck hurt. She couldn't lift her head to study the bodies pressing around her, so she looked at their feet instead. There were a few nice boots, and some scuffed, worn shoes.

"Here now, Miss Lorna." Pretty Lem squatted beside her. "Let me get you out of there." He spun her on her side to get access to the knots on her wrists, aggravating her injury again.

"Get away from her, you fool." Suddenly, Lem's flaxen curls were nowhere to be seen. In his place crouched a dark figure, his gray gaze merciless.

"Hello, Blackbird," said Brandon.

Chapter Thirty-Four

He knew.

The scorn with which he'd uttered the nickname left no doubt in Lorna's mind.

Brandon pivoted and handed a pistol to a man Lorna didn't recognize. Then he got to work freeing her. Lord Sheridan and Mr. De Vere edged into the room, while a giant in gentleman's clothing blocked the doorway, preventing other members of the Crib Cross Gang from entering.

Coop's face appeared below the large man's arm. "Bluebell!" he yelled. "Here, girl. Come on." The dog didn't respond.

As soon as she was free, Lorna scrambled across the floor to the bloodhound who had saved her life. The flow of blood had slowed to a thick seepage. "Bluebell?" she said. "No, no, girl, you can't..." Kneeling beside the animal, she lifted the heavy head into her lap and stroked the wrinkly face. Somehow, the great, slobbering beast had trotted her way into Lorna's heart. Despite their inauspicious beginning, the canine had given Lorna much-needed friendship and loyalty. Her simple, open heart loved small boys and resurrection men alike. Lorna's chin trembled.

She felt Brandon hovering over her shoulder. His presence bore down on her like an approaching storm. The weight of his gaze slumped her shoulders. Coward that she was, Lorna couldn't bear to look at Brandon and see condemnation in his eyes.

He crouched beside her and felt Bluebell's neck. "She's still alive," he said. Lorna risked a glance. Brandon's face was an emotionless mask. "I think the wound is mostly in the muscle, but she's lost too much blood."

Lorna's vision became watery. "How is Marjorie?"

"Laboring. Dying, most like," Brandon said, his voice bleak. "I must get back to Fenton House and help McGully."

Marjorie dying. Bluebell dying. Brandon hated her, now that he knew what she was. Soon, Elmwood would be gone, and she would lose Daniel, too. She stood on the precipice of unbearable loss, her toes dangling over the edge.

Brandon jerked to his feet and turned to go without offering her a hand, or so much as asking how she fared after her ordeal. His rejection cut deep. She stroked one of Bluebell's ears and tried to take a deep, calming breath. She couldn't; her ribs hurt. In fact, she seemed to hurt everywhere, she noted, with the beginnings of detachment.

Lord Sheridan and Brandon exchanged words Lorna could not hear. Brandon continued to the door, while Lord Sheridan stooped to lift Lorna into his arms.

"Your clothes will be ruined," she protested.

"Perfect," he said blithely. "Then I've no reason not to call upon my tailor on Monday and my glove maker on Tuesday. Heroism of this order demands a new ensemble."

The large man in the door stepped aside. Over the heads of the others, he regarded Lorna with friendly concern. One by one, the men filed out.

Coop grabbed Brandon's arm. "You said Blue's still alive. Help her," he snapped.

Brandon paused. "Fine," he replied.

"They say you're one of the best knifemen," Coop continued. "What good are you if you won't lift a finger to help a defenseless animal?"

Henry De Vere rolled his eyes. "Mr. Dewhurst agreed to your request. Weren't you listening? You won."

Coop clicked his mouth shut. "Oh." He sniffed. "All right then." With a jerk of his chin, he collected Pretty Lem. The two men made a basket with their arms and gently scooped Bluebell from the ground.

"Interesting friends you have, Miss Robbins," Lord Sheridan murmured into Lorna's ear. Having carried her outside, he ascended a short flight of stone steps and emerged in an alley behind a building. Considering Lorna had been convinced she was going to die in that dank little room, even the shards of sky glimpsed between rooftops felt like wide, open spaces.

"Where are we?" Lorna asked. "How did you find me?" Strangely, she felt like she was going to float away. She wanted to clasp Lord Sheridan's neck to prevent that fate, but her arms wouldn't cooperate.

"Two resurrection men came to Brandon's place. Something they told him led him to believe they might have information regarding your whereabouts. As there were only two of them, and all of us—and Norman should be counted as a brigade all by himself—it didn't take long to convince them that giving us your location was the best decision they could make for their continued well-being." He flashed her that charming, irrepressible smile of his. "As to where we found you: in the cellar of a fairly respectable tavern. Henry, Harrison, and Norman are going to have a word with the proprietor. I don't suppose this establishment will be considered respectable much longer." The light, polite tone of his voice couldn't fully conceal the threat of danger in his words.

"Are those other men Honorables, too?"

Lord Sheridan glanced at her in surprise. "You know of our little society?"

"Brandon told me." She blinked heavily. "Do you hate me, too?"

"You're quite the adventuress." Tucking her head close to his neck, the man maneuvered into a carriage and settled her on the seat beside him. "What's not to admire?" He made quick work of producing multiple handkerchiefs from his pockets and pressing them to her arms. Was it strange that the cuts had stopped hurting?

Part of Lorna wanted to explain to Lord Sheridan why he ought not admire her; a larger part saw no reason to convince the man to despise her. "I'm cold."

The space between his russet brows contracted. He released one of her arms to fish a blanket from beneath the seat. "We'll be to Fenton House soon," he said, tucking the blanket securely around her legs. His voice sounded far away.

"We will?" Lorna hadn't realized the carriage was in motion. Her lids, so heavy, slid home.

"No you don't." Lord Sheridan jostled her. Reluctantly, Lorna's eyes opened. "Dewhurst said you must stay awake. And because I value my own skin, I mean to follow his instructions—which means you must, as well."

Why should Brandon care what happened to Lorna? Before, certainly; but not now that he knew. This made her sad.

The numbness spreading through her limbs was pleasant. Much nicer than the pain, if a little unsettling. It spread to her mind; she welcomed it.

"Look at me, Miss Robbins," Sheridan said sharply, an edge to his tone. She tried to comply, but his face remained out of focus.

The seat disappeared from beneath her. There was another flash of sky. Outside? And then flat white. Inside? Her head jostled. Something soft supported her back. A firm pressure exerted itself against her lip.

Slee, forcing himself into her mouth.

And just like that, the blessed numbness was gone. "No," she cried, thrashing her head to the side, kicking and slapping with a burst of energy fueled by terror. "Get away!"

Hands grabbed her, forced her arms to her sides. "Miss Robbins! Lorna, please, calm yourself," the authoritative male voice compelled her. Her complaisance would only make it easier for Slee to hurt her. Lorna didn't want to be hurt. She didn't want to die. She wanted to live. And so she fought, and she screamed.

• • •

The scream echoed through Fenton House, filling the corridors and racing up the walls, until the entire structure reverberated with the essence of female suffering.

Brandon darted up the stairs and into Lady Fenton's chambers. She was on a birthing stool, one midwife clasping her hand, the other kneeling in front of her, and McGully off to the side, laying out an array of implements.

The laboring woman's mouth was frozen wide as the scream went on and on, a primordial shout of pain and rage. Florbela's face had been the same, but her scream had been a silent one. The sudden flash of memory shook Brandon's nerves, but he wrenched his mind back from that dark place.

At last, Lady Fenton's scream tapered into a groan. She slumped against the midwife at her side, who patted her brow and offered soothing words of encouragement.

"How is everything here?" Brandon asked McGully.

The Scotsman's gaze flicked to his employee. "Why have you saddled me with *them*?" He nodded toward the midwives, his derision evident. "Send them away, and hurry. I need your hands."

Brandon didn't have time for his mentor's professional prejudices. "Sir, you'll have to find a way to work with these worthy ladies. I have two more patients coming in who need my immediate attention."

McGully drew back. "What?"

Just then, a flood of voices filled the entryway downstairs; heavy steps thudded on the stairs.

The resurrectionists carrying the dog appeared in the door. "Where d'you want Blue?" asked the golden-haired one.

McGully's eyes bulged; he rounded on Brandon. "Are you mad?"

Another scream rent the air, but it didn't come from Lady Fenton.

Brandon's heart seized. *Lorna.*

It was still hard to believe that Lorna was the lady resurrectionist who had been a thorn in Brandon's side for a month.

He'd known it for certain when another wave of resurrectionists appeared, this time led by Bluebell, at Slee's hideout. So one of these ruffians was the "friend" who owned the hound. It had taken Brandon only a few seconds to deduce the identity of the new group—but had the Crib Cross men come to aid Lorna? Before he could deduce their intentions, a confused, three-way brawl had erupted between The Honorables and the two gangs of body snatchers.

In the melee, it had all fallen together with terrible clarity. The Lorna Robbins he knew had always been a criminal, but Brandon couldn't bring himself to care, not when she was in danger. When he'd seen her in that cellar, bound and abused, he'd nearly gone out of his head with rage and fear. And when Slee went after her with a knife, he had acted on pure instinct, snatching one of Harry's pistols and putting an end to the lowlife who dared threaten the woman he loved, the woman who was his entire world.

After that, all he'd wanted to do was grab Lorna into his arms and carry her to safety, but Brandon hadn't trusted himself to touch her. If he did, he wouldn't be able to focus on the other responsibilities demanding his attention. And so he'd placed his woman in the hands of an inveterate womanizer. Sheri might not have many scruples when it came to his bedroom activities, but he respected his friends and would never try to seduce the woman Brandon loved. He thought highly of Lorna, as well, and the two facts made him the best choice for tending her until Brandon could see to her himself.

"I've two patients to sew up," he told his mentor. "You're in good hands with Mrs. Fisher and Miss Watling," he said, nodding to the midwives. "I'll be back as soon as I can."

Behind him, McGully sputtered and yelled for Brandon to stop. Lady Fenton cried out with another pain. Brandon tucked his chin and kept moving.

Henry and Harrison stood in the hallway outside Lorna's room. Brandon brushed past his friends into the bedchamber. Lorna strained against the restraining hands of Sheri and Norman, obviously in the grips of one of her panic episodes.

Lorna's maid, Charity, pawed at her mistress's ruined bodice, trying to wrestle the buttons free. "I knew you'd want her undressed," the woman announced.

A drinking glass lay on the floor, contents spilled on the rug.

"Leave me alone!" Lorna cried, one eye wide. The other was swollen to a slit, the surrounding flesh red and purple from the viscous blows Slee had landed on her face. "I have to get out. Let me go. Please, *please!*" Her ragged respiration bordered on hyperventilation.

"Stop, all of you!" Brandon yelled. "Can't you see you're making her worse?"

Norman shot him an apologetic look and instantly made for the door, grabbing Sheri's arm and towing the other man behind him.

Sheri looked stricken as Brandon shooed them into the corridor. "I did what you said. I kept her awake."

"What can we do to help?" Harrison asked.

Brandon glanced over his shoulder. Lorna was lashing out at Charity. "Plenty of water and rags," he said, "and a bottle of brandy."

Harrison, Norman, and Henry headed off, but Sheri resolutely planted himself outside Lorna's door. "I'll be here if you need me," he said.

With a nod, Brandon turned back into the room. "You, too," he told Charity. "Out."

The maid swatted Lorna's slapping hands. "But Mr. Dewhurst…" she protested.

"Out."

The maid flung up her hands. "On your head be it," she huffed. "I'd mind your trinkets if I was you. She's got a mean punch."

Freed from grasping hands, Lorna struggled to push upright. The gashes in her arms bled freely once more, weeping down her arms, staining the coverlet.

Brandon took her shoulders in a firm, but gentle, grip.

Her arm swung up. Brandon allowed the blow to strike his face. She trembled from fear and possibly blood loss. If he didn't get her wounds closed soon, he worried she might do herself irreparable harm.

"Lorna, it's Brandon." He shook her gently. "Do you hear me? You're safe, Lorna. It's only me."

The wild-haired beauty regarded him with a feral gleam. Her bottom lip sported a cut that had already closed; dried blood crusted the gash. Terror slowly drained from her turquoise gaze as recognition dawned. "Brandon?" she whispered. "Is it over?"

The vulnerable sound pierced his heart. He wanted to take her in his arms and soothe her as he'd done before. *But she lied.* She was a resurrectionist, affiliated with murderers and thieves like Slee.

"It's over," he confirmed. Beneath his touch, her arms were feverish. "You must let me tend your wounds, or else they'll fester."

She turned her head, her curls shielding her bruised face from his scrutiny. "They all know, don't they?"

Betrayal flared through his chest, hollowing him. He removed his hands, needing to put physical distance between them. *They know? They?* Had she no thought for him? He'd offered her everything he had to give, his body, his love—he'd even told her about his son, something he'd never confided in another soul.

Wrenching open the door, he put his head into the corridor. "Where's that water?" he snarled at Sheri, who merely lifted a brow and strolled toward the stairs.

All the while he'd been making a lovesick fool of himself, Lorna had given him nothing in return but half-truths and outright lies. Raking a hand through his hair, he growled.

From the opposite end of the corridor, another of Lady Fenton's moans sounded, reminding Brandon he had other duties.

"Water!" he bellowed.

"Brandon?" came Lorna's plaintive voice.

Glancing back, he saw she'd pulled down the top of her dress and lain down. Her chemise, saturated with blood and sweat, clung stiffly to her torso, revealing her lithesome form. Even now, knowing what she was, his body responded to her. He closed his eyes and turned away, unable to bear the betrayal of his flesh on the heels of discovering her duplicity.

At last, The Honorables approached in a procession, bearing water and stacks of cloths. Sheri brought the requested brandy and two glasses, as though Brandon and Lorna might wish to share a toast. As they carried the supplies into the room, Henry lifted his arm, hoisting Brandon's bag. "Thought you might need this, old man."

After his friends filed back out, Brandon tried to concentrate on cleaning and sewing the wounds. Lorna had downed some brandy and now watched him with a steady, if slightly fuddled, gaze.

As he tied off a row of stitches, he finally responded to her concerns. "You can trust my friends' discretion," he assured her. "Lord and Lady Fenton know nothing. I'll tell them Slee abducted you opportunistically, after failing in his plot against Lady Fenton."

She sagged in relief. "Thank you."

A sharp retort formed on his tongue, but Brandon bit it back.

"I was going to tell you this morning," she said. "I hated keeping such a secret from you."

"That isn't a *secret*," he hissed. "How Lady Chambers achieves that unnatural shade of red hair is a *secret*. The precise number of women Sheri has bedded is a *secret*. This"—he gestured up and down her length—"is not a secret; it is—you are—a person I don't know."

"You do know me!" she protested, hurt shading her words. "Better than anyone else. You understand me and I think…I think I understand you, too." Tentatively, she reached a hand toward his face. She gasped at the strain of lifting her injured limb.

Brandon leaned back, out of reach.

Deflated, Lorna let her arm fall.

"If you didn't know me," she said in a small voice, gaze trained on her lap, "you wouldn't be the only person I can tolerate being near when these terrible fits are upon me." Her pink tongue darted out to swipe her bottom lip. "And I know *you*, Brandon. I know how much you hate resurrectionists." She lifted her face to him. Even with bruises eclipsing her constellations of freckles, Lorna looked young and guileless. Despite himself, Brandon's heart lurched. "I couldn't bear for you to despise me."

The confession was heartbreaking in its raw honesty. And it *was* the truth. He'd sensed there was something Lorna was keeping from him, something holding her back. But everything they'd shared—the friendship, the passion—had been real.

Carefully, Brandon wound lengths of linen around her stitched arms, glad to have the task as an excuse not to meet her pleading gaze.

Only too well could Brandon relate to the fear of being judged unworthy on the basis of one's profession. He grimaced as he recalled how he'd reflexively defended himself to Lorna the night they'd dined with the Freedmans, assuming she'd look down on him for being a surgeon, because so many others had.

But she hadn't scorned him. She had accepted him, had, in fact, praised his work as important.

"Brandon?" Her chin quivered. "Please say something."

He finished tying off the bandages. "Keep those clean." He packed his supplies into his bag and stood. "Bed rest until the swelling in your injuries decreases and the risk of infection has passed. Now, pardon me," he said with a curt nod, "I must see if there's anything to be done for Bluebell, then assist McGully with Lady Fenton."

There was nothing more to say, not until he'd thought things through.

Chapter Thirty-Five

Lorna stood in front of the door. The muscles in her arms flexed, tugging at the stitches. On the other side, feminine voices murmured. With everything that had happened, she was uncertain how she'd be received. *What would Blackbird do?* Blackbird, of course, would show no fear, not even in the face of social catastrophe. Squaring her shoulders, Lorna knocked.

"Come in," came the reply.

Sitting in bed, Marjorie looked lovely as ever in a silk robe of pale apricot. In her arms, she held a baby, snugly tucked in swaddling.

Marjorie glanced at Lorna from beneath a fringe of sooty lashes. Dark circles below tired eyes were the only signs of her recent ordeal. When she saw Lorna, her smile chased away even those small imperfections.

Nelly and Alice sat nearby; both ladies had bundled infants tucked in their arms. Nelly met Lorna's eyes. "Our dear Miss Robbins has come at last," she said, repeating some of the first words she'd said to her neighbor. Alice, likewise, favored Lorna with a welcoming smile.

"Are you feeling better?" Marjorie asked. "Come meet the terrible trio."

Despite the bravado she'd tried to imbue herself with, Lorna felt a decided surge of relief. "They don't seem terrible at all," she said, approaching the group. "They're all sleeping like sweet angels."

"Wait until they get hungry," Marjorie said dryly. "They were born about a month early, so they eat almost constantly. One wakes up wailing and sets off the other two. Then they all start snuffling and rooting at the breast like a farrow of truffle piglets."

Lorna laughed. "What a description! And the poor things only a week old. How will you describe them in a few years?"

The new mother fondly stroked the head of the baby cuddled to her chest. "As my miracles," she murmured, then bent to kiss the little brow.

Since the babies' birth, Lorna had been confined to her guest chamber while she recuperated from Slee's attack. The bruises on her face and ribs had begun to fade, and the stitches in her arms itched terribly, which meant the cuts were healing, according to Charity.

Brandon had not come to see her since tending her wounds, but he had sent a gift: a beautiful redingote of dove-gray silk, lined with fur and embroidered with blue-green scrollwork that matched her eyes. Lorna thought it far too fine to wear in inclement weather, but she had donned it in her room and admired herself in the mirror. The coat was deliciously warm and softer than any garment Lorna had ever owned.

There was a note tucked into the box: *We'll speak when you're feeling better.—BD*

The gift reassured her that Brandon might not hate her after all, but she didn't know what it meant. Some gentlemen gave ladies gifts when ending an affair, did they not? Could this be his way of easing the end of their association?

Trying not to think too much about it, Lorna had devoted herself to resting and recovering. Now that she was feeling better, the time had come to take her leave of Fenton House. She'd return to Chorley House today, then go on to Elmwood tomorrow. Whatever happened with Brandon, it was time to deal with the matter of Daniel's guardian.

Once she met Lord Huffemall, perhaps the man could be persuaded to loan Lorna the funds needed to repay Wiggins, thereby keeping the estate safe for Daniel, at least for now. Over time, she could repay him out of Elmwood's meager profits. The plan would mean more scrimping and doing without, but the sacrifices would be worthwhile, if they secured her brother's future.

"Won't you hold one of the little darlings?" Nelly asked, her expression soft and dreamy as she snuggled the tiny infant. "Not this one," she said, hugging her charge a little closer. "One of the others."

Chuckling, Marjorie offered the child she held. "Take this fine fellow." Lorna's arms ached, but she would not miss the chance. "This is our heir," Marjorie said. "We named him after you."

Lorna's hand paused mid-pat above the baby's bottom. "Me? What on earth for? And isn't *Lorna* a touch feminine for such a handsome young man?" She was being diplomatic in the way one must be with babies. Truthfully, the child looked like a wizened, little old man, all loose skin and wrinkles.

Marjorie's eyes misted over; her voice was thick with emotion. "You saved me and my children. His name is Robin."

Lorna's heart fluttered; warmth suffused her chest. She took another look at young Lord Robin. The infant opened his eyes, giving her a view of their fathomless blue depths. "Perhaps you really *are* handsome," she whispered to the boy, a slow grin spreading across her face. "The other names?" she asked.

Nelly turned to display her little friend. "This gentleman is Lonan."

Lorna's ears perked at the unusual name. "A family name?"

"Not directly," Marjorie said. "It's Irish, to honor Archibald's maternal heritage. It means 'blackbird.'"

Lorna's smile froze on her face.

Heedless of Lorna's sudden unease, her friend continued, "Since we chose a bird-related name for his brother, we decided to stay within the theme." Marjorie gave no indication of knowing about Lorna's own connection to the name.

To cover her discomfiture, Lorna bent to inhale Robin's scent, a heady combination of milk and powder.

"And this," Alice announced, "is the lovely Lady Branna. She has two brothers to watch over and protect her."

"Or to torment her," Nelly said.

"Or to rule over with an iron fist," supplied Marjorie.

The friends shared a laugh, then Lorna asked, "Another bird name?"

Marjorie shook her head. "Believe it or no, she's named for your Mr. Dewhurst."

Baby Robin screwed up his face and grunted. With no more warning than that, his whole head turned red and he let out a plaintive wail. As promised, the other two soon contributed their voices to the commotion. Lorna and Alice exchanged pained looks.

Three wetnurses trotted in and collected the babies. The sounds of the siblings' hungry complaints were audible until they reached the nursery and, one must assume, were provided with their sustenance.

Easing lower into the bed, Marjorie drew a deep breath and released it with a long sigh. "Oh, it's so lovely to be able to breathe again," she said. "Back to my daughter's name: The boys were born without more than the usual degree of difficulty, thanks to Mr. McGully and the midwives Mr. Dewhurst recommended. But the last baby wouldn't come out. I lost a great deal of blood, and was rapidly fading."

"Oh, Marjorie," Lorna said, sitting on the edge of the bed and taking the woman's hand. "But you're all right now, aren't you?"

Marjorie squeezed her hand reassuringly. "I am, or I will be, in any event. Mr. McGully wanted to use some positively medieval-looking torture device on me." Recalling the implements displayed at the anatomy school lecture, Lorna shuddered. "Thankfully, Mr. Dewhurst arrived at that very moment. He suggested moving me from the birthing stool to the bed, where they all poked and prodded at me, and determined the baby was lying sideways."

Alice snorted. "Her brothers had the poor little dear squashed into the corner."

"Undoubtedly," Marjorie agreed. "After that, Mr. McGullly permitted Mr. Dewhurst to turn the baby from the outside. He was adamant that no one actually…that is…" She blushed and cleared her throat. "He insisted no one reach inside to turn the baby. He said it would cause too much damage. Two pushes later, out came Branna."

Lorna's heart felt full to bursting with pride. It must have been terrible for Brandon to come into Marjorie's birthing chamber and find her in a bad way, reminding him of losing Florbela and his own son. But he'd kept his wits about him and preserved two lives. Because of him, a woman who had been fully expected to die would live to mother all three of her children.

All at once, Lorna yearned to tell Brandon just how much she loved him. She didn't know how he would react to such an announcement, given that uncovering her resurrectionist activities may have caused his love for her to wither and die, but…didn't she have to try?

As if on cue, Lord Fenton popped into the room. "Ladies." He nodded to the women in general, then turned to Lorna. "Shall we, Miss Robbins?"

Lorna took her leave of her friends, promising to see them all soon. In the foyer, his lordship helped her into her new coat. Lord Fenton handed her into his carriage, instructing the driver to take them to Chorley House.

"You know, Miss Robbins," the new father said as the carriage started forward, "while my children were making their unruly way into the world a week ago, I had some unexpected company in my study. Several persons delivered a dog in need of Mr. Dewhurst's surgical attentions. They were most devoted to the animal, and relieved me of a bottle of my finest Scotch while we paced and fretted over our respective concerns."

His light tone did not fool Lorna. She held her breath, cringing inwardly for what she knew must be coming. Lord Fenton did not make her wait long.

"These gentlemen also expressed apprehension over your well-being, Miss Robbins. It seems you suffered your injuries at the same time and place as the dog—Bluebell, I'm told she's called." His pale brown gaze sliced her to the quick. "I was startled to learn these men are friends of yours."

A chill suffused her. In spite of what Brandon had told him, Lord Fenton knew all, she was certain. He would order her to stay away from his wife and children. And why not? Lorna was an outrageously inappropriate friend for a viscountess.

It was nice to have some female friends, she thought glumly. Too bad she couldn't have kept them a little while longer. Ah, well. She'd infiltrated Society under false pretenses, and never meant to stay longer than the time it took to pay off Wiggins. She supposed it was just to be exposed for the imposter she was. Even if it caused her stomach to cramp and her cheeks to burn.

She stared at her gloved hands in her lap, placidly folded atop the silk of her fine new redingote. *Look at yourself*, she thought. *Still a fraud.* She had no more right to these small luxuries than she did to the acceptance of polite society.

"I won't bore you with the details of the activities of myself and my small army of solicitors over the last week," Lord Fenton continued. "I will merely tell you that you need no longer worry about a certain Mr. Wiggins."

Lorna's face snapped up to meet Lord Fenton's steady gaze. His sharp features softened as his expression gentled.

Bewildered, she frowned. "But the money I owe—"

"You need *never worry about it again.*" Lord Fenton spoke slowly, giving each word weight. "All the money you paid him has been returned to your solicitor, Mr. Gordon, for you to claim whenever you like. The matter is settled."

She could do nothing but stare, mouth agape. Lorna wished she had the pride to turn down Lord Fenton's generosity, but she had none where Daniel was concerned. Elmwood was secure. Daniel was safe.

"Furthermore," he went on, "you may wish to know that Lord Huffemall is a cousin of mine, and is a fair and reasonable man. I've taken the liberty of writing to offer him my witness of your character." Lord Fenton leaned forward and took her hands, a smile of compassion crinkling his eyes. "I assured him that you are as devoted to your brother as one person can possibly be to another, and that you have provided Lord Chorley a safe, happy home, from which he should not be removed. You have nothing to fear, Miss Robbins, not from any quarter."

Overwhelmed, Lorna burst into tears. She buried her face in her hands and sobbed. The heavy weight of her responsibilities slowly slid away, scouring her innards and leaving her feeling raw, exposed.

His lordship's hand settled on her shoulder. "You have friends, Miss Robbins. Do not forget. And now you are free."

• • •

Almost as soon as Lord Fenton delivered her to Chorley House, Lorna made ready to depart again. A fierce urgency to see Brandon swept through her. No longer could she abide being separated from him. Prepared to seek out the man she loved, she quickly washed her face in her room, then returned downstairs.

In the corridor, she halted. Oscar was escorting a guest toward the parlor.

That guest spotted Lorna and wagged her tail.

Bluebell slowly made her way down the hall, favoring her front left leg. Coop followed behind, gently encouraging the animal when she paused to catch her breath. The dog sported a bandage around her shoulder. A piece was missing from the end of one of her ears, the edge unmistakably a human bite mark.

Dropping to her knees, Lorna opened her arms and welcomed the canine's sloppy greeting. "Hello, Blue," she said, scratching the dog behind the ears and nuzzling her wrinkled neck. "Hello, dear girl."

She looked up at Coop. "Hello to you, as well. Won't you come in?" She led them into the parlor, asking Oscar for tea and whatever treat Cook could spare for Bluebell.

Coop sat awkwardly on the edge of a chair, looking decidedly ill at ease. His nose fairly glowed pink, fine veins prominent on flushed cheeks. One hand fisted on his knee; in the other, he clutched a cap. He wore the blue suit Lorna had seen him in the day they visited Manning and learned about Marjorie, pregnant with triplets, the greatest prize any resurrection gang could hope to claim.

With a tired groan, Bluebell lay at Coop's feet. Her head rested between her paws, jowls melting in a furry puddle around her nose.

"Good to see you up and about again," said the resurrectionist. "Can't nobody keep our Blackbird down for long, not even a scoundrel like Slee."

She smiled fondly, but couldn't keep a touch of sadness from her voice. "I'm just plain Lorna Robbins now, Coop. My resurrecting days are over."

Behind his lower lip, his tongue made a lump, flitted back and forth several times in quick succession. "'Bout like I figured." Reaching down, he patted Bluebell's haunch. "That Dewhurst is a cunning shaver. Cheated Old Grim out of how many just the other day? You an' Blue, that lady and her brood, too. Fine bit of work. Wouldn't mind selling to a tiptop surgeon like him."

"He'll be needing a new supplier, now that Slee's gang is out."

"An' our buyer, Manning, is charged with plotting murder against her ladyship." Coop sounded scandalized. Lorna marveled that a man in Coop's profession could keep such firm hold of his own particular morality. "He's going to dangle, mark my words." Coop toed a circle on the rug. "I'll have to see what I can work out with Dewhurst, seeing as we're both at loose ends."

Tea arrived, with a hearty portion of lamb for Bluebell.

Coop grasped the china cup gingerly, as though fearful it would spontaneously shatter in his hand. Setting it carefully to the side, he wiped his palm on his thigh. "Would you say I been square with you, Blackbird? I always treat my boys to round dealing. No cove never had cause to accuse me of being unfair."

"You've been nothing but honorable in our dealings, Coop. Thank you for taking me in like you did, for giving me a chance and sharing the profits—"

He cut her off with a gruff wave of his hand. "It's just, if I been good to you, maybe you can do somethin' for me."

"If it's within my power."

Coop swallowed hard. "Take Bluebell off my hands, would you? Tore up like this, she ain't no use to me no more."

The heartlessness of the words hit Lorna hard. How dare he discard the loyal beast? Then she noted the tremble of Coop's chin.

"Of course I'll take her," she answered gently.

The body snatcher, fearless in the face of death and lawlessness, sniffed. "You got a place out there in the country, yeah? Room for her to roam around?"

"Plenty of room for running, and squirrels and rabbits for her to chase to her heart's content." Picturing Daniel's joy at being reunited with Bluebell, Lorna beamed. "There's a little boy there who already adores her and will be delighted to explore the countryside with his faithful companion. She will have a happy life, Coop."

A cuff swiped across the man's nose. "Good." He nodded stiffly. "That's good. She'll like that. Sniffing birds and flowers and stuff, 'stead of quarrons all the damned time. Nose like hers should retire in proper style, yeah?"

"I couldn't agree more."

Coop slapped his thighs. "All right, then. S'pose I'd best be on my way, 'fore the Watch shows up, wanting to know what a blighter like me is doing in a fine house like this."

Lorna rose and took Coop's hands. Much to his chagrin, she kissed his cheek. "I would tell them you are a welcome guest."

The Crib Cross Gang would always have a place in her heart. Rowdy, rough, and borderline criminal they might be, but they were loyal and had their own kind of honor. Each man had made Lorna feel like an integral part of the team, for the first time giving her a taste of acceptance from someone besides her younger brother. They valued her for who and what she was, and helped Lorna find a reserve of determination—and a streak of recklessness—she hadn't known she possessed.

The experience had been terrifying and wonderful in ways she couldn't yet articulate. If nothing else, Lorna's adventures had led her to her friends—and Brandon.

The resurrection man's perennially chapped face turned a deeper shade of red. "Right. Well, then." Clearing his throat, he nodded at the dog. "Mind you take care of yourself, Bluebell, and that boy of yours, too. Don't be a nuisance, or Blackbird'll toss you on your lame ear. And don't you come running back to me, if that happens." He dropped to his haunches and stroked the canine fondly. "Ain't no spongin' in Crib Cross."

Bluebell's tail thumped against the floor. She whined.

"Don't you go and get tears in your peepers. Not over me. You got a good and proper home now."

The scene between resurrectionist and hound was so affecting, Lorna felt she was imposing. She turned away, only to see Brandon standing in the door. Their eyes met, silently communicating a world of emotion.

Coop heaved to his feet and started when he noticed Brandon. "Mr. Dewhurst! Damn if you ain't as quiet as the best sneaksman. You ever done any thieving?"

Brandon extended his hand to the body snatcher. "Nothing in a professional capacity, only mischief against my brothers when I was a lad. Good to see you again, Mr. Cooper."

For once, the gang leader didn't insist upon his preferred nickname. "And you, Mr. Dewhurst. I was just taking my leave." He glanced once more to Bluebell, and then to Lorna. "You take care of my favorite ladies now, yeah?"

Brandon clapped his shoulder. "Come by my place soon, won't you? I believe we should discuss business."

A happy grin split Coop's face. He nodded his way out of the room and whistled a jaunty tune on down the corridor.

The parlor door swung closed. Taut silence filled the space, broken only by a rumbling exhalation from Bluebell.

No words were exchanged. Acute awareness of one another held them rapt. Lorna ached for the feeling of his arms around her, for the sweet torment of his lovemaking. Her breath hitched in her throat. Slowly, she crossed the room.

Gently, he traced a finger along the sweep of her shoulder, hovered his palm over her stitched wound. The warmth of his hand seeped through the thin fabric of her sleeve.

Brandon's face dipped, stopping two excruciating inches from her mouth. Every nerve in Lorna's body tingled in anticipation. They stood that way, close but not touching, for an endless moment. He was waiting for her in that intense way of his, his silence demanding her response. The space between them was a trifle, the merest breath, but Lorna knew it would be insurmountable unless she finally gave herself to him as completely as he'd given himself to her.

"I love you," she said. The words hung in the air, given, but not yet accepted. A tentacle of the old, familiar anxiety slithered through her middle. What if he couldn't forgive her for misleading him, or accept her for what she was?

Brandon's eyelids slid home as he leaned their foreheads together, one hand cupping the back of her neck. At his touch, tension drained from her body. His fingers massaged her neck, relaxing her further.

"Your involvement with the resurrectionists kept us apart."

She nodded, dreading that it might ruin any chance they had of being together. "I wish you hadn't found out the way you did. I should have told you."

A shadow crossed the face that had become beautiful to her. "Will you tell me now? How did this happen?"

Impulsively, Lorna took Brandon's hand and led him to the settee. He stretched out with his legs across the cushions and back propped on the arm and pulled her into his lap, her back to his chest, carefully positioned so as not to disturb her injuries. One of his arms wrapped around her waist; his long fingers stroked her belly. His touch felt marvelous, but she tried not to read too much into it.

When they were settled, Lorna began to talk, telling her story from the day of Thomas's funeral, the fateful day she met both Wiggins and the Crib Cross Gang. Now that she'd given the words an outlet, they poured forth, unwilling to be stoppered again beneath a cork of shame and secrecy. And, oh, the blissful relief of finally, *finally*, telling another soul everything she'd been carrying alone for so long.

As she spoke, Brandon held his peace. He pressed kisses to the top of her head from time to time, or flattened his palm against her middle, hugging her closer as she recounted some of the more harrowing moments of her life as Blackbird.

"One of the most trying things," she said, turning so she could face him, "was discovering that you were watching over Lady Fenton, just as I was. I was terrified you'd learn my secret, but, at the same time, it made me feel that much closer to you. Even if you didn't know about the connection we shared, I knew you understood what I was going through, how miserable it was to try to be close to that lovely, lively woman while waiting for her to die. Knowing that you were going through it, too, helped me feel not quite so alone."

Some emotion she couldn't read contorted Brandon's features. His hands tightened, one fisting in her skirt, the other gripping her ribs. He seemed to be struggling with himself—about what?

"Thank you for the coat," Lorna finally said, attempting to change the subject. Her story had disturbed him. Now that he knew all she'd done, did he wish to be free of her for good? "It's the most beautiful thing I've ever owned," she prattled nervously. "It makes the rest of my clothes look that much shabbier."

On a moan, brought his mouth to hers, feeding her a kiss laced with anguish. Lorna whimpered, denying his pain. She regretted nothing that had transpired, for it had brought them together. In the dark world they shared, he was her beacon of light. Her feelings poured through her caresses, telling him without words just how dear he was to her. He fought back, kissing her fiercely, his tongue delving into her mouth with hot strokes that quickly sparked arousal low in her belly. His hands slid over her back and sides, kneading her soft flesh. Against her hip, she felt him harden and lengthen.

Ruthlessly he tore away, pupils blown wide, his sensual lips parted. "Don't thank me for a damned coat, Lorna. Already, I knew you were more than I deserved, but now…" His dark brows pulled together. "You were right there with me in that hell, offering me comfort and support, when I should have been giving you the same. But I didn't know you'd been plunged into the darkness beside me.

"When you convinced Lady Fenton to gift me her body, you sacrificed everything—your home, your family, *everything*—and I didn't even know." He grasped either side of her face, driving his hands into her hair, releasing the curls from the pins keeping them tamed. He shook her lightly, as though to import upon her the seriousness of what he was saying. "You gave up the only means you had of repaying your brother's debts. Not just for me, but for Lady Fenton, too, which makes your actions all the sweeter. Only you, walking in all three worlds—Society, surgeons, and resurrectionists, were perfectly placed to save her from a terrifying fate."

Lorna's hands floated up to cover his. "She was so afraid, Brandon. I couldn't let them fight over her body. It was the only way, and you were the only one I trusted to do right by her."

He searched her face, then kissed her, gently. It was slow and sweet, but no less affecting than his earlier, rougher kiss.

"This isn't the first time you've humbled me, Lorna, and I don't suspect it will be the last." Tilting his head, he asked, "If I'd listened to your refusal, you'd have let me walk away, none the wiser, wouldn't you?"

Yes, she would have, and he knew it.

"Then I suppose it's a good thing I'm stupidly determined when I put my mind to something," he said, a teasing glint in his eye. "I don't care that you worked as a resurrectionist, Lorna. I understand why you didn't tell me. How could you, when I'd expressed my distaste for them? Every night, I meet them at the threshold of my workplace and home. I do hate the violent criminality that goes hand-in-hand with the business. My work has forced me into association with killers, and no, I don't like them, and I won't apologize for looking down on murderers. But you managed to fall in with a good lot, thank God." He paused to draw breath.

"Feel better?" she asked wryly.

"Seems I had some things to relieve myself of, as well." He raked his hair. "In any event, I'm not here to cast judgment for doing as necessity demanded to save your home and family. To the contrary, I fiercely admire you, Lorna. You are simply stunning, in every conceivable way. My feelings haven't changed. If anything, I love you even more. If you'd let me, I'd give you everything that's mine, all that I am."

How could it be that such a fine man thought so highly of her? Brandon's whole life was dedicated to saving lives and teaching others to do the same. Every day, he somehow summoned the fortitude not only to face suffering and death, but to defy them. He was honor and valor personified, a gallant knight bearing a knife, rather than a sword. Yet he was every bit as much the champion of the defenseless as that shining-armored hero of old.

Ignoring the protests of her muscles, Lorna threw her arms around his neck. "If you're determined to love me, then I suppose I'm just going to have to let you. It works out nicely, since I'm hopelessly in love with you." She lifted her face and kissed him soundly. From what had seemed to be an endless quagmire of darkness had emerged this unexpected gift of love and grace. And she meant to keep it.

On the opposite side of the sitting area, Bluebell pulled herself to her feet. She limped across the rug and nudged Lorna with her snout.

Reluctantly ending the kiss, both Lorna and Brandon petted the animal. Bluebell groaned in ecstasy at the attention. "I'm taking her back to Elmwood, to live with me and Daniel." She took a deep breath then looked Brandon in the eye. "I'd like to take you to live with us, as well."

"Does that mean you've agreed to marry me?"

"Do the prince and princess marry at the end of the fairy stories?" she rejoined.

Brandon's gray eyes widened in mock horror. "I don't know! I'm told I'm hopeless with fairy stories. Do they?"

"Yes," Lorna said with a happy grin, her heart aglow with joy. "They do."

Epilogue

Ten years later

"Look here, Al." Brandon pointed to an internal structure with the tip of a knife. Once again, he'd forgotten his new spectacles on his nightstand and had to squint a bit. "That's the gizzard."

"Humans don't have those, right, Papa?" said his eight-year-old child. Wide eyes of a familiar turquoise turned to regard him somberly.

"Indeed not. What animals *do* have gizzards?"

"Birds, of course," said Al, indicating the dissected chicken laid before them on a table in Elmwood's conservatory—long since converted to Brandon's private dissection chamber. "But fish, too." Small, plump lips twisted to the side in a thoughtful expression. "Some reptiles, as well?"

"That's exactly right," Brandon said, leaning over to kiss the freckled temple. "How did you get to be so brilliant?"

The little girl giggled, the sound pure sunshine and fairy rings. Brandon and Lorna's daughter, Alene, tended toward the serious; coaxing a dimpled smile out of her always felt like a small victory.

"*You* taught me, silly!"

"Did I?"

"Yes."

"Are you certain?"

She clapped a hand to her mouth. "Yes!"

"Oh, well then, no wonder you're a prodigy. You have a brilliant teacher."

That earned him not only another smile, but a hug around the waist, as well. Brandon had enjoyed a happy upbringing, but his father had not been a physically affectionate man. He didn't mourn the lack for himself; rather, he regretted that his father had never fully enjoyed the pure, unfettered joy that came from openly demonstrating love for one's child.

"You should go inside and wash up," he said when Alene broke away to resume her inspection of the bird's anatomy. "Mr. and Mrs. De Vere will be here soon."

They hadn't seen Henry and his family since last fall, and Brandon looked forward to catching up with his friend. The rest of The Honorables would arrive over the next several days, for what had become an annual reunion.

Alene clapped her hands, bouncing on the balls of her feet, braids jouncing against her back. "Please, Papa, may Opal and I ride together?"

The reunion festivities kept growing in size, as wives, and then children, had been added to The Honorables' clan-by-choice. Brandon's and Henry's eldest children were only months apart in age, and the girls had been fast friends since infancy. When they weren't together, the girls were voracious correspondents.

"If her parents—"

Movement outside caught his attention. It was Lorna, strolling in the garden. For a long moment, he was raptly engrossed by the vision his wife presented. Her figure was a bit fuller than it used to be, having now borne two children, but the more generous curves suited her beautifully. Surrounded by early summer blossoms and a profusion of greenery, and with her hair loose around her shoulders—as he'd always loved it best—she was like some fey creature out of the storybooks he still never could keep straight. Lorna retained a youthful aura, with only smile lines faintly etched on her darling, freckled face.

In her arms, she carried Clive, their fifteen-month-old son. She stopped to point out some interesting bit of nature to the boy. The baby beamed at whatever it was his mother had shown him, then patted Lorna's cheek. She smiled in return, an easy expression free of the sometimes-crippling anxiety that used to haunt her.

A dog loped up the path behind Brandon's wife and child, shaggy tail wagging and beard wet from the slobber stringing from loose jowls. Sabo was an odd-looking beast, the result of his dam, Bluebell, mating with one of the neighbors' small terriers during one of her romps about the countryside. As an anatomist, Brandon still puzzled over how that particular pairing transpired.

Sabo was a genial creature, gentle with the children and always eager to accompany Brandon when he went out, whether for a ramble or calling on a patient. But Brandon still missed Bluebell, who had quietly passed away two springs ago, surrounded by her doting human family. They'd buried her beneath a shady oak, her resting place marked with a plaque. When she died, Brandon had written to Coop, whom they only saw rarely these days—and then just socially—when the family stayed in Town for the winter anatomy term. The old man had made the journey to Elmwood, accompanied by the former members of the now-defunct Crib Cross Gang. Daniel had come home from school, as well. Together, they'd held a memorial service in honor of the finest dog any of them had ever known. The little ceremony had fed village gossip for weeks, but Brandon didn't give a damn.

During her years with Brandon and Lorna, Bluebell had been a loyal friend to them all, her antics entertaining and exasperating in turn. Blue had had a particular fondness for Lorna, and had seen her mistress through the several panic episodes that occurred during the early months of Brandon's and Lorna's marriage, and which then recurred while she carried Alene. Most of all, Brandon never could forget that Bluebell had thrown herself between Lorna and that knife-wielding maniac, a service for which Brandon would always honor her memory.

On the garden path, little Clive lunged for Sabo. Lorna bent to safely lower the child to the ground, giving Brandon a perfect view of her sensually curved backside. His body responded at once, sweeping away any melancholy his ruminations had summoned.

She must have sensed his hungry gaze, for she straightened and turned, her eyes unerringly finding his. Even separated by a wall of glass and thirty-some feet, awareness between them flared, potent as ever, their connection now all the richer for the joys and sorrows they had shared through the years.

"Look, Papa! Uncle Daniel!" Alene's joyful cry pulled Brandon's attention back into the dissecting room, to notice his daughter pressed against the glass, facing the drive.

As she'd said, the young baron trotted up the drive, sitting tall on his mount. With the blessings of Lord Huffemall, his benign legal guardian, Daniel had stayed at Elmwood and grown up in the care of Brandon and Lorna. Once a year, his lordship had journeyed to Elmwood to check in on the lad in person. As he grew older, Daniel began spending a month of each summer in Wales with Huffemall. Brandon had educated the boy himself, with a tutor hired on to supplement lessons, until he'd made his way to public school at age thirteen.

Alene vibrated with excitement. Uncle Daniel was a great favorite, as he always arrived with sweets and little gifts.

"You'd better hurry with that washing up, then," Brandon said. No sooner were the words out of his mouth than his daughter tore out of the room like a fox with hounds nipping on her heels.

Brandon cleared up the morning's anatomy lesson, carefully cleaning every tool and surface used. By the time he found his family on the front lawn, Alene and Sabo were running circles around Daniel, who was on hands and knees in the grass, giving chase to Clive—himself crawling as fast as his pudgy arms and legs could carry him and screaming with glee.

Brandon wrapped his arms around Lorna from behind; her hands settled on his wrists. Together, they spent a moment quietly watching their family at play. Inevitably, though, Lorna's curls tickled his nose, inviting him to burrow in and inhale deeply of her familiar scent. She rocked against him even as he hardened, her nails nipping little crescents into his skin.

"How long until the De Veres arrive?" Lorna asked over her shoulder.

"An hour or so," Brandon murmured, pressing a kiss to her neck.

"Daniel can watch the children."

"Thank God."

His wife grabbed his hand and, laughing, they ran into the house.

THE END

More from This Author
(From *Once a Duchess* by Elizabeth Boyce)

1813

Isabelle Jocelyn Fairfax Lockwood, the former Duchess of Monthwaite, knelt on the stone hearth and prodded the weak fire in the grate of her small cottage in southern Leicestershire. The flames gave a half-hearted attempt to brighten before they settled back to a feeble glow. She blew into the coals. Again, the flames briefly intensified. She held her hands out for warmth, their cracked skin pained by the January chill.

"Another bit o' peat, do you think, Mrs. Smith?" asked Bessie, Isabelle's lone servant and companion.

The middle-aged woman's round cheeks were pink from cold, she noted with a pang of conscience. Bessie wore stout wool stockings under her dress, a shawl, cap, and fingerless gloves. Isabelle wore much the same; her attire was of only marginally better quality. She felt chilled, but she knew the cold did not seep into her bones the way it did Bessie's. It wasn't fair to make the woman suffer on account of Isabelle's thriftiness. "Certainly."

She rose from the hearth and picked up the dress lying across the back of a chair in the cottage's parlor. It was a fine gown at odds with the humble abode: sky blue silk with silver embroidery down the long sleeves and around the bottom hem, and seed pearls adorning the neckline. It was a heaven of luxurious elegance, a dress fit for a duchess, and it had several small moth-eaten holes in the skirt. Isabelle had cursed under her breath when she discovered the damage this morning. She had so few nice things left to her name, she'd be damned if this dress would feed those insidious creatures.

She settled into the chair near the fire, took up needle and thread, and began carefully repairing the fabric.

"Wouldn't you like me to do that for you, ma'am?" Bessie hovered beside her, one hand extended. "Such a lovely thing. Where've you been keeping it?"

Isabelle flinched inwardly. It was foolish of her to have the dress out where Bessie could see it. She ran the risk of spoiling the false identity she'd cultivated to escape notoriety. "Mrs. Smith," the parson's widow, had no business owning such an extravagant gown.

She should have sold it with the rest, she chided herself. Goodness knew she needed the blunt. Alexander was late with her allowance—again. The last money her brother sent in October was nearly gone.

But sentimentality had gotten the best of her. Everything she owned now was simple, serviceable, sensible. She had precious little left to remind her that she was a gentleman's daughter and, for a short time, a noblewoman.

"No, thank you," she said, pulling the gown against her stomach. Isabelle cast around the immaculate cottage for something to occupy the maid. "Do you have any mending of your own?" she asked.

Bessie frowned thoughtfully, deep lines marking her cheeks. "My nephew did drop off a few shirts when he brought the peat on Monday."

"There you are." Isabelle smiled brightly. "Go ahead and see about them." She watched the maid disappear into her small bedchamber. The door shut.

Foolish, stupid girl, she chided herself. If she weren't cautious, Bessie would discover Isabelle's true identity. The past year had passed in peaceful anonymity. Her only correspondents were her brother and her last remaining friend, Lily. They both knew to address their letters to Mrs. Jocelyn Smith.

Isabelle stroked her hand down the gown's limp sleeve, the embroidery's ridges a textural contrast to the slippery silk beneath. She'd never worn the dress. It was a winter gown, suited for a fête in London. That party never came.

What had come was her mother-in-law Caro, hurling accusations of adultery against Isabelle and Justin—while Isabelle was still bedridden with a broken rib.

What had come was Justin's disappearance. She never saw or heard from her friend again after Caro came to Hamhurst.

What had come was Marshall, confused and angry. He asked her over and over whether she had betrayed him. But what was the word of his wife of only months, compared to the wisdom of the woman he'd known all his life? He believed the worst: that Isabelle was the fortune-hunting, title-hungry jezebel his mother had always known her to be.

What finally came, after months of agonizing uncertainty, was the divorce.

• • •

Isabelle stood on the walk in front of the village's little posting office, clutching the letter from her brother. Finally, her allowance. She tore it open as she started toward the mercantile where the owner would exchange a bank draft for currency. There remained no money to purchase peat for the fireplace, nor tallow candles, or Bessie's wages—or much food, for that matter.

With fingers aching in the cold, she unfolded the letter and blinked in surprise. Instead of a bank draft tucked inside, there were only a few lines in her brother's hand. She stopped and read the note in the middle of the walk:

Having given the matter due consideration, I find I must discontinue my financial support. While I was obligated to look after your welfare when you were unmarried, and would be again if you were widowed and destitute, I simply cannot afford to maintain you further in your present situation. My own circumstances no longer allow for such an expense, as I'm sure you understand.

*A. Fairfax*Cut off. Alexander had finally done it. She'd wondered, with her pittance of an allowance coming later and later every quarter, whether this was where it was headed. She scanned the letter again, searching for any sign of filial affection. There was none. Rather, she detected anger behind his words. Her*present situation*could only refer to her being divorced. If he truly felt no obligation to support his divorced sister, why had it taken him nearly three years to say so?

Isabelle reversed direction and trudged back to her cottage with her brother's letter buried in the pocket of her heavy wool coat. There was nothing remotely feminine or decorous about her outerwear, but neither was there anything refined about the bitter wind that lifted last night's snowfall from the ground in swirling clouds that stung her eyes.

The mile-long walk would not have been so burdensome if she had money in her pocket, instead of the cruel letter. Twice she lost her footing on snow-covered ice.

"All it needs is a broken ankle to complete the Gothic tragedy," she muttered.

She passed the rest of the trip home playing out the novel in her mind: the ill-used maiden, broken in body and heart, taken to bed with consumption. The doctor shaking his head sadly. No hope for it, he'd say, nothing more to be done. Alexander, contrite, kneeling beside her bed, clutching her hand and weeping, begging her forgiveness and promising all the peat she could burn, if only she'd recover. She would turn her fevered eyes upon him, open her mouth as if to speak, and then sigh her last. Her brother would gnash his teeth, and pull out clumps of hair in his despair, cursing himself for being such a fool.

She opened the cottage door no richer, but a little lighter in spirits.

•••

The following Saturday, a visitor arrived to alleviate the winter doldrums. Though the cottage door opened into the front hall just off the parlor, Bessie took the unnecessary step of announcing the identity of the new arrival.

"Miss Bachman to see you, Mrs. Smith."

Isabelle was already on her feet, flinging her needlework aside to embrace her friend.

"Lily!" she exclaimed. "Whatever are you doing here?"

Lily's abigail sidled in behind her mistress, carrying a valise. She scrutinized her surroundings with a dismayed expression on her face.

Both women sported bright pink cheeks. "Never say you walked in this inclement weather!"

"Nothing like a bracing bit of exercise to shake off a post chaise trip," Lily said.

She divested herself of her fashionable bonnet and cloak, revealing a fetching red traveling costume. Isabelle took the items and passed them off to Bessie.

"You must be freezing," Isabelle said. "Can I offer you some—"

Behind Lily, Bessie emphatically shook her head. No tea.

"That is, perhaps you would care for some coff—"

Bessie shook her head again.

Isabelle's face burned. Oh, this was low. She silently cursed her brother and the Duke of bloody Monthwaite, but most of all, she cursed herself for being in this predicament.

Lily patted her lovely chestnut coiffure and pretended not to notice Isabelle's discomfiture. Her brown eyes lit up.

"I just remembered." She gestured to her maid who pulled a small wooden box from her own coat pocket and handed it to Lily. "I brought some tea. It's a new blend I haven't tried." The container was about the size of her palm and a couple inches deep. "I know you probably have your own favorite," she said apologetically, "but if it's not too much trouble, would you try this one with me?"

Isabelle blinked back the tears burning her eyes. Only Lily could come bearing charity and make it sound as though Isabelle would be doing her a favor by accepting.

She took the proffered gift, her fingers cradling the box. "Of course," she said, her voice thick. "Tea, please, Bessie." Her mouth twisted into an ironic half-smile. "In the good service." She only had the one.

Bessie gave the faintest of curtsies and bustled off, carrying Lily's outerwear and the tea. Isabelle directed Lily's Abigail to take her bag to Isabelle's own bedchamber. They would have to share a room, as they'd done when they were girls.

When the maids left, Lily started to sink onto the faded couch, but Isabelle scooped her up again in a fierce hug. "Thank you," she whispered against her friend's ear. They sat down and Isabelle took in her friend's lovely ensemble. "It's so good to see you in a cheerful color," she said kindly. "The black never suited you."

Lily nodded. "Believe you me, you cannot be happier to see me in a color than I am to be wearing it. What an odd thing it was, to mourn a man I scarcely knew—to be a widow before I'd even wed. I'm glad the year is over, but neither do I quite look forward to being thrust onto the marriage mart. My whole life, I never had to wonder who I'd marry; I always knew. But now my future husband is an enigma. Which makes me like every other female in England, I suppose," she finished matter-of-factly.

Isabelle smiled sympathetically. Through the designs of all parents involved, Lily had been born with her wedding date already set. She was to marry her betrothed the first of June, 1811, when she was twenty years of age. January of that year, however, Ensign Charles Handford and the rest of the Nineteenth Lancers were sent to reinforce Wellington's Peninsular force. Charles didn't make it home for the summer wedding, and in November 1811, he'd been killed in battle. Isabelle knew her dear friend did not truly grieve him, but neither was she glad to have escaped the match at the cost of the groom's life.

These dreary thoughts occupied her mind until Bessie brought the tea tray. While Isabelle poured, Lily pulled Bessie aside and murmured to her in a low voice. The maid nodded and collected Lily's abigail. The women donned cloaks and departed through the front door.

"What was that about?" Isabelle asked wryly, hoping to put aside the somber atmosphere. "You haven't sacked Bessie, have you? No one else worth a salt will work for such a miserable pittance. I shall never find another like her." She passed a cup and saucer to Lily.

"I've sent them to the butcher." Lily shrugged guiltily. "You know how particular I am about food. I'm a horrible guest."

Isabelle shook her head. Again, Lily made her gifts sound like a nuisance.

"Besides," Lily continued with the spark of the devil in her eyes, "I wanted your dear Bessie out from under our feet. I live in fear of slipping up and calling you Isabelle, instead of Jocelyn or Mrs. Smith."

Isabelle nodded. "Fair enough." A strand of her blond hair fell down alongside her cheek. She hooked it behind her ear. She couldn't remember the last time her hair had been styled by a lady's maid. "Why have you come, Lily?" She touched her friend's arm lightly. "Not that I'm not delighted to see you, of course, but I don't get many surprise visitors."

Lily set her tea on the small table beside the sofa. "I've come to issue an invitation."

Isabelle's ears perked. "To what? No one's invited me anywhere in years."

"A wedding," Lily answered. "My cousin, Freddy Bachman, is returned from Spain. He's getting married in a week. I hoped you'd come as my guest. It will be my first outing in quite a long time, too."

A wedding? Isabelle wrinkled her brow and buried her face in her teacup. A wedding was so respectable. Two people standing before God, pledging their lives to one another—surely they wouldn't want a divorcée there. She'd be like a leper at a garden party—completely out of place, abnormal, despised.

"Isabelle?" Lily ventured.

She raised her eyes over the rim of her cup.

"Shall I pour, dear?" Lily asked. "Your cup was empty before you lifted it."

Isabelle quickly lowered the vacant china. "Ah, so it is. Yes, please," she said with tight gaiety. She forced a laugh. "Who on earth is married in the dead of winter?"

"My cousin, for one," Lily said while she poured Isabelle a fresh cup. "His fiancée has been waiting these several years for his discharge from the army."

Isabelle's smile faltered. "She waited for him to come home from the war? For years?" Such a testament of devotion was humbling. Isabelle shook her head. "I can't. It wouldn't be right."

Lily's finely arched brows drew together and she tilted her head to the side. One gleaming curl rested prettily on the shoulder of her red dress. "Don't be ridiculous."

Isabelle shook her head again. "No."

"Why not?" Lily took Isabelle's cup and set it aside, then scooped both of Isabelle's hands in her own. "You must stop thinking of yourself as some kind of pariah. You're divorced, not diseased. No one else is going to…catch it." Her full lips turned up in a sympathetic smile. "You've been in exile long enough," Lily continued. "I assure you, no one is talking about you at all anymore."

Isabelle regarded her warily. "Really?"

Lily nodded. "You're not nearly as interesting as you think you are."

Isabelle laughed, then drew a nervous breath. "Oh, I just don't know. I would feel so conspicuous."

"It's just a family affair," Lily assured her. "You wouldn't know anyone there, and they don't know you, either—except for my parents, of course, and they adore you. It will be a perfect first step."

Isabelle sighed. "It does sound like an ideal reintroduction to respectable company. But, something has happened that may delay my plans." She went into her bedchamber to retrieve Alexander's letter and handed it to her friend.

Lily scanned the page, then clicked her tongue. "The absolute gall of the man." Her fist closed around an edge of the page. She shook it in front of her. "How dare he? Punishing you yet again? What does he hope to accomplish by cutting you off?"

"I don't know." Isabelle pulled her shawl tighter around her shoulders. "But you see, now is not the time for me to try to go back into society. I'll have to work first, save a little money—"

"Work?" The word fell from Lily's mouth like a bite of rotten egg. "What do you mean?"

"I have to earn money," Isabelle explained calmly. "I've given it a great deal of thought. I'll do something small to start, perhaps take in mending. I can't rely upon unexpected visitors to keep me in tea."

Lily blushed.

Isabelle stood and paced the length of the small room. "I should like to open a shop, eventually. Perhaps a millinery."

"You don't make hats," Lily pointed out.

"There is that," Isabelle agreed. "Perhaps I could import them. From Paris."

Lily's eyes widened. "Smuggled bonnets? I really can't imagine you mingling with the criminal element. Not at all a respectable endeavor."

"I suppose not." Isabelle tapped her chin. "There must be something!"

"We'll think about it this week, all right?" Lily reassured her. "I wonder, though, if you won't be in your dotage by the time you have enough money to launch yourself again."

Isabelle sighed and plopped back onto the couch in a rather unladylike fashion. "I just want a family, Lily. Is that really too much to ask? A respectable husband and a few children of my own?"

The familiar emptiness in her heart ached. Childbirth had taken both Isabelle's mother and the infant girl who would have been her little sister. Her father then fell into a melancholy from which he'd never recovered. Fairfax Hall went without the attention of its master for a decade. Isabelle had likewise gone neglected. Left to the care of doting servants and a tutor, she'd been permitted to do as she pleased.

Her treasured friendship with Justin Miller should never have gone on as long as it did, she now knew. It was not at all the thing for a young lady to be on such close terms with a young man, but no one bothered to put a stop to it. Justin was the one constant source of affection and amusement in her life.

Lily's family came from their home in Brighton only a couple times a year to visit Mrs. Bachman's parents, who were neighbors to Fairfax Hall.

Alexander had gone to Oxford, and Isabelle's papa spent his time in solitude—in the library, in his study, or wandering the estate. Several times, she and Justin had found him lying on the ground, sleeping beside the white marble tomb he'd built for his wife and child. There was room inside for him, too. It seemed to Isabelle as though he wanted to crawl inside and join her.

Isabelle sometimes wondered how her life would have been different if he had been dead in truth, rather than absent only in mind and spirit. She would have been properly provided for, she supposed, not allowed to develop such hoydenish tendencies. It had been painful, too. As a child, she tried and tried to cheer her father. She danced and sang silly songs. He smiled wanly with eyes devoid of humor and patted her head. Isabelle wondered why she and Alexander weren't good enough. She missed Mama, too, but there were still people she loved around her. Didn't Papa love her? She was certain there was something—some one thing—that would make him better. Isabelle spent countless hours trying to find it.

In time, when she was twelve, Papa did the only thing that would end his suffering. Isabelle heard the shot and got to his study first. He'd fallen sideways on the leather sofa, and what she noticed most was not the blood, but the peaceful expression on his face.

Isabelle returned to herself. She blinked a few times and said in a low voice, "I've never *had* a family, Lily. Is it too selfish of me to want one of my own?"

"Of course not," Lily cooed. "We'll get you there, Isa, never you fear." She straightened to a businesslike posture. "As much as I dislike the idea, I agree you must do something to generate income. I'll save up my pin money, too, and maybe in a few months—"

"No," Isabelle interjected vehemently. She clutched her skirt in her fists. "I'll take your tea, but I cannot accept your money." Lily started to protest, but Isabelle raised a hand to stop her. "Please. I have endured this situation for several years. This is just a new obstacle, and I *shall* overcome it. But not with your allowance."

Lily sighed. "All right, then. Do say you'll come to the wedding, though. I should dearly love your company."

The allure of polite society warred with Isabelle's practical concerns. At last, she shook her head. "I'm sorry, but I just can't, Lily. Not with things so tight here. The days I'd spend away are days I could be earning money to keep this place heated."

Worry lines bracketed Lily's mouth. "I wish you would let me do something for you, dear. Your bleak circumstances cannot persist."

A half-smile tugged Isabelle's mouth. "Things will improve. And I'll tell you something," she said, pulling her shoulders back. "It will be nice to have reliable income, rather than depend on a man's whim."

"Hmm." A thoughtful expression crossed Lily's pretty features. "I didn't think of that, but you're right. What a novel idea. Since you won't come to the wedding with me, I'll do what I can to help you find a position."

"Maybe it will even be fun," Isabelle said, her mood brightening. "This is a chance to make a new start. I've been living a kind of half-life ever since the divorce. Now I can start over."

Lily raised her chipped teacup. "To new beginnings."

Isabelle lifted hers to join the toast. "To new beginnings. And, to the devil with men."

• • •

Lily's brows shot to her hairline. "A cook? Really, Isabelle, what are you thinking?"

A week after her arrival, the maids bustled to prepare for Miss Bachman's departure to her cousin's wedding. In that time, Isabelle had approached every business in the area at which she might be at all useful.

Isabelle playfully swatted her friend's arm. "Yes, a cook. I'll have you know, I'm a reasonable hand in the kitchen. At home, Cook taught me out of Mother's French recipe books."

The taller woman cast her a dubious look. "Be that as it may, inns are frequently rather seedy."

"Oh, no, the George is a very clean establishment. Mr. Davies was so impressed with the stew I made, I was even able to negotiate a higher wage."

"Wage negotiations?" Lily's shoulders rose and fell with her sigh. "All right, Isabelle, you've impressed me. Go ahead and tumble into the working class. I suppose you're ready as you'll ever be."

Isabelle grasped her friend in a tight hug. "Thank you for everything."

Lily held her back at arm's length. "You can do anything you put your mind to, Isabelle. Your dreams of a husband and children—you *can* have those, you know. Go and cook for your villagers if you must, but you're still hiding. Come back to the world and take your proper place."

Isabelle's lips curved in a wistful smile. "This *is* my proper place now, Lily. This is the life I must live."

For more books by Elizabeth Boyce, check out

Once an Heiress

Praise for *Once an Heiress:*

"*Once an Heiress* combines everything readers love about historical romance with a twisting, suspenseful story that will have you on the edge of your seat ... I loved every second of *Once an Heiress*—it had the intrigue I love about historical romance combined with an excellent storyline that kept me on my toes."
—The Romance Reviews

"If you like historical romances with a strong heroine that doesn't stick to society rules and a scarred hero with a wonderful hidden heart then you will like *Once an Heiress* by Elizabeth Boyce."
—Harlequin Junkie

Once an Innocent

Praise for *Once an Innocent:*

"*Once an Innocent* by Elizabeth Boyce is a fantastic espionage romance that has some surprising action and gripping drama. If you are a 007 fan, you will be entertained by this novel."
—The Romance Reviews

In the mood for more Crimson Romance?
Check out *Once Upon a Wager* by Julie LeMense at
CrimsonRomance.com.

Printed in the United States
By Bookmasters